EIGHT LIGHT YEARS FROM HOME

"All is quiet on the perimeter, Captain," Aiken said. "Sounds like the Frogs're pretty riled up in the 'ville, though. Do you think they'll attack us?"

"It could happen," Pearson replied. "The ambassador still hasn't answered Geremelet's ultimatum."

"They're not talking about . . . surrendering, are they?"

"Not that I've heard, Master Sergeant. Don't worry, it won't come to that."

"Yeah. The Marines never surrender."

"That's what they say. Keep a sharp watch."

"Aye aye, sir."

Aiken turned and looked into the southern sky, where the first stars were beginning to appear. Eight light-years from home had not much altered the familiar constellations, though the dome of the sky was strangely canted against the cardinal directions. There was a bright star, however, in the otherwise dim and unremarkable constellation Scutum, not far from the white beacon of Fomalhaut.

Sol. Earth's sun. As always, the sight of that star sent a shiver down Aiken's spine. So far away, in both space and time.

Eight point three light-years. Help from home could not possibly arrive in time . . .

BOOK ONE OF
THE LEGACY TRILOGY

STAR CORPS

IAN DOUGLAS

An Imprint of HarperCollins*Publishers*

EOS
An Imprint of HarperCollins*Publishers*
10 East 53rd Street
New York, New York 10022-5299

Copyright © 2003 by William H. Keith, Jr.
ISBN: 0-380-81824-8
www.eosbooks.com

First Eos paperback printing: April 2003

HarperCollins® and Eos® are trademarks of HarperCollins Publishers Inc.

Printed in the U.S.A.

10 9 8 7 6

STAR
CORPS

Prologue

12 MAY 2138

Firebase Frog
New Summer
Ishtar, Llalande 21185 IID
72:26 hours Local Time

Master Sergeant Gene Aiken leaned against the sandbag barricade and stared out across the Saimi-Id River. Smoke rose from a half-dozen buildings, staining the pale green of the early evening sky. Marduk, vast and swollen, aglow with deep-swirling bands and storms in orange-amber light, hung immense and sullen, as ever just above the western horizon. The gas giant's slender crescent bowed up and away from the horizon where the red sun had just set; its night side glowed with dull red heat as flickering pinpoints, like twinkling stars, marked the pulse and strobe of continent-size lightning storms deep within that seething atmosphere.

The microimplants in Aiken's eyes turned brooding red dusk to full light, while his battle helmet's tactical feed displayed ranges, angles, and compass bearing superimposed on his view, as well as flagging thermal and movement targets in shifting boxes and cursor brackets.

The sergeant studied Marduk's blood-glow for a moment, then looked away. At his back, with a shrill whine of servomotors, the sentry tower's turret swiveled and depressed, matching the movements of his head.

He could hear the chanting and the drumming, off to the

east, as the crowds gathered at the Pyramid of the Eye. It was, he thought, going to be a very long night indeed.

"How's it going, Master Sergeant?"

Aiken didn't turn, not when he was linked in with the sentry. His battle feed had warned him of Captain Pearson's approach.

"All quiet on the perimeter, Captain," he replied. "Sounds like the Frogs're pretty riled up down in the 'ville, though."

"Word just came through from the embassy compound," Pearson said. "The rebel abos have seized control in a hundred villages. The 'High Emperor of the Gods' is calling for calm and understanding from his people." The way he said it, the title was a sneer.

Abos, abs, aborigines; Frogs, or *Froggers.* All were terms for the dominant species of Ishtar . . . ways of dehumanizing them.

Which was a damned interesting idea when you realized how *not* human the Ahannu were.

"Do you think they'll attack us?"

"It could happen. The ambassador still hasn't answered Geremelet's ultimatum."

A gossamer flitted in the ruby light, twisting and shifting, a delicate ribbon of iridescence. Aiken lifted the muzzle of his 2120 and caught the frail creature, watching it quiver against the hard black plastic of the weapon's barrel in bursts of rainbow color. Other gossamers danced and jittered in the gathering darkness, delicate sparkles of bioluminescence.

"They're not talking about . . . surrendering, are they?"

"Not that I've heard, Master Sergeant. Don't worry. It won't come to that."

"Yeah. The Marines never surrender."

"That's what they say. Keep a sharp watch. There've been reports of frogger slaves trying to gain entrance at some of the other bases. They might be human, but we can't trust them."

"Aye aye, sir." The Ahannu slaves, descendants of humans

taken from Earth millennia ago, gave Aiken the creeps. No way was he letting them through *his* part of the perimeter.

"Good man. Give a yell if you need help."

"You don't need to worry about *that*, sir." He hesitated, looking up at the vast and seething globe of Marduk. "Hey, Captain?"

"What?"

"Some of the guys were having a friendly argument the other night. Is Ishtar a planet or a freakin' moon?"

Pearson chuckled. "Look it up on the local net."

"I did. Didn't understand that astrological crap."

"Astronomy, not astrology. And it's both. Marduk is a gas giant, a planet circling the Llalande sun. Ishtar is a moon of Marduk . . . but if it's planet-sized and has its own internally generated magnetic field and atmosphere and everything else, might as well call it a planet, right?"

"I guess. Thanks, sir."

Pearson walked off into the gloom, leaving Aiken feeling very much alone. He turned and looked into the southern sky, where the first stars were beginning to appear. Eight light-years from home had not much altered the familiar constellations, though the dome of the sky was strangely canted against the cardinal directions. There was a bright star, however, in the otherwise dim and unremarkable constellation Scutum, not far from the white beacon of Fomalhaut. Aiken might not know astronomy from astrology, but he'd pulled downloads enough to know what he was looking at now.

Sol. Earth's sun. As always, the sight of that star sent a small shiver down Aiken's spine. So far away, in both space and time . . .

Eight point three light-years. Help from home could not possibly arrive in time.

1

Giza Complex
Kingdom of Allah, Earth
0525 hours Zulu

The trio of TAV Combat Personnel Carrier transports came in low across the Mediterranean Sea, avoiding the heavily populated coastal areas around El Iskandariya by crossing the beach between El Hammam and El Alamein. Skimming the Western Desert at such low altitudes that their slipstreams sent rooster tails of sand exploding into the pale predawn sky, the TAVs swung sharply south of the isolated communities huddled along the Wadi El Natrun, dumping velocity in a series of weaving banks and turns. Ahead, silhouetted against the brightening eastern horizon and the lights of Cairo, their objective rose like three flat-sided mountains above the undulating dunes.

The defenders would know that something was happening; even with stealth architecture, the three transatmospheric vehicles had scorched their radar signatures in ion reentry trails across the skies of Western Europe as they'd descended from suborbit, and the mullahs of the True Mahdi had been expecting something of the sort. The only question was how long it would take them to react.

Captain Martin Warhurst, CO of Bravo Company, sat hunched over in his travel seat in the rear of CPC Delta's red-lit troop compartment, crowded torso to armored torso with the men and women of 1st Squad, First Platoon. There were no windows in the heavily armored compartment, no viewscreens or news panels, but a data feed painted a small, brightly colored image within his Helmet Data Overlay, showing the outside world as viewed through a camera in the TAV's blunt nose.

There wasn't a lot to see, in fact—abstract patterns of light and darkness wheeling this way and back with the TAV's approach maneuvers. The area beyond the Giza complex, along the west bank of the Nile, was brightly lit. The extensive archeological digs behind the Sphinx and between the two northern pyramids, those of Khufu and Khafre, were bathed in harsh spotlights reflected from aerostats hovering high above the ground-based beam projectors.

He knew the mission orders, knew the lay of the land and the location of the company's objectives, but it was almost impossible to make sense of what he was seeing on his HDO display. Balls of yellow and red light floated up from the ground—fire from enemy antiaircraft positions. Colored lines and symbols glowed among alphanumerics identifying targets, way points, ranges, and bearings. His cranialink provided analysis, based on data jacked through from the CPC's combat computer. He could see the area marked as the platoon's drop-off point, midway between the Sphinx and Khafre's pyramid.

"Captain Warhurst," the phlegmatic, female voice of the TAV's AI pilot said in his helmet receiver. "Thirty seconds. Hot LZ."

"I see it," Warhurst replied. His grip tightened on his weapon, a General Electric LR-2120 Sunbeam pulse laser, with its M-12 underbarrel 20mm RPG launcher and data hotlink to his Mark VII armor. He'd been in the Marines for six years and made captain two years ago, but this would be his first time in combat, his first hot drop, his first time in command with a live enemy.

God, don't let me screw it up. . . .

The TAVs made a final course adjustment, shrieking low

above the sands between the middle and southern pyramids, their dead-black hulls slipping through crisscrossing targeting radar beams like ghosts, evading hard locks. Air brakes unfolded like ungainly wings as their noses came up, and billows of sand exploded from the hard-driving plasma thrusters arrayed at wing roots and bellies.

"Hold on," the AI's voice said, as deceleration tugged at Warhurst's gut and the steel deck tilted sharply beneath his booted feet. "We're going in."

"Hang onto your lunches, boys and girls," he called over First Platoon's comm channel. "We're grounding!"

A jolt . . . a moment of suspense and silence . . . and then another, harder jolt as the TAV decelerated on shrieking thrusters to a slow-drifting hover. With a shrill whine of hydraulics, the first CPC was extruded from the side of the TAV's fuselage on unfolding davits as raw noise banged and shrieked inside the sealed troop compartment. Plenum thrusters already spooling howled now as all four onboard hovercraft personnel carriers swung free of the floating TAV and detached their cables. Sand blasted around the hovercraft as they floated half a meter above the surface, skittering sideways to clear the overhang of their huge, black transport while the TAV engaged full thrusters and rose clear of the drop zone. "Good luck, First Platoon," the AI pilot's voice announced.

"We're clear of the TAV, Captain!" Lieutenant Schulman, the CPC commander, yelled over the vehicle's comm system. Hammer blows clanked and pinged and sang from the hull outside. They were taking small-arms fire. "Objective in sight, range two-three-five. Moving!"

"Roger that!" Warhurst's helmet display feed had shifted automatically to a pickup on the CPC's hull now that the hovercraft was free of its ride. He could see the flash and wink of gunfire in the darkness, the streaking tracers of heavy automatic weapons. Somewhere in the distance a round of HE went off with a deep-throated *crump*, briefly lighting the dune shadows nearby. The CPC's turret shrilled as it rotated in its collar above and forward of the troop compartment, and Warhurst felt the steady *thud-thud-thud* of the 50mm autocannon slamming high explosive rounds into an enemy gun position.

The armored Marines remained strapped in their seats, weapons muzzle up between their knees, silent while boiler room noise boomed and banged around them. Once, the CPC lurched heavily to the left as a near miss rocked the hovercraft over on its plenum skirts like a boat listing in heavy seas, but Schulman righted the stubborn, tough-hulled machine and swerved hard as armor-seeking missiles strobed in dazzling cacophony outside.

"Coming up on the drop-off, Captain!" Schulman warned. "Ten seconds!"

"Roger that!" He checked the map on his HDO. They were on target. With a focused thought, he shifted to the platoon freak. "Ten seconds, people! Go to IR!"

With a thought focused through his implant, Warhurst engaged his helmet's infrared overlay, and the red-lit shapes around him faded into gloom, nearly invisible, with only enough heat leakage from joints and peripheral gear to give each Marine in the compartment a faint, ghostly aura.

The hovercraft slewed sideways, and the aft hatch opened up, ramp dropping and shields unfolding to reveal a cold black sky above the grays and midnight blues and blackgreens of a chill desert landscape painted in infrared. Warhurst hit the quick release on his harness and was on his feet, ducking to step beneath the hatch. "C'mon, Marines!" he shouted. "Ooh-*rah*!"

In a double line, twelve Marines stormed down the drop ramp and onto the sand as point-defense lasers on the CPC's upper deck tracked incoming mortar rounds and flashed them to metallic vapor. Warhurst raced ahead, conscious only of the press of the Marines around him, of the rattle and pop of weapons fire, the flicker of muzzle flashes in front of him.

He threw himself down on the slope of a dune, scrambling

up and forward until he could bring his weapon to bear. The 2120's sighting camera was linked by computer to his helmet display. A red-glowing reticle crosshaired whatever the laser's muzzle was pointed at, together with flickering numbers giving range, bearing, and probable target ID. He took aim at the muzzle flashes fifty meters to his northeast and thumbed the lever to engage his RPG autolauncher. He let the weapon's sight record the target—dimly seen shapes of yellow emerging from the inky blue-green backdrop. His computer tagged the guns as teleoperated sentries, but the body heat of a dozen enemy soldiers showed as vague shapes through the dune itself and as pillars of moist heat moving above the sand. Field sensors detected the RF leaked by electrical systems, probably the sentries' motors and power packs.

Good enough. He squeezed the trigger. The boxlike hard plastic case of the weapon vibrated within the grip of his gloves as he loosed a burst of grenades, cycling at twelve rounds per second, fanning eight rounds in a spread along the crest of the sand dune ahead. Accelerated to eight hundred meters per second by the launcher's mag driver, each round unfolded in flight, a tiny ramjet engine kicking on as microvanes steered the projectile toward its chosen target. Like steadily glowing fireflies against the night, the string of ramjet-propelled grenades streaked through the darkness, rising high above the sand dune sheltering the enemy gunners, then angling suddenly and sharply down, detonating behind the ridge in a chain of explosions, each as powerful as the blast from a fist-sized lump of CRX-80.

Shrieks and screams rose from the target area as clouds of sand geysered into the sky, mixed with chunks of plastic, metal, and more grisly debris. A running figure showed briefly at the crest of the ridge; Warhurst thumbed his weapon to laser and triggered a pulse. The target flopped out of sight, but Warhurst wasn't sure whether he'd scored a kill or not.

Explosions continued to thump and boom all around

them. The other members of First Platoon had spread out along the dune, laying down a devastating curtain of explosive firepower, driving the enemy gunners to cover.

With a thought, he engaged his helmet's data link with the CPC. *What's up ahead?*

The CPC sensors were far sharper and more observant than those packed in a Mark VII combat armor suit. In addition, Lieutenant Schulman had by now deployed a small army of recon floaters, marble-sized sensor packs riding their magfields across the battlefield, allowing the CPC computer to build up a coherent and complete view of the entire engagement.

A picture inset opened for him at the top of his helmet's field of view. Symbols moved slowly across a 3D model of the surrounding terrain—green squares, circles, and triangles for Bravo Company's Marines; reds for known hostiles; yellows for unknowns. Dropping the resolution to a hundred meters, he was able to narrow the feed to just First Platoon, checking on their position, then open it again to the entire battlefield.

The sand dune ahead was clear. No living targets, no operating machinery or electrical devices. The flanks were clear as well, as Second and Third Platoons completed their deployments to either side. "First Section, First Platoon, move out!" he called over the platoon's command channel. "Second Section, overwatch."

He was struggling to find the right rhythm of command. In a sense, he was wearing two hats—commander of Bravo Company as well as CO of First Platoon. He couldn't neglect one for the other and needed to stay well-grounded in the scope and depth of the entire battle.

This despite the fact that he was only directly aware of the fighting in his immediate vicinity, at squad level. Even his HDO electronics and satellite-relayed downlinks couldn't entirely lift the eternal fog of war.

Scrambling to his feet, Warhurst jogged across the sand until he reached the explosives-chewed berm. A tangle of bodies lay on the far side—Kingdom militia, from the look of them, in a mix of dark fatigues, chamelecloth, and civilian clothing. A black beret on the sand bore the green and silver crescent flash of the True Mahdi. The weapons were mostly Chinese lasers and Shiite Persian K-90s; the charred and scattered fragments of casings, ammo boxes, and squat tripods were probably the remnants of Chinese Jixie Fangyu automated sentry guns, JF-120s.

The two squads of First Section fanned out along the slope, providing cover as Second Section moved up to join them. Ahead and to the left a blaze of light showed eerily luminescent in Warhurst's IR view. Several man-sized heat sources jogged past the base of a small building with lighted windows. He raised his weapon, switching to RPG and tracking the figures, but a targeting interrupt appeared on his helmet display, blocking the shot. The targets *were* hostiles, no question of that; he'd thought for a moment that his weapon had detected the IFF signatures of other Marines moving into his field of fire. The readout said otherwise. The company's primary objective lay in that direction, just behind the building. His rifle was telling him that a miss might cause unacceptable collateral damage.

Slapping the selector switch back to laser, he triggered a stuttering burst of laser fire on the hostiles, scoring at least one hit. He saw the man beneath the targeting crosshairs flail wildly and go down. The rest appeared to be scattering back across the desert, toward the river.

Advancing again by sections, First Platoon rushed forward, taking small-arms fire from the building but nothing powerful enough to more than ding their armor. A five-ton cargo hovertruck lay on its side half buried in the sand, its turbine box blazing against the darkness. The twelve CPCs drifted slowly among the dunes, laying down intense covering fire. Overhead, the airborne TAVs darted and hovered like immense black dragonflies while the ground units called down fire from the sky.

Warhurst ran up to the building, a squared-off office module of the sort designed to be moved by truck or floater to where it was needed temporarily. Throwing himself down on the sand, he took aim at the single door. "Come out!" he yelled. At his mental command, his suit's comm suite translated his words into Arabic. *"Yati!"*

Other Marines joined him, and a burst of automatic fire snapped from the module window. Warhurst sent a burst of laser pulses back in reply, burning through the thin plastic walls of the building and eliciting shouts and screams inside.

Someone shouted something in guttural Arabic, and Warhurst's suit translated: "Do not shoot! Do not shoot!" A moment later the door banged open and two KOA troops stumbled out, holding their Chinese lasers above their heads. A moment passed, and two more emerged, supporting a third man, a wounded comrade, between them.

"Out! Out!" Warhurst yelled, and Sandoval and Kreuger leaped forward. They pulled the weapons from the prisoners' hands, tossed them aside, and shoved the captives back and away from the building. Michaelson and Smith banged through the door and rolled inside, checking the building, then emerged again to report it secure.

Gunfire crackled in the distance as Second and Third Platoons established a company perimeter. At the building, though, there was momentary peace, an eerie calm. After ordering Kreuger to keep watch on the prisoners, now lying facedown on the sand a few meters away, Warhurst checked in with his other platoon commanders. Both reported the enemy on the run, light casualties, and a secure regimental LZ. Gunnery Sergeant Petro reported that First Platoon now controlled the main objective. The defenders were fleeing . . . or had been neutralized, one way or another.

Walking out across the desert toward the company's objective, Warhurst opened the command channel. "Backstop, Backstop, this is Sharp Edge One. Objective Stony Man secure."

"Sharp Edge One, Backstop. Roger that. You have some people back here who've been holding their breath ever since you went in."

"Well, don't let them breathe yet. There was heavy—repeat heavy—enemy activity in the LZ." So much for that easy in, easy out op they'd promised, Warhurst thought. "Local resistance has been broken, but I don't want to get too fat and happy out here."

Just ahead, Objective Stony Man rose from a broad, steep-walled pit carved into hard-packed sand and limestone bedrock . . . a long, low, weathered body lying on a pedestal like a crouching lion . . . the head ancient, secretive, facing east across the black sparkle of the Nile.

The Sphinx of Giza, sentinel of the Great Pyramids, still silent after all these millennia. He could make out a faint, reflective gleam from the plastic shell that had been added a century ago to prevent further erosion.

Warhurst's proximity motion detector chirped at him, and he turned in the indicated direction. A small, gray sphere, marble-sized and pulsing with a superconductor-driven magnetic induction field, was moving left to right ten meters away. He brought his weapon up, but his targeting interrupt cut in. The object IFFed as a Net News Network remote camera.

Damn, he thought, Triple N, as usual, had better intelligence than the Pentagon. How the hell had they picked up on the Giza op so quickly?

He considered overriding the cutouts and bringing the camera down. Troops in the field had the right to do so if a wandering news camera might reveal positions or movements to the enemy. In fact, the mullahs across the Nile in Cairo were probably watching live Triple N news coverage at that moment. He resisted a comic-relief impulse to wave.

Still, the networks were generally pretty good about keeping their equipment back from the immediate front lines, if only because those flying robotic eyes were damned expensive and tended to draw fire. If newsies were around, it was a good sign that the enemy wasn't. Anyway, the one he'd seen was traveling at a pretty good clip, heading toward the river. He let it go.

Warhurst returned his attention to the Sphinx once more. After a moment's thought, he slung his weapon, then reached up and unsnapped the catches on his combat helmet. He wanted to see that ancient wonder with unaugmented eyes.

The light surprised him and made him blink. The sky was bright and pale blue, only minutes from sunrise. The Sphinx continued to stare at the eastern horizon, as though patiently waiting for yet another in a chain of three million dawns.

He turned then, facing west, and caught sight of a glorious panorama—the three pyramids rising above the Giza Plateau; the nearest, Khafre's, just two hundred meters away. The upper half of each glowed a brilliant orange-yellow, bathed in light from a sun still below the horizon; the lower halves were still gray with night shadow.

Soldiers! Forty centuries look down upon you! So, it was said, Napoleon had addressed his men in 1798, just before the Battle of the Pyramids. Those enigmatic, artificial mountains had seen more than their share of blood upon the sand already.

Stuttering automatic gunfire punctuated that thought. It sounded like Cooper and Third Platoon were slugging it out with the locals near the base of Khufu's pyramid. He could hear the radio chatter in his earclip speaker.

"Shooters! Shooters on the pyramid, north side!"

"Roger that. I've got 'em."

"Haley! Wokowski! Circle left!"

"North side clear!"

The fighting was dying down . . . but this had only been the opening round. The angry mobs occupying the Giza Plateau had retired as usual last night to the comfort and security of Cairo, north and across the Nile, but they would be back as soon as they realized that the UFR/USA had intervened in the crisis militarily, and they would have Mahdi

Guards and crack Saladin with them. The Marines had seized the plateau just west of the Nile; now they would have to hold it.

Warhurst didn't know why the Marines were there, and frankly, he didn't care. Scuttlebutt had it that KOA was threatening to shut down the archeological digs in and around Giza and evict all foreign xenoarcheologists, but the premission briefing had stressed only that hostile forces in the area around the Sphinx and the Great Pyramids—including both regular troops and large numbers of poorly armed militia—were threatening vital American interests in the region and needed to be neutralized . . . *without* causing collateral damage to the monuments, archeological digs, and foreign personnel in the area. The three TAVs bearing First, Second, and Third Platoons of Bravo Company, 3rd Marines, had lifted off from Runway Bravo at Camp Lejeune just forty minutes ago, traversing the Atlantic south of Greenland on a great circle suborbital flight that had brought them down over Egypt. More troops—2nd Regiment's Alfa, Charlie, and Delta Companies—were on the way; Bravo Company was tasked merely with clearing the LZ and securing the perimeter.

He hoped the relief force came fast. Right now they were terribly exposed—eighty-four Marines, twelve lightly armored CPCs, and three TAVs, holding a few hundred hectares of sand and stone monuments that just hours ago had been swarming with screaming, religious-fanatic mobs.

And those mobs would be back. Guaranteed.

In the east the sun flared above the flat horizon, an explosion of golden light illuminating the dunes and casting long, undulating shadows that filled each depression and indentation in the sand. Warhurst settled his helmet back over his head, resealing the latches.

The counterattack, when it came, would come soon and from the direction of Cairo, fourteen kilometers to the northeast.

Esteban Residence
Guaymas, Sonora Territory
United Federal Republic, Earth
1055 hours PT

John Garroway Esteban relaxed in the embrace of his sensory couch, opening himself to the images flooding through his mind. Gunfire snapped and crackled in the distance, as a mob of swarthy men in a mix of military uniforms and civilian clothing swarmed across a bridge, some in trucks or cargo floaters, most on foot. The news anchor's voice-over described the scene as data windows opened with sidebar data. LIVE FROM CAIRO floated in blue letters above the confused and chaotic panorama.

"Demonstrations began in Cairo three days ago," the anchor was saying, "when the Mahdi declared that the monuments of Giza existed to declare God's glory and that attempts to excavate them in order to prove extraterrestrial influences in ancient human affairs were blasphemous and, therefore, illegal under the religious laws of the Kingdom of Allah. All archeological excavations in Egypt were ordered halted when—"

With a focused thought, John shifted feeds. *Show me the Marines.*

It felt as though he were drifting above the desert. It was mid-morning, and men in chamelarmor almost indistinguishable from the sand around them crouched in holes scratched into the shelter of a dune. Robot sentries, solitary pylons capped by laser turrets, scanned the horizon, as an American flag fluttered in the breeze from a makeshift pole. In the background the scarred and age-smoothed face of the Sphinx looked over the desert, and behind it rose the golden apex of one of the pyramids. A velvet-black, stub-winged aircraft circled overhead. *"Silim,"* he whispered, an Ahannu word currently in vogue with the xenophilic set, meaning "good" or "with it."

"Just before dawn this morning," the narrator said, "elements of the 3rd Marine Division were suborbited into Giza, neutralizing local forces and setting up a defensive perimeter, establishing what President LaSalle called 'a safe zone to protect both American and Confederation interests in the region.'"

For minutes more, he took in the scenes relayed from the battlefield, views of American Marines crouched under cover, of robotic fliers patrolling sandy wastes, of a team of Confederation archeologists debarking from a transatmospheric lander and being escorted by Marines to the base of the Great Pyramid.

The scene blurred and shifted, and John found himself sitting in a folding chair in the White House Rose Garden. President LaSalle stood behind a podium a few meters away, her face drawn and tired, as though she'd been up all night. "One of my predecessors," she said, "called the U.S. Marines the Navy's police force. In fact, for the past 150 years they have been the *President's* police force, the first of this nation's military forces to be deployed to any spot on the globe where our vital interests are being threatened. I did not make the decision to deploy our young men and women to this region lightly. Ongoing excavations at Giza are in the process of uncovering remarkable discoveries of inestimable value in understanding our past and the nature of repeated extraterrestrial interventions upon this world of ours thousands of years ago. It is vital to all of us that these discoveries remain intact, that they not fall into the hands of radical religious extremists. . . ."

For John, it was as though he were sitting right there with the reporters, listening to the President's speech. The clarity and realism of the noumen's sensory input were nearly as sharp as real life. His implant was an expensive, high-end set, with almost two thousand protein processor nodes grown from microscopic nanoseeds scattered throughout his cerebral cortex and clustered within the nerve bundles of the corpus callosum. His father had insisted on a top-of-the-line Sony-TI 12000 Series Two Cerebralink, complete with social interactive icon selection, high-speed interfaces, emotional input, and multiple net search demons, and for once John was happy that his father was who and what he was, able to pull that much thrust. The 12000 was an executive model, the sort of cranialink nanohardware favored by high-powered CEOs and techers, light-years beyond what the other kids had had for schoollinks.

John was eighteen and well into his first year of online university work. Carlos Jesus Esteban was determined that his son would get his degree in business management. John knew that his father might differ with him about his future career, but at least—

A yellow light winked against the upper right corner of the news window in John's mind. *Shit!*

He mindclicked the link, closing the window, but the warning program he'd written for his Sony-TI simply wasn't fast enough to beat the parental insertion. The window froze before it collapsed completely, then expanded again to show President LaSalle caught in foolish-looking mid-word.

His father's noumetic icon exploded into his consciousness, a mustached giant, vast and stern, in violet business smartsuit, with lightning flickering about his brow. "What the hell are you doing?" The elder Esteban's voice was like thunder, and John, out of long-polished habit, cringed, then flared back.

"This is *my* feed!"

"You think so, smart kid? *I* bought you that fancy nanoware, and I won't have you nouming that damned political pornography. Not as long as you're in *my* house!"

The image of President LaSalle winked out, and John floated alone in cyberspace with his father. He tried to adjust his own icon presentation so he felt less like a tiny satellite orbiting a planetary giant, but he found the mental input

controls beyond his reach. His father was running his
noumenal feed now.

Pretty soon I'll be able to noum what I want to. The
thought came to mind unbidden.

Somehow—could his father *do* that?—Esteban caught the
thought or its echo. "What do you mean by *that* crack?" his
father said. "Where do you think you're going?"

John felt the shifting cybercurrents of moving data packets. Damn! His father was sifting through his files. If he
found out—

"What are you hiding, *muchacho*? Huh? What do you
have in here?"

Abruptly, desperately, John mindclicked and severed the
link. He sat once again in his sensory couch, the familiar
surroundings of his home E-room around him. He lay there
for a moment, breathing hard. Damn, damn, *damn* his father! These encounters always left him shaking, weak, and
feeling violated. Just because his father felt that he had the
right to monitor everything that he did on the net . . .

Sometimes that translated as the right to monitor everything that he thought, and to John, that blatant invasion of
privacy, self, and boundaries was as personal and as direct as
a slap across the face.

If his father was angry at him for following Triple N's
coverage of the Egyptian crisis, he would have been absolutely furious to learn that in a few days' time his son
would be leaving home for good.

Tough, he thought. John Garroway Esteban had been a
free agent since turning eighteen three months ago. For
much of his life he'd dreamed about being a Marine, ever
since his mother had told him about her ancestors, the Garroways, and the roles they'd played in wars from Korea to
Mexico.

Soon he would be a Marine himself, and he could kick off
the mud of this damned planet and begin to see the worlds.

Silim! . . .

Marine Planetary Base
Mars Prime, Mars
1914 hours Zulu

Some 210 million kilometers from John Esteban's
E-center musings, Colonel Thomas Jackson Ramsey—"TJ"
to his friends—touched the announce pad at the doorway to
the office of his commanding officer. The door slid open in
response. "General Cassidy? Reporting as ordered, sir."

"Enter," William Cassidy said without looking up from
his work station.

Ramsey entered, centering himself on the hatch, hands
clasped stiffly at his back. He didn't know why he'd been
summoned here. He didn't think he was in trouble, but with
Brigadier General Cassidy—a tough, no-nonsense character
with dark mahogany skin, silver hair, and a hard-ass attitude
reputed to curdle milk at fifty meters—you never knew.

"At ease, at ease," Cassidy said after a moment. He pulled
the link circlet from his head and tossed it aside on the desk,
then rubbed his eyes. "Drag up a chair."

Ramsey floated a glider chair across the deck and an-
chored it with a thought. "You wanted to see me, sir?"

"Yes, damn it. You've got new orders."

Ramsey's eyebrows lifted themselves toward his hair line.
"Sir? I've only been here eight months." The usual length of
off-world deployments was two years.

"I know. And I'm going to hate like hell to lose you." Cassidy gave him a sidelong look. "What's your famsit?"

Curiouser and curiouser. A Marine's family situation was
only raised for offworld deployments. "No current contract,
sir. I had one before I shipped out for Mars." Cheryl hadn't
been willing to wait for him, and he couldn't say he blamed
her. It still hurt, though. . . .

"Any kids?"

"No, sir. Do I take it that I'm being reassigned out-Solar,
General?"

"I guess you could say that. It's volunteers only, and it's long term. *Very* long term. But it's carrying a Career Three."

"Goddess! Where are they sending me?"

"That," Cassidy said, "is classified. They won't even tell me. But they want you back on Earth so they can talk to you about it. Open up and I'll pass you what I have."

Ramsey uplinked to the local netnode with a coded thought and tuned to the general's channel. Information flickered through his awareness, resolving itself into stark words hanging before his mind's eye. There wasn't much.

FROM: USMCSPACCOM, QUANTICO, VIRGINIA
TO: THOMAS JACKSON RAMSEY, COLONEL, USMC
    HQ DEPOT USMC MARS PRIME
FROM: DWIGHT VINCENT GABRIOWSKI, MAJGEN, USMC
DATE: 2 JUN 38
SUBJ: ORDERS

YOU ARE HEREBY REQUIRED AND DIRECTED TO REPORT TO USMC-SPACCOM WITH YOUR COMMAND CONSTELLATION, DELTA SIERRA 219, FOR IN-PERSON BRIEFING AND POSSIBLE VOLUNTARY REASSIGNMENT.

THE IP PACKET *OSIRIS* (CFT-12) WILL BE MADE READY TO TRANSPORT COMMAND CONSTELLATION DELTA SIERRA 219 TO USMC SPACEPORT CAMP LEJEUNE, DEPARTING MARS PRIME NO LATER THAN 1200 HOURS LT 3 JUNE 2138, ARRIVING CAMP LEJEUNE SPACEPORT NO LATER THAN 9 JUNE 2138.

OFFERED MISSION REQUIRES FAMSIT CLASS TWO OR LOWER. RECENT CHANGES IN INDIVIDUAL FAMSITS SHOULD BE UPLINKED TO USMC-SPACCOM PRIOR TO SCHEDULED DEPARTURE.

OFFERED MISSION ASSIGNMENT CARRIES CAREER THREE RATING.

SIGNED: D. V. GABRIOWSKI

This, Ramsey reflected, would not be an ordinary duty reassignment. Career Three meant a *big* boost to his career track . . . the equivalent of a major combat-command assignment or a long-term independent command, possibly both. The famsit requirement could only mean a long deployment, a couple of years at least.

Where the hell were they sending him, Europa?

Which reminded him . . .

"They want my whole constellation to go Earthside with me," he said.

"I know Captain DeHavilland and Sergeant Major Tanaka are at Cydonia," General Cassidy replied. "A C-5 has already been dispatched to bring them in. The rest of them are here at Prime, aren't they?"

"Actually, sir, I was thinking of Cassius. He was seconded to Outwatch when I was assigned here. He's been on Europa for eight months."

"I don't have any information about your sym, Colonel. But this is damned hot. I would imagine that Quantico has already made provisions to bring him back as well."

If so, this assignment *was* hot, hotter than a class-four solar flare. The Corps was not in the habit of casually shuttling command constellations from Mars to Earth just for a briefing . . . and sure as Chesty Puller was a devil dog, it wasn't in the habit of ferrying a lone AI symbiont all the way back from Outwatch duty in the Jovians.

Where were they being sent?

He had a pretty good idea already—there weren't that many possibilities—and the thought both thrilled and terrified. . . .

2

Listening Post 14, the Singer
Europa
1711 hours Zulu

And further still from Earth, some 780 million kilometers from the warmth of a shrunken, distance-dwindled sun, a solitary figure crouched on top of the half-surfaced ruin of a half-million-year-old artifact, high above the swarming camps of humans who studied it. The figure was not human, and in this modality didn't share even a basic humanoid shape with his builders. Humans called this model "the spider," because of the low-slung, flattened body, the eight spindly legs, and the cluster of eye lenses and manipulators set into his forward armored casing.

He was patient, as only an artificial intelligence could be patient. AI-symbiont CS-1289, Series G-4, Model 8, known to his human companion as Cassius, had waited here in the icy cold for just over 4.147 megaseconds now, some forty-eight days in human terms. By slowing his time sense by a factor of 3,600, however, his wait thus far had seemed more like nineteen hours, and even those hours, passing uneventfully, were accepted without emotion or anxiety, as much a part of Cassius's environment as the ice and the near-perfect vacuum around him.

The surrounding landscape—*icescape* would be a more appropriate term—was a jumble of crushed and broken structures, towers, pylons, Gothic arches, and towering stacks of smoothed and round-cornered buildings, all encrusted with mottled gray-black and white ice. The swollen orb of Jupiter hung low in the sky, just above one of the radiation-blasted pressure ridges that crisscrossed the icy moon's frozen surface. Europa circled Jupiter in just over three days, thirteen hours. With the time compression, eighty-five hours passed in what seemed to Cassius like a minute and forty-one seconds; shrunken sun and unwinking stars drifted across the sky from horizon to horizon in just fifty seconds. The swollen orb of Jupiter itself always remained in the same area of the sky, bobbing with Europa's libration as the moon orbited in tide-locked step about its primary, but the banded disk waxed and waned through a complete cycle of phases, from full to crescent and dark, then back to full, all in a single time-compressed "day." The other Jovian moons, from the silvery disk of Ganymede to a handful of stars, circled the giant planet, each at a different pace. Beneath that spectacular light show, across Europa's frozen surface, shadows swung along the undulating ice, shrinking with the fast-rising sun, vanishing at high noon, then lengthening into the darkness of the short night, a cycle three days long compressed into a perceived handful of seconds.

From time to time Cassius was aware of humans moving through his circle of awareness, brief, blurred flickers of motion. He checked each, but at a subliminal, unconscious level. Had any lacked the requisite IFF codes or trespassed into unauthorized zones, his time sense would at once have defaulted to one-to-one, allowing him to challenge the interloper.

A human might have been lonely, but Cassius accepted the isolated duty as simply another mission within his design specs and parameters. He was aware of human activity in the area, of course. The tilted, roughly disk-shaped bulge of the Singer exposed above the frozen wastes of Europa's world-ocean ice cap was ringed by a dozen small camps, pressure domes, habs, and radshield generators providing access to the mountain-sized mass of alien technology locked in the broken ice. Lights blazed around the perimeter, each casting pools of warm yellow radiance to hold the cold and darkness at bay, but Cassius was more aware of the radio chatter and telemetry, voices and streams of data whispering just above the eternal hiss and crackle of Jupiter's radiation belts.

The human activity was all routine, electronic exchanges depersonalized to the point of tedium.

Seventy-one years before, the Singer had been discovered deep in Europa's ocean, locked away beneath the eternal, planetwide ice cap. Europa's seas were host to teeming, myriad life-forms—sulfur-based thermovores thriving around the Europan equivalent of deep-sea volcanic vents. The Singer, however, was from somewhere else, somewhere outside the Solar system, a product of an advanced technology that had mastered star travel at just about the same time that *Homo erectus* was evolving—or was being evolved, rather—into archaic *Homo sapiens*. Half a million years ago the Singer had been involved in a fight of some kind, a battle that resulted in the destruction of a colony of different aliens then thriving on the surface of Mars, at Cydonia. Damaged, it had crashed through the Europan ice cap and was stranded.

But not killed. The bizarre machine intelligence that called itself Life Seeker, which humans dubbed "the Singer" because of its eerie, ocean-locked wail, had waited out the millennia, eventually sinking into insanity—some believed out of sheer loneliness. When humans had approached it seventy-one years before, it roused itself from schizophrenic dreamings and attempted to break free. Piercing the ice, it transmitted a broadband radio pulse of incredible power to the stars and then, its scant energy reserves exhausted, died.

The Singer had been silent ever since.

Silent, that is, save for the noisy monkey-pack swarmings

of human explorers, archeotechnologists, xenosophontolo-
gists, and exocyberneticists. As soon as the brief Sino-
Confederation War of 2067 had ended, a steady stream of
human ships made their way into the Deeps beyond the orbit
of Mars, voyaging to the coterie of moons circling Jupiter.
The Singer might be dead, but the kilometer-wide corpse was
a solid mass of advanced alien technologies, an immense
computer, essentially, that once had housed a self-aware intelligence far exceeding humankind's. For seven decades human science had been plumbing the depths of the Singer,
gleaning a host of technological tricks, arts, and secrets.
There were endless promises of new and near-magical means
of generating limitless power, of bending gravity to human
will, of generating nucleomagnetic fields powerful enough to
block a thermonuclear blast and sever the fabric of space itself, of new structural materials millennia beyond current
manufacturing understanding, of computers and AIs of su-
perhuman speed and capability, even—whisper the mere
possibility softly—of the chance that one day humans might
venture to the stars at speeds vastly exceeding that of light.

Such were the promises of the inert Singer . . . promises
still far from being realized. In seventy-two years, Earth's
best scientists had barely begun to catalog the wonders still
locked away inside that dead and ice-bound hulk. It might be
centuries more before hints, guesses, speculations, and gru-
eling work in the frozen hell of Europa's 140-degree-Kelvin
embrace generated useful technology.

Those promises, however, were so golden that accredited
scientists were not the only mammals scavenging through
the Singer's dark, cold corridors. Five years ago a couple of
research assistants with a Pakistani archeotechnological
team had been caught by Marine security personnel with
nearly forty kilos of Singer material—bits and pieces of
structural support members and paneling, the equivalent of
computer circuit boards, dozens of the fist-sized crystals believed to be used as memory storage media, and several

oddly shaped artifacts of completely alien design and unknown purpose.

That hadn't been the first time site robbers managed to infiltrate the legitimate science teams and smuggle out pieces of the alien ship. Bits of Singer technology had been appearing on Earth for at least the past ten years. Collectors reportedly had paid as much as fifteen million newdollars for fragments mounted and privately displayed as . . . art. The most startling case on record was the three-meter-wide slice of alien hull metal found hanging behind the altar of the Church of the Gray Redeemers in Los Angeles. When *that* had been smuggled back to Earth, and how, was anybody's guess.

The U.S. Marines had been the guarantors of the Singer archeological site's security ever since the end of the Sino-Confederation War. Once it was realized that covert looters were making off with fragments of the alien ship and selling them as curios, as art, and even as religious relics, the newly formed Confederation Department of Archeotechnology authorized the use of military AIs as sentries. Cassius had been assigned to Outwatch duty eight months ago, when the rest of his constellation—the twelve Marine officers and NCOs of cybergroup Delta Sierra 219—had been deployed to Cydonia. There was little need of team AIs on Mars, where the duty was routine and the local net provided reliable data and technoumetic access. On Europa his considerable skills and more-than-human senses could be put to good use patrolling the Singer artifact, protecting it and the Confederation science teams.

In eight months there'd been no incidents. Everything was strictly routine . . . which was, after all, the best way for things to be. Another sixteen months, and he would be able to rejoin his constellation back on Earth. Though it was difficult to say whether what he felt for his teammates was truly akin to *human* emotion, he did miss them. . . .

A radio signal caught his attention, and he instantly

shifted back to standard temporal perception. The sun stopped its rapid drift across the sky, coming to a halt just above the golden-orange crescent of Jupiter. The shadows froze motionless in the patterns of mid-afternoon.

A Navy lander was descending from the west, balancing itself down gently with plasma thrusters against Europa's 131-centimeters-per-second-squared gravitational tug. IFF tagged the dull black and silver sphere as a lander from the Outwatch frigate *Kamael,* currently in Europa orbit.

And a radio transmission from the Singer main base was already calling him in. "Cassius, this is Outwatch Europa. RTB, repeat, RTB."

Return to base? He was not scheduled to leave Listening Post 14 for another 105 hours.

But more so than for a human, even for a human Marine, orders were decidedly orders. He extended his spider legs to full length and began picking his way down the icy slope of the Singer's hull, making his way rapidly toward the main base.

The lander had been sent for him. He wondered why.

Giza Complex
Kingdom of Allah, Earth
1815 hours Zulu

"Here they come!" Captain Warhurst yelled. A thousand armed men, at least, sprinted into the open, screaming and firing wildly. Most were on foot, but a number of vehicles were mixed in with the surging mob—open-topped flatbed trucks with gun crews in the back, and light cargo hovercraft of various sizes and descriptions. "Commence firing!"

Warhurst leaned forward against the low wall of sandbags, moving his weapon to drag the targeting reticle into line with one of the charging Mahdi shock troops, a big man in mismatched pieces of Chinese and Persian armor, carry-

ing a K-90 assault rifle. A touch of the firing stud, and the
LR-2120 hummed, the vibration of the charge cycler flywheel barely perceptible through his armor.

There was no flash or visible pulse of light. Such wasteful
displays of pyrotechnics belonged solely to the noumenal
fantasies of VR thrillers. The laser pulse lasted for only one
hundredth of a second, far too brief a period to register on
the human eye even if there'd been dust or smoke in the atmosphere to make the light visible. The LR-2120 had a
pulse output of fifty megawatts; one watt for one second
equals one joule, so the energy striking the target equaled
half a million joules—equivalent to the explosive power released by the detonation of fifty grams of CRX-80 blasting
compound, or a tenth of a stick of old-fashioned dynamite.

The pulse explosively vaporized a fist-sized chunk of the
man's polylam breastplate as well as the cloth, flesh, and
bone underneath, slamming him back a step before he crumpled to the sand. Warhurst shifted targets and fired again . . .
and again . . .

The attack had been gathering all day. Kingdom of Allah
troops and Mahdi fanatics had begun spilling across the
Giza and Duqqi bridges out of Cairo early that morning,
shortly after the Marines secured their slender perimeter
about the Giza complex, but they stayed within the cluttered,
narrow streets between Giza and the river, mingling with a
fast-swelling crowd of civilians who chanted and waved
banners. The Marines found it amusing. The signs and banners, for the most part, were in English, as were the chants.
Clearly, the demonstration was for the benefit of the net
news services and their floating camera eyes, which by now
saturated the battlefield area as completely as the Marines'
own recon probes.

By mid-afternoon, however, the demonstrators had dwindled away, most of them crossing the Nile bridges back into
Cairo proper. The shock troops and militia had remained,
and the Marines braced themselves, knowing what to expect.

The attack finally came, boiling out from among the ramshackle buildings and narrow streets and into open ground. The Marines had orders not to fire on civilian structures, but they had deployed a line of RS-14 picket 'bots fifteen hundred meters from the Marine perimeter. The baseball-sized devices had buried themselves in the sand and emerged now to transmit data on the range, numbers, and composition of the attacking force, and to paint larger targets, like trucks and hovercraft, with lasers.

With accurate ranging data transmitted from the pickets, Marines inside the perimeter began firing 20mm smartround mortars, sending the shells arcing above the oncoming charge, where they detonated, raining special munitions across the battlefield. Laser-homing antiarmor shells zeroed in on the vehicles. Shotgun fléchette rounds exploded twenty meters above the ground, spraying clouds of high-velocity slivers across broad stretches of the battlefield. Concussion rounds buried themselves in the sand, then detonated, hurling geysers of sand mixed with screaming, kicking bodies into the air.

Only one TAV was airborne at the moment. They were being kept up one at a time to conserve dwindling supplies of the liquid hydrogen used to fuel them. One was sufficient, however, to stoop like a hawk out of the sun, scattering a cloud of special munitions bomblets in a long, precisely placed footprint through the middle of the crowd. A truck and two hovercraft exploded, sending a trio of orange fireballs into the intense blue of the late afternoon sky.

All of the Marines along the northeastern sector of the perimeter were firing now, along with robot sentries and gunwalkers. Warhurst switched his weapon to burst fire; laser rifles had to recycle between each shot, so true full-auto wasn't possible, but he could trigger up to six bursts at a cyclic rate of two per second before the weapon had to take a three-second pause to recharge. Another truck exploded.

Dozens of KOA troops were falling, caught in a devastat-

ing fire from the Marine positions and from directly overhead. The front ranks wavered, hesitating in the face of that
deadly wind as those farther back kept pressing forward. In
another moment the attack had dissolved into a bloody,
thrashing tangle of people, some holding their ground, most
trying desperately to flee to the rear and the imagined safety
waiting for them back across the Nile.

"Cease fire!" Warhurst called over the command channel.
"All squads, cease fire. They've had it."

The attackers continued to flee, leaving several hundred
dead and wounded in the desert; none had come within
twelve hundred meters of the Marine lines. Most had fallen
well beyond the range of their own weapons. No Marines
had been hit.

"Good old Yankee high-tech scores again!" Private Gor-
don called over the tac channel. "They didn't even touch us!"

"Belay the chatter," Warhurst warned. "Keep alert. Petro?
Anything in front of you?"

He had to assume that the brash, frontal rush had been a
feint, something to pin the Marines' attention to the northeast while the real attack was staged from another quarter.

"Negative, sir," Gunny Petro replied. She was in charge of
the northwest sector. "No targets."

"Rodriguez?"

"All clear, Skipper."

"Cooper?"

"Nothing on my front, sir."

The robot sentries out in the desert were very sensitive,
fully able to detect the approach of a single man by his body
heat, his movement, his radar signature, even his scent.
When Warhurst called up a tactical overhead view of the
perimeter, he could see his own troops huddled in their fighting positions . . . but no sign of enemy troops closer than
three kilometers.

But there would be another attack, and soon. He looked
up into the early evening sky and wondered what the hell
was happening to their relief.

Esteban Residence
Guaymas, Sonora Territory
United Federal Republic, Earth
1545 hours PT

"The *Marines*?" his mother cried. "Goddess, why would you want to join the *Marines*?"

John Garroway Esteban stood a little straighter, fists clenched at his side. "You had no right!" he said, shouting at his father, defiant. "My noumen is mine!"

"It's *my* house, you're *my* son!" his father shouted back, raging. The elder Esteban had been drinking, and his words were slurred. "*I* paid for your implant, and I can goddamn do anything in, to, or through your goddamn noumen I goddamn want!"

"Carlos, please," John's mother said. She was crying now. This was going to be a bad one.

They'd had this argument before, many times. John's Sony implant created the inner, virtual world through which he could access the World Net, communicate with friends, and even operate noumenally keyed devices, from thought-clicked doors to the family flyer. *Noumenon* was the conceptual opposite to *phenomenon*; where a phenomenon was something that happened outside a person's thoughts, in the real world, a noumenon was entirely a creation of thought and imagination, a virtual reality opened within his mind . . . but the one was no less real than the other. As the saying went, just because it was all in your head didn't mean it wasn't real.

It was also personal, keyed to John's own thoughts and implant access codes. His father, however, insisted on supervising him through the implant, and the almost daily invasions of his privacy gnawed at John constantly.

Lots of kids had implants with parental controls, if only to monitor their study downloads and keep track of the entertainment Net sites they visited. Carlos Esteban went a lot further, eavesdropping on his conversations with Lynnley, reading his private files, and now downloading his conversation with the Marine recruiter three days ago. Every time John managed to assemble a counterprogram, like the yellow warning light, his father found a way around it . . . or simply bulled his way right in.

And his father was, of course, furious at his decision to join the Marines. He'd expected his father's anger but had hoped his mother would understand. She was *del Norte*, after all, and a Garroway besides.

"No son of mine is going to be part of those butchers," his father was saying. "The Butchers of Ensenada! No! I will *not* permit it! You will join me in the family business, and that is that!"

"I don't want to be a part of the damned family business!" John shot back. "I want—"

"You are eighteen years old," his father said, his voice rich with scorn. "You have no idea what it is you want!"

"Then maybe this is how I'll find out!" He swung his arm angrily, taking in the quietly sophisticated sweep of the hacienda's E-room and dining area, including the floor-to-ceiling viewall overlooking the silver waters of the Sea of Cortez below Cabo Haro. "I won't if I stay *here* the rest of my life!"

A tone sounded. The house was signaling them: someone was at the door. He wanted to snatch the excuse, to pull up the visitor's ID through his implant and go open the door . . . but his father was glaring into his eyes, furious, and the brief wandering of his thoughts would have been immediately noticed.

"You have here the promise of a good education!" Carlos continued, shouting. If he'd heard the announcement tone, he was ignoring it. "Of a place in the family business when you graduate. Security! Comfort! What more could you possibly need or want?" Carlos Jesus Esteban took another long sip from the glass of whiskey he held. He'd been drinking more and more heavily of late, and his temper had been getting shorter.

"Maybe I just want the chance to get those things for myself. To get an education and a job without having them handed to me!"

"Eh? With the Marines? What can *they* teach you? How to kill people? How to shed whatever civilized instincts you may have acquired and become an animal, a sociopathic *murderer*? Is that what you want?"

The house butler rolled in. "Excuse me," it said. "There is—"

"Get out!" the elder Esteban screamed.

"Yes, sir." Obediently, the robot spun about and glided out of the room once more, as though it was used to Carlos's violent moods.

"You just want to go with those worthless gringo friends of yours," his father continued. "You think military service is some sort of glamorous game, eh?"

"Have you thought about joining the Navy, Johnny?" his mother asked helpfully, with a worried, sidelong glance at his father. "Or the Aerospace Force? I mean, if you want to travel, to go offworld—"

"*All* of the services are parasites!" Carlos shouted, turning on her. "And the Marines are the worst! Invaders, oppressors, with their boots on our throats!"

"My grandfather was a Marine," John said with more patience than he felt. "As was *his* father. And *his* mother *and* father. And—"

"All your *mother's* side of the family," his father snapped. He drained the last of his whiskey, then moved to the bar to pour himself another. He appeared to be calming down. His voice was quieter, his movements smoother. A dangerous sign. "Not mine. Always, it is the damned Garroways—"

"Carlos!" his mother said. "That's not fair!"

"No? Please excuse me, Princessa del Norte! The gringos are *always* in the right, of course!"

"Carlos—"

"Shut up, *puta*! This worthless excuse for a son is *your* fault!"

The house had been signaling for several moments, first with an audible tone, then with a soft voice transmitted through John's cerebral implants. No doubt the butler had been dispatched with the same warning: someone was still at the front door. A quick check with the house security camera showed him Lynnley Collins's face.

Now might be his only chance.

"I'll, um, see who's at the door," he said, and slipped as unobtrusively as possible from the room. His father was still screaming at his mother as he rode the curving line of moving steps from the E-center to the entranceway, alerting the house as he descended to open the door.

Lynnley was standing on the front deck, looking particularly fetching in a yellow sunsuit that bared her breasts to the bright, golden warmth of the Sonoran sun. Her dark-tanned skin glistened under her body's UV-block secretions. Her eyes, with her sunscreen implants fully triggered, appeared large and jet-black.

"Uh, hi," he said, slipping easily into English. Lynnley was the daughter of a *norteamericano* family stationed at the naval base up at Tiburón. She spoke excellent Spanish, but he preferred using English when he was with her.

She glanced past him as he stepped outside, brushing back a stray wisp of dark blond hair. The door hissed shut, cutting off his father's muffled shouts.

"Whoo," she said. "Bad one?"

He shrugged. "Pretty much what I expected, I guess."

"That bad?" She touched his arm in sympathy. "So what are you going to do?"

"What can I do? I already thumbed the papers. We're *Marines* now, Lynn."

She laughed. "Well, not quite. There are a few minor formalities to attend to first. Like basic training, remember?"

He walked to the side of the deck, leaning against the redwood railing and staring out over the glistening waters of the Gulf of California. La Hacienda Esteban clung to the summit of a high hill overlooking the cape. The sprawl of the town of Guaymas, the harbor crammed with fishing boats, the clutter of resorts along the coast, provided a bright, tropical splash of mingled colors between the silver-gray sea and the sere brown of the hills and cliff sides. *God, I hate it here,* he thought.

"Having second thoughts?" Lynnley asked.

"Huh? Hell no! I've got to get out of here!"

"There are other ways to leave home than joining the Marines."

"Sure. But I've always wanted to be a Marine. Ever since I was a kid. You know that."

"I know. It's the same with me. It's in the blood, I guess." She moved to the railing beside him, leaning against it and looking down at the town. "Is it just the Marines your dad hates? Or all gringos?"

"He married a gringo, remember. And she was a Marine's daughter."

"Hell, the war was over twenty years before he was born, right? What's his problem?"

John sighed. "Some of the families down here have long memories, you know? His grandfather was killed at Ensenada. He doesn't like the government, and he doesn't like the military."

"What is he, Aztlanista?"

"I don't know anymore. Some of his drinking buddies are, I'm pretty sure. And I know he subscribes to a couple of different Aztlan nationalist netnews sites. He likes their ideas, whether he's a card-carrying member or not."

"S'funny," Lynnley said. "Most of the Aztlanistas are poor working class. Indios, farmers. You don't usually see the big landowners messing with the status quo, joining revolutionary organizations and all that." She tossed her head, indicating the hacienda and the surrounding hilltop lands. "And your family *does* have money."

He shrugged. "I guess. We don't talk about where the money came from, of course." His father's family had become fabulously wealthy in the years before the UN War, when parts of Sonora and Sinaloa—then states of the old Mexican Republic—had furnished a large percentage of several types of illicit drugs for the huge and wealthy northern market.

"But it's not just the money," he went on. "There's still such a thing as national pride. And all of the big-money families around here stand to come out on top of the heap if Aztlan becomes a reality. The new ruling class."

"Huh. You think that could happen?"

"No," he replied bluntly. "Not a snowball's chance on Venus. But the possibility is going to keep the locals stirred up for a long time."

Baja, Sonora, Sinaloa, and Chihuahua were the newest dependent territories of the burgeoning United Federal Republic, a political union that included the fifty-eight states of the United States plus such far-flung holdings as Cuba, the Northwest Territory, and the UFR Pacific Trust. Acquired during the Second Mexican War of '76–'77, all four north Mejican territories were in line to be granted statehood, as the fifty-ninth through the sixty-second states, respectively, pending the outcome of a series of referendum votes scheduled in two years. Heavily dependent both on Yankee tourism and on northern markets for seafood and marijuana products, the region of old Mexico surrounding the Gulf of California had closer ties to the UFR than to the Democratic Republic of Mejico, and statehood was likely to pass.

But many in the newly acquired territories favored independence. The question of Aztlan, a proposed Latino nation to be carved out of the states of northern Mejico and the southwestern United States, had been one of the principal causes of the UN War of almost a century ago. The then–United Nations had proposed a referendum in the region, with a popular vote to determine Aztlanero independence. Washington refused, pointing out that the populations of the four U.S. states involved were predominantly Hispanic and almost certain to vote in favor of the referendum, and that federal authority superceded local desires. The war that followed had raged across the Earth, in orbit, and on the surfaces of both the Moon and Mars.

In the end, with the disintegration of the old UN and the rise of the U.S./UFR-Russian-Japanese–led Confederation of World States, Aztlan independence had been all but forgotten . . . save by a handful of Hispanic malcontents and disaffected political dreamers scattered from Mazatlan to Los Angeles.

The dream remained alive for many. John's father, his family long an important clan with connections throughout Sonora and Sinaloa, had been more and more outspoken against the gringo invaders who'd migrated south since the Mexican War. *"Carpetbaggers,"* he called them, a historical allusion to a much earlier time.

But he'd not been able to convince John, and for the past four years their relationship, already shaky with Carlos's drinking and his notoriously quick temper, had grown steadily worse.

"Have you ever thought," Lynnley said quietly, "that you and your dad could end up on opposite sides, if fighting breaks out?"

"Uh-uh. Won't happen. The government can't use troops on federal soil."

"A war starts down here, and all it would take is a presidential order. The Marines would be the first ones to go in."

"It won't come to that," he said, stubborn. "Besides, I want space duty."

She laughed. "And what makes you think they'll take what you want into consideration?"

"Hey, they gave me a dream sheet to fill out."

"So? I got one too, but once we sign aboard, our asses are theirs, right? We go where they tell us to go."

"Yeah . . ." The idea of coming back to Sonora to put down a rebellion left him feeling a bit queasy. He thought he remembered reading, though, that the government never used troops to put down rebellions in the regions those troops called home. That just didn't make sense.

It wasn't going to come to that. It *couldn't.*

"You need to get out of the house for a while?" Lynnley asked him. "I thought we might fly out to Pacifica. Maybe do some shopping?"

John glanced back at the front door. He could hear the faint and muffled echoes of his father, still shouting. *"You stupid bitch! This is all your fault! . . ."*

"I . . . don't think I'd better," he told her. "I don't want to leave my mom."

"She's a big girl," Lynnley said. "She can take care of herself."

But she doesn't, he thought, bitter. *She can't.* He felt trapped.

After talking with the Marine recruiter over an implant link three days ago, he and Lynnley had gone to the Marine Corps recruiter in Tiburón the next day and thumbed their papers. In less than three weeks they were supposed to report to the training center at Parris Island, South Carolina. Somehow he had to tell his parents . . . his mother, at least. How?

More than once in the past few years, Ellen Garroway Esteban had left the man who was, more and more, a stranger. Two years ago John had tried to get between his parents when his father had been hitting his mother and he'd received a dislocated shoulder in the subsequent collision with a bookcase. And there'd been the time when his father chased her out of the house with a steak knife . . . and the time she ended up in the hospital, claiming to have fallen down the stairs. John had begged her to pack up and leave, to get out while she still could. Others had done the same— her sister Carol in San Diego, the social worker who'd counseled her after her stay in the hospital, Mother Beatrice, their priest. Each time, she'd agreed the marriage was unsavable and nearly left for good . . . but each time, she found a reason to stay or to come back home.

One day, John was terribly afraid, she was going to come back home and Carlos was going to kill her. It would be an accident, of course. Injuries he inflicted on others always were.

John hated the thought of leaving his mother, of just walking out and abandoning her. He felt like a coward for running away like this. At the same time, he knew there was nothing else he could do to help her. Goddess knew, he'd tried, but, damn it, she kept coming back, she refused to press charges, she covered up for her husband when the police showed up in response to his panicked calls, made excuses for his behavior: "Carlos is just under a lot of stress right now. He can't help it, really . . ."

His mother would have to decide to help herself. *He* would be gone.

But not just yet. "No," he told Lynnley. "You go ahead. I'd better hang around and see how this plays out."

"Suit yourself," she told him. "Just remember, you won't be able to protect her when you're with the Corps off on Mars or someplace."

"I know." *Am I doing the right thing?*

He wished there was an answer to that.

3

IP Packet Osiris
En route, Mars to Earth
1337 hours Zulu

Colonel Ramsey lay snug within the embrace of a linking couch, only marginally aware of the steady, far-off vibration that was the packet's antimatter drive. It converted a steady stream of water into plasma and hard radiation, blasting it astern to accelerate the blunt, bullet-shaped vessel with its outsized heat radiators at a steady one gravity. Twenty hours after boosting clear from Mars orbit, the *Osiris* was already traveling at over 700 kilometers per second and had covered well over 25 million kilometers.

Within his thoughts, stroked by the virtual reality AI of the *Osiris* communications suite, he was in a huge auditorium, the Pentagon Briefing Center, located some kilometers beneath the Potomac River. The faint, steady thrum of the packet's main drive, starcore furies rattling just above the level of detectability in deck and titanium-ceramic bulkheads, was all but submerged by the incoming sensations of the padded auditorium seat, the murmured conversations and rustling movements of people around him, the glare off the big screen behind the podium, magnifying the features of the speaker.

"Gentlemen, ladies, AIs," General Lawrence Haslett said, addressing both those gathered physically in the briefing center and the much larger audience present electronically as well, "as of zero-nine-thirty this morning, Operation Spirit of Humankind is go. President LaSalle signed the executive order authorizing the Llalande Relief Expedition, and both House and Senate approval are expected by tomorrow. Admiral Ballantry has cleared the use of our newest IST, the *Derna*, for the op, and given the orders to begin rigging her for the voyage."

Haslett, Army Chief of Staff for the UFR/U.S. Central Military Command, gripped the sides of the podium as he spoke, his words as clear as if he were physically standing in the cramped comm suite on board the *Osiris*. It was hard for Ramsey to remember that the images he was seeing were already ten minutes and some seconds old. That was how long it took the comm lasers bearing the sensory data to reach *Osiris* from Earth.

"I needn't tell all of you," Haslett went on, "that this is a singularly important deployment, demanding diplomacy, tact, and a clear set of mission objectives and priorities." He paused. "I also needn't remind you that time is very much against us. While the FTL communicator on Ishtar provides an instantaneous link with the comm array on Mars, it will take ten years, objective, for the *Derna* to reach the Llalande system. By that time, of course, anything can have happened. New Sumer may have fallen, almost certainly *will* have fallen, if the situation continues as it has for the past few weeks. We need to proceed on the assumption that our colony will have been overrun by the rebels by that time, and craft the expeditionary force's orders with that in mind."

A chirp sounded over Ramsey's implant, a question signaled from someone in the audience.

"Yes," Haslett said.

"Yes, sir," one of the men seated in the auditorium, an Aerospace Force colonel, said, his image thrown up on the big screen at Haslett's back. Biographical data scrolled down the right corner of Ramsey's vision, identifying him as Colonel Joshua Miller. "If the Llalande contact mission is already doomed, what's the point of sending another ship out there? Is this a punitive expedition?"

"Not punitive, Colonel Miller. Not *solely* punitive, at any rate. You must know what the polls are saying about the situation on Ishtar."

"I didn't realize we were running our wars according to the poll numbers," another officer put in, and a number of people in the auditorium chuckled.

Haslett scowled and cleared his throat. "The mission commander will have full discretionary powers to deal with the situation as he sees fit, once he arrives at Ishtar. We will be sending along firepower enough that a full range of possible military options will be available."

"They'd damned well better," the woman on the recliner to Ramsey's left muttered, sotto voce, as if the people within the virtual reality transmission playing itself out within their heads might hear. "It's a hell of a long way to call for reinforcements if the Marines get into trouble!"

"You noticed that, did you?" Ramsey said, and smiled. Major Ricia Anderson was his executive officer within their constellation. "This op is going to be a logistical nightmare."

"Nothing new there, Colonel. The Corps always gets the short end."

"Seal it, Rish. I want to hear."

"This operation was originally conceived as a task force comprising a single Marine expeditionary unit," Haslett was saying in response to another question. "The Ishtar garrison is a Marine unit, and Spirit of Humankind is being presented to the public as a relief operation."

Ramsey brought up a text readout and scrolled down through the last few moments. Yeah, there it was. A Confederation liaison officer had asked about the possibility of a multinational task force. There'd been a lot of speculation about that in the netfeeds over the past few months.

"Even so," Haslett went on, "New Sumer Base is a multinational expedition. Euro-Union, Japan, Russia, the Brazilian Empire, Kingdom of Allah, the People's Hegemony, they all have science teams and contact specialists on Ishtar or in orbit. And every other nation with interests in the Llalande system wants a piece of the action. Whether we make this a multinational task force or not, we can expect at least four other nations to launch expeditions of their own within the next year or so.

"The latest word from the National Security Council is that there will be *two* expeditionary forces sent. The idea will be to get the American relief force to Ishtar as quickly as possible, which means assembling, training, and launching it within the next few months. Meanwhile, a second contingent, probably Army Special Forces, will be assembled to accompany any multinational force sent to Llalande, both as backup for the MEU and to safeguard American interests with the multinationals.

"This dual-force strategy has a number of advantages. Perhaps most important, the second force will be able to take direction from the first during its approach and alter its strategy to conform with the situation on the ground. And, of course, we'll also have the advantage of already being in control of key targets and bases when the multinationals arrive."

Ramsey sighed. Politics and politicians, they never changed. Was Washington more afraid of the rebellion spreading among the Ahannu or of the possibility of Chinese or Brazilians gaining control of Ishtar's ancient, jungle-smothered secrets?

Well, it didn't matter much, really. As usual, the Marines would be going in first.

Burning curiosity—and some fear—gnawed at him, though. As yet, no one had told him or the other members of his constellation *why* they were being summarily redeployed to Earth, but his private suspicions were validated when a laser comm message to *Osiris* had directed him and the other members of his constellation to link in for Haslett's Pentagon briefing.

Ever since he'd been called into General Cassidy's office at Prime three days ago, Ramsey assumed that the mysterious new orders would involve the Llalande crisis. Nothing else he could think of could possibly justify the expense of loading an entire Marine administrative constellation on board an antimatter-drive packet and shipping them back to Earth on an expensive, high-speed trajectory. Marines—even Marine colonels and their staffs—rarely rated such first-class service. Interplanetary packets, with their antimatter drives capable of maintaining a one-g acceleration for their entire transit, cut the flight time between Earth and Mars from months to five days, but even now, a century after their first deployment, they were hellishly expensive to operate.

What else could it be? As always, there were a few dozen hot spots and minor wars scattered across the face of the Earth. The recent Confederation intervention in Egypt had been much in the news of late; Marines had landed in Giza a couple of days ago to seize vital archeological sites from the hands of Mahdi religious fanatics. There was still the threat of a major political break with the Kingdom of Allah, even the possibility of war, but they wouldn't ship twelve Marines back from Mars just for *that*.

Same for the unrest in the American Southwest. There'd been rumblings in the states of Sonora and Chihuahua for years now, the possibility of civil unrest, even civil war. But again, there were plenty of Marines and other UFR forces on hand to deal with that.

Besides, there was the Famsit Two requirement, which suggested a long deployment off-Earth, the sort of deployment that would destroy marriage contracts and long-term relationships. The Corps had begun classifying men and women with family-situation ratings shortly after the UN War, when they'd begun assigning personnel to out-Solar duty in the thin, cold reaches beyond the orbit of Mars.

The Outwatch had been created as a joint UFR/U.S./Confederation military force with the awesome responsibility of patrolling the asteroid belt and the Jovian system. The destruction of Chicago in 2042 during a French warship's un-

successful attempt to drop a small asteroid on the central
United States had alerted the entire world to the threat of
small powers being able to nudge large rocks into Earth-
intercepting orbits that would wreak incalculable havoc
when they struck. No fewer than twelve large vessels were
kept in solar orbit within the belt or beyond, tracking and intercepting all spacecraft that might rendezvous with a plane-
toid in order to alter its course . . . and they'd been given the
responsibility for watching over Confederation interests on
Europa, with the Singer excavations, as well.

With the beginning of large scale mining operations
within the Belt, the Outwatch's personnel needs had sky-
rocketed. There were plans to increase the Navy-Marine
presence in the Belt to twenty ships within the next five
years, and there would be a desperate need for Famsit One
and Two personnel to man them.

But even that wouldn't justify bringing constellation
Delta Sierra 219 to Earth. Outwatch assignment needs were
ongoing and long-term, typically lasting a couple of years.
Any emergency need to fill an out-Solar billet could be
taken care of by screening new Marines coming out of
Camp Lejeune.

Which left the Ishtar crisis.

Everyone in the constellation felt the same sharp curiosity, sharing scuttlebutt and speculation with urgent fervor.
Ricia and Chris DeHavilland had both already told him that
they thought 219 was being tapped for command of the
Ishtar relief force.

It was a pretty good bet. Delta Sierra 219 had a lot of experience under its communal belt, including command of a
regiment in the Philippine Pirate War six years ago. That
was before Ramsey had come aboard, but he'd downloaded
all of the sims and data stores, all but experiencing directly
that savage guerrilla conflict at sea and in the jungles of Lu-
zon. They'd also done plenty of air inserts and during the
past eight months on Mars had trained with the new combat
suits in an extraterrestrial environment.

It was only beginning to sink in for Ramsey now. He was going to be offered a chance to go to the stars. The *stars* . . .

And with a regimental command, no less. *He* would be in charge of the Marine air-ground components of the MEU, probably under a general's overall mission command. That was the sort of plum assignment that came along once in a Marine's career, and it could well open the door to a general's stars in his future.

"Final selections for the expeditionary command staffs are being made now," Haslett was saying. "We should have the command teams by the end of next week. The selection boards are still reviewing the records of several general officers for Mission Command. In the meantime, all Earthside Marine Corps evolutions for Operation Spirit of Humankind will fall under the command of Major General Gabriowski." Haslett looked off to the side. "General? Would you care to add anything?"

General Dwight Gabriowski walked across the stage to the podium, a stout, muscular man with a bullet-smooth head and a Marine DI's scowl. Gabriowski. That clinched it, then. He was the man who'd ordered DS 219 back to Earth.

"Thank you, General Haslett," Gabriowski said. "I don't have much to say . . . except that I consider it an honor that the Marine Corps has again been called upon to lead the way. We've been hearing a lot lately about the Corp's redundancy . . . again . . . and it's a pleasure to be able to prove that we have as important a role in safeguarding our national interests, *wherever* they might lie, in the twenty-second century as in the twenty-first, or the twentieth, or the nineteenth. I want to add that . . ."

"Oh, Goddess, give me strength," Ricia said from the couch next to Ramsey's.

"Politics as usual," Ramsey said. These days, it seemed that the Corps spent as much money and attention on public relations—on the delicate job of persuading each President and each session of Congress that the Marine Corps was not the anachronism its enemies claimed. "You'd think that after Garroway's March—"

Gabriowski was still talking. "By the end of the month, we will be able to begin building the MEU from volunteer candidates Corpswide. This is an extraordinary mission, of extraordinary importance. It demands the best of our people, the very best of us, all of us together. Marines. Army. Navy. Aerospace. *Ad astra!*"

"Too bad he doesn't have a full marching band playing behind him," Ricia observed. " 'Stars and Stripes Forever' . . . or maybe the 'Luna Marine March.' "

"Ooh-rah!" But he couldn't completely share her sarcasm. It was a moving moment for him. "The Corps is going to the stars, Ricia," Ramsey said. "It'll sure as hell count for something come time for the next military appropriations, right? Semper fi!"

"Yeah," his exec said, dark and bitter. "Semper fucking fi."

Giza Complex
Kingdom of Allah, Earth
1615 hours Zulu

Captain Martin Warhurst pulled himself up and onto the final tier of stone blocks, grateful that he was in good enough shape to have made the climb, irritated that some of the Marines made the trek look easy. Sergeant Maria Karelin watched him with wry amusement as he paused to catch his breath, then stood up and walked over to the sniper's nest where she and Lance Corporal Lambeski, her spotter, had constructed their perch.

And perch it was, an eagle's eyrie. They were halfway up the eastern face of the Great Pyramid, some seventy meters above the desert floor. Their vantage point, in the pyramid's afternoon shadow and behind a low, sandbag wall erected on one of the two-and-a-half-ton stone blocks that made up most of the mountainous structure, gave them a magnificent view out over the desert and the tumultuous sprawl of the city Cairo. Ramshackle stone buildings shouldered one another in cluttered confusion on both sides of the Nile, tumbling across the silver-blue sheen of the river to the very edge of the Giza excavations. The hundreds of bodies that had fallen on the sand during the battle three days ago were gone.

Right now it looked as though the entire civilian population of Cairo had spilled out across the bridges over the Nile and begun gathering at the edge of the Giza complex two kilometers away, a vast, seething throng of humanity carrying banners and chanting slogans. Warhurst stepped up his helmet's magnification to study the angry, upturned faces in the crowd.

"We've got one of the high muckety-mucks tagged, Captain," Karelin told him. She stroked the butt of the massive MD-30 gauss sniper rifle propped up on the sandbags by its bipod. "Want us to pop him?"

"Let me see." He slaved his helmet display to her rifle. She leaned into the stock and swung the muzzle slightly. The image shifted left and magnified some more, coming to rest with red crosshairs centered on a bearded, angry-looking man in a turban and caftan, gesticulating savagely from the hood of a military hovertruck as he harangued the crowd. Warhurst queried his suit's computer, uplinking the image to Mission G-2. An ID came back seconds later, the words scrolling down the side of Warhurst's helmet display. "Abrahim ibn-Khadir," Warhurst said, reading it. "One of the Mahdi's number-one mullahs."

"Say the word, Captain," Karelin said, "and he'll be one of the Mahdi's *former* mullahs."

"That's a negative," Warhurst replied. "We shoot in self-defense. No provocative acts. You know the drill."

"Yes, sir," she said slowly. "But we don't have to like it. I'm in favor of proactive self-defense. Nail the bastard before he nails you."

"Yeah, or before he stirs up his pet fanatics, gets 'em to launch a suicide charge," Lambeski added.

"Orders is orders," Warhurst said lightly. He'd been concerned about just such a possibility, though the op commanders didn't seem to be at all worried. A suitable demonstration of superior force and firepower, they'd told him, would be enough to hold the Islamic forces at bay.

The Marines had provided that demonstration of force and firepower . . . but Warhurst wasn't at all sure the lesson had been learned.

"Shit," Karelin said. "You think the fat asses back in Washington know what they're doing? We were supposed to be relieved two days ago, as I recall!"

"Affirmative," Warhurst replied. He continued to study ibn-Khadir's face on his helmet display. "And the political situation has changed. You'll recall *that*. So we will sit right where we are, defend our perimeter, and wait for the relief . . . which will be deployed soon. You have a problem with that, Sergeant?"

"No . . . sir," she replied, but he heard the bitterness in her voice, and the touch of sarcasm.

The situation, he thought, was rapidly getting out of hand.

The original op plan had called for the assault force to seize the Giza Plateau and establish a perimeter, then hold it until a detachment of Confederation peacekeepers arrived to relieve them. That deployment was to have taken place at dawn on June 3.

Late on the second, however, while the Marines fought off the counterattack by the Mahdi's forces, the Chinese delegation had called a special meeting of the Confederation Security Directorate. The CSD, successor of the long defunct UN, provided a legal arena for the world's nation-states, including those, like China, that were not Confederation members. China had declared the deployment of American troops to Egypt to be an act of aggression as defined under Article II of the Confederation Charter and demanded a withdrawal. The issue was now being fought not in the desert outside of Cairo, but in the council chambers and meeting rooms of the CSD headquarters in Geneva.

The Confederation Joint Military Command had elected
to hold back the relief expedition until America's legal
standing on the issue was better defined. And, after all, so
long as the Marines were not under direct attack . . .

Unfortunately, Warhurst knew, that left Marines in a precarious position, holding a perimeter far larger than tactical
doctrine allowed, growing short on sleep as they stood
watch and watch, with supplies of food and especially water
tightly rationed. The water supply to the Giza complex had
been cut at the pumping stations on the Nile and not restored. Every indication suggested that another attack was
imminent. The Pentagon had promised that reinforcements
were only thirty minutes away, should the Marines' position
grow too precarious.

But a hell of a lot could happen in thirty minutes.

"Let's see what he's telling them," Warhurst said.

Uplinking again to Brigade Intelligence, he requested a
consecutive translation. The wildly shouting mullah was too
distant for the Marines to pick up his words through their armor sensor suites, but the AI he connected with had been
programmed both for Arabic and for lip-reading. Within another few seconds, a flat, atonal voice began speaking over
his helmet headset, the emotionless quality of the words
oddly contrasting with their evident content.

"The Western satans think to deprive us of our heritage,"
ibn-Khadir was saying. "They poke and dig among our
monuments, desecrate our grave sites and holy places, then
tell us that these symbols of our people, these holy testa-
ments to the power of Allah, were constructed by *another*
people, by foreigners . . . with the aid of demons from another star. They corrupt these holy places and defile the
name of Allah!" Ibn-Khadir turned his head, and the AI lost
the next few lines of his speech.

It sounded like the standard propaganda line, though.
Archeological discoveries over the course of the past two
centuries had proven that the principal structures on the Giza
Plateau—the three Great Pyramids of Khufu, Khafre, and

Menkaure, and the Sphinx—all had been raised, at least in preliminary form, eight thousand years before the traditionally accepted dates of their building, long before the Neolithic tribes who would later be known as Egyptians had migrated to the Nile Valley. The Egyptian government and, later, after the Mahdi had unified the far-flung Kingdom of Allah, the Principiate of Cairo, had insisted that the Sphinx and Great Pyramids were an expression of the soul of the Egyptian people and not of alien invaders who'd established colonies on Earth over ten thousand years ago.

That battle was not new. Variants of it had been ongoing since the last decade of the twentieth century, when American archeologists and geologists had first noted that erosion patterns in the flanks of the Sphinx were characteristic of rain, which suggested that it was considerably older than the traditionally assigned date of 2400 B.C. Dr. David Alexander, the noted Egyptologist who later gained fame as the father of xenoarcheology on Mars, had been expelled from Egypt because his theories and finds contradicted long established traditions of Egyptian history.

Seventy years had passed, but the delicate balance of politics, religion, and national pride hadn't changed. Two months ago archeologists from both the European Union and the UFR had opened a new chamber hewn from bedrock almost fifty meters beneath the hindquarters of the Sphinx. Artifacts discovered there tended to support the theory of extraterrestrial design, and a new tunnel had been found— one hinted at by Herodotus and other ancient writers—leading back toward the Great Pyramid of Khufu, where recent sonar and deep radar imaging suggested that a vast labyrinth of chambers remained yet undiscovered.

A deep bedrock labyrinth that could not possibly have been chipped out with the use of stone tools and wooden mallets.

A preliminary publication on the find in an archeological journal had triggered excitement worldwide, as well as a sharp rejection by the Islamic Kingdom of Allah. The local government authorities had ordered the Giza excavations closed down and all foreign archeologists to leave the country. From then on, all excavations in Egypt and other Kingdom of Allah states would be carried out by approved Islamic archeologists, under the direct supervision of the Islamic Directorate of History in Baghdad.

To Warhurst, it sounded like a hell of a stupid way to do science.

"We will not let the foreign satans take *truth* and twist it into blasphemy!" ibn-Khadir was shouting to the crowd. "The time has come to throw the foreigners out, to reclaim our history for ourselves, in the blessed name of Allah!"

The cheer that went up from the mob was audible across two kilometers of open ground. Warhurst felt an uneasy chill, despite the heat of the afternoon. Ibn-Khadir was bringing their fervor to a boil, and it wasn't hard to guess what would happen next.

"They're going to try a goddamned puppy rush," Karelin said, echoing Warhurst's own thoughts.

A puppy rush. Shit. Most of the people in that crowd were unarmed, as far as Warhurst could tell from the MD-30's magnified sniperscope image, though a few Chinese and Iranian assault rifles were in evidence. Many were women, many more teenagers and younger. The KOA militia leaders might well have decided to rush the Marine perimeter with civilians, hoping that the Americans wouldn't "kick the puppies," that they would at least hesitate and not open fire until armed militiamen could get close enough to begin killing Marines.

The hell of it was that a civilian charge, or an assault shielded by unarmed civilians, was a lose-lose proposition for the Marine defenders. If they held their fire, the enemy would break through the perimeter and be among them; no matter how good the Americans' mil-tech, they would be too badly outnumbered to survive a close-quarters battle.

But if the Marines opened fire, the up-close-and-personal images of unarmed Islamic civilians being slaughtered at long range would be uploaded to every e-news server on the Net, to be replayed time after time in gory and colorful detail on the viewalls and HVs of half the people on the planet. It would be a moral nightmare from which the UFR might never recover.

But maybe there was a different way.

"Downsize a click," he told Karelin. "And fire up your see-through."

"Aye aye, sir."

The generator in her rifle began spooling up to speed. The view of ibn-Khadir seemed to pull back twenty meters, revealing all of the truck he was standing on and more of the surrounding crowd. "Smile for the camera," Karelin said, and she fired the X-ray scatter pulse.

The image in Warhurst's display blanked out, showing nothing but green light. In a few seconds, however, the gun's computer built up a composite image from the back-scattered X rays, an image that turned sheet metal, plastic, cloth, and flesh into faint translucence, revealing denser structures like bone and the solid titanium steel of the hover-truck's engine block in light green, yellow, and pale green-white.

To avoid burning people in the target area, the pulse lasted for only a handful of nanoseconds, so the initial image was frozen in time. The computer superimposed that image on the real-time view, however, animating it to match the moving reality.

"There," Warhurst said. "See the flywheel on the drive train?"

"Roger that," Karelin said. The targeting reticle shifted again, coming to rest over the circular mass of the hover-truck's flywheel. Dopplered readings on the back-scatter radiation showed that it was in motion.

The Egyptian hovertruck was powered by pretty old tech, a hydrogen-burning power cell array that in turn powered the turbine compressors of two large lift fans in the vehicle's chassis. The fans were off, the vehicle grounded on its plenum chamber skirts, but the power assembly was still running, storing energy in the massive, fast-spinning flywheel that provided both extra power on demand and gyroscopic balance.

"See if you can nick that wheel," Warhurst said.

"Ay-firmative, Skipper!" Karelin leaned into the stock of her weapon again. There was a faint whine as its magfield generators came up to full power, and then a piercing crack as she squeezed the trigger.

Gauss rifles, rail guns, mass drivers—all terms for the same simple concept. The MD-30—MD for "mass driver"—was a sniper's rifle, using an electromagnetic pulse to launch a 250-gram sliver of steel-jacketed depleted uranium with a muzzle velocity of approximately Mach 25.

The truck beneath ibn-Khadir's feet jerked sharply with the impact, the engine access panels snapping open, the plastic windshield shattering. The impact smashed the engine block wide open, smashed the durasteel-armored flywheel housing, and cracked the flywheel itself. In an instant the truck's body was flipped into the air, sending the Mullah ibn-Khadir flying in a thrashing tangle of robes and limbs. The vehicle's steel and plastic shell absorbed most of the high-speed shrapnel from the flywheel, but torque ripped the vehicle open and bounced it onto its roof.

The crowd, cheers turned to shrieks of terror, broke and scattered in all directions. The hovertruck's hydrogen cells, ripped open by the impact, ignited, sending a ball of orange hydrogen flame blossoming into the sky. In an instant the more or less orderly gathering was reduced to chaotic pandemonium, as civilians and militia troops fled the burning wreckage. Several dozen bodies lay around the truck, hit by shrapnel or stunned by the sonic crack of the hyperprojectile—it was impossible to tell which. Ibn-Khadir was sprawled ten meters from the wreck, weakly moving as two of his braver supporters tried to help him to his feet.

"Taking kind of a chance, aren't you, Skipper?" Lambeski

asked with a matter-of-fact expression. "Burning civilians like that . . ."

"Burning hydrogen rises," Warhurst replied. "That's why only thirty-some people died on the *Hindenburg*."

"The what?"

"Never mind. We might have hit a few civilians with flying chunks of truck, but it happened so quickly, I doubt the newsie remotes saw what happened or could reconstruct it. And I *don't* think they'll be eager to try another mob rush, do you?"

"You got that right, sir," Karelin said. "Look at 'em run!"

She'd stepped the magnification on her scope down to take in the entire sweep of the west bank of the Nile, from El Giza north to the University of Cairo and beyond to the district of El Duqqi. The panicked mob was dispersing back across the Gama and Giza bridges.

The mullahs might be able to assemble the mob again, but it would take time.

And maybe help would arrive by then.

Maybe.

4

Giza Complex
Kingdom of Allah, Earth
1838 hours Zulu

Like a large and exceptionally ugly beetle, all angles and planes and outstretched landing jacks, the first dropship drifted down out of the evening sky on shrieking plasma thrusters, moving toward the bare patch of desert south of the Sphinx marked by the brilliantly pulsing green landing beacon.

Unlike the suborbital TAVs that had brought in the Marines, these were true spacecraft, big UD-4 Navajo cargo landers generating a million pounds of thrust through their six Martin-Electric plasmadyne jets. Air scoops gaped now, fans howling, gulping down air as reaction mass, saving precious water for higher altitudes, where the air ran thin or trailed away into vacuum.

Sand exploded in swirling clouds from beneath the lander as it touched down, sagging slightly as its hydraulics took up the shock of landing. Belly doors gaped open, interlocking square teeth sliding apart to disgorge eight light Rattlesnake robot tanks, four Cobra medium MBTs, a pair of massive Gyrfalcon mobile artillery crawlers, two twenty-ton cargo floaters, and four armored personnel carriers. The dropship lifted again in a sandblasting whirlwind as soon as its cargo was clear. Other dropships were touching down at marked LZs elsewhere across the Giza Plateau.

Warhurst trotted up to the lead APC, which was just beginning to unbutton. The markings indicated American rapid-deployment infantry. He was surprised, having expected a joint Confederation unit coming in by TAV from the UK, not American troops. And the UD-4s meant they'd deployed from orbit, probably from the Army's Rapid Deployment Force Orbital Station in low orbit.

A man in an Army active-camo armor cuirass and brown fatigues, with a major's oak leaf insignia painted on his shoulder pieces and the RDF's lightning bolt insignia on his breast, clambered down the aft ramp as a line of fully armored troops piled out of the APC and jogged out onto the sand.

"Who's in charge here?" the major demanded.

"Captain Warhurst, 2nd Regiment, U.S. Marines." He didn't salute. Standing orders required a suspension of any military protocol that might allow the enemy to target officers.

"Major Rostenkowski, 5th Light Infantry."

"Welcome to Egypt, Major."

"Good to be here. You are relieved, Captain," the major said. "The Army has the situation in hand."

"About damned time, Major," Warhurst said. He turned his head to watch the soldiers falling into line as a sergeant bawled orders at them. "What happened to the Confed relief?" The last he'd heard, his relief was supposed to be a couple of Russian platoons, some light German armor, and a detachment of Brits.

Rostenkowski grinned. "Bogged down in politics, as per SOP. Washington is getting it from all sides these days, and the Confederation isn't sure they want to play along. The Joint Chiefs elected to send us instead. You and your boys and girls are to hustle ass back to Quantico for debrief. What's your tacsit?"

"Give me your feed channel, sir."

They matched 'ware frequencies, and Warhurst thought a packet of detailed tactical data to Rostenkowski's biocybe system, providing him with detailed information on the initial assault, the counterattack, and the overall situation since.

"Nice twist, using a sniper to discourage that attack," the major said. "Any civilian casualties?"

"We're not sure. Our spotters saw ambulance crews picking up four people, but we don't know if they were dead or just badly hurt when the truck exploded."

"Well, the important thing was to keep that sort of thing out of the newsies' eyes. Good work, Captain."

"Thank you, sir." He was somewhat irritated by Rostenkowski's brusque manner. His Marines had done a hell of a job these past four days, and he was being congratulated for his public relations skills in keeping the collateral damage he'd inflicted out of the netnews downloads.

"This is an Army deployment area now, Captain. Tell your people to stand down unit by unit as we relieve them."

"Aye aye, sir."

"Oh, and you'd better get yourself presentable."

"Sir?"

"A special TAV is being vectored in to pick you up. Should be grounded within fifteen mikes."

Warhurst looked down at himself. He was wearing his armor, sans helmet and gauntlets, and the active camo surface was sand-pitted, gritty, and streaked with grime. His one-piece underneath was sweat-soaked and rank; he'd not had a bath in four days, and he knew his depilatory had worn off a couple of days back, leaving him with a distinctly unregulation shadow on his face.

He'd not brought much in the way of toiletries or spare uniforms . . . not for a deployment that was supposed to last for a day, two at the most.

"A TAV? Taking me where?"

Rostenkowski shrugged. "Back to Quantico. Don't know why. All I know is to tell you to be ready to go . . . and to leave your people in charge of your number two." Rostenkowski turned then and began shouting orders at the soldiers unloading supply crates from one of the transport floaters.

Warhurst used his internal mapping biocybes to locate his XO. He would have to let her know what was going down.

And where the *hell* was he going to find a clean uniform?

Esteban Residence
Guaymas, Sonora Territory
United Federal Republic, Earth
0902 hours PT

"I'm leaving, Mom. I have to."

They strolled along the stone-strewn beach, the oily gray surf of the Sea of California lapping at their feet, the muddy breakers just ankle high. The sun blazed low above the mountains in the east, promising another sweltering day. Both John and his mother wore lightweight bodysuits against the UV and the heat, and their faces glistened with blocking oils generated by antisun nanotreatments.

"I know, Johnny. I just wish you weren't joining the Marines, is all."

"Why?" He tried a grin. "It's not like we don't have it in our blood. Garroway's March?"

"Oh, it's in your blood, all right. Damn it."

"The thing is, I don't want to leave you. Dad can be . . . tough to live with."

She sighed. "Don't I know it? But . . . he means well. He's just . . . under a lot of stress lately, is all. . . ."

"Damn it, Mom, I wish you'd quit making excuses for him. He drinks too much, and when he's drunk, he loses his temper. The cybercontrols don't seem to be helping him much."

"He disabled them."

"What?"

She nodded. "About six months ago. He admitted it to me, during a fight. He said the control implant made him feel like he wasn't himself."

"Does his doctor AI know?"

"I don't know. It's his business, not mine."

"It's your business if he hits you! If he makes your life miserable!"

"He's only . . . gotten physical a couple of times. . . ."

"That's a couple of times too damned many!" He shook his head. "Maybe I shouldn't leave after all. . . ."

"No, Johnny. No, you were right the first time. You've *got* to go. Maybe if you do, there won't be as much holding me here."

"I worry about you, Mom."

"Don't. I can look out for myself."

"Mom, I've been researching this, downloading stuff from the psych library in Hermosillo. Dad is an abuser. A clinically abusive personality. If we stay here—if *you* stay here—he'll hurt you. Maybe worse. You've got to get out."

"It's not that bad, Johnny. Really. It's just sometimes he can't control himself."

"Bullshit."

"What?"

"I said, bullshit. Look . . . the last time he hit you . . . if there'd been a cop in the living room that time, or even a security robot, recording what happened, do you think he would have touched you?"

"That's not—"

"Would he have hit you if anyone was there?"

She struggled with the thought for a moment. "Well . . . no."

"Then he *can* control himself. Don't you see? He hits you because he *can,* because he knows he can get away with it, and it's a way of exercising power. And it's not just the hitting. Words can hurt as much as fists sometimes, you know? What the downloads I've been looking at call emotional abuse. And the way he spies on us, tries to go through our private cyberfiles . . ." John shook his head, feeling desperate. "That's why I've got to leave, now. I just can't take it any longer. If I don't leave now—"

"I know, son. I want you to go."

"But I don't want to abandon you."

"You're not. I *told* you to go, didn't I?" She managed a smile. "Don't worry about me. I've been thinking . . . I've been thinking about my sister in San Diego, maybe going up and seeing her."

"If you do, Mom, don't come back. Please?"

"We'll see. As for you . . . you'll be careful?"

"As careful as they'll let me be."

"It's just that . . . Wouldn't the Navy be . . . well . . . cleaner?"

He laughed. "No muddy foxholes on a high guard cruiser, that's for sure. But, no. I've wanted to go with the Corps ever since I read *Ocher Sands*." He'd liked the downloaded drama so much that he'd bought the hardcopy book as well. He'd been enticed by the fact that it was about his great-grandfather, "Sands of Mars Garroway," and his grandmother, Caitlin. But he'd been permanently hooked by the tales of Marine men and women serving off-world, on the moon, Mars, and the Jovian satellites.

"I hear it's awfully hard. The training, I mean."

He reached down, picked up a flat stone the size of the palm of his hand, and sent it skipping out across the waves three . . . four . . . a fifth skip before it sank. "Yeah. And I'll tell you the truth, Mom. I don't know if I can cut it. But I know I have to *try*."

"I imagine with that kind of attitude, you'll make it. I'm proud of you, Johnny."

"Thanks, Mom. Are you . . . you're sure you'll be all right?"

"I'll be fine. Will *you* be okay?"

"Sure! Plenty of fresh air and exercise? Plenty to eat? And plenty of friendly, helpful drill instructors to remind me of

Dad in his more emotional moments, just so I don't get home-sick." He didn't add that Lynnley would be there too. His mom knew he and Lynnley had been seeing each other, but he didn't think she would understand their pact. She might think he was joining the Marines just because Lynn was joining, and that wasn't the way things were at all.

"One question, son."

"Shoot."

"Do you still want to be assigned to space duty?"

"Well . . . sure. I'll take SMF if it's offered. That's where the real excitement's at, you know."

She made a face. "Yes. I know. But you might be gone . . . a long time."

"Probably. A couple of years, maybe, for a hitch on Mars. That's not so bad." He hadn't told her that he'd already dreamsheeted for Space Marine Force duty with the recruiter. Not that he was all that likely to land a space billet, but he wanted the chance, and bringing that bit of news into the conversation would . . . complicate things.

"Let's just wait and see what happens, okay?" he told her.

She smiled. "Okay."

They turned around and began strolling back up the beach toward the steps leading up the cliffs to the house.

IP Packet Osiris
En route, Mars to Earth
1847 hours Zulu

Dr. Traci Hanson was still furious, two days after she'd left Mars. How *dare* they interrupt her work at Cydonia? There couldn't be anything so demanding of her particular attention and expertise back home that warranted dragging her away from the Cydonian xenocomplex, to say nothing of the sheer, insane cost of stuffing her on board a constant-g packet that would have her back on Earth within a week.

"The hell of it is," she growled at one of her cabin mates, "the institute ordered me home, but I think *your* people are pulling the strings." She was lying on her couch, flat on her back and feeling miserable.

Gunnery Sergeant Athena Horst snorted. "Who? The Corps?"

"No. The Pentagon. The government. Hell, whoever it is who's running the show these days."

"You didn't do so hot in civics in school, did you, babe?"

"Only the federal government can afford to give us a cruise back to Earth in such luxury," Hanson said with a sneer, glancing around the cramped, gray-green compartment that was quarters to her and three Marines for the duration.

"Well, they're not my people. We're as much in the dark about this redeployment as you are."

"I was talking with Lieutenant Kerns a little while ago," Staff Sergeant Krista Ostergaard put in. "The scuttlebutt is that we're being reassigned to a new mission. An out-Solar mission."

"That means Llalande," Master Sergeant Vanya Barnes said. "Shit."

"You don't want to go to the stars, Van?" Ostergaard said.

"I don't want to be gone twenty years."

Horst shrugged. "Hell, why not? The time'll pass like that," she snapped her fingers, "thanks to old Einstein. And it's not like we have families back home."

"The *Corps* is home," Ostergaard said.

"Fuckin'-A," Horst said, and she exchanged a high-five hand slap with Ostergaard. "Semper fi!"

Hanson frowned and looked away. She was uncomfortable with these women, with the posing and the brassy-cold hardness of body and of mind that she was coming to associate with all of the members of this peculiar subspecies of human known as U.S. Marines.

The *Osiris* was a small vessel, mounting an eighty-five-ton hab module normally outfitted for eight people, two to a cabin, not counting the AIs at the controls. A small lounge area, a galley, and the communications suite completed the amenities. For this passage, though, the admin constellation of Marines on board, composed of six women and six men, had been packed into the four compartments, with the one extra slot—for the ship's sole civilian passenger—provided in the lounge. Hanson had been given a choice of sleeping there or in one of the two compartments assigned to the women. She'd chosen to share quarters because the lounge, which connected all four cabins and the galley, was less than private, with Marines of both sexes tramping through at all hours of the vessel's artificial day and night.

She'd begun regretting the decision within hours of boosting out of Mars orbit. These female Marines made her nervous with their bad-ass attitudes and nanosculpted bodies. They were rough, strong, and as foul-mouthed as their male Marine counterparts, flat-chested and hard-muscled, with technically enhanced eyes that seemed to look right through her.

They'd been polite enough, true, but her forced incarceration had left her irritable and sour. She was at least a borderline claustrophobe, and none of the compartments on board the *Osiris* was larger than a small bedroom. It wouldn't have been so bad if they'd been in free fall; even the tiniest hab compartment seemed roomy with three-dimensional floating space in microgravity. But the steady one-g acceleration—three times what she was used to after a year on Mars—kept her pinned to the deck, and most of the time strapped into her couch. She didn't understand how Horst and the others could move about with such casual disregard for the acceleration dragging at them every minute of the long ship-day.

Then something one of the Marines had just said managed to register in her weight-numbed mind. "Wait a minute," she said. "What was that about Llalande?"

"Llalande 21185," Barnes said, staring at her with her peculiarly dark nanoaltered eyes. "It's a red dwarf star about eight light-years from—"

"I *know* what it is," Hanson snapped. "We've been watching it from Mars. What did you mean about an out-Solar mission there?"

"Stands to reason, honey," Ostergaard said, grinning. "That's where the action is. My money's riding on a relief expedition. You're an archie, right?"

"Xenoarcheotechnologist," she replied.

"Whoa, the lady's using damned big words," Barnes said.

"Positively sesquipedalian," Horst said, with just a hint of a sneer.

Ostergaard laughed. "I'll bet a month's pay they want you out on the Llalande planet to check out the xenotech they've been finding. Right, Marines?"

"Fuckin'-A," Barnes said. "Assuming there's any left when we get there, ten years from now."

"I'm *not* going to Ishtar!" Hanson said. She didn't want to admit it, but these people were scaring her now. "My work is here, on Mars."

"You're not on Mars now, honey," Horst reminded her. "You're en route to Earth on *very* special orders. Either you really pissed someone off back there or you're headed for Ishtar." She grinned, an evil showing of teeth. "And maybe both!"

Traci Hanson was used to having things her own way, to charting her own course and the hell with what others thought. It had gotten her this far, head of mission research at the Cydonian complex, and only a few scars the worse for wear. If they thought they could just order her to drop everything to go haring off to the stars, they were crazy. What did they think AIs were for?

Robinson. She would take this up with Robinson as soon as she got back.

Or . . . as soon as she was able to get up and walk around again, after this brutal week of acceleration.

Then she remembered that the packet's acceleration matched the gravitational acceleration of Earth itself, that this hell was going to go on and on.

Shit . . .

Headquarters, PanTerra Dynamics
New Chicago, Illinois
United Federal Republic, Earth
1455 hours CT

   Gavin Norris had never seen a demonstration like this.
The chanting throngs filled the circular PanTerra Plaza and
spilled over into all of the surrounding thoroughfares. Police
in full armor were everywhere, trying to maintain order and
keep the main walkways open. The demonstration, he gathered, was an anti-An gathering, and tempers were burning
high. Pro-Anners were there as well, and demonstration and
counterdemonstration were threatening to erupt into full-
scale civil war.

   Norris ignored the chanting crowds as best as he could,
making his way toward the slender, black pinnacle that was
his destination. The PanTerra Building soared two kilometers into the thin, cold air of the midwestern sky, rising from
the Highland Park district to look down on a cloud-mottled
Lake Michigan to the east and the still empty ruin of the
Barrens to the south.

   The destruction of Old Chicago during the UN War a century ago had killed millions—no one would ever know the
precise death toll—and extinguished one of the largest and
most prosperous cities on the planet. Plutonium from the reaction mass heating grid of the French spacecraft that had
broken up above Lake Michigan had scattered radioactive
dust southwest across the city, leaving a poisoned footprint
fifty kilometers long burned into the soil of northern Illinois.
Detox robots and crews in sealed crawlers continued to
work both in the desert ashore and in the waters offshore,
but the most optimistic calculations indicated that the Barrens would remain hazardous for another five centuries at
least.

   North of the Barrens, though, the rebuilding had been
proceeding with an enthusiasm born of victory in the deter-

mination not to see the brawling, big-shouldered city of
Sandburg's poem forever extinguished. The cities of Highland Park and Waukegan had merged, becoming the nucleus
of the new metropolis. The lake itself was all but dead now,
but construction had begun extending out over the water almost as soon as the radiation there dropped to reasonable
levels.

The PanTerra Building, with its distinctive black panther logo perched high atop the revolving dome that
housed its executive suites, had foundations sunk deep
within the bedrock beneath what once had been open water. The PanTerra Plaza consisted of open grounds and
pavement immediately in front of the main entrance, centered on a towering water fountain symbolizing the Spirit
of Chicago.

The demonstration was well under way by the time Norris approached the building. All traffic—ground and air—
had been blocked from the Highland Park district as far
south as Central and as far west as Sheridan, and the slide-
ways had been turned off. He had to park his flier at a port
garage near Central Park and walk five blocks through
streets packed with thronging mobs. When he saw how
packed the plaza was, he turned away and found an entranceway to the transit levels. Most of the major buildings
in New Chicago were connected by floater tubes beneath the
ground level.

An elevator took Norris from the PanTerra Building's
transit access bay to the lobby. A separate elevator, one with
a security check panel that tasted the DNA on his palm and
electronically probed his briefcase and his clothing, took
him then to the 540th floor, so far above the demonstration
that the mobs simply vanished into the geometrical intrica-
cies of street, building, and plaza.

Allyn Buckner met him in another lobby, this one with
soaring, curving walls that were either completely transpar-
ent or remarkably large and seamlessly joined viewall pan-

els. The PanTerran panther hung above the entrance to the
conference center, ten meters high, muscles rippling in real-
istically animated holography.

"Mr. Norris," Buckner said, extending a hand. He was a
thin, acid-looking man with an insincere smile, one of the
small army of PanTerran vice presidents whom Norris had
dealt with in the past. "Thank you for coming in person."

"Not a problem, Mr. Buckner," Norris replied. "You
never know who's got access to your VR link codes. I prefer
face-to-face."

"Indeed. We can guarantee the security of our conversation here. This way, please?"

Norris jerked his head to the side, indicating the crowds
far below. "So, what the hell is *that* all about?"

"War, Mr. Norris," Buckner said as he led Norris beneath
the giant panther and into the conference suite. "There is going to be a war very soon now. The first war, I might add, to
be fought across interstellar distances."

"Llalande?"

"Of course. The people are quite upset over the, um, slavery issue."

"There was a pretty sizable pro-An contingent down
there too."

"Religious nuts, Mr. Norris. The lunatic fringe. The *people* are demanding that the human slaves on Ishtar be
freed."

That, Norris thought, was something of an oversimplifi-
cation. The number of separate factions on Earth clashing
over the issue of contact with the An and the sociopolitical
situation on distant Ishtar was simply incalculable. True, the
loudest voices right now were those of outrage over the discovery of the Exiles—descendants of humans taken from
Mesopotamia thousands of years ago and transplanted to
the An world as a slave population. But there were other
voices as well. The entire Islamic block wanted all dealings
with the An halted . . . and an end to archeological research

both on Earth and off-world that tended to relegate humankind to a less-than-glorious set of beginnings. That was what the fighting right now in Egypt was all about. And then there were the countless religions, cults, and movements worldwide that viewed the An as gods, figuratively or even literally.

But there were also groups who saw considerable profit in closer ties with the An. Most of the major megacorporations of Earth were vying now for the technological spin-offs coming out of the xenoresearch off-world.

And of course that was where the real power lay, Norris thought . . . not with the "people," but with the multitrillion-newdollar corporate entities who truly controlled the planet.

Inside the conference suite, Buckner guided Norris to a carpeted, soundproofed room with an elaborate array of viewalls, link centers, and screens. "Computer," Buckner said, addressing the air. "Security, level one."

"Security, level one initiated, Mr. Buckner," a female voice replied. "Do you require a record?"

"No. Switch off."

"Switching off, Mr. Buckner."

"I don't even like the AIs listening in to some of this," Buckner explained. "What we're on to here is so fantastic—"

"Are you sure the mikes and recorders are really off?"

"Of course. The software was developed in this very building. Have a seat."

Norris sank into the embrace of a chair that molded itself to his back and shoulders. "So, I gather you have another assignment for me."

"We do." Buckner took a seat opposite his. "A very important one. A *lucrative* one."

"You've got my attention, Mr. Buckner."

"We have been scanning our personnel records for a particular person. You were the first of the troubleshooters on our list. And the best, I might add. You have all of the qualities we are looking for—young, dynamic, ambitious. No family to speak of, no long-term commitments or contracts. Not even any casual lovers."

Norris raised an eyebrow. They didn't know about Claire, evidently. Good. "What's your point?"

"We need a liaison, Mr. Norris, on a very, very special operation."

"What kind of operation?"

"You'll be fully briefed later, if you accept."

"How can I accept if I don't know what it is?"

Buckner smiled, an oily tug at the corner of his mouth. "Oh, we may be able to offer suitable inducements."

"Such as?"

"We are offering you a long-term contract. A very long-term contract, in fact. Minimum time—twenty years."

Norris's eyes widened. "Is that a business proposition or a prison term?"

"A little of both, I fear. If you accept, you won't be able to terminate. Not . . . conveniently, at any rate."

A twenty-year contract? Buckner must be out of his mind. "This doesn't exactly sound like a promotion, Mr. Buckner. What are the inducements you mentioned?"

"A nice, round figure, Mr. Norris. One billion newdollars, *and* a shot at senior management, when you return. Perhaps even a seat on the board."

"One *billion!*" Norris hung on the shock for a comic moment, mouth gaping. "One *billion?*" Then he heard the rest of Buckner's sentence. "What do you mean, when I return? Where are you sending me?" He already knew he was going, wherever it was. A billion newdollars? Was the man serious?

The viewwalls at Buckner's back lit up in response to a linked thought. A swollen gas giant hung low in a russet sky. Oddly twisting, purple-hued vegetation clotted an undulating landscape. Pyramids reflected the gold-red light of a tiny, shrunken sun.

"Ishtar, Mr. Norris. We're sending you to Ishtar, eight light-years away."

"My God!"

He hoped Claire wouldn't be *too* hurt when he told her goodbye.

5

*U.S. Marine Corps Recruit Train-
ing Center
Parris Island, South Carolina
0215 hours ET*

"Now I want you maggots off of my bus . . . *move! Move!
Move!*"

John stumbled down the steps in a sleep-deprived haze,
crowding forward with the other recruits as they piled off the
ancient and weather-beaten magbus that had brought them
there from Charleston in the middle of the night. The Marine
sergeant who'd ridden the bus with them all the way from
the Charleston skyport, a grimly taciturn man in spotless
khakis, had been singularly uncommunicative for the entire
trip. Now, though, he was bellowing at the recruits, chivvy-
ing them from their seats and into line. Lights glared overhead, casting weirdly moving shadows and making it light
enough to see the footprints painted on the ground, neatly
spaced in a single long rank.

Another sergeant was waiting for them, hands on hips,
the infamous "Smokey Bear" hat square-set on his head.
"Fall in! I said fall *in*, damn it! Feet on the prints! *Stand at
attention!*"

The mob of civilians shoved and bumped into line, each
of them taking on his or her own semblance of standing at
attention . . . or at least a half-informed guess as to what

such a posture might be like. John's loving study of the
Marine Corps in past months had included a download of
several Corps training manuals, and he'd been practicing in
front of the E-center's holopickup a lot lately. The footprints on the ground were closely spaced, so close that each
recruit was shouldered in tightly to left and right, ahead
and behind, a single, anonymous mass of tired humanity.

"Jesus, Quan Yin, and *Buddha!*" the second sergeant
bawled. "I ask for recruits and they send us *this*? The boss is
not gonna like it!"

John stood rigidly in line, eyes fixed on the letters reading
U.S. GOVERNMENT on the sloping gray side of the magbus,
endeavoring to keep them fastened there as the sergeant
stalked past his line of sight. The night air was steamy, a
blanket of heat and humidity that dragged at each breath and
brought sweat dripping from brow and nose.

The sergeant from the bus prowled down the line of
scared and sleep-deprived recruits. "You! Square away!
Shoulders back! Get rid of any cigs or gum. And you! Yeah,
you, maggot! Quit gawking around and hold those eyeballs
front and center or I will personally *pop* them out of your
miserable maggot's skull and *eat* them for breakfast!"

John was pretty sure he knew what was coming, courtesy
of family stories from his mother about life in the Corps—
disorientation, confusion, controlled but deliberate terror,
sleep deprivation, all in the name of breaking down civilians
and rebuilding them as Marines. Forewarned was fore-
armed, as far as he was concerned. Whatever they dished
out, he could take. He was a Garroway now, in name as well
as by birth.

He did wish Lynnley were here, though. She'd flown out
from Tiburón to Charleston, while he'd accompanied his
mother north to San Diego first, then caught a sub-O flight
out of Salton Spaceport. They'd planned to meet up at the
Charleston skyport yesterday, but all incoming female recruits had been rounded up as soon as they arrived and
whisked off to some other receiving area. He'd found him-

self herded on board the ancient magbus with thirty-seven other young men and the taciturn Marine sergeant.

That sergeant was taciturn no longer. "*On* behalf of Major General Phillip R. Delflores, commanding officer of this installation, and *on* behalf of the United States Marine Corps, *welcome* to Parris Island," he bellowed, somehow making the ear-ringing yell effortless, somehow doubling the volume of select words for emphasis, as though a bellow was his normal and everyday manner of speech. "I *am* Staff Sergeant Sewicki, and my assistant here is Sergeant Heller. I *will* keep this short and simple, so that even brainless civvy maggots like you can understand.

"This is *my* island, this is *my* Marine Corps, and you maggots are *my* responsibility! Today you are embarking on a twenty-one-week course of Marine Corps recruit training, commonly known as boot camp. You are *not* at home any longer. You are *not* at school, you are *not* in your old neighborhood, you are *not* back in the world that you once knew. During these next few weeks, you *will* obey all orders given to you by *any* Marine. Just so there's no confusion on this point, you people are *not* Marines. You are *recruits*. You must *earn* the title of U.S. Marine. To do that, you must prove to your officers, your drill instructors, your comrades, *and* yourselves that you are *worthy* of the uniform and the title of a United States Marine! *Do* you recruits understand me?"

The question was greeted by a mumbled chorus of "Yes," and "Yes, sir," and even the occasional "Sure."

Sewicki exploded. "*When* you open your maggot mouths, the very first word you utter will be the word *sir!* The very *last* word your maggot mouths utter will be the word *sir!* . . . *Do* you understand me?"

"Sir, yes, sir!" was the response, somewhat ragged and quavering.

"*No! No! No!*" Sewicki's eyes bulged, his face reddened, and for an instant John wondered if the man was going to have a stroke. "*What* do you people think this is, the goddamn Army? *When* I ask if you understand me, *when* I give you an order, the correct and *proper* response is, 'Sir, aye aye, sir!' *Do* you understand me?"

"Sir, aye aye, sir!"

" 'Aye, aye' means '*I* understand and *I* will obey!' *Do* you understand me?"

"Sir, aye aye, sir!"

"What? I can't hear you!"

"Sir, aye aye, sir!"

"Again! Louder!"

"Sir, aye aye, sir!"

He cupped a hand to his ear. *"What?"*

"Sir, aye aye, sir!"

"You!" He spun suddenly, face and forefinger inches from the face of a terrified recruit three men to John's right. "What is your name?"

"Sir! H-Hollingwood, sir!"

"Hollywood! What kind of a name is that?"

"Sir—"

"Let me see your war face!"

"S-Sir! Aye . . . what?"

"Let me see your goddamn war face! Do you know how to make a war face? *This* is a war face! *Arrrr!* Now *you* do it!"

With his eyes rigidly front, John could only imagine what was going on, but he heard the recruit give a terrified yelp.

"That is *pathetic!* You do *not* frighten me, Hollywood! Hit the deck! Ten push-ups!"

The recruit dropped.

"*On* your goddamn feet, Hollywood! *What* did I just tell you?"

"Sir, I—"

"*When* I give you an order, you *will* respond with 'Sir, aye aye, sir!' *Do* you understand me?"

"Sir, aye aye, sir!"

"What was that? I can't hear you!"

"Sir, aye aye, sir!"

"Now hit the deck and give me twenty push-ups!"

"Sir, aye aye, sir!"

As the recruit began grunting through his push-ups, attended closely by the other sergeant who was shouting out the cadence, Sewicki continued his prowl in front down the ranks.

"I am an *easy* man to get along with. *All* you need to do to get along with me is *to* obey my commands instantly, *without* hesitation, *without* argument, do you understand me?"

"Sir, aye aye, sir!" the ranks chorused.

"You!" Sewicki moved so fast he appeared to dematerialize, rematerializing in front of a recruit in the front rank four to John's left, face glowering, finger pointing. "What's your name?"

"Sir! Garvey! Sir!"

"Gravy, is that *gum* you have in your mouth?"

"Uh, sir, I mean, it's—"

"Is that or is that not gum you have in your maggot mouth?"

"It's—It's counterhum, sir."

"Remove it."

Garvey spat the offending wad into his hand.

"Place it on your nose."

"S-Sir . . . ?"

"On your nose, recruit."

"Sir! Aye aye, sir!"

"And it had better stay there until I tell you to get rid of it!" He spun, addressing them all. "As for the rest of you, we are going to march—or perform the best simulation of a march that you yahoos are capable of performing—into that building behind you, and there you will deposit in a bin that we will provide any and all contraband you may have on your persons, including guns, knives, weapons of any kind, cigs, lighters, candy, food, soda, liquids of any type, gum, stims, *all* drugs including analgesics, mem boosters, and sleepers, nano dispensers of any kind *including* hummers and joggers, game players, personal communications and recording devices, personal entertainment systems, neural plug-ins, pornographic material of all types—including naked holopics of your girlfriends, boyfriends, and/or parents—*do* you understand me?"

"Sir! Aye aye, sir!"

"I don't care what you used, smoked, tapped, smacked, licked, drank, charged, plugged, or popped back in the World. You people with electronic enhancements *will* be losing them tomorrow. While you are in *my* Corps and on *my* island, you will be *clean*."

John blinked. He couldn't mean *all* electronics, could he?

Sergeant Sewicki's face suddenly filled his vision, glowering down at him, a mask of red fury. "*You!* What's your name?"

"Sir! Garroway! Sir!"

Sewicki's war face softened a bit with surprise . . . but *only* a bit. "That name has a special meaning around here, recruit," he growled. "You big enough to carry it?"

"Sir, I hope so, sir."

"There's no *hope* for you here, recruit. And in the future, you will not refer to yourself as 'I' or 'me' or 'my.' You will refer to yourself as 'this recruit.' Now, do you know who Sands of Mars Garroway was?"

"Sir, he was one of my . . . uh, one of this recruit's ancestors, sir."

Sewicki's eyes glazed over for a moment, as though he was studying something within, an implant download, perhaps. "Says here on my roll that your name is Esteban."

So the bit with Sewicki demanding the names of individual recruits had been simple theater.

"Sir, I had—"

"What did you say?"

"Uh, sir, I—"

"You are *not* an *I*! *None* of you maggots rates an I! The *only* first person on this deck is me! The *only* time you maggots say the word 'I' is when you declare that you under-

stand and *will* obey an order, and you *will* do so by saying
'aye aye'! *Do* you understand me?"

"Sir! Aye aye, sir!"

"*Every* time you wish to refer to yourselves, you will do
so in the third person! You will say 'this recruit' and you will
not say the word 'I'! *When* you refer to yourselves, you will
do so as 'recruit,' followed by your last name. *Do* I make
myself clear?"

"Sir, aye aye, sir!"

"Jesus, Quan Yin, and *Buddha*, are you that *stupid*, maggot? You say 'aye aye' when you understand and will obey
an order! If I ask a question requiring of you a simple yes or
no answer, you *will* reply with the appropriate yes or no! *Do*
you understand?"

"Uh . . . Sir, yes, sir!"

"What was that? I heard some static in your reply!"

"Sir! Yes, sir!"

"Now, what is it you had to say to me?"

John had to grope for what it was Sewicki had originally
asked him. Exhaustion and disorientation were beginning to
take their toll, and his mind was fuzzy.

"Sir! This recruit had a naming last week. I . . . uh . . . this
recruit took his mother's name. Sir."

"You're a little old for that, aren't you, son?"

Save for the members of a handful of conservative religious groups, women rarely took the names of the men they
married anymore, which meant that a person's last name
was now a matter of conscious choice. Throughout most of
western culture, for at least the past fifty years, boys took
their father's last name, girls their mother's, until about the
age of fourteen, when the child formally chose which name
he or she would carry into adulthood. John originally had his
naming ceremony on his fourteenth birthday at his father's
church in Guaymas.

There was nothing in the rules, though, that said he
couldn't have a second naming and change his last name
from Esteban to Garroway. He'd gone to a notary in San

Diego with his mother as soon as they'd left Sonora, paid the twenty-newdollar fee, and thumbed the e-file records to make it official. He would never be John Esteban again.

"Sir—" he began, wondering how to explain.

"I think you're a goddamn Aztie secessionist, maggot, trying to hide your Latino name."

The sheer unfairness of the charge surged up in his throat and mind like an unfolding blossom. "Sir—"

"I think you're trying to be something you're not. I think you're an Aztie trying to infiltrate *my* Corps—"

"That's not true!"

"Hit the deck, maggot!" Sewicki exploded. *"Fifty push-ups!"*

"Sir! Aye aye, sir!"

Face burning, John dropped to hands and toes and began chugging off the repetitions. As Sewicki pounced on another victim farther down the line, the other sergeant loomed over him, counting him down. His Marine career, he decided, was off to a very rocky start. It wasn't that he thought the Garroway name would buy him any favors, exactly, but he sure hadn't figured on it buying him any trouble.

He'd only reached fifteen, arms trembling, when Sergeant Heller swatted him on the back of his head and barked, "On your feet, recruit!" Sewicki was leading the rest of the group off to a building behind the paved area at a dead run, and he had to scramble to catch up, jogging through the humid night.

By now he was beginning to wonder if he would *ever* catch up.

The building was a featureless gray cinder-block structure, unadorned and almost unfurnished, save for a desk with a nano labeler operated by a bored-looking civilian. As the recruits filed in, the civilian touched each on the back of the left hand with the wand. Within seconds the numeral 1099 began gleaming from each recruit's hand in self-luminous neon-orange light.

"That," Sewicki told them, "is the number of your recruit

training company, Company 1099. It *is* your address. It *is* who you are and where you are in the training schedule. You *will* be required to memorize it!"

Next, they filed past a large, plastic bin beneath the hawk-sharp gaze of Heller and Sewicki, dropping into it everything the two sergeants considered to be "contraband." Most of what they collected were handheld electronics and microcircuit jewelry, hummers, sensory stims, and the like.

A few of the more expensive units were sealed in plastic with the recruit's name, to be returned to him after he left boot camp. Most, though, went into the bin, along with a growing pile of gum, candy, pornoholo cards, prophylactic pills, analgesics, wakers, sleepers, memmers, magazine sheets, and disposable personal comms. One recruit, a bulky, heavy-set guy who claimed to be from Texas, surrendered a bowie knife he had strapped to his leg, claiming with a broad, easy drawl that he was an experienced knife fighter and that he'd heard Marines could choose their own *personal* blades.

Sewicki held out a hand. "Hand it over, recruit," he said with a dark and surprising gentleness, "or I will *take* it from you, and I might accidentally break an arm doing it." The recruit looked like he was going to argue but then appeared to think better of it, much to John's relief. He knew that one troublemaker could make it hell for the entire company, and he didn't like the idea of his comfort depending on what some hypertestosteroned commando wannabe with more bravado than brains thought was a cool idea.

John had nothing on him but a wadded-up sheet of magazine card, e-loaded with the latest issues of *Newtimes* and *Wicca Today*, that he'd picked up at the skyport in San Diego to read on the trip. He tossed it into the bin with the rest of the trash, thinking of the gesture as a symbolic break with his civilian past. Whatever Sewicki said, he was a *Marine* now, at very long last.

After that they were told to sit on the linoleum tile floor and were given more facts to memorize.

"Listen up, all of you. You are not yet Marines, but you are no longer civilians. Your lives are no longer governed by the Constitution of the United States, which all of you have sworn to uphold and protect, but by the Uniform Code of Military Justice.

"During the next few weeks, you *will* become familiar with the UCMJ, but for now you will memorize only three articles of that document. Article 86 of the Uniform Code of Military Justice prohibits absence without leave. Article 91 prohibits disobedience to any lawful order. Article 93 prohibits disrespect to any senior officer. Now feed 'em back to me! Article 86 of the Uniform Code of Military Justice prohibits absence without leave!"

The recruits repeated the phrase in a ragged, partly mumbled chorus, barely intelligible among the echoes from the bare concrete walls.

"I think I just heard a freaking mouse squeak," Sewicki yelled, cupping his right hand to his ear. "*What* did you maggots say?"

They repeated the article, stronger this time, and more in unison.

"*Again!*"

Half an hour later, the three UCMJ articles still ringing in their ears, they were brought to attention and run back into the night, this time to another building nearby. There, a trio of bored-looking civilians buzzed flat palm depilators over their scalps, leaving them completely bald as the discarded hair piled up on the floor to ankle depth. John had just begun to recognize some of the other members of the recruit platoon by sight . . . and now all were transformed into curiously subhuman-looking creatures with glazed eyes and hairless scalps gleaming in the overhead fluorescents.

As he stood at attention waiting for his turn with the barber, he decided that he could accept most of what was happening philosophically, though his run-in with Sewicki earlier still rankled. The stories he'd heard about boot camp were proving to be fairly accurate. The name-calling and constant, shouted verbal harassment didn't bother him. He'd heard that in the old days, a couple of centuries back, drill instructors had actually been forbidden to hit their men, to use racial or personal slurs, even to swear in front of them or call them names.

That had been an ideologically charged era, a scrap of ancient history when the Corps had been forced by circumstance and a fast-changing American culture to adopt a politically correct attitude requiring that recruits be handled with gentleness, understanding, and respect.

"*Damn* you, maggot! Get those eyeballs off of me *now* if you want to keep them!"

Those days were long gone now. The purpose of boot camp had always been to reduce all incoming recruits to a common level, break them of their civilian habits and attitudes, and rebuild them as Marines. The breaking had begun the moment they'd stumbled off the bus, and it was proceeding apace, with no sign of letup.

It took all of twenty seconds for John's longish brown hair to join the furry blanket on the floor. After that they ran to yet another building, this time to pass through a web of laser light while computers measured his body, then to receive a seabag and pass down a line of tables where still more bored civilians dropped item after item of clothing and gear into the bags as the recruits held them open and sergeants bellowed for them to move it up, move it up. The gear they were issued included everything from "Mk. 101 cleaning kit, M-2120, laser rifle, for care of" to "shoes, shower" to "cream, facial depilatory." Uniform items included multiple sets of underwear, shorts, T-shirts, socks, shoes, work caps, and the ubiquitous utilities known as BDUs—battle dress uniforms—all but the underwear and shoes in the same shade of basic olive drab.

The sun was just coming up over the broad, silver-limned reach of the Atlantic Ocean when at last they were run into their barracks, exhausted, dazed, and drenched with sweat. Their course took them past a transients' barracks, where young men leaned out of open windows with hoots, wolf whistles, catcalls, and cheerful cries of, "Man, you maggots are in a *world* of *shit!*"

Home for the next several days was a receiving barracks, a long, narrow room with ancient wooden floors, lined with beds stacked two high, each bunk separated from the next in line by a gray double locker.

Here, the recruits were again assembled on the floor, where they were given a long and detailed lesson in the strange and alien new language they were now required to use. It was not a floor, but a *deck*; not a ceiling, but an *overhead*; not a door, but a *hatch*; not stairs, but a *ladder*, not a bed, but a *rack*. You didn't wear pants, you wore *trousers*; you didn't wear a hat, but a *cover*. Upstairs was *topside*; downstairs was *below deck*. This area where they were assembled was the *squad bay*. The area just outside the drill instructor's office at the far end of the room was the *quarterdeck*. A room was a *compartment*. The bathroom was the *head*. Left was *port*, right was *starboard*.

It seemed as though the Marines had a different name for everything, and the Goddess help anyone who forgot or slipped into his old patterns of civilian speech.

The drilling continued for another hour, followed by a session where they were assigned racks and gently instructed in how to lay out, fold, and stow the clothing and gear they'd been issued. Next, they were ordered to strip, and with shower clogs on their feet, a towel in the left hand and soap in the right, were marched to the head. "Let's go, ladies, anytime you're ready! Close it up! Close it up! Nuts to butts! Make the guy in front of you *smile!*"

Showering was done, literally, by the numbers, with Sergeant Heller looking on from behind a glass window in the bulkhead above the shower pit and barking orders over a needlemike. "*First!* Place your towels on the overhead bars. *Next!* Take your positions on the footprints painted on the deck! Reach up with your right hands! Grasp the shower chain and pull down, while standing in the stream!" Shrieks, groans, and giggles accompanied the icy torrent. "Belay that racket in there! No one told you to talk! One! Two! Three! Four! Five! *Release* the shower chain! Now! Lather up the soap and wash your head and face! Reach up with your right arm and grasp the shower chain. Pull down and rinse off. One! Two! Three! *Release* the chain! . . ."

It was a bizarre experience for John. The shower facility was downright primitive, with cold water dumped on their heads when they yanked on the pull chain. No temperature selector. *Bar* soap, for Goddess's sake, instead of a disinfect mixture or dirt solvent or skin cleanser added to the water stream. No sonic wash or infrared bake. No pulsing spray or steam mist, and definitely no civilized ten-minute soak in the hot tub to finish off the ritual. And having someone barking out at them what to wash, when to wash it, and how long to rinse it . . .

"*Next!* Lather up your right arm . . . that's your *right* arm, maggot . . . yes, you! Twelve from the end! Grasp the pull chain. Pull to rinse . . . One! Two! Three! *Release* the chain! . . ."

They were being treated, he realized, like children . . . no, worse, like incompetents, like brain-damaged incompetents too slow to understand the simplest command. He could understand the need for this kind of guidance, intellectually, at least, but the process itself was humiliating in the extreme.

"Now lather your crotch. Do *not* be embarrassed. No one is looking. No one would *want* to look, believe me! Lather thoroughly! Now, reach up and grasp the pull chain. Pull to rinse . . . One! Two! Three! *Release* the chain! . . ."

After showering and drying off, they marched nuts to butts back to the squad bay, where they stood in line, arms stretched out at shoulder level, while Sewicki, Heller, and a

Navy corpsman walked down the line, inspecting each shivering recruit for wounds, cuts, abrasions, bruises, or signs of ringworm or other fungal infections. Only then were they allowed to don for the first time the uniform of their new service . . . olive drab BDU trousers, T-shirts, and utility covers. The only technical aspect to their garb was in the heavy black boondockers, smartshoes that sighed and hissed as they adjusted themselves to the size and shape of each recruit's feet. There were no sensors in their BDUs, no fitting mechanism, no heaters or coolers, not even a link to a smartgarb channel for weather advice.

John thought about that pile of discarded electronics in the disposal bin. He'd always thought of the Marines as high-tech, with their armored suits and APCs, flier units and M-2120 lasers, combat implants and e-boosters. What they were wearing now was about as back-to-basics as it was possible to get.

Another hour passed as men who'd somehow missed getting vital items of clothing or gear or who'd ended up with extras were sorted out and discrepancies corrected. Civilian clothing was carefully sealed in plastic bags, labeled for storage, and collected. It would be returned when they completed boot camp . . . or when they washed out and gave up the new uniform.

Only then were they herded once more into ranks, then marched across the parade field outside—no, that was a *grinder*—to the mess hall. John thought at first that he would be too tired to eat, but found instead that he was ravenous. Even when he was eating, though, the constant barrage from Heller and Sewicki never let up. They paced among the tables, continuing the sharp-barked litany of correction, guidance, and downright bullying. "Food is *fuel*. You need *good* fuel to do what we expect you to do. No sliders! No rollers! No goddamn pogey bait! *Good* food, and lots of it! Regulations say *three* thousand *two* hundred calories *per* meal. And you *will* need it! . . ."

And there *was* a lot, but with just twenty minutes precisely in which to eat it. Chipped beef piled over toast, scrambled eggs, salad—a *salad* for breakfast!—orange juice, fresh oranges . . .

But as he wolfed down the meal, he was already wondering if he'd made a terrible, terrible mistake. . . .

6

Building 12, Xenocultural Mission
Terran Legation Compound
New Sumer
Ishtar, Llalande 21185 IID
27:13 hours Local Time

"Come *on*, Moore! They're coming over the north wall!"

Dr. Nichole Moore kept retrieving her data mems, pulling double handfuls of the domino-sized crystalline chips from the lab's storage compartment and stuffing them into the Marine seabag Sergeant Aiken had given her.

"I'm almost done," she replied.

Carleton, the senior PanTerran representative, pounded on a desktop with a clenched fist. "Damn it, they'll be here any minute! *Forget* that crap!"

She whirled on him, eyes blazing. "This is five years of research, Carleton!" she yelled. "Five years of my *life!* I'm not leaving it to be burned!"

"Stay then!" Carleton snapped, and vanished into the passageway outside. She could hear the wail of the assembly siren over in the Marine compound. She knew Carleton was right. There wasn't much time.

But she had to save her records. Five Terran years of patient work with the An and their human pets. She raked the last of the mems into the bag, added her personal recorder and the desktop computer, which still had several thousand

photographs and several megabytes of notes that hadn't
been mem-stored yet, then sealed the opening.

The Marine seabag had little in common with the all-
purpose stowage bags of centuries past. It was more like a
square satchel, but with smartthreads woven into the fabric.
A couple of tugs on the carry straps unfolded it into a backpack; as she pushed her arms through the straps and hoisted
it into place, she heard the whine of servos adjusting the balance on her back and felt the grip of shoulder distributors
snugging down over her shoulders. She had nearly thirty kilos of notes, mems, and electronic gear inside, and lugging it
out of the compound would have been a real bitch without
the technic assist.

Nichole took a last look around her office, feeling the tug
of regret. Five years . . .

Damn Geremelet and his Destiny Faction anyhow . . . and
damn the High Emperor for trying to appease them, and
damn the Trade Mission for interfering with the millennia-
old balance of social forces on this world, and damn the
Humankind Party on Earth for stirring things up, and, yes,
damn herself and her xenocultural team for digging into
questions that perhaps should not have been uncovered.
Of *course* slavery was immoral, unjust, and obscenely
wrong . . . but when the slaves were actually happy with
their lot, had been bred to be happy for generation upon un-
told generation . . .

Satisfied at last that she'd managed to grab the most critical of her research data, she accessed her neurimplants, log-
ging onto the Legation network one last time. The main
network AI was still offline, though, and all she could see
within her electronically enhanced mind's eye was the same
warning that had been up and broadcasting for the past
twenty hours—all civilian personnel were to gather a minimum of necessary belongings and report to the Pyramid of
the Eye for evacuation. The base's two ground-to-orbit
transports had been shuttling up and down constantly for the
past twelve hours or so, hauling people up to the relative

safety of the *Emissary*, in Ishtar orbit. The evacuation was perhaps half complete. According to the posting on the net-cast, another transport would be lifting within forty minutes.

And she would be on it. She took a last look around the room, then, on impulse, used a stylus to scrawl a brief message on a notebook, leaving it on a countertop. Someday she might be able to return. More likely, though, it would be someone else, someone trying to figure out what had gone wrong here. The message might help. She hurried out into the hallway, palm-locking the door behind her. *As if I'll be back to work here at the next shift,* she thought, bitter.

Building 12 was a gray, ground-extruded nanocrete dome near the east side of the XC Mission quarter, ugly as sin, as her grandmother back in Michigan used to say, but it had been home and office for five Terran Standard years. She emerged from light and air-conditioned coolness on the elevated walkway halfway up the side of the curved wall, plunging into the steamy heat outside.

Spread out below her within the tight perimeter of the Legation walls, the embassy compound was submerged in murky red twilight, with only the bright gleam of a handful of lights in scattered windows to show where Earthers had left them burning after leaving for the evacuation pickup. Gunfire crackled and snapped from the north, where a company of Marines was trying to hold off the incoming tidal flood of Anu god-warriors and their Sag-ura slaves. Smoke stained the red sky at a dozen different points—most of them marking burning 'villes outside the wall, but a few were inside, set by fanatics within the embassy compound or by firebombs lobbed over the wall.

It was late morning—not that the Terran Legation staff ever paid much attention to local time. Ishtar circled giant Marduk in 133 hours, which meant that its day-night cycle was five and a half Earth days long. The Legation's work and rest periods were based on a standard twenty-four-hour cycle matched to Greenwich Mean Time on distant Earth, a necessary concession to the biological needs of a much different world's evolution. In any case, the light from the primary, red-dwarf Llalande 21185, was so wan that the landscape always seemed to be shrouded in twilight, even at high noon.

At the moment, the sun was a red-ember pinpoint gleaming high in the eastern sky, well above the haze-shrouded Ahtun Mountains, too tiny and too distant to lend Ishtar more than a trickle of heat. In the west, above the black cone of God Mountain, Marduk hung against the deep green and purple sky, a baleful scarlet eye poised to fall upon the exotically lush landscape of Ishtar and crush it. Though gibbous and waning now, the sliver of Marduk's night side visible at the moment glowed almost as brightly as the sunlit side. Stirred and stressed by the constant gravitational tug-of-war with its largest satellite, the gas giant radiated far more heat than it received from its star, heat sufficient to warm its Earth-sized satellite to tropical temperatures on the side forever facing Marduk in tide-locked captivity.

Nichole spared only a moment for the red-gloom beauty of the landscape. The gunfire in the north was growing steadily in intensity, and she could see the black sprawl of Geremelet's hordes surging through the shattered main gate. A cluster of rockets rose from the jungle beyond, trailing orange flame. The flames winked out; moments later, a scattering of flashes popped and strobed across the northern quarter of the compound, followed seconds later by the dull thud of the explosions. The Marines wouldn't be able to hold that army of Ahannu fanatics back much longer.

A Marine Wasp droned overhead, its insectlike body painted in stripes of yellow and dark blue-black. It angled across the compound toward the north, and she guessed that it was searching for the launch site of those rockets.

Shouldering her pack, she moved quickly down the stairway curving along the wall of Building 12. The streets of the city were almost lost in the near-darkness. Not for the first time, she wished she had microimplant optics like the

Marines used, to help her pick her way through the shadows. Normally, the Legation's streets and walkways were brilliantly lit, but the power had failed hours before and the streetlights were out. The ground was littered with debris—scattered chunks of rock and broken nanocrete from the Ahannu rocket barrages—and twice she nearly stumbled with her heavy load.

"Halt! Who's there?" a voice demanded from the shadows to her left.

"I'm Dr. Moore," she said. "Xeno-C Mission."

A figure stepped forward from the shadows, man-shaped but bulkier, heavier, and clad in black military armor. Gauntlets grasped a massive laser rifle, which was connected to the armor's backpack by a trio of thick cables. The armor was dented and scarred in several places. The name AIKEN, G. was stenciled across the top of the helmet, above where the visor would have been had it had one, and a master sergeant's insignia decorated the upper left arm, painted in dark gray against the darker black of the armor.

"Hey, Doc," Aiken said. His voice, amplified through the suit's speaker system, echoed off nearby walls. "I hoped that was you. Lemme give you a hand."

She pulled back. "I . . . I can manage just fine, Master Sergeant."

"Sure you can." The speaker's volume was lower now. "But I can do it faster." He reached out and lifted the pack from her shoulders as lightly as if it were empty. "We've got to hustle."

"What are you doing here, anyway? I thought you guys were holding the north wall."

"That's Company G. Companies C and E are checking to make sure all the civilians get out. And we're late for rendezvous with our transport. Anyone else back there?"

She knew he meant the mission and shook her head. "I don't think so."

The armored figure seemed to be listening or hesitating . . . and then she realized Aiken was talking to someone else on his radio. "Okay. The rest of my team will go through the mission, just to make sure. You come with me."

He turned and strode down the rubble-littered street without looking back to see if she was following. She hesitated . . . but then realized he had all of her notes and records. She had to follow to keep her claim to them. *Damn* him.

Nichole didn't like the Marines, didn't like their presence here on Ishtar. She felt that militarism had no place on an alien world, had no place at all for a first contact with a sentient alien species. As far as she was concerned, the Marine contingent accompanying the science and diplomatic missions only increased the tension and mistrust between the humans on the one hand and the Ahannu on the other.

Even so, she had to admit that when things turned sour with the locals, the Marines were all that had stood between members of the civilian missions and death. She couldn't help wondering, though, if things would have been different had there been no military to provoke Geremelet and his fanatics in the first place.

Well, the Marines were here, and the damage done. She wondered how things could be patched up with the locals, wondered if there was any way, now, to find a common ground with them. Goddess! Between Geremelet here and the Humankind Party back on Earth . . .

Another Ahannu rocket banged into the roof of a compound building nearby, sending up a shower of swirling red sparks. Ahannu technology was such a bizarre mix of the antiquated and the advanced. Some few among their elite warrior units carried weapons more advanced than anything in the Terran arsenal . . . and yet they used gunpowder rockets, primitive firearms, swords, and *chakhul*—a kind of pike or spear with a long and wickedly curved blade. The high-tech stuff was believed to be working artifacts left over from the Ahannu glory days of ten thousand years before—*god weapons*, the Ishtaran natives called them. Ishtar was all that was left of a spacefaring empire that once had spanned at least a dozen worlds, including ancient Earth. The Ahannu and the humans they'd brought with them from Earth had survived the collapse of their civilization, which continued only here in sharply abbreviated and primitive form.

Current xenoarcheological thought was sharply divided at the moment between two mutually opposing theories. Traditional dogma held that the Ahannu Empire had been utterly destroyed ten thousand years ago by the enigmatic race known as the Hunters of the Dawn, that somehow the Hunters had overlooked this oddball world, largest moon of a gas giant in a red dwarf star system.

Nichole preferred the newer, more daring theory, advanced by Dr. Hayakawa and others. It posited that the Hunters of the Dawn were long dead when the Ahannu first reached Earth sometime toward the end of the last ice age. The Hunters had been a predatory species ranging this part of the galaxy perhaps half a million years ago, at the time when an earlier cycle of galactic civilization called the Builders had been terraforming Mars and tinkering with what would become the human genome. They and their technology, represented by the immense artifact discovered almost eighty years ago on one of Jupiter's moons, had destroyed a thriving interstellar community encompassing some hundreds of races scattered throughout this region of space. The Hayakawa Solution held that the Ahannu had been destroyed in a war with themselves, a civil war that devastated all but one of their handful of worlds—Ishtar. It was much easier to accept that idea than the notion that any technic species could have survived—and still be wiping out potential competitors—in nearly historical times.

It was also a bit more comforting. Any killer species like the near-mythical Hunters that could survive half a million years would have godlike powers by now . . . and it was arrogant presumption to assume they'd lasted long enough to destroy the Ahannu Empire, then conveniently faded into extinction. No, the Hunters *must* have destroyed themselves, she believed, or simply retired from the galactic stage at some point in the distant past, perhaps hundreds of thousands of years ago.

Not that any of that was of any great importance now, she thought, as another rocket exploded overhead, and bits of red-glowing, smoking shrapnel clinked and chattered on the pavement. "You okay, Doc?" Aiken asked her.

She nodded, then realized he couldn't see her with his back to her. "Yes," she said. "Homemade rockets. Primitive stuff."

"It's still deadly enough," he replied. "Especially if you're not wearing armor. C'mon. Down this way."

He led her sharply right, into the mouth of a narrow alley between a storehouse and Building 4, the Mission Recreational Center. He was moving at a jog that ate up the ground, and she found herself having to run all out to keep up with him. *Damn, I'm not used to this*, she thought. *Too much sitting around in the office trading gossip and eating native sholats.* She was sweating heavily in the humid heat, and her jumpsuit was rapidly soaking through.

They emerged on Alexander Boulevard, at the edge of the native compound, and turned southeast, toward the Pyramid of the Eye.

Traditional Ahannu architecture ran heavily toward step pyramids and conical, two- and three-story huts. Some xenoarcheologists thought the ziggurats of ancient Mesopotamia had been inspired by the buildings of the An colony destroyed there in about 8000 B.C., though there was ample evidence that the Builders had used the same design much earlier, on Mars and elsewhere.

In fact, the structure dubbed the Pyramid of the Eye was almost certainly *not* Ahannu but something much older, erected in the Ishtaran jungle by the Builders as much as half a million years ago.

Perhaps the ancient An had gotten the idea of the step pyramid from the Builders.

Or perhaps it was simply a very common, very sturdy and easily raised architectural style, common to hundreds of civilizations across the galaxy. Nonetheless, the stark power of the ancient ziggurat contrasted sharply with the low, dome structures of mud and brick clustered around its base.

She was reminded again of something she'd seen on Earth—the ruins of ancient Egyptian temples, palaces, and workers' huts clustered about the bases of the three much older, enigmatic pyramids on the Giza Plateau on Earth.

Aiken abruptly stopped, spinning to his left. Nichole saw nothing but shadows beneath an awning extended from the side of a native shop, but the Marine triggered his laser, firing from the hip. The heavy weapon gave a low-throated hum, deep and loud enough to make her teeth ache, and the beam, made visible by dust particles and ionizing air, sparkled in yellow-white brilliance for nearly a full second.

Rock exploded from the face of the storefront. By the brief glare of incandescence, Nichole saw a shape—a *human* shape—stumbling from the scattered shadows.

It was a man, a Sag-ura, naked and shaven-headed. Judging by the fine network of tattooed scales all over his body, the colorful face markings, and the keen-edged *chakhul* in his hands, he was one of the Sag-ura slave warriors of the God's Hand. Aiken's shot had sliced at an angle down across his torso, nearly severing his head and left arm from his chest in an explosion of blood and charred flesh.

Nichole didn't scream, not quite, but she let out a yelp. "*What have you done?*"

"Getting you the hell out of here. Come on!"

"You *killed* him!" But then she realized how stupid that protest sounded. The slave soldier had certainly been trying to kill them, and if his spear was useless against a Marine's battle armor, he wouldn't have had much trouble with the light plasweave fabric of her mission jumpsuit. According to some of the stories collected by the Sag-ura Cultural Studies Group, the Sakura-sag were not known for taking prisoners.

The Pyramid of the Eye loomed ahead now, its truncated peak bathed in harsh, white light. A pair of Wasps orbited the structure, protecting a larger, more massive flier resting on the uppermost platform. She could see people up there, tiny black stick figures moving against the lights.

There was a flash and a loud bang, and Aiken stumbled. Nichole could hardly see what happened next, so quickly did it unfold, but she had the blurred impression of more humanoid figures emerging from shadows between several of the buildings along the north side of the boulevard.

Aiken dropped to one knee, recovering, pivoting with his cumbersome laser. The weapon hummed again, and by its flash she saw the attackers, a handful of Sag-ura led by a full-caste Ahannu warrior.

It was a big one, taller than a man, and more massive. The folks back home called them reptiles, though they were more properly classified as parareptilians. The scales, the slit pupils, the cranial crest, the fighting claws, all contributed to the lizard-like feel of the thing. Literally designed for fighting, it didn't have the intelligence of Ahannu godwarriors, but it was quick and it was cunning. The godweapon clutched in its six-fingered hands didn't help either.

It fired a second time, and something exploded against Aiken's armor. It staggered him, but he brought the laser to bear, firing into the Ahannu's chest. It was wearing a quilted cloth uniform or armor of some kind, but that provided scant protection from the Marine's return fire. It keened, a shrill, baying wail, then dropped to the pavement, heavily muscled legs kicking and twitching.

The Sag-ura warriors that accompanied it slashed at Aiken with their spears, then scattered as he triggered the laser again and brought down two of them. Two more armored Marines trotted up. "Hey, Master Sergeant!" one said over his suit's external speaker. "You called?"

"Where the hell were you guys? The freakin' Annies are all over the place."

"Roger that. They're coming through the North Gate like nobody's business. We're not holding them."

Aiken stooped, picking up the god-weapon dropped by

the Ahannu warrior. "Let's move it. We have a transport to catch."

The trio led Nichole through the East Gate of the Legation compound to the west face of the pyramid just beyond. Other people, civilians and military, were moving up the broad steps. A rocket exploded in the distance with a hollow thump. "Go on up and get on the T-40," Aiken told her. "Here." He handed her the pack.

"What . . . what about you guys? Aren't you coming?"

"We'll be going out later," he replied. With that, he turned and trotted toward the northwest, the other two Marines at his heels.

Nichole started up the pyramid's steps. The satchel, slung over her shoulder, was heavier than she'd remembered it, and she was out of breath from the ragged jog through the Legation compound's streets. Her jumpsuit was supposed to be self-drying and cooling, but its microcircuitry just couldn't keep up with the heat or her exertions, and she felt her strength waning.

Three-quarters of the way up, she stopped, dropping the pack and sagging onto the step for a breather. From there, the compound and the surrounding city were spread out below and around her in magnificent, twilit panorama. Heavy columns of smoke stained the sky to the north and northwest, and she could see hordes of attackers surging through the streets and plazas a kilometer away. Many carried torches and were burning anything they could find that was flammable. It was a scene out of Hell, of an alien Armageddon.

Shouldering her pack again, she started up the last of the steps. They were awkwardly placed, steeper and more narrow than was comfortable for human legs. Ahead, the stairway split to either side of an alcove opening into the pyramid's interior, creating a stone-walled chamber that opened onto the steps. Light spilled from the inside, and she saw people moving within. She decided to enter the alcove and see who was there.

The Chamber of the Eye, from which the pyramid took its

name, was featureless and bare, the walls, floor, and ceiling highly polished black stone, with no carvings, no paintings, no decorations of any kind. The lights came from high-power lamps erected by human technicians; the only furnishing that had been in the room when the first expedition arrived from Earth was an ellipsoid of what looked like polished rock crystal two meters across, suspended from the ceiling by a slender but rigidly inflexible tether. Its dark interior gave it the look of a huge eye—hence the name.

At the moment, a man's head and shoulders hovered within the eye's pupil. Behind him was the corporate logo of PanTerra, a stylized graphic of Earth floating within a canted ring. The usual pair of Marine sentries stood inside the door, expressions blank. Carleton stood in front of the eye, along with three other PanTerran reps, speaking with impassioned urgency. "Damn it, Roth, this is *your* screw-up! I'm not taking a fall for it!"

"No one is asking you to, Mr. Carleton," the face within the eye said with a bland lack of emotion. "And, of course, we take full responsibility for all decisions made at the *corporate* level. Still, our field personnel must be held accountable for losses incurred due to any mishandling of the local situation—"

"There was no mishandling, damn it! We carried out Corporate's directives to the letter!"

"That will be determined at the review. We'll keep you informed, of course."

"Jesus Christ, have you been listening to me, Roth? We're losing the interstellar link! We're eight light-years from help! An hour from now we could all be dead!"

"Well, we certainly hope that won't happen, Mr. Carleton," Roth said. "As you point out, though, you are eight light-years and some away . . . a ten-year journey at best. There is absolutely nothing any of us here can do . . . but wish you luck. Goodbye, Mr. Carleton. I hope your fears about the situation there . . . prove meritless."

The face in the Eye blanked out, replaced by the standard

carrier wave signal of ICLI. The government organization known as Interstellar Communications Link International was the entity responsible for maintaining the faster-than-light comlinks between several far-flung planets—here on Ishtar, among the melancholy ruins on Chiron at Alpha Centauri A, on inhospitable Hathor at Wolf 359, and of course in the Cave of Wonders on Mars. Within the Cave of Wonders, beneath the barren Cydonian mesa known as the Face, an array of thousands of viewscreens, product of a technology seemingly magic by current human standards, showed that once, half a million years ago, the Builders had created an instantaneous communication network linking thousands of worlds. Most of the screens at the Martian Builders site were dead, evidence that their empire, like so many others, had fallen to the Hunters of the Dawn.

Of the rest, a handful had been identified with nearby stars, and, as the new antimatter-torch technology gave humankind a means of approaching near-light speed, three of those worlds—Chiron, Hathor, and Ishtar—had been visited. The first two were dead worlds, the detritus of a war of interstellar extinction fought half a million years before; Ishtar, however . . .

"Bastard!" Carleton snapped.

"What's the matter, Carleton?" Nichole asked. "Your books showing a loss for the quarter?"

Carleton whirled. "What are *you* doing here?"

"Hey, I just came in out of the cold."

The irony was lost on the PanTerra agent. "You shouldn't be in here."

"Why not? Free access . . ." One of the absolute rules of ICLI's stewardship of the FTL comm links was that access to the Builder technology was never to be restricted to any person or group, for any purpose. It was a rule more often honored in the breach than in fact.

"We're not going to *have* access in another few moments," he said, apparently trying to steer the conversation away from PanTerra business. "Those idiots!"

"Blaming the home office for your own stupidity isn't going to cut it," she told him. "Anyway, PanTerra has no business exploiting the natives or their technology."

"That, Doctor, is not your decision. C'mon, let's get to the transport."

He brushed past her and out onto the pyramid steps, followed by his assistants. Nichole hesitated a moment, staring at the Eye, then turned and followed them.

That Eye had provided humans with their first glimpse of living An a century ago, when Dr. Alexander himself had entered the Cave of Wonders on Mars and seen for the first time the arrayed viewscreens providing two-way real-time links with a thousand worlds. Studies of the sky—the slow-moving stars and a spectroscopic analysis of the distant red sun glimpsed through the open, west-facing opening of the chamber—had identified the site as a world of Llalande 21185, and a relatively easy goal for one of Earth's early interstellar attempts. The chances for profound scientific and historical investigation and discovery had been staggering.

But so too, unfortunately, had been the opportunity for corporate greed. Nichole hated Carleton, hated the whole idea of having PanTerra and a consortium of other corporate and government business interests present on this expedition . . . but as Carleton had so bluntly pointed out, that had not been her decision. The Lima Accord of 2125 had promised the right of corporate entities to trade with the Ahannu, in order to define, create, and realize new markets and products, and to provide diplomatic and cultural ties between the two races.

Who could have foreseen that their interference would have caused a damned war?

At the truncated peak of the Pyramid of the Eye, a T-40 Starhauler rested on massive landing jacks, its cargo ramp down. A line of Marines was trying to maintain order in the crowd attempting to board the transport. "Take it easy, people!" one Marine bellowed over an amplified suit speaker.

"There's room enough for all of you! Take your time, and take your turn!"

"Move along! Move along!" another Marine called from the top of the transport's ramp. "Plenty of room. Don't panic."

Plenty of room . . . but the Marines weren't coming, not on this trip. The T-40 had been detailed to haul the last of the Legation compound's civilian population up to the *Emissary*, in orbit five hundred kilometers above Ishtar.

Nichole took her place in line and filed up the ramp, just behind Carleton and his assistants. The Starhauler had been designed as a transatmospheric cargo carrier, not a people mover, but its capacious cargo bay could hold thirty people or so in claustrophobic discomfort.

Nearly two hundred civilians had already been transported to the *Emissary* on previous trips. About 150 remained, most milling about outside the Marine guard perimeter waiting to board a shuttle, but they were fast running out of time, just moments ahead of the Destiny Faction's attack on the compound.

A Marine at the edge of the waiting crowd took her name, checked his implant data, and said, "*There* you are, Dr. Moore! Where've you been, anyway? You're on top priority."

"I'd just as soon wait my—"

The Marine cut her off. "Key admin personnel and people with expert knowledge of Annie customs and language have immediate clearance to orbit, ma'am. Come on through."

He ushered her through the Marine barricade as the crowd grumbled and surged forward. A real nasty scene in the works, she decided . . . and decided, too, that she didn't envy those Marines their job.

She stood in line beneath the thrust of the transport's stub wing but had not yet reached the ramp when someone screamed and pointed.

People around her stopped talking, and several wandered out of line, walking toward the north parapet of the pyramid.

In the west, the peak of the conical mountain known as An-Kur—"God Mountain"—was . . . *glowing*.

"What the hell?" Carleton said, turning on the ramp ahead of her to stare back at the sight.

"It's a volcano!" a young media rep shouted.

It was no volcano, that much was obvious. To Nichole, it looked as though the top of that far-off mountain had just peeled itself open, and now a pinpoint of light brighter than the local sun, brighter even than Earth's sun seen from Earth, was shining out of the cavity within.

The blue-white thread of light snapped on abruptly, connecting the mountain peak with the sky at a ten-degree angle from the vertical, a beam so bright that Nichole covered her eyes as more of the watching civilians screamed or yelled.

An instant later a soundless flash blossomed in the deep green of the sky.

Long seconds passed, breathless, and then the shockwave from the mountain reached them, a dull, thundering rumble and a gust of heavy, heat-scorched air. The flash in the sky had faded to a scattering of starlike embers, slowly fading.

Only then did the enormity of what had just happened sink in. "Goddess!" she cried. "They've destroyed the *Emissary*!"

And then the panic set in atop the Pyramid of the Eye.

7

Briefing Room 401
White House Subbasement, Level D
Washington, D.C., Earth
1425 hours ET

"They're coming in over the walls now!" the Marine cried, his eyes wide and staring. He couldn't have been older than twenty. *"They're inside the compound and closing in on the pyramid!"*

The young Marine's face filled the darkened briefing room's wallscreen, which stretched floor to ceiling across one end of the cool, wood-paneled chamber. A number of men and women sat at the long table, watching quietly. The atmosphere was heavy with emotions ranging from grim acceptance to shock.

"We got the last of the civilians out a couple hours ago," the Marine continued. *"There's a place in the mountains east of here—an Uhsag village the scientists've managed to make contact with. We might be able to hold out there for quite a while.*

"Of course, ten years is a long time. And maybe you guys—"

Moisture trickled down the huge face on the wallscreen. It was impossible to tell whether it was sweat or tears, but his eyes were glistening. He broke off, then shook his head.

"Screw that. Anyway, if you send relief, watch out for An-

Kur. That's the big, lone mountain ten klicks west of the compound. There's some kind of god-weapon there, a big son of a bitch, hidden inside the top. We had no idea it was there. It picked the Emissary *right out of the sky, one shot. Don't know what the range is, but it's at least five hundred klicks. I . . . I . . . damn it! They're supposed to be primitives here! What are they doing with a freakin' planetary defense system?"*

A loud explosion banged nearby, and voices could be heard in the background, shouting commands, yelling response. The Marine looked around, shouted, *"Right!"* Then he looked back into the Eye. *"They're comin' up the pyramid steps! Gotta go. Uh . . . look, remember us to our families, for those of us that got 'em, okay? Man, this really sucks vacuum."*

The Marine's face spun away from the pickup. The quietly watching military officers and civilians in the room could make out a vertical slice of green-violet sky stained by what might have been a distant cloud of smoke, the doorway into the Chamber of the Eye, looking out across the city of New Sumer. Several sharp sounds emanating from the screen—the hiss and snap of high-powered lasers, the shrill whine of power packs—filled the air. Movement, a tumble of half-glimpsed shapes, blocked out the sliver of sky momentarily. Someone screamed.

Several moments passed, punctuated by more sounds, like the cold scrabblings of claws on stone, the clink of metal, a low-voiced grunt. For just a moment another face filled the wallscreen, flat and emotionless, a reptilian face dominated by enormous, oddly shaped eyes of metallic gold, horizontally slashed by elongated pupils. The skin was green and faintly scaled, the skull elongated and topped by a low, bony crest, the mouth a black-rimmed slash. Nictitating membranes flickered over those hypnotic eyes once . . . twice . . . and then the apparition vanished.

The wallscreen flickered, then winked out. General Haslett, Army Chief of Staff for the UFR Central Military

Command, stared into the dark emptiness for a moment, shocked and afraid. *My God*, he thought. *What are we sending our people out there to face?*

General Dahlstrom, the National Security Council's senior briefing officer, stood as the lights came up.

"Madam President," she said, "Gentlemen, ladies, that was the last transmission monitored by our ICLI station on Mars. Since about ten hundred hours our time yesterday there has been no further transmission from the Llalande system—only the usual open-channel carrier wave. We still have a visual of the Chamber of the Eye, but there's been no activity that we can make out."

"Then the rebels haven't destroyed the Builder FTL unit," President Katharine LaSalle mused aloud. "That's one good break for us, at least."

Dahlstrom nodded. "Yes, Madam President. However, our xenosoc analysts believe that it would be extremely unlikely for them to damage the unit in any case. The Eye is as sacred to Geremelet's faction as it is to the High Emperor."

"Right," Admiral Knudson, the head of the Joint Chiefs, said. He was a brusque, hard-bitten man with long service in the Naval Space Forces. "Part of their campaign, remember, was to liberate the Eye from the evil offworlders."

"Just what the hell happened out there, anyway?" the President demanded.

"The situation is . . . complicated, ma'am," Samantha Van Horne, Director of Central Intelligence, said. She gestured at the empty wallscreen. "It's hard enough to get good intel on human opponents, let alone aliens. In this case, we have only the tiniest glimmer of how the Ahannu think and, in particular, what they think of *us*."

"They can't still be thinking of us as escaped slaves," General Karl Voekel, the Aerospace Force representative of the Joint Chiefs, said. He gave David Billingsworth, the SecState, a hard look. "The State Department has been working on that issue for the past five years!"

"This is hardly the time for recriminations," Billingsworth

said. He looked across at Warren Boland, the Secretary of Science. "Besides, we worked with what DepSci gave us."

Boland shrugged. "As Samantha said, it's tough reading nonhumans or guessing how they'll react to anything we do."

"Every report coming through *my* data feed indicated that relations with the God-Emperor and his court were good and getting better," Billingsworth said.

"*Its* court," Dahlstrom reminded him. "The Ahannu have no sex."

"It must make their Saturday nights damned boring," Haslett observed dryly. "No wonder they're so riled up. In any case, this—this Destiny Faction, as they call themselves, appeared to be a minor nuisance, nothing more."

Voekel chuckled. "Jesus, General, a minor nuisance? It's a damned civil war, and it's been brewing for years! How did we miss it coming?"

"It's not exactly a civil conflict," Van Horne said. "The Ahannu God-Emperor seems to be waiting to see whether it should openly support Geremelet's horde. It hasn't come out with a public disavowal, at any rate."

"So is the Destiny group working for the Emperor?" the President asked. "Or against it?"

Billingsworth shook his head. "We just don't know, ma'am."

"Our best reports suggest that the Destiny Faction is independent of the Ahannu government," Van Horne added, "but that the imperial court is tolerating it and possibly even helping it along privately." She shrugged. "Maybe the God-Emperor is just letting Geremelet do what the Emperor itself can't do."

"Playing both ends against the middle," Haslett said. "With *us* as the middle."

"Something like that," Billingsworth said. "Now that the Legation compound has been overrun, we have to assume that the God-Emperor will bring Geremelet into the government formally and probably adopt Geremelet's foreign policy as well."

"Do we know what that will be?" President LaSalle asked.

"No, ma'am, but we can take a guess. Geremelet's faction came to power on the platform that humans were renegade slaves . . . uh, what was the word?"

" 'Sag-ura,' " Van Horne told him. "It means, roughly, 'foreign slaves.' "

"Right. They don't have the technology to strike at Earth, of course, but that's probably just rhetoric. What they do want is us off of Ishtar, permanently."

"Ishtar for Ishtarans," Knudson said with a sneer. "Is that it?"

"Basically, Admiral, yes. They feel they were shamed as a people by appearing inferior to us technologically. Remember, they still think of us as their property, slaves or pets that they domesticated thousands of years ago. If we're not around to remind them, they can feel better about themselves."

"So what's the solution, then?" the President wanted to know.

"Let 'em have their damned planet," Voekel said. "God knows we don't need trade with the Annies. The xeno people can study 'em from orbit."

"Not if they have the technology to shoot a starship out of the sky," Dahlstrom pointed out.

Voekel shrugged. "They've had five years to study these critters. That ought to be enough."

"Five years," Boland pointed out, "isn't enough time to even begin mapping out the problem. This is a whole world, a whole culture, a history, a language, a people unlike anything we've ever known—"

"The fact is," Voekel said, "we don't need these Annie jokers nearly as much as they need us. And starships are damn expensive. I just think we ought to take a real careful look at what we have invested here, before sending any more of our assets out there to Llalande."

"Are you saying we should call off Operation Spirit of

Humankind?" Haslett asked. He pursed his lips, a sardonic acknowledgment of the pretentiousness of the cumbersome title. "At *this* late date?"

"What's late?" Voekel asked. "The ships haven't launched yet. The relief force hasn't even been assembled. We could call the whole thing off this afternoon. Damn it, I say we *should* call it off. The cost—the risk—it's just not worth it."

"Which means we write off our people on Ishtar," Admiral Knudson said. "Unacceptable. Absolutely unacceptable!"

"Karl may be right," Thomas Wright, the Secretary of Human Affairs, said. "The cost of each interstellar expedition is . . . quite literally astronomical." He chuckled at his own wit. "Attempting to enforce our political will on aliens is lunacy at best. DepHA regrets the loss of life, of course, but I remind you that we advised against the original involvement at Llalande when contact was first established ten years ago. The Ahannu are primitives and no longer understand those fragments of advanced technology they still possess. It's not as though they can teach us anything, right?" He made an unpleasant face. "As for the xenohistorical crap, that's been out of control since First Contact and the Genesis Awareness. I don't think anyone really understands the Frogs or what they supposedly did on Earth thousands of years ago. I don't think we *need* to. It's all moot."

"We'd damned well better understand them, Mr. Wright," Van Horne said, her voice sharp, "if we're going to understand the psychoreligious mania that's infected the American population over the past few decades."

That, Haslett thought, was certainly true. The knowledge that aliens, the ancestors of the Ahannu, had colonized Earth over ten thousand years earlier, enslaving the human inhabitants of the Fertile Crescent, had struck humankind's collective awareness like a thunderbolt. The idea that those aliens had actually tinkered with the human genome, somehow been responsible for what humans were like today . . . that bit of information had utterly and forever transformed the way man would look at himself.

"Just the American population?" Billingsworth asked with a wry grin. "Whether people think they're gods, devils, or alien slave raiders, the whole damned world has gone nuts over the Ahannu, one way or another."

"Be that as it may," Voekel said, "certain inescapable facts remain. We cannot support a major military operation at interstellar distances against the determined resistance of an entire planetary population. Further, there is no compelling reason to do so. The loss of our people already in the Llalande system is regrettable, certainly, but we must recognize and accept that even if some have survived the debacle at Ishtar, ten years is a long time. There will be no survivors by the time the *Derna* and her support group arrives in the Llalande system."

"Madam President," Admiral Knudson said, turning to face the woman at the head of the table. "The voters will never forgive a . . . a *betrayal* of this magnitude! We must at least attempt to relieve the Llalande mission. Anything less would be criminal!"

"Sending more people after them to die would be stupid," Voekel said. "If military history teaches us anything it's that we should know when to cut our losses and get out."

"There's more to it than that," the President said. "There are . . . certain political considerations that must be taken into account."

"Aren't there always?" Billingsworth asked with a wry twist to his mouth.

"It's this issue of human slaves on Ishtar," the President continued. "The people are up in arms. Protests. Demonstrations. Marches. Riots, even. Some pro-An, of course, mostly the religious groups, but the worst are the anti-An movements. More and more groups are appearing everywhere now, here and in other countries too. The Human Dignity League. The Earth First Coalition. The Humankind Abolitionist Union. I've never known *any* issue to unite so many people from so many countries across so much of the entire globe!"

Again Haslett had to agree. Descendants of human slaves taken by the An to the Llalande system ten thousand years ago now numbered anywhere from hundreds of thousands to millions—no one was sure how many there were—and their bondage had become a rallying point for all of the anti-An groups on Earth.

"And the violence is completely out of hand," President LaSalle continued. "That riot in New Chicago a couple of weeks ago . . . what was the final tally on that?"

"Fifty-one killed, Madam President," an aide with an open cerebralink seated just behind him said, a vacant expression on his face as he pulled the requested data down off the White House AI-Data Net. "Over three hundred injured. Perhaps 800 million in property damage."

"Fifty-one killed," President LaSalle repeated, shaking her head. "And there have been riots all over. Here in Washington. Detroit. Los Angeles. New Miami. And in other countries too. Johannesburg. Rome. Kiev. Madrid. Rio. The people want those human slaves on Ishtar—these Saguras—they want them *free*. If we abandon the planet, it's going to count heavily against us in the congressional elections this year and even worse in the presidential election in 'forty."

"Madam President," Voekel said, "surely we can't base our policy—our military policy—on a world eight light-years away, on the antics of a few damned malcontents!"

"General, those 'few damned malcontents,' as you call them, pull a hell of a lot of political weight. You know how unsettled things have been all over the world since the discovery of human slaves on Ishtar. If we back out now, if we abandon the relief mission, we could conceivably find ourselves facing civil unrest at home *and* a shooting war with the rest of the Federation. I will not be the President who signs that order!"

The men and women gathered at the table were silent for a moment. General Haslett finally spoke. "General Colby?

You've said nothing so far. They're *your* Marines. What do you think?"

General Anton Colby, Commandant of the U.S. Marines, shook his head gravely. "The Marines go where they're told to, General. For the record, I am opposed completely to abandoning our people on Ishtar, but you all knew that already." There were a few subdued chuckles from around the table.

"With the situation on Ishtar," Colby continued, "we are faced with a strategic problem unlike anything we have faced before. As General Voekel pointed out, the battlefield is so far away that the tactical situation is likely to have changed beyond recognition by the time our boys and girls get there. The length of the deployment is such that we will need to use a specially derived and trained unit, one without close family ties to home. By the time they return to Earth, everyone they know will have aged twenty years at least, while they will have aged only months . . . depending on the rho-delta-tau and the efficiency of the onboard hibertechnic equipment.

"Gentlemen . . . ladies . . . Madam President . . . there is an old saying in the Corps, one dating from the first half of the twentieth century. 'Send in the Marines.' That saying was a reflection of the Corps' flexibility and hitting power in situations where it just didn't pay to declare war and send in the entire army, but where military might or the threat of an all-out war was necessary to achieve the President's goals, whatever they might be.

"The Marine Interstellar Expeditionary Unit will have the training and the hardware necessary to rescue our mission in the Llalande system. If we're too late for a rescue, well, they can secure our property there, show the folks back home that we at least goddamn tried, and if necessary send a message to the Ahannu that humans don't take kindly to being pushed around.

"I would like to add that some eighty of the people on

Ishtar are Marines serving with the Terran research mission there. The Corps does not forget its own. If the decision is made to abandon those brave men and women out there, then I am prepared to immediately tender my resignation as Commandant of the Marine Corps. A number of my staff and other senior Corps officers are prepared to take the same steps. That, Madam President, is all I have to say at this time."

"Well spoken," Billingsworth said. "Madam President, I must agree with General Colby. Operation Spirit of Humankind must go on, whatever the cost in dollars or lives. We lose too much if we let the Ahannu scare us off."

"This council is not a democracy," the President said, her voice cold. "There will be no vote. The decision rests entirely with me."

"Ah, and with Congress, Madam President," the Secretary of Human Affairs said. "We can't forget Congress. They're paying the bill, after all, and have the responsibility to declare war."

"You needn't remind me, Tom," she told him. "And you needn't worry. Congress will declare war when I ask them to. They're the ones whipping up all of these anti-An resolutions lately, remember. It's good political capital for the folks back home."

"An interesting public relations problem there, Madam President," Haslett said. "We declare war, but it will be ten years before our strike force reaches the target. Do you think Congress, or the public, will still be interested in fighting this war in 2148? A decade is a long time in politics and in the public's memory."

"Frankly, General Haslett," the President said, "that will be my successor's problem, not mine." She chuckled. "I plan to win my second term in 'forty, retire with dignity in 'forty-four, and be safely ensconced as an elder statesperson teaching metapolitical law on the WorldNet by the time our people even get to the Llalande system."

"But that also means, Madam President, that your successor, or the next Congress, might not want to continue paying for a war that *we* started. Our troops could find themselves eight light-years from home with no hope of further reinforcements or supply."

"Then the Joint Chiefs and the Federal Military Command will just have to see to it that we win with the one expeditionary force, won't they?"

Haslett nodded but felt deep reservations. This unexpected Ahannu god-weapon that could shoot starships from the Ishtaran sky . . . it was disturbing, even frightening. If the transport *Derna* was destroyed while the Marines were on the ground, they would have no way home, no matter what provisions Earthside Command made in advance. And Haslett was politician enough to know that the public wasn't likely to support *another* expensive mission to Llalande to rescue the first two, no matter how up in arms they were at the moment over the Ahannu's human slaves.

General Haslett glanced across the table at Colby and wondered what the Marine commandant was thinking.

The Mall
Washington, D.C., Earth
1840 hours ET

Secretary of State David Randolph Billingsworth rarely visited what he thought of as the tourist city. The special government service maglev subway generally whisked him straight from the underlevels of the White House–Executive Building complex to the station less than a block from his suburban Bethesda home, so his only glimpses of downtown Washington were through the odd window or on the big wallscreen in his office. The coded message that had come through on his cerebralink's priority comm channel had been as explicit as it had been terse, however. He'd checked a robot floater out of the Executive Office motor pool and ridden six blocks to the Fourteenth Street entrance of the Mall Dome, right next to the Smithsonian Museum of American History.

The Dome, actually a long, narrow ellipsoidal geodesic, stretched from the foot of Capitol Hill almost to the base of the Washington Monument, arching high above the historic Washington Mall. The largest freestanding geodesic in the world when it was built in 2069, it was widely praised as a modern wonder of the world . . . and equally vilified as a monumental eyesore in the City of Monuments.

Billingsworth had no feeling about it one way or another. It was possible for him to get anywhere within the government office warrens by maglev, from the Pentagon to the Capitol Building to Central Intelligence at Langley to the White House, so he never needed to go up on the surface and actually *see* the thing. But he had to admit it was rather pleasant . . . a cool escape from the heat and humidity of midsummer D.C., with late afternoon sunlight filtering through the transparencies to the west, from behind the slender dark spike of the Washington Monument.

He took a seat on a park bench next to a riot of forsythia. Tourists strolled or hurried past on the walkway or slid silently along on the glidepath. A naked couple snuggled on a blanket on a hillock nearby. A young woman—a congressional aide, perhaps—jogged past with a determined gait, her head completely enclosed in a sensory overlay helm, wearing nothing else but a sports bra and shoes. Near the Mall entryway, a gaggle of teenagers resplendent in iridescent Ahannu scale tattoos and shaven heads were passing out pro-An vidfliers to any who would take them.

No one seemed to recognize him, and that was good. He'd considered wearing an overlay helm himself . . . but that would have broadcast his ID out to anyone else with the requisite electronics and an unhealthy curiosity. Besides, people knew the President . . . but how many knew what the SecState looked like or even what his name was?

"Mr. Billingsworth?"

He turned. Allyn Buckner sat down on the other end of the bench and casually pretended to read a newsheet. He was wearing a conservative green and violet smartsuit and dark data visor.

"Buckner. Why'd you drag me out here?"

"Security, of course. I can't very well come to your office, or even your home, not without my presence being noted on a dozen e-logs. Nor could you visit me unnoticed. And hotel rooms, restaurants, and places like that all have so many electronics nowadays there's no way to guarantee a private conversation."

Billingsworth took another long look at the people passing by. This hardly seemed *private* . . . and even an open park had more than its fair share of police surveillance floaters, security scanners, and even roving news pickups.

But Buckner had a point about other possible meeting places. Public establishments were entirely too public, while offices and government buildings were heavily wired for all manner of electronic communications and data access. He would have preferred to meet with the PanTerran VP in one of his own secure meeting rooms—there were ways to avoid the log-in and ID protocols—but this, he supposed, would have to do.

"Well?" Buckner asked with brusque matter-of-factness. He scanned a fast-moving live newsfeed of a religious riot in Bombay, then folded the sheet and dropped it on the bench. "Let's have it."

Billingsworth sighed. "Operation Spirit of Humankind is still go," he said. "Scheduled departure is four months from now . . . October fifteenth."

"Give me the details."

Billingsworth reached out and took Buckner's hand, shaking it as if in greeting, pressing the microelectronics embedded in the skin at the base of his thumb against similar nanocircuitry in the PanTerran officer's palm. The ultimate in secret handshakes, the transfer of files stored in the Sec-State's cerebralink to Buckner's files took only a few milliseconds, with no RF or microwave leakage that might be intercepted and monitored.

"Excellent." Buckner seemed satisfied, in his acidic way. "My people were afraid that the government was going to backstep on this."

"I don't understand why you need me to be your . . . your spy."

"Not a spy, Mr. Billingsworth. Our *associate*. In twenty years, if all goes well, our very, very wealthy associate."

"Twenty years . . ."

"Think of it as long-term investment. You'll be . . . what? Eighty-one? Eighty-two? Young enough to benefit from a complete rejuvenation program, if you wish. And still be rich enough to buy that Caribbean island you want to retire to."

Billingsworth felt a sharp stab of alarm as a floater with the WorldNet News logo on its side drifted past, its glassy eye on the lookout for anything newsworthy. Humans might forget a face, but not a news bureau AI; he turned his head away, studying the foreplay antics of the couple on the hillock behind them. With a soft whine of maglifters, the flying eye drifted past, moving slowly toward the Fourteenth Street entrance.

"But I still don't understand what you need with these briefing records," he said when the snoop-floater was out of range.

"They help us plan, Mr. Billingsworth. The government is notoriously unreliable when it comes to long range planning. You can never really count on anything past the next round of elections. When dealing with business opportunities light-years away, that can be a distinct disadvantage. With this," he tapped the right side of his head, "we know we can proceed with certain plans, long range *expensive* plans, without risking the loss of our investment when the government waffles, or changes its mind, or decides to have a war. Besides, you need to do something to justify your shares in this venture, right?"

"I suppose so. But the scandal if this gets out—" he broke

off as another congressional jogger bounced past, oblivious and anonymous in his sensory helm. Next time, Billingsworth thought, he would definitely wear one of those, but with the ID functions off. There had to be a way to rig that, somehow.

Buckner gave a thin smile. "Then it's in both our best interests not to let it get out, right?"

"Yes, damn you."

"Good. You'll let me know if there's any change or new development. The usual e-drop." He stood up, dropping the newsheet in a nearby recycler. "And cheer up! You're going to be rich and live to be two hundred, easy. And no one will ever hear about those bad investments of yours last year."

Buckner turned and walked away, heading toward gardens filling the Mall interior.

Billingsworth watched the couple having sex on the hillside a moment longer, then used his cerebralink to signal the robocar, stood, and walked toward the Fourteenth Street entrance to meet it.

He was sweating, despite the Mall's air-conditioning, and his breath was coming in short, hard gasps. Damn it, he *had* to find a way to guarantee better privacy for his meetings in the future.

8

DI's Office, Company 1099
U.S. Marine Corps Recruit Train-
ing Center
Parris Island, South Carolina
0920 hours ET

"Garroway! Center yourself on the hatch!"

Garroway leaped into the DI's office, moving at the dead run that had been demanded of him and all of his fellow recruits in Company 1099 since the day they'd arrived at Parris Island.

"Sound off!" Gunnery Sergeant Makowiecz barked without looking up from his desk display.

"Sir!" Garroway snapped back as the toes of his boots hit the white line painted on the deck and he came to rigid attention, eyes locked firmly on an ancient water stain on the cinder-block bulkhead above and behind the DI's left shoulder. "Recruit Garroway reporting to the drill instructor as ordered, sir!"

"Recruit," Makowiecz said, his voice still as razor-edged as a Mamaluk sword, "your indoctrination classes are complete and you are about to enter phase one of your training. Are you fully aware of what this entails?"

"Sir! This recruit understands that he will be required to surrender all technical and data prostheses still resident within his body, sir!"

"Well quoted, son. Right out of the book. Stand at ease."

The sudden change in his DI's manner was so startling that Garroway nearly fell off his mark. Almost reluctantly, muscle by muscle, he relaxed his posture.

"Why do you want to be a Marine, son?" Makowiecz asked.

"Sir, this recruit—"

"Belay the third person crap," Makowiecz told him. "This is off the record, just you and me. You've seen enough of boot camp now that you must have an idea of how rough this is going to be. You are about to go through twelve weeks of sheer hell. So . . . why are you putting yourself through this?"

Garroway hesitated. He felt like he was just starting to get the hang of automatic recitations in the third person—"this recruit"—and it somehow didn't seem fair for the DI to suddenly come at him as though he were a normal, thinking human being. It left him feeling off balance, disoriented.

"Sir," he said, "all I can say is that this is what I've wanted ever since I heard stories from my mother about my great-grandfather."

Makowiecz placed his palm on a white-lit panel on his desk, accessing data through his c-link. "Your great-grandfather is one of the Names of the Corps," he said. "Manila John Basilone. Dan Daly. Presley O'Bannon. Chesty Puller. Sands of Mars Garroway. That's pretty good company. His name is a damn fine legacy.

"But you know and I know that there's more to being a Marine than a *name* . . ."

He paused, waiting expectantly, and Garroway knew he was supposed to say something. "Sir . . . this recruit . . . I mean, *I* don't know what you want me to tell you. I can't go back to what I was. Sir."

"You have an abusive father."

The change of topic was so sudden, Garroway didn't know how to respond. "Uh, it's not that bad, sir. Not sexual abuse or anything like that. He just—"

"I'm not interested in the details, son. But hear me, and hear me loud and clear. *All* abusive behavior by parents or stepparents or line-marriage parents—or by anyone else in authority over a kid, for that matter—does incalculable damage. Doesn't matter if it was sexual abuse or physical abuse with routine beatings or 'just' emotional abuse with screaming fits and head games. And it doesn't matter if the adult is alcoholic or addicted to c-link sex feeds or is just a thoroughgoing abusive asshole. It's really impossible to say which is worse, which kid gets hurt the most, because every kid is different and responds to the abuse in different ways."

"My father yelled a lot," Garroway said, "but he never hit me. Uh, not deliberately, anyway." He didn't add that Carlos Esteban *had* hit his mother, frequently, and threatened more than once to do the same to him, or that he was an alcoholic who'd disabled the court-appointed cybercontrols over his behavior.

"Doesn't matter. It says here your mother has filed for divorce. She's out of the house?"

"Yes, sir. She's staying with a sister in California now."

"Good. She's better off out of this guy's way, and you'll be better off knowing she's okay." He got a faraway look in his eyes as he scrutinized the data feed flowing through his link. "It says here you were hospitalized once with a dislocated shoulder after a domestic altercation."

"That was an accident, sir."

"Uh-huh." The sergeant didn't sound at all convinced. "Your father has been cited seven times . . . domestic violence . . . disturbing the peace . . . assault . . . This bastard should have been locked away and rehabbed a long time ago."

"There are . . . political factors, sir. He's a pretty big man in Sonora, where we live. He's good friends with the local sheriff and with the governor."

"Shit. Figures."

"Sir . . . I don't understand where this is going. Are you saying I'm not qualified to be a Marine because my father—"

"You're qualified, son. Don't worry about that. What we're concerned about right now is your c-link. Your implant is a Sony-TI 12000 Series Two Cerebralink."

"Uh, yessir. It was a birthday present from my parents."

"Do you have a resident AI?"

"A personality, you mean? No, sir." Most cerebralinks had onboard AI, for net navigation if nothing else. He didn't have one with a distinct personality, though. His father hadn't believed in that sort of thing.

"Cybersex partner?"

"Uh . . . no . . ." He'd linked into a number of sex sites, of course, for a few hours of play with various fantasy partners. Everyone did that. But he didn't have a regular playmate.

"Cyberpet?"

"No, sir." His father had been pretty insistent about his not having any artificial personalities—a waste of time and money, Carlos had said, and a threat to his immortal soul—and he'd done a lot of e-snooping to make sure his orders were obeyed.

"What did you do for companionship?"

"Well . . . there's my girlfriend. . . ."

"Lynnley Collins. Yes. You're pretty close with her?"

"Yes, sir."

"A fuck buddy? Or something closer?"

"She's a *friend*. Sir." He had to bite back his rising anger. This kind of cross-examination was the sort of thing his father did, stripping him of any semblance of privacy.

Of course, he'd known he would be surrendering most of his privacy rights when he signed up. But this prying, this spying into his private life . . . damn it, it wasn't *right*.

"I know, son," Makowiecz said gently, almost as if he was reading Garroway's mind. "I know. This is as intrusive, as downright abusive, as anything your old man ever did to you. But it's necessary."

"Sir, yes, sir. If you say so, sir."

"I do say so. Does it surprise you that we pay pretty close attention to a recruit's private life here? We have to." He pulled his hand off the contact panel on the desk and leaned back in his chair. Outside, clearly audible through the thin walls of the DI's barracks office, a boot company jogged past, sounding off to a singsong cadence to the beat of footsteps thundering together.

> *"Am I right or am I wrong?*
> *Each of us is tough and strong!*
> *We guard the ground, the sea, the sky!*
> *Ready to fight and willing to die!"*

"It's a damned paradox, Garroway," Makowiecz said as the chanting faded away across the grinder. "Lots of kids join the Marines who had bad childhoods. For a lot of 'em, the Corps is their mother and father put together. I know. That's the way it was for me. And we have to put you through six kinds of hell, have to *break* you in order to build you up into the kind of Marine we want. If that's not abuse, I don't know what is."

"A history feed I downloaded once said that it used to be that Marine DIs couldn't even swear at the recruits. Sir."

Makowiecz nodded. "True enough. That was back, oh, 150 years ago or so. We couldn't lay hands on recruits then either. A number of Marine DIs were discharged, even court-martialed and disgraced, for not following the new guidelines. They'd grown up in the old Corps, after all, and they thought that harassment and even physical abuse toughened the recruits, made them better Marines.

"We know better now. Still, the rules have relaxed a bit since then, because it was discovered that we couldn't make Marines without imposing discipline . . . and sometimes some well-placed profanity or grabbing a recruit by the stacking swivel and giving him a shake is just what is needed to get the message through his damned thick recruit skull. You copy?"

"Yes, sir."

"We *have* to invade each recruit's private life, right down to his soul—if he has one. We need to know what makes him tick. How he'll react under stress. And how we can transform him into a U.S. Marine."

"I understand that, sir." And he did, reluctantly . . . and with a few reservations.

"Good. You understand too that we have to remove your cerebralink."

"Yes . . . sir."

"You don't sound so sure of that."

"Well, it's kind of scary, thinking about being without it. I'll be getting a Marine Corps model, right?"

"That's affirmative. Eventually. But first you will learn how to function without any electronic enhancement at all."

"Without . . . any? . . ." The thought wasn't scary. It was terrifying.

"Right. Look . . . you know the cerebralink is nothing but a tiny set of parallel computers nanotechnically grown inside your head and connecting to certain parts of your nervous system, like the linkpads in the palm of your hands. It lets you link head-to-head with others with compatible hardware, lets you connect with the WorldNet and pull down the answer to any question, gives you a whole library just a thought-click away. You can see anything, call anyone, make reservations, even download the whole history of the Corps just by thinking about it. The thing is, too many kids nowadays rely on the net, know what I mean?"

"I guess so. But . . . are you saying it's wrong to link on?"

"Wrong? Hell no. Direct net access is one of the great cornerstones of modern technology and culture. But you as a Marine need to learn that you can get along without any technic prosthesis whatsoever . . . not just learn it, but know it right down to your bones. Our ancestors went a long way without implants or c-links. You can too.

"However, we've found a special problem with kids coming from families with major dysfunctions. Alcoholism. Net addictions. Violence. Kids who don't get the love and care they need at home tend to grow up relying on surrogates, like AI companions, cyberpets, or e-mates. When they're separated from their comfort-of-choice, whatever it is, it can be pretty rough."

"Why don't you just keep them from enlisting, then?" Damn it, if they were going to kick him out of boot camp for *this* . . .

"If we did that, son, we'd have to exclude the majority of our volunteers. And some of our best people came from bad home situations. Myself included. But we do take them aside first, like I'm doing with you, and give them a final chance to think about it, think about what they're in for. When we pull your hardware, you're going to feel more alone, more lost, more isolated than you've ever felt in your life. It's going to be hell. And you're going to have to ride it out. Eventually, you will be issued with a Marine Corps implant. *If* you make it through."

"And if I don't?"

"If you don't, the government will stand you to a replacement, though I'm afraid it won't be as fancy as a Sony-TI 12000. Government issue, IBM-800 series. But you can upgrade that for anything you want later."

"What . . . what are my chances, sir?"

"Oh, pretty good, actually. We lose maybe fifteen percent of our recruits at this stage. But the proportion is higher for kids from dysfunctional families, like yours. We could lose, oh, maybe thirty, thirty-five percent. A lot of kids have formed attachments they can't get along without. You have an edge, because you haven't bonded with an AI construct yet."

"I can handle it, sir."

"Good. Because our best Marines are fighters, the ones who've had bad shakes and had to fight to make it through. Tough. Survivors. We *want* that in our people. But we need to give you the chance to back out now, before we yank your plug-in."

"Thank you, sir."

"You have twenty-two hours to think it over. Tomorrow, at zero-seven-thirty, you will report to recruit sick bay for processing. You may, at any time until then, refuse the treatment. At that time you may opt either for a full discharge or transfer to one of the other military or government services. One less demanding than the U.S. Marine Corps. Do you understand me?"

"Yes, sir."

"Very well." He paused, and his voice hardened again. "Back to the routine. Dismissed!"

That, Garroway knew, was his cue to slip back into his recruit persona. "Sir! Aye aye, sir!"

He pulled a sharp about-face, then fairly lunged from the compartment, on the run.

Headquarters, PanTerra Dynamics
New Chicago, Illinois
United Federal Republic, Earth
1545 hours CT

A scarlet-uniformed attendant ushered Dr. Traci Hanson into the briefing chamber on the 540th floor of the PanTerra Dynamics Building in New Chicago and toward her seat at a large, crystalline-topped conference table. A viewall behind the table showed the gold, scarlet, and purple panorama of Ishtar, the vast orb of Marduk hanging low in the sky above clustered pyramids, obelisks, and the low, rounded domes of native habitations.

She was still having some trouble getting around on Earth, three weeks after her return from Mars, but she waved off the proffered arm and made the final walk to her seat on her own. She wore an earth-return EW suit, a utilitarian-looking green jumpsuit with an exoskeleton walker frame invisibly woven into the fabric. It helped her stand without falling, and supported the weight that, to her, still felt three times greater than normal. At least now she could stand. For the first few days after her return, she'd been all but confined to a wheelchair. Now she could get around pretty well without any artificial aid at all, resorting to the EW suit only when she knew she was going to be standing or walking for long periods.

Rising with solemn formality, Allyn Buckner introduced himself and the others already seated.

"Dr. Hanson," he said in a raspy voice. "So good of you to come. May I present Gavin Norris . . . Clarence Rafferty . . . Lee Soong Yi . . . Mary Pritchard . . . and I believe you already know Conrad Robinson and Marine Colonel Thomas Jackson Ramsey."

She nodded to each in turn. Conrad Robinson was her department head at the American Xenoarcheological Institute, though she barely knew him. And Ramsey . . .

"Colonel Ramsey," she said. "Yes. We shared the packet hop back to Earth." She noted with a small stab of irritation that Ramsey was wearing a dress Marine uniform, with no sign of the braces at neck or wrists indicating that he was wearing a walker.

"Hello again, Dr. Hanson," Ramsey said with a grin. "Gotten your Earth legs yet?"

"More or less," she replied brusquely, in no mood for casual talk. She looked at Buckner as she sank into her seat, grateful to be off her feet. "So. I understand you want me to go out-system. Why? Or perhaps I should say, 'Why me?' "

"Because you are one of our best xenoarcheologists, and an expert on the An or Ahannu or whatever they call themselves."

"*An*," she replied in a clipped, offhand manner, "is what primitive humans in the Mesopotamian region called the species when they first arrived on Earth, some ten to twelve thousand years ago. Their name for themselves is *Ahannu*, which means, approximately, 'the Holy People.' "

"Er, yes. Exactly," Buckner said.

"You see, ladies and gentlemen," Robinson said quickly, "why I said Dr. Hanson would be perfect for this mission."

"But you haven't asked me if I want to go," she said. "I am flattered, Mr. Buckner, but I am not prepared to sacrifice twenty years or more of my career . . . not when there is so much yet to do *here* and on Mars."

"Sacrifice? Who said anything about sacrifice? Upon your return, you will only be some five years older, not twenty . . . and thanks to cryohibertechnics, you'll experience none of the actual voyage. And you will be able to study the Ahannu in person, on their homeworld."

"Not their homeworld," she said, correcting him. Damn the netnews media. With sloppy reporting and sheer carelessness, they'd perpetuated the popular misconception that Ishtar was the world where the An had originally evolved. "The world we call Ishtar was an An colony world, like Earth. The Hunters of the Dawn appear to have overlooked Ishtar when they—"

"Yes, yes, as you say. In any case, the chance to meet the Ahannu face-to-face would have to be the chance of a lifetime for a dedicated research scientist such as yourself."

"A dedicated research scientist such as myself," she said, "depends on the timely publishing of papers to stay current and to stay known in a highly competitive field. I will not waste twenty years *sleeping* while my colleagues are continuing to publish in my absence!"

"Not even for, say . . . fifty million newdollars, plus the chance at royalties from discoveries this corporation may make on Ishtar?"

She opened her mouth, then clamped it shut again. Had she heard right? "Fifty . . . million?"

"I would think, Doctor, that that much money might go a long way toward paying you back for any professional . . . inconvenience. And upon your return, you will, of course, be *the* expert on the Ahannu. I expect we could promise you a position with PanTerra Dynamics, in fact."

"What happened to Nichole Moore?"

"Eh?"

"Nichole Moore is the xenoculturalist assigned to the Terran Legation on Ishtar," she said, "working under a government grant for the Smithsonian Institute. She's been in the New Sumer compound for five years now. *She* would be the leading expert on the Ahannu at the moment, unless . . ."

"We have . . . lost touch with Dr. Moore," Buckner told her. "We are assembling an expedition to go to Ishtar, rescue any survivors, and reestablish a Terran presence in the Llalande system. Since it will be ten years before the relief mission can arrive, we must assume that Dr. Moore and the rest of *Emissary*'s people are all dead or will be dead by the time you arrive."

She nodded slowly. "I see." She'd suspected as much, of course, both from what she'd picked up at the Cydonian complex and from her conversations with the Marine women on board the *Osiris*. Geremelet's Destiny Faction had won considerable power among the Ahannu, and there'd been growing danger of a coup or at least of a civil war on Ishtar, one that would threaten the tiny human contingent stationed at New Sumer. "They killed Dr. Moore, and now you're sending me?"

"You'll have considerably more firepower behind you than Dr. Moore did," Buckner said. "A full Marine Expeditionary Unit, in fact. One of its primary tasks will be to protect you."

"No," she said. "Find another victim."

"I beg your pardon?"

She looked at her boss. "Mr. Robinson, the institute is largely funded by the federal government, but we are not soldiers to be ordered about! They can't just pack me off to another goddamn star for twenty years!"

"Actually, Dr. Hanson," Robinson said, "I put your name in the running. You will be ideal for this mission. And you must admit that the financial remuneration package is, well, quite generous."

"I don't care about that! You can't transfer me eight light-years! What about my work here?"

"Carter and Jorgenson will be more than able to fill in for you at Cydonia, Dr. Hanson."

"Carter and Jorgenson! Carter is a second-rate hack who can't see beyond his fringie religious beliefs! And Jorgenson is so determined to try and prove that some mythical ancient human culture was the Hunters of the Dawn that—" She stopped, eyes widening. So that was it. Jorgenson was her chief rival within the institute. She'd crossed academic swords with the man more than once, and was convinced that he owed his current power and prestige more to the people he knew in government than to any real ability in his field. He'd also failed more than once to get her into his bed, and had taken to twisting her words whenever he had the opportunity, as if in petty revenge. Hell, he'd delivered one paper that had made *her* look like the fringie nutcase, by misrepresenting her contention that the An had introduced the concept of religion to the early native population of Earth.

He'd been silent ever since she threatened to expose him as a fraud. Was this his way of getting even?

"If I were you, Doctor," Robinson went on, "I would give some thought to my future with the institute and where else you might be able to apply your considerable talent and experience."

She blinked. "Is that a threat?"

"There are no threats here, Dr. Hanson," Buckner said gently. "Think of it as . . . an incentive."

"Is that what you call it?"

"Fifty million newdollars?" Buckner chuckled. "Compounding interest at ten percent over ten years? Or . . . let's make it seventy-five million. *And* a contract with PanTerra Dynamics naming you research director of your own exo-studies department upon your return to Earth. You will be extraordinarily rich . . . and able to apply your talents toward any area of research you might desire. Who knows? Working with the Ahannu directly . . . you might open up whole new, undreamed of areas of study. . . ."

Traci felt light-headed, almost dizzy. This was everything she could ever have dreamed of. Freedom of research, and the money to let her pursue that research wherever it took her. No longer dependent on the institute, or anyone else. It seemed almost too good to be true. . . .

Which in her book meant that it *was* too good to be true.

"Wait a minute," she said. "Wait just a damned minute. How can you afford to throw money around like that? Fifty million, seventy-five million. What's your annual salary, Buckner? About ten, maybe twenty million, at a guess? Hell, I don't care if seventy-five million is nothing but loose credit chips to you, even a company as big as PanTerra has to show a profit. And you won't show a profit spraying newdollars around like water."

"Believe me, Dr. Hanson, when I say that there is a great deal of profit to be made in a new market, an entire new *world* market, for this company. I can offer you, oh, let's say an even one hundred million. That's five million per objective year, and I assure you that the profit potential for an entire world is *many* times greater than that."

"That is an interesting point, Mr. Buckner," Ramsey, the Marine colonel, said. His hands were clasped together on the desk before him, and his eyes were like gray ice. "A fascinating point. What is it about a planet that makes it so worth PanTerra's attention?"

"What do you mean? An entire *planet*. Do you have any idea what the gross domestic product of the Earth is right now, Colonel?"

The Marine showed a cold smile. "Large. But that's not the point. I've done some research, sir, into the economics of interstellar trade. I think both Dr. Hanson and I would be most interested in just what it is you expect to find in the Llalande system that could be worth such a whopping big investment on your part."

"Well, the trade alone with the Ahannu—"

"Isn't enough, sir. The Llalande system has no raw materials that our own system doesn't have in vast abundance. We've barely begun to tap the raw material resources of our own asteroid and Kuiper belts, and the nickel, iron, and heavy metals we find right here in our own backyard are just as good as anything we could haul back across eight light-years, and a hell of a lot cheaper. Native products? The Ahannu are primitives, millennia behind us in technology. There would certainly be a market for Ahannu artwork and crafts . . . but nothing worth the cost of shipping them eight light-years."

"There is one commodity, Colonel, that always pays in the long run," Buckner said. "*Knowledge.* Information. You're right, of course. We may never have merchant ships plying the galactic trade routes. But the knowledge we could pick up from an entire new, alien culture is staggering, and literally incalculable.

"Consider. Knowledge of the fact that there has already been contact between the Ahannu and humans, in our own prehistory, has utterly transformed the way we think about ourselves, how we think about our place among the stars. The new philosophical insights, the new religions—"

"Have already been more trouble than they're worth," Traci put in. "I'll grant you that knowledge is the one trans-portable resource that might make interstellar trading worth-while. But you can send information by FTL comm or even laser or old-fashioned radio. Why do you need to send people out there?"

"To get the information, of course." Buckner sighed, crossing his arms. "AIs are still limited in what they can do, especially in a situation involving an alien species. If you don't want the job, there's nothing more we can do about it. I have other contacts, other agencies. Perhaps we could approach Dr. Chaumont, at the Institute Française Xenobi-ologique. . . ."

"Damn it, Dr. Hanson," Robinson said, half rising from his chair. "Consider what you're doing!"

Traci could see that her department head had a pretty hefty stake in this affair as well. If PanTerra went to the EU, the institute might lose grant money . . . or worse, prestige.

She still didn't like it. Colonel Ramsey had a point: Pan-Terra was being just a little too free with their money, and she had the feeling there was more to the corporate giant's interest in Ishtar than they were willing to admit.

On the other hand . . . a hundred million newdollars, and the chance to write her own ticket when she returned? There was such a thing as too good to be true . . . and such a thing as too good to pass up. This was literally the chance of a lifetime.

"Okay, okay," she said. "Don't get your underwear in a twist. I can hardly pass this one up, can I?"

"Excellent," Buckner said. "I knew we could count on you, Dr. Hanson. You *won't* be sorry."

Traci smiled as she shook his hand, but the smile was forced. She found herself trusting Buckner about as far as she could throw him in a ten-g field.

Just how long would it be before she *was* sorry?

9

Recruit Sick Bay
U.S. Marine Corps Recruit Train-
ing Center
Parris Island, South Carolina
0800 hours ET

"Sir, Recruit Garroway, reporting as ordered, sir."

"Have a seat, recruit," the Navy corpsman, a hospitalman first class, said, gesturing at the white-draped table. "We'll be right with you." The man's data badge gave his name as HM1 D. LOGAN.

"Sir, yes, sir!"

"Drop the 'sir' crap," Logan said. "I work for a living."

Garroway sat on the table, watching apprehensively as the corpsman passed a small, handheld device in front of his head and torso. A monitor on the console nearby displayed Garroway's vital signs: temperature, pulse, respiration, blood pressure, EEG output, and cyberneural feed frequencies.

"Corrective optic nano?"

"Yes . . ."

"We'll write you a scrip for glasses."

Garroway had no idea what that word meant, though the context suggested something to correct his nearsighted vision. He suppressed an urge to do a search on the net; Parris Island was shielded from regular library services, and he didn't have the codes to navigate the base military data stores.

"Your heart rate's a bit high," Logan said. "And your BP is up."

"Of course they are," Garroway replied stiffly. "I'm . . . scared."

It was an honest response, at least. He'd thought about what he was doing thoroughly, as his DI had suggested, and in the end decided he had no choice but to go through with this. But of course he had second thoughts . . . and third . . . and fourth. He'd spent the last thirty minutes standing in formation outside the medcenter, waiting as one member of his company after another vanished into the building.

Thirty minutes to reflect on whether he really wanted to go through with this.

But the thought of pulling out now, of transferring to another service—or, infinitely worse, of going back home to Guaymas—was far more disagreeable. Besides, if he wanted to be a Marine, *this* was his path.

"Scared? Of the procedure?" The corpsman grinned. "I thought you wanted to be a big, rough, tough Marine?"

"Hey—"

Logan shrugged. "Don't sweat it. Most guys make it through okay. Just remember that . . . if you feel strange, y'-know? It's all up here." He tapped the side of his head. "You can *think* your way through and come out fine. How many channels you got?"

"Four hundred eighty."

"Library feed?"

"Local Hermosillo Node, and a direct feed from Global-Net Data."

"Ow. That'll hurt, losing all that. Pretty hot stuff. Full graphic capability? Visual overlay?"

"Yes . . ."

"And comm, of course. What kind of math coprocessor?"

"Sony-TI 12000. Series Two, with nonlinear math processing. Extensions for hypertrig, Calculus Four, and poly-logmatics."

"Well, I'm afraid you're going to be counting on your fingers and toes for a while." Garroway watched as the corpsman picked out the injector and loaded it with a vial of what looked like clear water. Placing the device on the table, the man then looked toward the wall and said, "Right. He's ready."

Part of the wall unfolded then into a tangle of gleaming tubes, arms, and sensors. Cables with EEG contacts touched Garroway lightly at various points on his scalp. Thoughts flickered through his consciousness, downloading through his cerebralink . . . a burst of violet light, a chord of organ music, and words, a gentle, female voice saying, "Please relax."

Garroway had been in AI-doctor treatment rooms before—each time he'd been given an injection of medical nano, in fact—but the experience always verged on the unsettling. A pair of robotic arms gently clasped his head and shoulders, immobilizing them in thick-padded fingers. A third hand, lighter and more delicate, reached down with glittering fingers and plucked the loaded injector off the table, then approached his neck with the injector clasped tightly in its metallic grip. Garroway felt a brief stab of fear . . . but then a gentle current flowing through the link dispersed the emotion, replacing it with a sense of quiet, placid euphoria. He barely felt the touch of the jet spray against his throat, just below the angle of his jaw at the left carotid artery.

He imagined he could feel the antinano fizzing up inside his brain, seeking out the nanochelates clustered within the deeper rifts of his cranial sulci and dissolving them. It was imagination, of course, since he had no sensory nerves inside his brain, but the feeling was real and distinctly odd nonetheless. In another moment he thought he could feel the chelated contact points in the palms of his hands softening as weil, as the silver-gold-carbon alloy of the palmlinks was absorbed back into his bloodstream.

One feeling that was decidedly not in his imagination, though, was the sense of diminishment . . . a kind of shrinking of mind and awareness. For one confused and near-panicky moment, it felt as though he was somehow being muffled in layers of unseen insulation. His hearing felt . . . *dead,* as well as his sense of touch, and something like a translucent gray mist dropped across his vision. Dozens of separate sensations shriveled, as though drawing back from his consciousness . . . smells, sounds, sensations of touch and temperature, and even vision itself becoming less intense, less there.

"Goddess . . ." he said, his voice sounding distant in his ears. He felt a little dizzy, a bit light-headed, and he might have fallen over if the robotic doctor hadn't been gently but firmly holding him upright on the table.

"Kind of rocks you, doesn't it?" the corpsman said. "How ya doing?"

"I'm . . . not sure. . . ."

"Can you stand?"

"I think so." He slid off the table, then braced himself as the dizziness returned, threatening to drop him to his knees. He swayed, then steadied, trying to clear his head. *Damn it, where had the room gone?*

No, the room was still here, but he felt so oddly detached. He remembered what Logan had said about it all being inside his head and tried to focus on what he *could* see and sense around him, not on what was no longer there.

Damn, he had never realized that the cybernanochelates in his brain had added so much to his perception of his surroundings. With his cerebralink operating, he'd been aware of everything within his range of vision. Now he found his visual focus only included a relatively limited area directly in front of his eyes, that he had to consciously shift his awareness to notice objects at his visual periphery. A moment before, he'd been aware of dust motes hanging in the air, of a scuff mark on the otherwise brilliant finish of the sick bay deck, of a three-K-cycle low frequency hum from the lighting panels overhead, of a small scrap of paper in the sick bay's far corner . . . all without consciously focusing on them. They were simply *there*. Now, to his increasing dismay, he had to really look to see something and note what it was. The corpsman's data badge no longer automatically transmitted rank and ID; he had to actually *read* the printed letters that spelled out HM1 D. LOGAN.

And . . . what had happened to his vision? Everything was slightly fuzzy now, though he found he could tighten things up a bit by squinting. Ah. His corrective optic nano, that was it. He no longer had microsilicate structures reshaping his eyeballs to give him perfect focus.

Was this really what it was like without cyber enhancement?

"Man, where'd the world go?" he asked.

"It's still there," Logan told him. "You just don't have the sensory enhancement or the electronic processing tied into your cerebral cortex anymore. Don't worry about it. You'll be amazed what you can do with the equipment nature gave you."

Garroway blinked, trying to assimilate this. He'd been expecting something more or less like this, of course, but the reality carried a lot more impact than the expectation. Damn, he felt so slow, so muzzy-headed.

He suddenly realized that he didn't know which way was north . . . and he no longer carried a small, internal map of where he was and where he'd been for the past several minutes.

For that matter, he no longer had an internal clock. He'd walked into the sick bay at 0800 hours . . . but how long had he been there? Several minutes, at least . . . but how long exactly?

He didn't know, had no way of knowing.

"Go out that way," Logan told him, jerking a thumb at a different door than the one he'd entered through. "Follow the blue line and join the rest of your company on the grinder."

The door had a touch pad, but it didn't open when he laid his palm across the slick, black surface. He had to *push* and engage the manual control so that the door slid open to let him out.

The blue line was painted on the wall, and if it had a cyber component to it, he couldn't feel it, not anymore. It led him down a corridor, through several lefts and rights, depositing him at last on the steps below the sick bay's back door. The rest of Company 1099, those who'd already gone through the process ahead of him, were waiting in ranks. Sergeant Dolby, one of 1099's three assistant DIs, motioned him into line without comment.

The other recruits appeared as dazed as he felt. Most, he knew—the ones who'd not been able to afford more than a basic-level cerebralink system or who'd had to rely on government-issue implants—weren't feeling nearly as dazed as he was, but all of them looked stunned, and several looked like they were about to be sick or pass out. Dolby walked up one rank and down the next, pausing occasionally to stop and talk quietly to a recruit who looked particularly bad off. The sergeant passed him without stopping, so perhaps, Garroway reasoned, he wasn't as bad off as he felt.

He tried to remember what it had been like before he'd gone to the medical center at Hermosillo on his fourteenth birthday and received the injections for his Sony-TI 12000. Before that he'd had a government-issued school model, of course, implanted when he was . . . what? It must have been around age four or so, but school models weren't sensory-enhanced, as a rule, and didn't store detailed memories unless a teaching code was downloaded in order to store a specific lesson. He remembered being taught how to read, how to research any question he could imagine on the WorldNet, even how to feel good about himself, but his day-to-day memories from that time were pretty hazy.

It took him a moment or two to realize that an hour ago, those memories *would* have been crystal clear. His cerebralink helped access memories, even those that had not been cataloged in downloading. He felt . . . diminished . . . shrunken, somehow . . . barely present.

The next thing he knew, he was lying on the pavement, looking up into the less than appealing features of Sergeant Dolby. He felt dizzy and sick, light-headed and cold. Dolby slapped him lightly on the face a couple of times. "You okay, recruit?"

"S-Sir." He tried to formulate the correct response—*This recruit is okay*—but failed. "Yes, sir."

"Stay put. A doc'll be along in a second."

Five other recruits of Company 1099 had passed out as well. They were helped back into the sick bay by unsympathetic corpsmen, who laid them out on cots, took their vitals, and gave them spray injections in their arms. There was no autodoc or treatment room; without cerebralinks, they couldn't be hooked into a diagnostic system. That thought alone was enough to leave Garroway wondering what could *possibly* have possessed him to voluntarily give up his cyberimplants.

After receiving the injection and being allowed to rest for twenty minutes, he felt well enough to return to the rest of the group. Another hour dragged by as the rest of Company 1099—those who'd agreed to lose their cybernano, at any rate—passed through the sick bay and the ministrations of the AI examination room. Out of the original complement of ninety-five men in Company 1099, fifteen had refused to allow their nanochelates to be removed, and three more had been rejected by the AI treatment room for one reason or another. Most of them were on their way back to civilian life by that afternoon, processed out on a DD-4010—"Subject unsuitable for Marine Corps service," a convenience-of-the-government discharge. Two volunteered instead for a transfer to the Navy, and three others elected to join the Aerospace Force.

"Why," Gunnery Sergeant Makowiecz bellowed at the ranks later that morning, "did we take away your implants? Anyone!" Several hands went up, and Makowiecz chose one. "You!"

"S-Sir, this recruit believes that you will issue Marine implants," Murphy, a kid from Cincinnati, said. "Civilian implants may not be compatible with military-issue gear or with each other. Sir."

"That," Makowiecz replied, "is part of the answer. But not *all* of it. Anyone else?"

Garroway raised his hand, and Makowiecz snapped, "You!"

"Sir," Garroway said, "it is Marine Corps policy to have all recruits begin at the same level, with no one better or worse than anyone else, sir!"

"Again, a piece of the answer, but not all of it. And not the most important part. Anyone else?" No one moved in the ranks. "All right, I'll tell you." Makowiecz pointed at the sky. "Right now, there are some 2,491 communications satellites in Earth orbit, from little field relays the size of your thumb in LEO to the big library space stations at L-4 and L-5. They all talk to one another and to the Earth stations in all of the major cities down here. As a result, the air around us is filled with information, data streams moving from node to node, access fields, packets uploading and downloading so thick if you could see 'em with your eyes you'd think you were in a snowstorm.

"With the right hardware chelated into your brains, all you have to do, anywhere on the surface of the Earth, is think a question with the appropriate code tag, and the answer is there. You want to talk to another person, anywhere between here and the moon, all you do is think about them and *bang*, there they are inside your head. Right?

"If you go to Mars, there are 412 communications satellites in orbit, not counting the big stations on Deimos and Phobos. Same thing holds. You don't have as many channels or as much of a choice in where you get your data from, but you can have any question answered, any spot on the planet mapped down to half-meter resolution, or talk to anyone at all, just by thinking about it.

"Even if you were to go all the way out to Llalande 21185, to the moon Ishtar, you'd find a few dozen communications satellites in orbit, plus the mission transport. Same deal. The Llalande net is a lot smaller even than the one on Mars. Highly specialized . . . but it's there.

"But what happens if you find yourself on some Goddess-forsaken dirtball *that doesn't have a GlobalNet system?*"

He let the words hang in the air for a moment, as Garroway and the other recruits wrestled with the concept. There was *always* a GlobalNet. Wherever man went, he took his technology with him . . . and that meant the net, and the myriad advantages of constantly being online. Life without the net would be as unthinkable as . . . as life without medical nano or zollarfilm or smartclothing or . . . *food*.

Their access to the net had been limited since they'd arrived on Parris Island, of course, but even that knowledge didn't carry the same impact as the DI's grinning words.

"Don't look so shocked, kiddies," Makowiecz went on. "People got on just fine without instant net access, back before they figured out how to shoot nanochelates into your brains. And you will too. Trust me on that one! Awright! Leh . . . *face!* Fowah . . . *harch!* Left! Left! Your left-right-left . . ."

Garroway was willing to accept the idea of learning how to live as a primitive, at least in theory. He'd expected to go the camping and survival route, learning how to make a fire, orienteer across the Parris Island swamps, catch his own dinner, and treat himself or a buddy for snakebite. The Marines were famous for being able to live off the land and get by with nothing much at all. He had no idea just *how* primitive things would get, however, until that afternoon after chow, when Dolby marched half of them back to the recruit sick bay to be fitted with glasses.

Glasses! He'd never heard of the things, though he realized now that he had seen them before, in various downloads of historical scenes and images from a century or two back. Two pieces of glass ground to precise optical properties, held just in front of the eyes by a plastic framework that hooked over the ears and balanced on the bridge of the nose . . . Once, evidently, they'd been quite fashionable, but the advent first of contacts, then of the dual technologies of genetic engineering and corrective visual nano, had sent them the way of the whalebone corset and silk necktie.

Those recruits whose parents had selected for perfect vision before their births didn't need visual correction. About half of the company, however, had had nano implants as part of their cerebralinks—submicroscopic structures that both allowed images and words to be projected directly onto the retina and, as an incidental side issue, subtly changed the shape of the cornea and of the eyeball itself to allow perfectly focused vision. Contact lenses, it had been decreed, were too dangerous, too likely to be smashed into the eye in pugil stick practice, a fall on the obstacle course, or hand-to-hand training. Glasses, with unbreakable transplas lenses, might fly off the face but they wouldn't blind a careless or unlucky recruit. And, unlike contacts, glasses could be taken off and cleaned in the field with the swipe of a finger after a fall in the platoon mud pit.

They just *looked* as ugly as sin . . . and twice as silly. Why, Garroway wondered, couldn't they just inject them all with a specialized antinano that neutralized the neural chelates but left stuff like vision correctives?

Several times so far in his service career he'd heard people refer to how there were three ways of doing anything—the right way, the wrong way, and the *Corps'* way.

He decided that he was going to have to get used to the occasional seeming irrationality, to accept it as a normal part of this new life.

It was that or go mad.

Headquarters, USMCSPACCOM
Quantico, Virginia
United Federal Republic, Earth
1415 hours ET

Colonel T. J. Ramsey wondered what megalomaniac had designed this program.

A dozen Marine officers hovered in space, like gods looking down upon the glowing red-gold, brown, and violet sphere representing distant Ishtar. A window had opened against the planet, revealing an orbital survey map of the New Sumer region along the north coast of the continent called Euphratea. The sense of sheer power was almost hypnotic.

Colonel Ramsey was completing the mission briefing. "That's it, then," he said. He gestured, and lines of green light flared against the map of the city, outlining perimeters, zones of fire, and LZs. "The initial landings will seize control of the city of New Sumer and the immediate area, with special attention paid to gaining control of the Pyramid of the Eye. That will be the Regimental Landing Team HQ." Another window opened, enlarging the map area around a prominent rise west of the city. "Before that happens, however, we will need to neutralize Mount An-Kur. That will be the particular task of your Advance Recon Landing Team, Captain Warhurst."

The briefing room, if it could be called that, was being projected inside the minds of the participants, some of whom were at Quantico, others as far away as the *Derna*, in high Earth orbit. The icon representing Captain Martin Warhurst wore Marine grays, which were somewhat outmoded on the fashion front. Just three weeks back from Egypt, he'd not had time to update his personal software, what with endless rounds of debriefings and the work he was putting into his latest assignment—the Llalande Relief Expedition ARLT. In contrast, most of the others at the virtual briefing flaunted the latest Marine officer's fashion, duotone white and gold tunics over blue trousers, both with red trim, and with a holographic globe-and-anchor projected above the left breast. Ramsey wondered how many of them wore the new uniforms outside of virtual reality. They looked peacock-gaudy in the briefing feed; few field commanders, however, bothered with the game of fashion keep-up so popular with the stateside Corps brass.

"I'd still feel better about this if we just rocked 'em from orbit," Warhurst said. "This giant gun or whatever it is they have inside the mountain . . . if it can claw starships out of the sky, how the hell are we going to even get close?"

Colonel Ramsey nodded. "I know. But we have very specific orders on this one. I already tried to sell the commandant on a bombardment from space, but his orders are to deliver that weapons system to our experts . . . intact. If we reduce that mountain to a crater, the Joint Chiefs are not going to be happy with us."

"So?" Major Ricia Anderson said, grinning, her voice just low enough that the colonel could convincingly ignore it. "They'll be ten years away! What are they gonna do, write us a nasty e-note?"

"Fortunately," Ramsey went on, "the Annies don't know we have to take that mountain instead of flattening it. That gives us a possible edge tactically, a slim one. From the description provided in the last transmission from the pyramid, we estimate that the beam weapon hidden inside An-Kur must generate a bolt of energy measuring at least 10^{16} joules.

"Now, we don't know how they generate that kind of power. Like all of the Ahannu god-weapons, it's pretty much magic so far as we or they are concerned. But that much energy takes time to generate and store, even if they have some kind of antimatter generator down there. We're counting on the fact that they'll have a limited number of shots, with a goodly recharge time between each one. That, Captain, will operate in your favor."

"Aye aye, sir."

Ramsey smiled. What else could Warhurst say? The man had volunteered for this mission as soon as it had been described to him. The chance to deploy to another star system . . . hell, don't quibble. The chance at an assignment with a Career 3 rating meant promotion points as well as a whopping big combat-hardship pay bonus. If Warhurst survived this op, his career would be *made*.

"Our biggest problem right now," Ramsey told his staff, "is manpower. Volunteers only, of course . . . and because of the objective mission duration, the pick is limited to Famsit One and Two. Our original TO and E called for a full regimental MEU . . . about two thousand people. With the logistical limitations of a *Derna*-class IST, we're reconfiguring that as an MIEU, a Marine *Interstellar* Expeditionary Unit, with a roster of twelve hundred. Even with that, though, we may have trouble filling out the roster."

Lieutenant Colonel Lyle Harper, the Regimental Landing Team's CO, raised a hand. "We could put in a special request at Camp Lejeune, Colonel. There are sixteen companies in training right now, and a fair percentage of those people won't have close family ties. Hell, they might see it as an adventure."

"Not to mention returning to Earth with five years objective under their belts," Major Lyssa DuBoise, commander of the MIEU's aerospace element, said. "Eligible for discharge and a hell of a lot of hardship pay!"

"Since when did the Corps become a mercenary unit?" Major Samuel C. Ross, the Regimental G-2, said. He was in charge of mission intelligence—a particular bastard of a job, Ramsey thought, since no one knew exactly what was happening on Ishtar right now, and there was no way in hell they could guess what it would be like ten years hence.

"Our people will do their jobs because that's the way they were trained," Ramsey said. "As for the rest, it's about time they got some financial recognition for what they do. There's little enough material gratification in the peacetime Corps."

"Amen to that," someone in the watching group muttered aloud.

"In any case," Ramsey continued, "Major Anderson will be responsible for recruiting volunteers at Lejeune. Because of the mission's subjective length, we'll need a high percentage of young men and women right out of boot camp. They'll all be eligible for sergeant's stripes and better by the time they get home."

Subjective versus objective time was becoming more and more of a problem in the modern military, especially in the Navy and the Marines. While career-military officers and senior NCOs were "lifers"—meaning they expected to be in the service for a full twenty or thirty years, at least—the vast majority of enlisted personnel signed up for an initial four-year hitch. Some small percentage of those opted to extend their enlistment for an additional six years, to "ship-for-six," as the old saying went, and a smaller percentage of ten-year veterans decided to go the full twenty or more to retirement.

If a young Marine rotated through various duty stations on Earth, or even on the moon or one of the orbital stations, there was no problem. That's the way things had been run in the military for centuries. But it was expensive to ship large numbers of men and women plus their equipment to other worlds within the Solar system, and so time on-station offworld tended to be measured in years rather than months.

And now that Marines were being sent to the worlds of other stars, the problem of finding unattached personnel who didn't mind leaving Earth and all they knew there for years, even decades at a time, was becoming critical. Nanohibernation technology and time dilation might make subjective time on board the Marine transport seem like days or weeks, at most, but objectively the voyage would last a decade—two before the mission personnel saw the Earth again. Those young Marine men and women would return to an Earth aged twenty years or more. And even the most optimistic mission planners expected the deployment to the Llalande system to require no fewer than two years of ground-time at the objective.

Finding the best Marines who were also Famsit One—no close family ties on Earth—or Famsit Two—FOO, or Family-of-Origin only—was becoming damned near impossible. If anyone could deal with the details and the delicacies of such a search, Ramsey knew it was Ricia.

"I have one final piece of business for this briefing," Ramsey said. He thought-clicked a new connection, allowing another image to form within the shared noumenal conference space. "Ladies, gentlemen, may I present our mission commander, Brigadier General Phillip King."

In fact, the image was a secretarial AI, projecting General King's thin face and dour expression into the group noumenon, and identified as such by a winking yellow light at his collar. Ramsey mentally shook his head at that; one never knew for sure if the construct one met in noumenal space was a real-time projection or an AI secretary, unless the other party put up an AI tag like King's insignia light. For most senior officers, secretary stand-ins for briefings and presentations were a necessity if they wanted to get any real work done at all.

In King's case, though, the light was a kind of message board proclaiming, "I am a busy man and have no time to spare for you." Ramsey had served under King once before, back in '29, and hadn't enjoyed the experience. The man tended to be fussy, rigid, and a bit of a prima donna.

He was also a superb politician, with a politician's connections and oil-smooth sincerity, at least on the surface. The word from on high was that King—thanks to postings to various ambassadorial staffs over the past few years—had the blessing of half a dozen other national governments involved in the international relief force.

"Thank you, Colonel Ramsey," the image said in King's

somewhat nasal tones. "I look forward to getting to meet each of you personally in the coming months.

"For now, I wish to impress upon each of you what an honor it is to be chosen for Operation Spirit of Humankind. I expect each of you to do your best, for the Corps, for America, for the Confederation, and for *me*.

"We are engaged in a deployment of tremendous . . . ah . . . diplomatic importance. As you all know, the Marine expeditionary force was to be followed by a second American expedition. That has now changed. The follow-up expedition is now envisioned as a true multinational interstellar task force, one including personnel from the European Union, the Brazilian Empire, the Kingdom of Allah, the Republic of Mejico, and others, besides our Confederation allies. The Confederation Council has decided that this is an expedition of truly human proportions, one in which all of humankind has a stake.

"It will be our task not only to defeat enemy forces on Ishtar, but to maintain the peace with the disparate members of the multinational task force. We *will* present a united front to the Frogs. . . ."

Somehow, Ramsey stifled an inward grimace that might otherwise have projected into the noumenon. The fighting in Egypt with KOA religious fanatics was only the most recent bit of terrestrial bloodshed going down. The European Union had been sparring with Russia as recently as the Black Sea War of '34, and the Brazilians and Japanese were going at it over Antarctic fishing rights just last year. And things had been simmering between the United Federal Republic and Mejico since long before the Second Mexican War.

Frankly, facing a planet-full of hostile Ahannu god-warriors was infinitely preferable to facing the politics, red tape, and outright blood-feuds that were bound to entangle Earth's first interstellar expeditionary forces. Ramsey knew that not even King, for all his diplomatic experience, was going to have an easy job keeping those factions straight.

And as a *military* commander . . . well, he had serious doubts that General King was the best man possible for the command.

10

*Field Combat Range
U.S. Marine Corps Recruit Training Center
Parris Island, South Carolina
0640 hours ET*

"Crawl, you sand fleas! *Crawl!* You *will* become *one* with the *dirt!"*

Makowiecz stood on the beach like an implacable giant, hands on hips, khaki uniform, as always, immaculately clean and sharp-creased, despite the unmitigated hell flying around him. The sound was deafening and unremitting, with explosions going off every few seconds and live rounds, both solid and optical, cracking through the air a meter above the ground.

John Garroway wondered why the ordnance never came near the DI, and decided, like the others in his company, that no bullet or laser pulse would dare threaten to muss the man's uniform, much less actually hit him. Break-room speculation had it that the DIs on the combat range wore smartclothes that communicated with the robotic weapons laying down the fire on the beach, blocking any fire aimed too close to any of the exercise supervisors, but that couldn't be proven. Besides, shrapnel and spent rounds were mind-less and didn't care where they flew. A low-powered round glanced off John's helmet—a spent rubber bullet, by the dull thump it made—and left his head aching.

"Garroway, you stupid asshole!" Makowiecz screamed. Damn, the man had been thirty meters up the beach; he had never seen him approach. "What do you think, that this is some kind of VR sim? Get your fucking head down!"

"Sir, yes, sir!" John screamed back through a mouthful of gritty sand. He pressed himself flatter as a close-grouped trio of explosions detonated meters away. Makowiecz didn't flinch.

"And keep moving! The enemy's *that* way! *That* way! What, are you waiting for him to come give you a personal invitation? Move your damned, tin-plated ass! *Move it!"*

John kept moving, forcing himself ahead with an odd, uncomfortable twisting of the hips, inching forward in his dead-man armor.

The grim sobriquet was an old term for Mark XIV polylaminate impact armor, obsolete since the Second Mexican War or before. Unpowered, unenhanced, the suit was heavy and drunk-clumsy, and moving in it was like dragging along the weight of another man. The outer chamelearmor layer had been stripped off, leaving a stark, bone-white surface shiny enough that the recruits could be easily seen on the combat range, at least in theory. At the moment, the recruits were so mud-covered that they might as well have been fully camouflaged.

They hadn't even been given fully enclosed helmets; learning how to use HDO displays was still weeks away in their training. Instead they wore ancient bucket helmets with swing-down laser-block visors and just enough built-in comm linkage to let their DIs talk to them, usually in blistering invective.

Not that Gunny Makowiecz needed technical assistance to chew out the recruits. He seemed to be everywhere on that live-fire range, yelling, swearing, admonishing, cajoling, raging, relentlessly using every trick of the drill instructor's handbook to motivate his struggling charges.

For three weeks now Company 1099 had been all but living in the antique Mark XIVs, marching in them, exercising in them, standing fire watch and sentry duty in them, and when they weren't wearing them, cleaning them. Twice now John had been ordered to hit the rack wearing his armor as punishment for being too slow hitting the mark with his ready kit at morning muster. That bit of motivational guidance, as it was called, had left him sore, chaffed, and tired, and a hell of a lot more eager to jump out of bed at a zero-dark-thirty reveille.

Another explosion thundered nearby, and John felt the thump of the detonation through the ground. Gravel rattled off his armored back. He was by now thoroughly miserable. Wet sand, mud, and grit had worked its way, inevitably, past the armor suit's seal at his neck and chafed now against tender places too numerous to mention. The platoon had started this morning's exercise twenty minutes ago at the surf line on the beach, leaving all of them soaked and coated with sand. Their objective was to belly-crawl three hundred meters up the shelf of the beach, over the dune line, and across the mud pit beyond. Explosive charges buried in the sand and the constant laser and projectile fire overhead kept things interesting . . . especially with the word from the DIs that one in a hundred of the bullets whizzing overhead was steel ball, *not* rubber, just to keep the men focused.

John stopped for a moment, trying to rub against a suddenly insistent itch on his side, beneath the armor. Sand fleas. They infested the beaches of Parris Island, seemingly as thick as the sand grains themselves, and when they got inside the armor, they bit and bit and bit, leaving long chains of fiery welts.

He was up to the line of dunes now, dirty gray sand slopes capped by straggling patches of grass rising like mountains in his path. Robot gun towers and sensors were spaced along the crest of the ridge, entrenched behind ferrocrete bastions, but the recruits were to ignore those and keep moving. The finish line for this sadistic race lay beyond the mud pits on the far side of the dunes.

"If you *stop*, you're *dead*." Makowiecz's voice grated in

their ears, an ongoing litany, chiding, needling, threatening. "When you're under fire out in the open this way, you keep moving or you stay put and get killed. *That's* your choice, ladies. That's your *only* choice! Now *hump* it! Fox! Paulsen! Stop your malingering, you two! Garroway! You're not being paid to scratch! The last ten men to the finish give me fifty push-ups, *in* armor!"

John humped it, wiggling up the dune slope faster, ignoring the grating pain of sand-rasped sores in armpits, neck, and groin, ignoring the burning itch of the flea bites. He'd managed to place himself so he would pass close to one of the robot sentry guns, the idea being that explosives and the fields of fire from the array of field emplacements wouldn't come too close to other gun mounts. Maybe he could make up for some lost time, then, crawling over the crest of the dune without having to worry about one of those damned towers winging him.

He'd been tagged for armored push-ups more than once before when he couldn't keep pace, and he did *not* like it.

The sun was still low above the teeming, reeking swamps of Parris Island to the east, still burning through the early morning mist. South, the gleaming facade of the new hospital facility, aerospace port, and depot HQ rose on pylons from the sea halfway to the skytower complex at Hilton Head, on the outskirts of Greater Savannah. Another world, that . . . an alien world, as far removed from the mud and stink and sweat and sand fleas of Parris Island as the fabled Ruined Cities of Chiron were from Earth.

No. That was just four light-years and some. Make it the An world at Llalande.

John squirmed onto the crest of the dune, up on knees and elbows now, scuttling ahead as fast as he could. The next thing he knew, a hammer-blow caught him smack in the tailbone, toppling him over and sending him sprawling back down the seaward side of the dune. Lying on his back, blinking up at the sky, he next became aware of Gunny Makowiecz leaning over him. "You okay, recruit?"

"S-Sir! Yes, sir!"

Makowiecz appeared to be listening to someone else—tapping into his link, perhaps, to the monitor AIs that kept track of all of the personnel on the range. "They say you caught a round in the ass, sweet pea. Maybe next time you'll learn to keep your damned ass down, where it belongs! You hear what I'm saying?"

"Sir! Yes, sir!"

"How do you cross an exposed ridge crest?"

"Sir! Flat on the belly and using all available cover to avoid showing a recognizable silhouette against the sky, sir!"

"Back in the action, then! And this time keep your mind on what you're doing!"

How the hell did Makowiecz know what was going on in his head? The man was uncanny. "Aye aye, sir!"

His hips and buttocks felt numb, but he rolled over and crawled back up the slope, careful this time to keep flat on the ground. Even rubber bullets packed a hell of a wallop, and he was going to be sore for days after this.

Worse, the rest of the platoon was well across the mud pit by now, plowing ahead as explosions sent columns of mud geysering into the air and bullets smacked and chopped into the mud around them. He'd lost a lot of time.

He thought-clicked to check his time, then groaned when nothing happened. Damn it, he still kept instinctively trying to trigger his Sony-TI 12000, even though almost a month had passed since he'd lost it. The worst was not being able to talk with Lynnley.

Makowiecz was waiting for him with an evil grin when he straggled in at the finish line fifteen minutes later . . . one of the last three or four to arrive.

"Assume the position, recruits!" Corporal Meiers, an assistant DI, barked. "Push-ups! And *one*! And *two*! And . . ."

John's legs were aching now, but he went into the exercise set with grim determination.

"Remember, ladies!" Makowiecz bellowed over his assistant's cadence. "*Pain* is the feeling of *weakness* leaving your body!"

"And twenny-*eight*! And twenny-*nine*! And . . ."

Lagrange Shuttle King Priam
In approach to IST Derna
Orbital Construction Facility 1, L-4
1320 hours Zulu

Half a million kilometers from Parris Island, the Marine Interstellar Transport *Derna* fell in her month-long orbit about the Earth. Built around a long, slender keel with a cluster of antimatter drive engines at the aft end, she had a length overall—her loa—of 622 meters. The massive, dome-shaped ablative shield and reaction-mass storage tank ahead of the three hab-cylinders gave her the look from a distance of a huge mushroom with a needle-slender stem. Aft, the broad flare of heat radiators resembled the fletching on a blunt-tipped arrow.

When under drive, the hab cylinders were folded up tight behind the RM dome, safe from the storm of radiation and high-energy dust impacts resulting from near-c velocities. Under one g of acceleration, aft was down. When the drives stopped—even AM-charged torchships couldn't haul enough reaction mass to carry them onward for years at one g—the three hab cylinders folded out and forward on arms extending ninety degrees from the ship's central keel, though still protected by the overhang of the RM dome. Rotating around the ship's axis, they provided out-is-down spin gravity for the passengers without requiring a rearrangement of the deck furniture, consoles, and plumbing.

At the moment, the IST *Derna* was in orbital configuration, her hab modules spread and rotating slowly. Beyond her, twenty kilometers away, Antimatter Production Facility *Vesuvius* gleamed in the sunlight, its vast solar array back-lit by the glare of the sun.

Strapped into one of the passenger seats on board the Lagrange Shuttle *King Priam*, Gavin Norris watched the approach on the viewscreen set into the back of the seat in
front of him. The shuttle was making her final orbital insertion maneuver with short, sharp taps on her thrusters; she
was still several kilometers out from the *Derna*, but the immense transport still all but filled the screen.

Norris was on his way at last, with unimaginable wealth
at the end of the journey. He let his gaze stray from the
screen and move about the passenger cabin. Every seat was
taken by hard-muscled men and women in gray fatigues—
the Marines who would be his fellow travelers for the next
two decades.

He was glad that most of that time would be spent asleep.
These were not exactly the sort of people he would choose
as companions on a vacation cruise. The woman in the seat
next to him, for instance . . . an argument against genetic
manipulation and somatic nanosculpting if ever he'd seen
one. Big-boned, lean, muscular, she looked like she could
snap him in two with a glance from those eerily black aug-
mented eyes. Her hair had been close-cropped to little more
than fuzz, and if she had anything like breasts under those
fatigues, she kept them well hidden. Hard, cold, asexual . . .
he tried to imagine himself in bed with her, then decided
that was a noumenon he did *not* want to file in permanent
memory.

He wondered why they were here. This was a volunteer
mission, of course; you didn't simply order young men and
women to leave homes and families for a twenty-year mission to another star, not if you wanted to avoid a full-fledged
mutiny. They certainly weren't offering these grunts money.
What, then? Rank? Glory? He snorted to himself. To Norris,
the military mind was something arcane and incomprehen-
sible.

"What the fuck are *you* gawking at, civ?"

He blinked. He'd not been aware that he was staring. "Uh,
sorry," he told her. A thought-click picked up her name-tag

data. She was Gunnery Sergeant Athena Horst, of something called ComCon DS 219. The mil-babble told him nothing. "I was just wondering why you Marines would sign up for a party like this."

She grinned at him, an unsettling showing of teeth. "Hey, this is the Corps," she told him. "Just like they say in the recruiting blurbs. 'See exotic worlds, meet fascinating lifeforms, kill them. . . . '"

"Uh . . . yeah . . ."

"Why are you here?"

"Me? I'm the corporate rep for PanTerra. They have . . . interests on Llalande, and I'm going to see to it that they're protected."

"What, you're a lawyer?"

"As a matter of fact, I am. My specialty, though, is CPM."

"What's that?"

"Corporate problem management." When her face remained blank, he added, "I'm a troubleshooter. I make certain that small problems do not become large ones."

"Troubleshooter, huh?" She chuckled. "That's rich. A civilian Marine!"

"What?"

"A civilian Marine! We're troubleshooters too, y'know. There's trouble, we shoot it!" She cocked her thumb and forefinger, mimicking a gun. "Zzzt! Blam!" She blew across the tip of her finger. "Problem down. Area secure."

"I see."

"I doubt that. Ha!"

"What?"

"I was just thinking," she said, grinning. "When we get to Ishtar, let me know how your troubleshooting works with the Frogs."

"Uh . . . frogs?"

"The Ishtaran abs. The Ahannu. What are you going to do if they get out of line, slap 'em with a lawsuit?"

"I will assess the situation and report to the PanTerran director's board with my recommendations. I'll also be there

as a corporate legal representative should there be, um, juris-
dictional or boundary disputes, shall we say, with any of the
other Earth forces going to Ishtar."

"I like my way better," Horst said. She shook her head.
"Give me a twenty-one-twenty with an arpeg popper any
day."

"A . . . what? Arpeg?"

"The Remington Arms M-12 underbarrel self-guiding
rocket-propelled 20mm grenade launcher, RPG Mark Four,
Mod 2, select-fire, gas-actuated, laser-tracking, self-homing
round in high-explosive, armor-piercing, or delay-detonated
bomblet or intel submunitions," she said, rattling off the
words as though they were a part of her, "with select-fire
from an underbarrel mount configuration with the Marine-
issue GE LR-2120 Sunbeam pulse laser with detachable
forty- or ninety-round box magazine and targeting link
through the standard Mark Seven HD linkage—"

"Whatever you say," he replied, interrupting when she
took a breath. "I'll stick to legal briefs, thank you."

She laughed. "Washington must really be pissed with the
Frogs," she said. "Being taken down by a self-homer arpeg
round is a hell of a lot cleaner than being fucking lawyered
to death."

He smiled blandly, then looked away, pointedly taking an
interest in the docking approach on his seat-back screen.
Clearly, he shared little in the way of language or attitude
with the Marines. He wondered if PanTerra was paying him
enough for this assignment.

The shuttle docked with the *Derna,* drifting gently into a
berthing rack mounted on the flat underside of the reaction
mass dome. A number of other TAV craft were already
docked, their noses plugged into a ring of airlock modules
circling the transport's core just forward of the slowly spinning hab-module access collar.

There was a slight pop as cabin pressures matched, then
the Marines around him began unbuckling, floating up from
their seats and forming a queue in the central aisle. He un-

buckled his own harness but kept hold of the seat arm, un-willing to let himself float into that haphazard tangle of legs, arms, and torsos.

"Mr. Norris?" a voice said in his head. "Have you had zero-g experience?"

He thought-clicked on the noumenal link. "Yes," he said. "A little, anyway." He'd had other offworld assignments with PanTerra—on the moon, on Mars, on Vesta, and twice on mining stations in the Kuiper Belt. All had been steady-g all the way—PanTerra always sent its executives first class—but he'd endured weightlessness during boarding and at mid-trip flipovers.

"Even so, it might be best for you to remain in your seat until the Marines have moved out. A naval officer can help you board the transport and get to your deck."

"Who is this?" He didn't recognize the noumenal ID: CS-1289. An artificial intelligence, obviously, but ship AIs generally went by the name of their vessel, and this one felt a bit broader in scope than a typical ship AI.

"You may address me as 'Cassius,'" the voice said. "I am the executive AI component for the command constellation on this mission."

"I see."

"Colonel Ramsey regrets that he cannot receive you in person," Cassius went on, "but he is still on Earth attending to the details of mission preparation. And Cicero has not yet uploaded to the *Derna*."

"Cicero?"

"General King's AI counterpart."

"Who's General King? I thought Ramsey was the mission commander?"

"Colonel Ramsey is the regimental commander and, as such, will have operational command on the ground at Ishtar. General King will have overall mission command, in-cluding all ground, space, and aerospace units."

"The CEO, huh? He supervises the whole thing from or-bit?"

"The analogy is a fair one, Mr. Norris. Once the Pyramid of the Eye has been secured, and assuming direct real-time communications can be reestablished between the Legation compound and Earth, General King will likely transfer his headquarters from the *Derna* to New Sumer."

Norris nodded, then wondered if the disembodied voice in his head could see the gesture. "Gotcha," he said. His briefing at PanTerra had covered Marine space-ground command structures and procedures in some detail, but he would need to know the people involved, not just the TO&E. General King, evidently, would be his primary target, but Ramsey would be the one to watch. He would have to get close to both men if his assignment for PanTerra was to succeed.

Waiting, only somewhat impatiently, he watched the last of the Marines float out of the aisle and through the *King Priam*'s forward lock. Patience had never been one of Norris's best or most reliable assets; he needed to keep reminding himself that he was committed to a twenty-year-plus contract in objective time, that even in subjective time there was no need for hurry at all.

Angry with himself, he thought-clicked through some meditative subroutines in his implants, seeking peaceful acceptance. Within moments the medical nano in his body was subtly altering the balance of several neurochemicals, lowering his blood pressure, slowing his heart rate, inducing the patience he required.

"Mr. Norris?"

It was an external voice a human voice this time. He opened his eyes. "Yes?"

A Navy officer floated in the aisle next to his seat row. He wore dress whites and appeared very young. "I'm Lieutenant Bolton. Will you come with me, please?"

"Of course."

The lieutenant gestured toward a storage case forward. "Uh, pardon my asking, but do you need a drag bag?"

"Drag bag?"

"Microgravity Transit Harness, sir. An MTH. To help get you—"

Norris frowned. He'd seen MTHs used in civilian space-craft, and a more undignified mode of travel was hard to imagine. "That won't be necessary, Lieutenant. I've been in zero g before."

"Very well, sir. If you'll just follow me?"

Grasping fabric handholds on the tops of the seats around him, Norris pulled himself gently from his seat and maneu-vered his way into the aisle. For a dizzying moment his vi-sual references spun and shifted; he'd been thinking of the cabin as having the layout of a suborbital shuttle or hyper-sonic TAV, with seats on the floor. During acceleration out from Earth, of course, down was aft, toward the rear of the cabin, and he felt as though he were lying on his back, but it was easy to translate that in terms of the acceleration one felt during the suborb boost from New York to Tokyo.

Now, though, all references of up and down were lost. The seats were attached to the wall, he was hanging in midair above a long drop toward the cabin's rear, and Lieu-tenant Bolton was swimming straight up, toward the for-ward lock.

It's all in your mind, he thought, angry again. He closed his eyes, grasped the next handhold forward, and grimly pulled himself along. When he opened his eyes, just for a moment, perspectives had shifted again and he was now moving down, head first, into a well, with Lieutenant Bolton looking up at him with a worried expression. "Mr. Norris?"

"I'm *fine*, damn it," he said. "Lead on!"

The worst parts were the twists and turns, though the air-lock was small enough and without contradictory visual cues, so he could catch his breath. Damn it, when was some-one going to find a way to provide constant gravity, no mat-ter where you were on a ship or what the ship was doing at the time?

Inside *Derna*'s inner hatch, a sign had been attached to

one wall saying QUARTERDECK, next to an American flag stretched taut by wires in the fly and hoist. Lieutenant Bolton saluted the flag, then saluted again to another naval lieutenant who floated there. "Permission to come on board."

"Permission granted."

An asinine ceremony, Norris thought with distaste. How did one stand at attention in zero g? Once the military got hold of one of these little rituals, they never let go.

At last they floated through a hatch and entered a cylindrical compartment with the words DECK and FEET TOWARD HERE painted in red letters on one end. Using straps on the wall, they aligned themselves with the deck, and Bolton used his implant to activate the elevator.

The device loaded into one of the rotating hab arms like a shell locking into the firing chamber of a rifle. For a disorienting moment Norris felt like he was upside down, feet hanging toward the ceiling, while the elevator's gentle acceleration away from the ship's spine induced a momentary feeling of weight. Then the sensations of spin gravity took hold and he drifted, feet down, to the deck.

The returning feeling of weight did little to soothe his bad mood. He'd never liked being weightless, with conflicting clues as to what might be up or down. The hatchway opened at last on Deck One of Hab Three. Uppermost of five decks in the module, this deck had rotation sufficient to create the sensation of about half a g, a bit more than the surface of Mars. Relishing the feeling of a solid deck beneath his feet once more, Norris strode into the lounge area surrounding the central elevator shaft.

He wrinkled his nose as he stared about the room. "What the hell is that smell? I thought this was a new ship?"

"It is, sir. New wiring, new fittings, new air circulators. All new ships smell a bit funny. Just wait until you wake up in ten years! It'll smell a lot worse, believe me!"

Norris didn't doubt the man. The interior of the hab module was clearly designed to cram as many humans into as small a space as possible. The walls—no, on a ship they would be called bulkheads, he reminded himself irritably—the bulkheads were covered by hexagonal openings, some open and lit within, some closed, giving him the impression of being inside an immense beehive. The central area was divided into thin-walled cubicles. He glimpsed men and women in some of them, sitting at workstations or jacked into entertainment or education centers. There was also a lounge with a table—not large or spacious, but with chairs enough to sit in small groups.

"The head—that's the bathroom on board a ship—is over there," Bolton said, pointing. "There's a common area in each hab module . . . Deck Two, one down from here. That's where the mess deck is, too."

Norris eyed the hexagonal cells all around him. Each appeared to be a tiny, self-contained cabin, two meters long and a meter across, only slightly larger than a coffin. A person could lie inside, but there wasn't room to stand. "My God, how many people do you have in here?"

"On this deck? Eighty. But these are the luxury quarters, sir . . . for the command constellation and the officers. Decks Three and Four house two hundred personnel apiece."

He looked around the compartment in disbelief. "Five hundred people? In *here*?"

Bolton cleared his throat. "Uh . . . actually, 480 just in this one hab module, sir. The *Derna* carries an entire Marine Interstellar Expeditionary Unit. An MIEU consists of a Regimental Landing Team, headquarters, recon, and intelligence platoons, and an aerospace close-support wing. That's twelve hundred Marines altogether, sir, plus 145 naval personnel as ship's crew. Of course, only about a quarter of that complement are on board now. The rest will be coming up over the course of the next three months."

"Thank you for the lecture," Norris replied dryly. "Where do you keep them all?"

"In the cells, of course," Bolton said. "Yours is over here, sir."

He would have to climb a ladder to reach his hexagonal cell, he found . . . located four up from the deck, just beneath the chamber's ceiling, or "overhead," as Bolton called it. Inside was a thin mattress, storage compartments, data jacks and feeds, access to the ship's computer and library, and a personal medical suite; altogether, a wonder of microminiaturization.

"It's not very big, is it?" Norris was reminded of the traveler hotels, common worldwide now, but first designed in Japan a century or two back, a person-sized tube with room to sleep in and not much else.

"You won't need much space, sir," Bolton told him. "You're scheduled for cybehibe in . . ." He closed his eyes, accessing the ship's net. ". . . twelve more days, sir. At that time, you'll be plugged into the ship's cryocybernetic system, and you won't know a thing until we reach Ishtar."

"Twelve days." He wondered how he was going to endure the crowding until then, and gave himself another nano boost. *Acceptance.* "Twelve fucking days."

11

Sick Bay
U.S. Marine Corps Recruit Train-
ing Center
Parris Island, South Carolina
1430 hours ET

"Garroway!"

"Sir, yes, sir!"

"Through that hatch!"

"Aye aye, sir!"

Garroway banged through the door that had already swallowed half of Company 1099. Inside was the familiar, sterile-white embrace of seat, cabinets, AI doc, and the waiting corpsman.

"Have a seat," the corpsman said. It wasn't the same guy he had met in there before. What was his name? He couldn't remember.

Not that it was important. New faces continually cycled through his awareness these days. Without his implants he could only memorize the important ones, the ones he was ordered to remember.

Of course, that was about to change now. He suppressed the surge of excitement.

"Feeling okay?" the corpsman asked.

"Sir, yes, sir!"

"No injuries? Infections? Allergies? Nothing like that?"

"Sir, no, sir!"

"Do you have at this time any moral or ethical problems with nanotechnic enhancement, implant technologies, or nanosomatic adjustment?"

"Sir, no, sir!"

The corpsman wasn't even looking at him as he asked the questions. He wore instead the far-off gaze of someone linked into a net and was probably scanning Garroway now with senses far more sophisticated than those housed in merely human eyes or ears.

"He's go," the man said.

The AI doctor unfolded from the cabinet. One arm with an airjet hypo descended to his throat, and Garroway steeled himself against the hiss and burn of the injection.

"Right," the corpsman said. "Just stay there, recruit. Give it time to work."

This was it, at long last. It felt as though he'd been without an implant now for half his life, though in fact it had only been about six weeks. Six weeks of running, of learning, of training, all without being able to rely on an internal uplink to the local net.

It was, he thought, astonishing what you could do without a nexus of computers in your brain or electronic implants growing in your hands. He'd learned he could do amazing things without instant access to comlinks or library data.

But that didn't mean he wasn't eager to get his technic prostheses back.

Outside of a slight tingle in his throat, though, he didn't feel much of anything. Had the injection worked?

"Okay, recruit. Off you go. Through that door and join your company."

"Sir . . . I don't feel—"

"Nothing to feel yet, recruit. It'll take a day or two for the implants to start growing and making the necessary neural connections. You'll be damned hungry, though. They'll be feeding you extra at the mess hall these next few days to give the nano the raw materials it needs."

He fell into ranks with the rest of his company and waited as the last men filed through the sick bay. Damn. He'd been so excited at the prospect of getting his implants that he'd not thought about how long it might take them to grow. He'd been hoping to talk to Lynnley tonight. . . .

He hadn't seen her, hadn't even linked with her, since arriving on Parris Island. Male and female recruits were kept strictly apart during recruit training, though he had glimpsed formations of women Marines from time to time across the grinder or marching off to one training exercise or another. The old dream of serving with her on some offworld station seemed remote right now. Had she changed much? Did she ever even think about him anymore?

Hell, of course she's changed, he told himself. *You've changed. So has she.*

He'd been on the skinny side before, but two months of heavy exercise and special meals had bulked him up, all of the new mass muscle. His endurance was up, his temper better controlled, the periodic depression he'd felt subsumed now by the daily routine of training, exercise, and discipline.

And a lot of things that had been important to him once simply didn't matter now.

He had been allowed to vid family grams to his mother, out in San Diego. She was still living with her sister and beginning the process of getting a divorce. That was good, he thought, as well as long overdue. There were rumors of unrest in the Mexican territories—Recruit Training Center monitors censored the details, unfortunately—and scuttlebutt about a new war.

He kept thinking about what Lynnley had said, back in Guaymas, about him having to fight down there against his own father.

Well, why not? He felt no loyalty to that bastard, not after the way he'd treated his mother. So far as he was concerned, he'd shed the man's parental cloak when he'd reclaimed the name Garroway.

"Garroway!" Makowiecz barked.

"Sir! Yes, sir!"

"Come with me."

The DI led him down a corridor and ushered him into another room with a brusque "In there."

A Marine major, a tall, slender, hard-looking woman in dress grays, sat behind a desk inside.

"Sir! Recruit Garroway reporting as ordered, sir!" In the Corps, to a recruit, *all* officers were "sir" regardless of gender, along with most other things that moved.

"Sit down, recruit," the woman said. "I'm Major Anderson, ComCon Delta Sierra two-one-nine."

He took a seat, wondering if he'd screwed up somehow. Geez . . . it had to be something pretty bad for a major to step in. During their day-to-day routine, Marine recruits rarely if ever saw any officer of more exalted rank than lieutenant or captain. From a recruit's point of view, a major was damned near goddesslike in the Corps hierarchy, and actually being *addressed* by one, summoned to her office, was . . . daunting, to say the least.

And a comcon? That meant she was part of a regular headquarters staff, probably the exec of a regiment. What could she possibly want with him?

"I've been going over your recruit training records, Garroway," she told him. "You're doing well. All three-sixes and higher for physical, psych, and all phase one and two training skills."

"Sir, thank you, sir."

"No formal marriage or family contracts. Your parents alive, separated." She paused, and he wondered what she was getting at. "Have you given much thought yet to duty stations after you leave the island?"

That stopped him. Recruits were *not* asked to voice their preferences, especially by majors. "Uh . . . sir, uh . . . this recruit . . ."

"*Relax*, Garroway," Anderson told him. "You're not on the carpet. Actually, I'm screening members of your platoon for potential volunteers. I'm looking for Space Marines."

And that rocked him even more. He'd wanted to be a Marine for as long as he could remember, true, ever since he'd learned about his famous leatherneck ancestors, but the real lure to the Corps had always been the possibility of offworld duty stations. The vast majority of Marines never left the Earth; most served out their hitches in the various special deployment divisions tasked with responding to brushfire wars and threats to the Federal Republic's interests around the globe.

A very special few, however . . .

"You're asking me to volunteer for space duty?" Excitement put him on the edge of the seat, leaning forward. "I mean, um, sir, this recruit thinks that, uh—"

"Why don't we drop the formalities, John? That third-person recruit crap gets in the way of real communication."

"Thank you, si—uh, ma'am." He sighed, then took a deep breath, trying to force himself to relax. The excitement was almost overwhelming. "I . . . yes. I would be *very* interested in volunteering for a duty station offworld."

"You might want to hear about it first," she cautioned. "I'm not talking about barracks duty on Mars." She went on to tell him, in brief, clipped sentences, about MIEU-1, a Marine expeditionary unit tasked with a high-profile rescue-recovery mission at Llalande 21185 IID, the Earthlike moon of a gas giant eight light-years distant.

"That's where the human slaves are, right, ma'am?" he asked her. The newsfeeds had been full of the story around the time he'd signed up. The enforced e-feed blackout during his training period had pretty well cut him off from all news of the outside world, but there'd been plenty of rumor floating around the barracks for the past couple of months. "We're going out there to free the slaves?"

"We are going to protect federal interests in the Llalande system," she replied, her voice firm. "Which means we'll do whatever the President directs us to do. The main thing you have to think about right now is whether you want to volunteer for such a mission. Objective time will be at *least* twenty years. Ten years out in cyhibe, ten back, plus however long it takes us to complete our mission requirements. Things change in twenty years. We won't be coming back to the same place we left."

That sobered him. His mother was, what? Forty-one? She'd be sixty-one or older by the time he saw her again. Regular anagathic regimens and nanotelemeric reconstruction made sixty middle age for most folks nowadays, but twenty years was still a hell of a chunk out of a person's life. How much would he still have in common with any of the people he left behind?

"We'll be in hibernation for the whole trip?"

"Hell, yes! That transport is going to be damned cozy for thirteen hundred or so people. We'd kill each other off long before we reached the mission objective if we weren't. Besides, they wouldn't be able to pack that much food, water, and air for that long a flight."

"No, ma'am." In a way, he was disappointed. Part of his dream included the thrill of the journey itself, flying out from Earth on one of the great interplanetary clippers or boosting for the stars on a near-*c* torchship.

Anderson was accessing some records with a faraway look in her eyes. "I'm checking your evaluations," she told him. "Your DI thinks highly of you. Did you know you're up for selection for embassy duty?"

"Huh? I mean, no, ma'am." The way Makowiecz and the other DIs kept riding him, he'd not even been sure they were going to recommend him for retention in the Corps, much less . . . embassy duty? That was supposed to be the softest, best duty in the Corps, standing guard at the UFR embassy in some out-of-the-way world capital. You had to be absolutely top-line Marine for a billet like that, and be able to keep yourself and your uniform in recruiting poster form. But the duty was the stuff dream sheets were made of . . .

"It's true," she told him. "And I won't bullshit you. The Ishtar mission *is* a combat op. We'll be going in hot, weapons free, assault mode. The abos are primitive, but they have some high-tech quirks that are guaranteed to raise some damned nasty surprises. So . . . what'll it be? A soft billet at an embassy? Or a sleeper slot and a hot LZ?"

He knew what he wanted. Plush as embassy duty was supposed to be, he'd always thought the reality would be boring. In fact, most duty Earthside would be boring, punctuated by the occasional day or two of truly exciting discomfort, pain, and fear during a combat TAV deployment to some war-torn corner of the planet. The Llalande mission might be hardship duty and combat, but it was offworld . . . as far offworld, in fact, as he was ever likely to get.

It would be what being a Marine was all about.

"Um, ma'am?"

"Yes?"

"I have a friend who joined up the same time I did. Recruit Collins. She's in one of the female recruit training platoons."

"And . . . ?"

"I was just wondering if she was being asked to volunteer too, ma'am."

"I see." She looked thoughtful for a moment. "And that would determine your answer?"

"Uh, well . . ."

"John, you presumably joined the Corps of your own free will. You didn't join because she joined, did you?"

"No, ma'am." Well, not entirely. The idea of signing up together, maybe getting the same duty station afterward, had been part of the excitement. Part of the thrill and promise.

But not all of it.

"I'm glad to hear it. Contrary to popular belief, the Corps does not want mindless robots in its ranks. We want strong, aggressive young men and women who can make up their own minds, who serve because they believe, truly believe, that what they are doing is right. There is no room in my Corps for people who simply follow the crowd. Or who have no deeper commitment to the Corps than the fact that a buddy joined up. Do you copy?"

"Sir, yes . . . I mean, yes, ma'am."

"I'm sure your DI has drilled this line into your skull, even without implants. The Corps is your family now. Mother. Father. Sib. Friend. Lover. In a way, you cast off your connections with everyone else when you came on board, as completely as you will if you volunteer for Ishtar and report on board the *Derna* for a twenty-year hibe slot. You will have changed that much. You've already changed more than you imagine. You'll never go back to that old life again."

"No, ma'am." But he wasn't talking about a civilian friend. Why didn't she understand?

"And you also know by now that the Corps cannot be run for your convenience. Sometimes, like now, you're given a choice. A carefully crafted choice, within tightly defined parameters, but a choice, nonetheless. You must make your decision within the parameters that the Corps gives you. That's part of the price you pay for being a Marine."

"Yes, ma'am."

"So. What'll it be? I can't promise you'll end up stationed with Recruit Collins, no matter what you decide. No one can. The question is, what do you want for yourself?"

He straightened in his chair. There still was no question what he wanted most. "*Sir,* this recruit wishes to volunteer for the Ishtar billet, *sir,*" he said, slipping back into the programmed third-person argot of the well-drilled Marine recruit.

"Very well, recruit," Anderson replied. "No promises yet, understand. We're still just screening for applicants. But if everything works out, and you complete your recruit training as scheduled, it will be good to have you on board."

"Thank you, sir!"

"Very well. Dismissed."

"Aye aye, sir!"

He rose, turned, and banged through the door, scarcely able to believe what had happened.

The stars! He was going to go to the fucking stars! . . .

Headquarters, PanTerra Dynamics
New Chicago, Illinois
United Federal Republic, Earth
1725 hours CT

"PanTerra Dynamics *is* going to the stars, gentlemen," Allyn Buckner said. "We have personnel on our payroll on the *Derna*, and they will be on Ishtar at least six months before you. Now . . . you can work with PanTerra, or you can be left out in the cold. What's it going to be?"

The virtual comm simulation had them standing in a floating garden, high above the thundering mist of Victoria Falls, in the Empire of Brazil. The building actually existed—a combination of hotel, conference center, and playground for the wealthy. Terraced steps, sun-sparkling fountains, riotous tangles of brightly flowering greenery to match the remnants of rain forest around the river below, Orinoco Sky was an aerostat city adrift in tropical skies.

Buckner, of course, was still in New Chicago. His schedule hadn't allowed him the luxury of attending this conference in person. In fact, perhaps half of the people in the garden lounge in front of him were there in simulacra only. Haddad, he knew, was still in Baghdad, and Chieu was linking in from a villa outside of Beijing.

Through the data feeds in their implants, however, each of the conference attendees saw and heard all of the others, whether they were in Orinoco Sky in the body or in telepresence only.

Buckner was glad he was there in virtual sim only. The decadence of the surroundings fogged the brain, sidetracked the mind. It was easier to link in for the meeting he'd called, get the business over with, and link off, all without leaving the embrace of the VR chair in his New Chicago office.

For one thing, it meant he could cut these idiots off if they imposed on his time.

"You Americans," Haddad told him with a dark look. "For a century you've acted as though you own the Earth. Now you are laying claim to the stars as well. You should remember that Allah is known for bringing down the proud and arrogant."

"Don't lecture me, Haddad. You're lucky even to be here, after that business the KOA pulled in Egypt." He grinned mirthlessly. "Besides, I thought you Mahdists didn't believe in the Ahannu."

"Of course we believe in them." He gave an eloquent shrug. "How could we not? They are there, on the Llalande planet, for all to see. We do not believe, however, that they are gods. Or that they shaped the course of human destiny. Or that they . . . they *engineered* us, as some ignorant people, atheists, suggest."

"Our friends in the Kingdom of Allah are not the blind fanatics you Americans believe them to be," Dom Camara said. "They are as practical, and with as keen a sense of business, as we here in the Brazilian Empire. Your scheme could upset the economies of many nations here on Earth. We wish to address that."

"You want to be in on the distribution of goodies, is what you mean," Buckner said. "I can accept that. But PanTerra is going to be there first. That means you play by our rules."

"And what, precisely," Raychaudhuri asked, "are the rules, Mr. Buckner?"

"PanTerra Dynamics will be the authorized agent for Terran economic interests in the Llalande system. *All* Terran economic interests. We welcome investment on Ishtar, but the money will go through us. We expect, in time, to form the de facto government on Ishtar."

Camara chuckled. "Mightn't the abos have something to say about that?"

Buckner made a dismissive gesture. "That's what the American Marines are for," he replied. "The human slavery issue has all of North America ready to kick the Ahannu where it hurts most."

"What do you mean?" Koslonova, of Ukraine, said. "You're saying the Marines are going to wipe out the Ahannu?"

Buckner smiled at her. "That, of course, would be the ideal."

Pelligrini, one of the other Euro-Union representatives, looked shocked. "Signor Buckner! You are talking about annihilating the population of a planet!"

"Calm yourself, Aberto. I said that would be the ideal, from our perspective, but we are realists. The MIEU will only have about a thousand Marines or so, and Ishtar is a world, a damned big place. They wouldn't be able to wipe out something like ten million aborigines all at once. Hell, even if they could, public reaction back on home would be . . . counterproductive.

"But we do see the game playing out like this: we all know they won't find any of our people alive when they get there, not after ten years. The Marines will have to assault the Legation compound and, of course, secure the Pyramid of the Eye to reestablish real-time communication with Earth. The Frogs, the abos, are practically stone age, but they're tenacious little bastards. They'll put up a fight. The Marines will have to smash them down pretty hard in order to regain control.

"Once the local government is forced to see reason, our people will form an advisory council and oversee the creation of a new abo government. We can expect the defeat of the current government to result in the surfacing of lots of new factions, and we'll selectively help those factions who go along with our plans for Ishtar. Within two years, three at the most, we should have a functioning Ahannu government in place, one completely friendly to PanTerran interests and compliant to the directions of our representatives. And, of course, the Marines will be there to provide the stick behind PanTerra's carrot."

"The *gwailos* of the western world followed a similar policy once on the shores of the Middle Kingdom," Chieu said quietly. "The end result was revolution, economic ruin, the collapse of empires, and unspeakable human suffering. Do you really expect your policies on Ishtar to have any different outcome?"

Buckner wasn't sure at first what Chieu was talking about. He thought-clicked through some download references, pausing just long enough to confirm that the Hegemony's representative was referring to the virtual land rush in China during the nineteenth century. Hong Kong. Macao. The Opium Wars. The Boxer Rebellion. A dozen nations had staked claims to various trading ports along the Chinese coast, intervening in Chinese affairs, forcing China to trade with the foreigners and on the foreigners' terms.

"Mr. Chieu, PanTerra has already invested heavily in the development of our franchise on Ishtar. We wish only to see a return on that investment. Frankly, when Ishtar ceases to be a profitable venture, we will be quite happy to return full control of Ishtaran affairs back to the Ahannu. In the meantime, we offer the aborigines peace, technical advancement, the advantages of technic civilization in so far as they're able to handle them, and stability. Think of it! Ahannu culture has advanced scarcely at all since the collapse of their interstellar empire ten thousand years ago. Within a few generations, they could undergo an industrial revolution and even contemplate a return to space."

"It's not like PanTerra to encourage potential competitors," Camara said. His smile robbed the words of their edge.

"Not competitors," Buckner said. "Trade partners. *Business* partners. The point is, all of that won't happen for a century or two. We don't need to worry about it. All we need do is think about the money we're going to make from this one investment!"

"Yes," Haddad said. "Money. A return on your investment. I believe I speak for a number of us here when I say that your scheme for using the human slaves on Ishtar as an additional return on your investment . . . this has a very foul smell to it. Am I to understand that PanTerra intends to im-

port slaves, *human* slaves, from Ishtar? That you intend—if
I understand this correctly—to use a campaign to free those
slaves, only to ship them back to Earth for use as slaves
here?"

"Please, Mr. Haddad," Buckner said with a pained expression. "We prefer the word '*domestics.*' Not 'slaves.' There
are entirely too many negative connotations to that word."

"Whatever you choose to call it," Haddad said, pressing
on, "the concept is neither moral nor economically viable."

"Representative Haddad has a point," Chieu said. "The
population of Earth would never accept such a moral outrage."

Buckner scowled at the assembly. "You want to lecture
me on morality? You, Haddad—when for at least the past
two hundred years or more your upper classes have im-
ported domestic servants from various parts of Asia and
Pacifica and paid them so poorly they cannot return home if
they wish? When pockets of outright slavery still exist
throughout the KOA in places like Sudan and Oman, and
when women still have fewer rights than male slaves?"

"We are all slaves of Allah—" Haddad began.

"Can the sermon. I worship at a different church, the
Church of the Almighty Newdollar." Haddad bristled, but
Buckner raised a hand. "Please. I mean no disrespect to anyone here. But it does give me a tremendous pain when people start making a major bleeding poor-mouth about moral
outrages when it's *their* comfort and *their* security and *their*
wealth that they're really concerned about. I don't like
hypocrisy."

"According to the report you've uploaded to us," Raychaudhuri said evenly, "you plan to partly defray PanTerra's
development costs on Ishtar by bringing freed human Sag-
ura back to Earth and selling them as servants. If that, sir, is
not hypocrisy—"

"And in your country, Raychaudhuri, a poor man can still
sell his daughters," Buckner said. "But that's not the point, is
it? Everything depends on how it is packaged. You've seen

PanTerra's reports . . . in particular, the reports on these Saguras. For ten thousand years they've been raised, been bred, as slaves to the Ahannu. They think of the Ahannu as gods . . . would no more think about disobeying them than you, Mr. Haddad, would think about disobeying Allah. They are conditioned from birth to accept the living reality of gods who direct every part of their lives.

"And now, we're going to arrive there, backed up by the Marines, and stand their world on its ear. What do you think would happen if we just walked in, gathered up all the Sagura, and said, 'Congratulations, guys. You're free.' Hell, they'd starve to death in a month! They don't even have a word in their vocabulary that means 'freedom'! Like Orwell pointed out a couple of centuries ago, you can't think about something if you don't have a word for it.

"At the same time, we have half the people on Earth clamoring for their release. 'Humans being held in slavery by horrible aliens! Oh, no! . . . We must set things right, must free those poor, wronged innocents from their bondage!'

"So PanTerra is proposing a social program that will satisfy the people of Earth, help the Ishtaran humans, and, just incidentally, help PanTerra recover what we've put into this project. As we send interstellar transports filled with Marines, scientists, and researchers out to Ishtar, we will begin bringing back transport loads of ex-slaves. They will be reintegrated slowly and carefully into human society. They do not understand the concept of 'money' or 'payment' or 'salary,' so they will be hired out to people willing to provide them with room and board in exchange for their domestic services.

"*Status*, my friends, is an important coin in human relations. The upper classes on Earth of nearly every culture still derive considerable status from the employment of human servants. And, as they used to say, good servants are *so* hard to find. Well, PanTerra has found the mother lode of domestic servants. Happy, healthy, beautiful people conditioned to take orders and provide service because that's the way they were raised, because that's the only thing they know. And those Sag-ura who are shipped back to Earth, I might add, will derive considerable status from the mere fact of being chosen to return to the fabled home planet. *And* they will have the chance to slowly assimilate into Earth-human culture.

"And if PanTerra charges for providing this service . . . what of it? People, don't you see? Everybody wins! You. The Sag-ura. And PanTerra."

"Mr. Buckner," Chieu said, "I thought PanTerra's sole interest in Ishtar was the possibility of acquiring alien technology?"

Buckner nodded. "It's our interest, certainly. Not our *sole* interest, but an important one. We expect to reap enormous profits from our research on Ishtar. The greatest profits of all may well come from aspects of their history and technology and biology and culture yet to be uncovered, things that we're not even aware of yet. But that is all so speculative at this point, it would be insane to count on that to balance the accounts. We *know* we will make a profit by bringing a few thousand Sag-ura back to Earth and acting as agents on their behalf. Anything else is, as they say, gravy."

The French representative, Xarla Fortier, folded her arms, radiating disapproval. "What arrogant assumption, monsieur, gives you the right to dictate this way to us? Ishtar, its wealth and its lost knowledge, should be the inheritance of all of humanity, not the playground of a single corporate entity! What you propose is nothing less than the wholesale rape of an inhabited world, to *your* benefit."

"Worse, Madame Fortier," Raychaudhuri said, "he proposes to let us watch but not participate. PanTerra intends nothing less than a complete monopoly over Ishtar and all her products, subsidized by the United Federal Republic and backed by the muscle of the U.S. Marines. I, for one, protest."

"Tell us, Mr. Buckner," Chieu said, eyes narrowing to hard, cold slits, "what happens if the population of Earth at large gets wind of this scheme of yours? You realize, of course, that any one of us here could upset your plans simply by net-publishing your report."

"Is that a threat, Mr. Chieu?" Buckner sighed. "I'd thought better of you. Each and every one of you answers to your own corporate interests. You will need to consult with them before taking such an irretrievably drastic step . . . one, I might add, that would reveal your own complicity in these deliberations. PanTerra would respond as necessary to minimize the damage, to put a good spin on things. We would emphasize the benevolent nature of our business dealings on Ishtar, the great public good we were providing. Even slavery, you see, can be presented as good, as a social or an economic or a religious necessity, if there is a carefully nurtured will to believe. . . . Am I correct, Mr. Haddad? True, our profits might be adversely impacted to some degree, but I doubt there would be major problems in the long run.

"Of course, whoever leaks that information would find their corporate interests cut off from the deal. My God . . . we're not leaving you out. We're making you our partners! Secrecy, you see, is more in your interests than in ours. Play along, and each of you becomes the sole agent for the distribution of what we bring back from Ishtar to your own countries. New science. New knowledge. New medicines, perhaps, or new outlooks on the universe. And, of course, the chance to offer Ishtaran domestics to the upper strata of your populations, at a *very* healthy profit for yourselves.

"Mr. Chieu, why would you possibly want to jeopardize that for yourself or the people of the Chinese People's Hegemony?" He shrugged. "You all can discuss it as much as you want. Take it up with the Confederation Council, if you like. The simple fact is, PanTerra will be at Ishtar six months before the joint multinational expedition gets there. And I happen to know that the Marines will have orders not only to safeguard human interests on the planet, but to safeguard Confederation interests as well . . . and that means UFR interests, ladies and gentlemen. PanTerran interests. I tell you this in the hope that we can avoid any expensive confrontations, either here or on Ishtar." He spread his hands, pouring sincerity into his voice. "Believe me when I say we want a reasonable return on our investment—no more. PanTerra is not the evil ogre you seem to believe it is. We are happy to share—for a fair and equitable price. Ishtar is a *planet*, a *world*, with all of the resources, wonders, and riches that a planet has to offer, with fortunes to be made from the exchange of culture, philosophy, history, knowledge."

"And if anyone can put a price tag on that knowledge," Haddad said wryly, "PanTerra can. Friends, I think we have little alternative, at least for now."

"I agree," Fortier said. "Reluctantly. We don't have to *like* it. . . ."

"We understand the need for secrecy, Señor Buckner," Dom Camara said. "But how can you guarantee that word of this—this plan of yours will not leak anyway? You can threaten to cut us off from our contracts with you . . . but not the Marines. Or the scientists." Camara cocked his head to one side. "This civilian expert you've hired . . . Dr. Hanson? Suppose she doesn't go along with your ideas of charity and enlightenment for the Sag-ura?"

"Dr. Hanson is, quite frankly, the best in the field there is. We brought her on board to help us identify and acquire xenotechnoarcheological artifacts that may be of interest. She is a PanTerran employee. If she doesn't do her job to our satisfaction, we will terminate her contract."

He didn't elaborate. There was no reason to share with these people the darker aspects of some of the long meetings he'd held here in New Chicago with other PanTerran executives. The truth of it was that anyone who got in PanTerra's way on this deal would be terminated.

One way or another.

"And the Marines?" Camara wanted to know.

"They work for the FR/US government, of course, and are not, as such, directly under our control. They will do what they are sent out there to do, however. And we have taken . . . certain steps to ensure that our wishes are heard and respected.

"Believe me, people, we are not monsters. We are not some evil empire bent on dominating Earth's economy. What we at PanTerra are simply doing is ensuring that there is not a mad scramble for Ishtar's resources." He cocked an eye at Chieu. "We certainly do not want an unfortunate repeat of what happened in China three centuries ago, with half the civilized world snapping like dogs at a carcass. We propose order, an equitable distribution of the profits, and, most important, profits for everyone."

"Including the Ahannu, Mr. Buckner?" Chieu asked.

"If they choose to accept civilization," Buckner replied, "of course. They cannot wall off the universe forever. But as they adopt a less hidebound form of government, a freer philosophy, they will benefit as our partners and as our friends." He was quite sincere as he spoke.

He almost meant everything he said.

12

Combat Center, IST Derna
Orbital Construction Facility 1, L-4
0810 hours Zulu

"Maybe we should get up," Ramsey said. "The day's half over."

"And just what," Ricia Anderson asked, "do you mean by *up*?"

"Insubordinate bitch!" he said playfully. "You know what I mean!"

In fact, there was no up, no down, no sense of direction save the words neatly stenciled across one bulkhead: THIS END DOWN DURING ACCELERATION.

"Bitch," Ricia said, cheerful. "That's me. Beautiful . . . intelligent . . . talented . . . creative . . . and hard to please."

He chuckled. "Hard to please? You didn't sound hard to please a little while ago."

She snuggled closer. "Mmm. That's because you're rather talented and creative yourself."

They floated together, naked, still surrounded by tiny glistening drops of perspiration and other body fluids adrift in microgravity. The compartment they occupied was small, only a couple of meters across in its narrowest dimension, an equipment storage space and access tunnel to the *Derna's* logic centers. The electronics housing the various AIs run-

ning on board—including Cassius and the *Derna*'s own artificial intelligence—lay just beyond an array of palm panels
on the "ceiling" and one bulkhead. Tool lockers and storage
bins took up most of the remaining surfaces, with a narrow,
circular hatch in the deck leading aft to the centrifuge collar.
Ramsey could hear the gentle, grinding rumble of the centrifuge beyond the hatch.

"Yeah, well," he said, ripping open the Velcro closure on
the body harness joining them. "If somebody comes up forward through that hatch to check on the logic circuits, we'll
have some explaining to do."

He pulled the harness off their hips and they drifted
apart, reluctantly. Ricia rotated in space, plucking from the
air behind her a towel she'd brought for the purpose, and
began sopping up the floating secretions. Ramsey grabbed
his T-shirt and helped, taking special care to wipe down
the gleaming surfaces of the storage bins and lockers
around them. He knew that every Marine on board must
know what went on in there, even those who didn't use it
for recreational purposes, but it wouldn't do to leave behind such obvious evidence of their tryst. The *Derna*'s
Navy crew could get testy about the grunts and the messes
they made.

Getting dressed together in those close confines was almost as much fun as getting undressed earlier. It was easier
when they helped one another, since there was hardly room
enough to bend over. It would be nice, Ramsey thought
with wry amusement, if the people who designed these
ships would acknowledge that people needed sex, and included sufficient space for the purpose—maybe a compartment with padded bulkheads and conveniently placed
hand- and footholds—not to mention locker space for
clothing and perhaps a viewall for a romantic panorama of
a blue-and-white-marbled Earth hanging against a backdrop of stars.

But unfortunately, that just made too damned much sense.
The *Derna*, first of a first generation of interstellar mili-

tary transports, was designed with efficiency of space, mass, and consumable stores in mind, not the erotic frolickings of her passengers. She had to keep thirteen hundred people alive for a voyage lasting years, even with relativistic effects, which meant that every cubic centimeter was carefully planned for and generally allotted to more than one purpose.

If the damned sleep cells had been just *a little* larger . . . but they were designed for one occupant apiece. Having sex in one of those hexagonal tubes was like coupling in a closed coffin. Ramsey knew. He'd tried it during the past month . . . twice with Ricia and once with Chris DeHavilland. They would be claustrophobic in micro-g; they were impossible under spin-gravity. Besides that, everybody on the hab deck would know who was sleeping with whom, and the Corps simply wasn't that liberal yet.

Everyone knew it was done, of course. The whole point of command constellations was *supposed* to be that teams that worked well together should be kept together, especially on long deployments. There was nothing wrong with that. But the fact that they'd been deliberately chosen because they had few family ties on Earth meant that there *would* be ties, both casually recreational and seriously romantic, among team members. They were, after all, human.

But few things about human nature ever changed, or, when they did, the change took a long time to manifest. The likely response among civilian taxpayers who paid for the Marines—not to mention their spartan accommodations in deep space—would have been horror at such scandalous goings-on. And the senior staff was always at pains to make certain that nothing scandalous about the Corps ever got into general circulation among civilians . . . *especially* civilian lawmakers.

Ramsey thought of an old Corps joke—the image of a Marine kept perpetually in cybehibe, with a sign on the sleep tube, "In case of war, break glass." Marines weren't supposed to have families, friends, or lives.

And they certainly weren't supposed to have *sex*.

They finished dressing—shipboard uniform of the day was black T-shirts, khaki slacks, and white sweat socks—gently spun one another in midair for a quick once-over for incriminating evidence of their past few hours, then pulled close in a parting hug. "Again tonight, after duty?" he asked.

"Sorry, T. J.," she told him. She kissed him gently. "I'm going to be with Chris. And tomorrow I'm shifting to the third watch. Maybe in two weeks?"

He nodded, masking his disappointment. "Sure." Relationships within the command group created what sometimes amounted to a large, polyamorous family. Social planning, however, could be a real problem at times, especially when complicated by ever-shifting duty schedules.

Well, it beats the hell out of living with civilians, he thought. He'd been married once—a five-year contract that Cindy and George had elected not to renew with him. If you were going to sleep with someone, it helped if they had some notion of what it was you did for a living, what it cost you, and why you did it.

Making their way aft through the docking bay, they paused on the quarterdeck to chat with Lieutenant Delgado, floating at his duty station in front of the big American flag. "Logic center is clear," he told Delgado, sotto voce.

"Aye aye, sir." Zeus Delgado was not a member of the command constellation, but he knew what went on forward. He'd promised to flash Ramsey over his link if someone was heading toward the logic center access who couldn't be turned aside.

At the centrifuge collar, Ramsey followed Ricia into an elevator and together they swiftly dropped outshaft into the familiar tug of spin gravity once more. Emerging on Deck 1 of Hab 3, they stepped into a crowded, hot, and noisy bustle of activity.

Eighty percent of the MIEU's troop complement was on board, but so far fewer than half of those had entered cybehibe. That meant crowding on all decks and a battle for the shipboard environmental systems as they struggled to vent all of that excess heat. Supplies were arriving at the L-4 space docks at the rate of two freighters every three days, most of them carrying either water or C-sludge, the hydrocarbon substrate used in the nanoprocessor tanks to make food. The *Derna* needed water especially, a small ocean of water, in fact, filling the huge mushroom cap forward. Water was *Derna*'s primary consumable, necessary not only for the drinking and washing needs for her crew and passengers, but also as their source of oxygen, their AM-drive reaction mass, and as radiation shielding at near-*c* velocities.

But the MIEU's weapons and equipment were arriving on board as well, and those Marines who hadn't yet gone into cybehibe were busy unpacking gear, checking it for wear, damage, or missing parts, and stowing it for the long voyage ahead. Everything from Mark VII suits and laser rifles to spy-eye floaters and TAL-S Dragonflies had to be unpacked, examined, up- or down-checked for maintenance, and entered into the virtual ship's manifest. Each individual Marine was responsible for her or his personal gear, including armor and primary weapon, so the hab deck was packed with men and women unshipping, inspecting, and cleaning everything from LR-2120s to KW-6000 power packs to M-780 grenades and CTX-5 demo packs. It was a job that would have been more happily carried out groundside, especially in the case of the high explosives, but the troops were arriving piecemeal, as were their weapons, on different flights from different spaceports scattered across the Earth. Especially considering the need to check all equipment after it had made the trip up to L-4, the most efficient place to bring the two together was on board the *Derna*.

But it made for a hell of a lot of chaos.

As Ramsey threaded his way past busy groups of enlisted Marines, he reopened his implants to shiplink traffic. He'd shut them down to afford some peace for his tryst with Ricia, and now he had to brace himself against the onslaught of messages and requests that had backlogged during his virtual absence.

"Good morning, Colonel," Cassius said. "You have forty-seven link messages waiting, twenty-nine of them flagged 'urgent' or higher. Two are flagged as Priority One. You also have seventeen requests for face meetings, and twenty-one requests for virtual conferencing. Also, there will be a delay in the shipment of the Dragonflies from Palo Alto. This may mean an additional delay in mission departure time."

Take a couple hours off for a quick docking maneuver, he thought, and all hell breaks loose.

"Two Priority Ones?" he asked the AI-symbiont aloud. "Shit, why didn't you tag me?" The command group's AI could reach him at any time, whether his link was online or not, and standing orders were to let Priority One and Two messages come through no matter what his link status.

"I felt you needed the downtime, sir," Cassius replied. "You've been pushing quite hard and showing both emotional and physiological signs of stress. I exercised discretionary judgment according to the specific parameters of—"

"Can it. What were the calls?"

"One from General King. He wished to know the status of the Dragonfly shipment. In your persona, I routed him through to the TAL-S maintenance center at Seven Palms."

"I see." He would have done the same. "And the other?"

"From General Haslett, sir, requesting an immediate virtual conference on the political situation. I pointed out that *Derna* is on Zulu, that you had been up quite late overseeing the arrival of the last stores freighter and were currently on sleep shift. I offered to wake you, and he said it could wait. I have scheduled you for a virtual conference with the general in . . . two hours, seventeen minutes from now."

Again he couldn't fault the AI's judgment . . . which was the reason they made such exceptional personal secretaries.

Both priority calls had been less than truly urgent, but both
needed handling by means both courteous and expeditious.

"Very well," he told Cassius. "Let's see the urgents."

"You may wish to greet Captain Warhurst first, sir."

"Eh?" Warhurst's dress khakis were a bit more up-to-date
than his icon garb, Ramsey noted. "Oh. Of course."

Warhurst was uncovered so he did not salute, but he came
to a crisp attention. "Captain Martin Warhurst reporting on
board, sir."

"Ah, Captain Warhurst, yes," Ramsey replied. "Welcome
aboard."

"Thank you, sir."

"Check with my exec, here, Major Anderson, for your
berthing assignments. Are your people getting settled in?"

"Yes, sir. But my company is only at half strength . . .
eighty-two troops out of 150 on my TO and E."

"Affirmative, Captain. But I'm afraid the rest of your team
will be newbies." He saw Warhurst's face fall at that news.
"Don't worry, son. You'll have time to whip them into shape
before deployment."

"Yes, sir. Uh . . . fresh meat out of Lejeune, sir?"

"Yup. Volunteers from recruit companies 1097, 1098, and
1099. They'll be arriving over the next three weeks or so."

"Yes, sir."

"Major Anderson has the specs and stats. You can review
their recruit records online, of course, and you can interview
them, if you wish, before they embark. Problem, Captain?"

Warhurst made a face. "No, sir. It's just . . ."

"Yes?"

"My mission brief has my company hitting Objective
Krakatoa. I would have thought you'd want an experienced
Mobile Assault Team on that one, sir."

"Ideally, yes. I'm afraid we don't have that luxury, however. Groundside HQ is holding back the best MATs against
the situation in Mejico and the Southwest territories. We get
what's left, I'm afraid."

"I see, Colonel."

"Don't worry, son," Ramsey said with an easy grin. "If your people aren't experienced now, they sure as hell will be by the time they've taken Krakatoa!"

"The ones who survive will be experienced, yes, sir," Warhurst told him. "The rest will be dead."

"That's the way it always is, Marine. You have your orders. Carry on!"

"Aye aye, sir!"

Warhurst was not happy, but that couldn't be helped. Weeks ago, Ramsey had downloaded the captain's combat record and guessed that Warhurst was at least as worried about his own qualifications for the assignment as he was about the experience of his men. He'd only taken part in one combat mission so far—the brief, bitter assault on Giza last June—and he must be wondering about why he'd been recruited for a berth with the MIEU, much less why he was supposed to lead the first assault onto Ishtar.

No matter. He was a good man and would come through when he had to.

Or he would be dead. But he would do his honest-to-Chesty-Puller best.

Semper fi. . . .

U.S. Marine Corps Recruit Train-
ing Center
Parris Island, South Carolina
0730 hours ET

Time, which had crawled forward at a seemingly imperceptible pace, with each day very much like the one past, at last began to accelerate. Garroway's training entered phase three as his nanochelates began to kick in, then phase four, when all of the pain and sweat at last began coming together. He might be, in Makowiecz's cordially bellowed invective, a scum-of-the-Earth lowlife-maggot recruit, but by the Goddess, he was a *Marine* scum-of-the-Earth lowlife-maggot recruit.

"Fire teams advance, by the numbers!" Philby called over the squad comm channel. "Fire Team One . . . *go!*"

Recruits Myers, Kilgore, and Garvey rose from cover, their combat suits mottled with the same ocher and gray tones of the rock and sand of the desert. They were still a bit clumsy with the new suits; Kilgore slipped in a soft patch of sand and fell heavily, dropping his laser rifle as he hit.

"Any time you're ready, Kill-girl!" Makowiecz's voice cut in, harsh and sarcastic. "I'm sure the enemy will happily sit down and wait until you're freaking ready!"

"Sorry, sir!"

"Yes, you are! Now *move! Move! Move!*"

Garroway heard the exchange spoken inside his head, a kind of technological telepathy generated by the chelated nanoconnections growing in key areas of his brain.

The full range of vision and hearing available to him was breathtaking, and he was still getting used to a sensory input that could be overwhelming at times. With a thought-click, his helmet's AI could adjust his visual input to anything from monochrome to full HSD, a hyperspectral display combining every wavelength from deep infrared to X ray. By clicking through a mental menu, he could see in the dark, filter out harsh light, and easily tell the difference between natural vegetation and camouflage.

"Fire Team Two!" Philby called. *"Go!"*

Mendelez, Jaffrey, and Kaminski rose from the sand, rushing forward in short, zigzagging bursts of speed, their goal a low, rock-strewn ridge crest a hundred meters ahead. Simulated laser fire—hell, it was *real* laser fire, Garroway thought, but stepped down in wattage until only suit sensors could register it—flashed and strobed from a pair of automated gun emplacements concealed among the boulders ahead and to the left. Explosions detonated somewhere behind him. The word was that the AIs triggering each burst knew how close they could get without actually hurting any of the recruits, but scuttlebutt also said there'd been plenty of injuries in other recruit companies during this part of the training already, and even a few accidental deaths. Dead was still dead, whether you were fighting frog-faced aliens eight light-years away or taking part in a routine training exercise right in your own backyard.

The excitement of the moment pounded in Garroway's skull. This might be just an exercise, but it was being played in deadly earnest against both AIs and flesh-and-blood opponents. His company—what was left of it now, eleven weeks into training—had been TAV-lifted to the Marine Corps training facility at Guardian Angels, in the Baja Territory, to play war games with SpecOps commandos and other Marines. They'd been told off in threes, grouped according to the Corps' current three-four-two doctrine: three men to a fire team, four fire teams to a squad, two squads to a platoon section. Owen Philby, a short, wiry agro from Niobrara, Nebraska, was the ARNCO—the acting recruit noncommissioned officer in command of Third Platoon's 1st Squad. They'd been given their orders—to take and hold that ridge up ahead—and except for Makowiecz's acid commentary over the comm channels from time to time, they were largely on their own.

Shit. Mendelez was down, the servos in his suit killed by his own AI. He would lie on the ground, a simulated casualty of a simulated fight, until the exercise was over. Garroway thought-clicked to his squad status display and saw that Kilgore and Garvey were down as well. Those guns up there were chopping the squad to bits.

"Fire Team Three! *Go!*"

Three more suited figures rose from cover, zigzagging across the open ground. One of them stumbled and fell . . . Fox. Then Lopez. And Hollingwood. Three up, three down. The enemy guns had the range.

"Fire Team Four! *Go!*"

That was Garroway's cue. Scrambling to his feet, he began dashing toward the ridge crest, dodging and weaving across the rocky ground. Philby and Yates rose with him, clumsy in their Mark VIIs. Philby took three lumbering steps, then fell heavily facedown as his suit servos cut out. Garroway saw the AI-generated flash of a rapid-fire laser skittering across the slope but couldn't make out where it was coming from. There was a wrecked and rusted hulk at the top of the ridge—the wreckage of an old magfloater APC, it looked like. The fire might be coming from there, but it was impossible to tell for sure.

Yates stumbled and fell, another simulated casualty. . . .

Garroway dropped to cover behind a sand-polished boulder, his shoulder slamming painfully against the rock despite the internal padding of his suit.

He thought-clicked to the tactical display again, superimposing the remaining members of 1st Squad on a color-coded map of the immediate area. Myers was halfway up the ridge, pinned down behind a scattering of boulders. Kaminski was also pinned, thirty meters behind Meyers. And . . . *damn!* Jaffrey had just gone down as well, yet another casualty.

And Garroway had barely gotten started, tail-end Charlie, a hundred meters from his objective.

Three men left, out of a twelve-man squad, strung out across the laser-blasted boulder field. Not good. Not good at all. Gunny Makowiecz was ominously silent. Had he already written the squad off for this exercise?

Garroway sagged inside his armor, almost overcome with frustration and, more, with exhaustion. This week in the Baja was an old Corps tradition—*"Motivational Week,"* more often referred to by the recruits who endured it as "Hell Week." In a solid week of exercises and evolutions, each man in the company could expect to get perhaps seven hours sleep in seven days, as his physical and mental limits were tested to the snapping point.

This was day two of Motivational Week. How the hell was he going to see this thing through for five more days? And what was the point? Things had been getting steadily worse ever since he'd arrived at Parris Island. He knew now he'd never make it as a Marine. All he needed to do was flash-link Makowiecz with the words "I quit."

An hour from now he could be enjoying a hot shower followed by a hot meal as he waited for them to process him out of the Corps. It would be so easy. . . .

Yeah? he asked himself. *Then what? Transfer to the Aerospace Force? Go back to live with your mother? Maybe you could get a job boss-linking construction robots on the moon. . . .*

He sighed, as another round of explosions detonated nearby. He'd had this discussion with himself before, and frequently. It was just getting harder and harder to see the answer clearly.

Still, there was one answer he could see, and that was an advantage, a small one, to the tactical situation he found himself in. The three surviving recruits of 1st Squad were so widely scattered that they were tougher targets for two automatic gun positions. More important, the three of them had more line-of-sight data to work with, with three widely spaced perspectives. Those guns might be invisible to all three men individually, but if they put their AI heads together, as it were . . .

"Myers!" he called over the tactical channel. "Ski! This is Garroway! Link in with your HSD data!"

He knew he was begging to be slapped down, and kept expecting Makowiecz to step in with his sharp-edged sarcasm and ask what he thought he was doing. He was taking over the responsibilities of the squad leader here . . . but Philby, the squad ARNCO, was lying helpless among the rocks a few meters away now, his suit dead and his comm suite offline. Somebody had to take charge, and Garroway's position at the far end of the strung-out line gave him a slightly better overview of the tactical situation.

His helmet AI picked up the data feeds from both Myers's

and Kaminski's suits. With a thought-click, he could now see what the other men were seeing from their vantage points . . . and he could let his own AI sort through all three hyperspectral arrays and build up a more detailed, more revealing image of what was really up there.

For over a century, now, military technology had witnessed a race between high-tech camouflage and the high-tech means of seeing through it. The first primitive hyperspectral arrays had been developed late in the twentieth century, allowing analysts to see the tanks, gun emplacements, and other equipment masked beneath camo netting and cut branches. Paint that changed color to match the surroundings had been harder to distinguish, but even the best reactive paint still had slightly different optical properties than steel, plastic laminates, or ceramics, especially at both long infrared and at UV and long X-ray wavelengths.

Nowadays, reactive camo paints used nanotechnology to mimic textures and UV refractive properties and to better mask distinctive heat signatures at all IR wavelengths. While targets like vehicles, which shed a lot of heat, couldn't be masked completely, relatively cool targets like robot gun emplacements were almost impossible to spot.

And yet . . .

His helmet AI brought three sets of data together, repainting the landscape in front of him in enhanced colors. A laser flashed again—the muzzle was carefully shielded, so he couldn't pinpoint the weapon that way—but Myers's helmet scanners had also detected something else, something critical . . . a telltale shifting of reflective frequencies that suggested *movement*.

"Myers, can you work your way farther to the left?"

"I'll try," Myers replied. "But every time I move, those damned guns—"

His voice was chopped off as the comm link was cut. But Garroway had the last bit of necessary input now, relayed just as Myers had shifted position. One of the two guns was there, well to the left and halfway up the ridge. The other was straight ahead, close to that wrecked APC but a little below it and to the right, a position calculated to misdirect the recruits into thinking the laser emplacement was somewhere on the wreckage itself. Sneaky . . .

His helmet marked both guns for him in bright red.

"You see them both, Ski?" he called.

"Got 'em, Gare."

"You take the one on the left," Garroway told him. "I'll get the one by the APC."

"Roger that."

"On my command, three . . . two . . . one . . . *now!*"

Garroway rolled to the left side of the sheltering boulder, coming to his knees and dropping his laser rifle into line with the chosen target. His weapon projected a crosshair onto his helmet display; he leaned into the boulder, bracing himself, as he dropped the targeting reticle onto the patch of enhanced color that marked the enemy gun, bringing his gloved finger tight against the firing button. The weapon cycled as the enemy gun spotted him and swung around to target him.

Garroway was a fraction of a second faster. The enemy gun didn't fire.

"Got him!" Kaminski yelled. "One echo down!"

"Two echoes down," Garroway added, using mil-speak shorthand for a gun emplacement. The ridge should be clear now, but he checked it out carefully before moving again. There could be backup positions, well-hidden and kept out of action until the first guns were killed.

"Sea Devil, this is Devil One," he called, shifting to the platoon frequency.

"Devil One, Sea Devil," the voice of the platoon controller replied. "Go ahead."

"Objective positions neutralized, but we've taken eighty-two percent casualties. If you want that fucking ridge, you'd better send support ASAP."

His phrasing wasn't exactly mil-standard, but the exhaustion and despair of a few minutes ago had just given way to a surge of adrenaline-laced excitement. Rising, he trotted forward, making his way up the face of the ridge to join Kaminski, who was already crouched in the shadow of the wrecked APC.

"Quite a view, Gare," Kaminski told him.

It was . . . and a familiar one. From up here, Garroway could look east across the silver-gray gleam of the Sea of California.

It was a bit strange being so relatively close to his old home at Guaymas, a place he honestly expected never to see again. The training range in the desert scrub country of Isla Angel de la Guarda was just across the Gulf of California from Hermosillo and only a couple hundred miles northwest of Guaymas. Even in late September the air simmered with the familiar dry but salt-laden heat of home, a baking, inhospitable climate ideal as a test range for the recruits as they learned to handle their new Mark VII armor.

I'm not going back, he thought, the emotion so fierce his eyes were watering. *I'm not going to quit.*

The thought came unexpectedly, unbidden, but he thought he recognized the surge of emotion that rode with it. He was over the hump.

Time after time in the past weeks, Makowiecz and the other DIs had hammered at the recruits of Company 1099: "Sooner or later each and every one of you will want to quit. You will beg to quit! And we're going to do our best to make you quit! . . ."

Every man and woman going through recruit training, he'd been told, hit a period known as "the wall" somewhere around halfway to three-quarters of the way through, a time when it felt like graduation would never come, when the recruit could do nothing but question the decision to join the service in the first place.

For those tough enough to endure, the wall was followed by "the hump," a time when training became even tougher, when the questions, the doubts, the self-criticism grew ever sharper, and then . . .

"Garroway!" Makowiecz's voice snapped in his head. "What the hell did you just do?"

"Sir!" he replied. "This recruit took command of 1st Squad when the acting squad leader was incapacitated, sir! We then took the objective, sir!"

He braced for the inevitable chewing out.

"Well done, Marine" was Makowiecz's surprising reply. "What would you have done differently if you had been in command from the start?"

"Sir, this recruit would have attempted to reconnoiter the objective with one fire team in the lead, the other two in support, and attempted to correlate hyperspectral data from all vantage points before moving into the open. Sir."

Philby, frankly, had screwed up, ordering the squad to advance into the open, knowing those guns were up there but without knowing their exact positions. In any race between man and laser, the laser *was* going to win.

Garroway kept his opinion of Philby's tactics to himself, however. They were all in this together, after all. *Gung-ho* . . .

"Outstanding job, Marine," Makowiecz told him. "Your support is on its way. Second Squad lost its ARNCO. When they reach your position, you will take command. Sit tight until then."

"Aye aye, sir!"

He was over the hump.

Graduation might be another five weeks off, but he felt like a Marine.

Makowiecz had *called* him a Marine!

Even getting killed an hour later didn't dampen the feeling. The Army SpecOps commandos were literally buried behind the ridge, their heat signatures masked by solid rock, their fighting holes hidden by boulders. They waited until 2nd Squad arrived and was just settling in, then rose like ghosts from their positions and cut down the recruits with simulated laser and plasma gun bursts before they knew what was happening. "You're dead, kid," one of the black-armored commandos had said as he grabbed Garroway from behind.

It didn't matter. He was a *Marine*. . . .

13

Pacifica
Off the California Coast
1105 hours PT

Garroway grinned at Lynnley. "You know, this would be a *lot* more fun in zero gravity."

"You!" she retorted, giving him a gentle punch in the chest. "Aren't you ever satisfied?"

"Well, if anybody can do it, you can," he replied. He checked his inner timer. "I guess we'd better be moving."

"Unless we want to be listed as AWOL, yeah," she told him. She stroked his arm gently. "It's been good, being with you like this. Thanks."

"Real good. I'm . . . going to miss you." He shook his head as she rolled out of the bed.

The walls and ceiling of the room showed a view of space—Earth, moon, sun, and thick-scattered stars, slowly circling. The view was an illusion, of course; for one thing, even in space the stars weren't that bright when the sun was visible.

"I'll miss you too," Lynnley said.

"I still don't want to believe we can't see each other again. Maybe ever."

"Don't say that, John! We don't know what's going to happen!"

"Sure we do! I'm on my way to Ishtar, and you're going to Sirius. I checked a star map download. We'll be farther away from one another than if one of us stayed on Earth!"

She shrugged. "That doesn't make any difference, does it? Even one light-year is too far to think about."

"Well, you know what I mean. We're going in two different directions. And I'd hoped we'd get deployed together."

"Damn it, we both know how unrealistic that idea was, John. The needs of the Corps—"

"Come first. I know. But I don't have to like it." He balled his fists, squeezing tight. "Shit." He got out of the bed and began picking up his clothes. He and Lynnley had been fuck buddies off and on for a couple of years now . . . nothing serious, but she was fun to be with and therapeutic to vent at and fantastic recreation in bed. He'd thought of her as his closest friend and somehow never even considered the possibility that they would end up in different duty stations.

"Simulation off!" he called, addressing the room. The view of space vanished, replaced by empty walls that seemed to echo his loneliness.

"Look," she told him, "we're both getting star duty, right? And we're both going about eight light-years. There's still a good chance we'll be tracking each other subjectively when we get back."

"I guess so." She meant that their subjective times ought to match pretty closely. Since they were both heading eight light-years out, they'd be spending about the same times at the same percentage of c and aging at about the same subjective rate.

But he didn't believe it. Things never worked out that neatly in real life, especially where the Corps was concerned. If he ever saw her again, one of them might well be years older than the other.

He sighed as he started pulling on his uniform. How much did that matter, really? They both knew they would be taking other sex partners. With the future so uncertain, there was no sense in meaningless promises to wait for one another. It wasn't like they shared a long-term contract.

"I think," he said slowly, sealing the front of his khaki shirt, "I'm just feeling a bit cut off. Like I'll never be able to come home again."

"I know. Everything, *everyone*, we leave here is going to be twenty years older when we see them again. At least. My parents aren't happy about it, but at least they understand. And they'll only be in their sixties when I get back."

"I just don't understand my mother," he said. "*How* can she consider going back to that . . . man?"

"Like I told you once before, you can't protect her. You can't live her life. She has to make her own decisions."

"But I keep wondering if she's going back to him because of me. Because I'm going to Ishtar."

"That's still her issue, right? You have to do what's right for *you*."

"But I don't know what that is. Not anymore. And I feel . . . guilty. She wasn't happy when I saw her yesterday. About my going to Ishtar, I mean."

"I think you're giving yourself a lot more power over your mother than you really have. You've been around before when she's left, and she's always gone back, right? What made you think this time would be any different?"

"I don't know. I don't know anything anymore. You ready?"

Dressed now in her khakis, she pulled on her uniform cap and tugged it straight. "Ready and all systems go," she told him. "You feel ready for lunch?"

He brightened, with an effort. "You bet." If they only had a few more hours together, he was determined to enjoy them, instead of brooding about the might-have-beens and the never-would-bes.

They left the room, stepping out onto the hotel concourse. Pacifica was a small city erected on pylons off the southern California coast, halfway between San Diego and San

Clemente Island, a high-tech enclave devoted to shopping, restaurants, and myriad exotica of entertainment. Two days after their graduation from boot camp, they were in the middle of a glorious seventy-two—three whole, blessed days of liberty. They'd already been to the Europa Diver, paying two newdollars apiece to take turns steering a submarine through the deep, dark mystery of Europa's world-ocean, all simulated, of course, to avoid the speed-of-light time lag. After that they'd checked into the pay-by-hour room suite and entertained themselves with one another.

Now it was time to find a place to eat. The restaurant concourse was that way, toward the mall shops and the sub-O landing port. White-metal arches reached high overhead, admitting a wash of UV-filtered sunlight and the embrace of a gentle blue sky.

In another forty-eight hours he would be vaulting into that sky, on his way to the *Derna* at L-4.

And after that . . .

"What do you do," he wondered aloud, "when you know you're not going to see Earth again for twenty years?"

"You are gloomy today, aren't you? We won't—"

"I know, I know," he interrupted her. "Our subjective time will only be four years or so, depending on how long we're on Ishtar . . . and most of that time we'll be asleep. From *our* point of view, we could be right back here a few months from now. But all of this . . ." He waved his hand, taking in the sweep of the Pacifica concourse. "All of this will be twenty years older or more."

"Pacifica's been here for forty-something years already. Why wouldn't it be here in another twenty?"

"It's not Pacifica. You know what I mean. All of these people . . . it's like we won't fit in anymore."

"Take a look at yourself, John. We're Marines. We don't fit in *now*."

Her words, lightly spoken, startled him. She was right. In all that crowded concourse, Garroway could see three others in Marine uniforms, and a couple of Navy men in black. The rest, whether in casual dress, business suits, or nude, were civilians.

Their uniforms set them apart, of course, but he also knew it was more than the uniform.

And now he knew what was bothering him.

It was as though he'd already left on his twenty-year deployment, as if he no longer belonged to the Earth.

It was a strange and lonely feeling.

Hab 3, Deck 1, IST Derna
Orbital Construction Facility 1, L-4
1240 hours Zulu

Keep thinking about the money, she told herself with grim determination. *Keep thinking about the money . . . and the papers you're going to publish . . . and winning the chair of the American Xenocultural Foundation. . . .*

Traci Hanson lay halfway out of the hot and claustrophobic embrace of her hab cell, flat on her back on the sleep pad, eyes tightly shut as the technicians on either side of her made the final connections. She hated the prodding, the handling, as if she were a naked slab of meat.

Which, of course, in a technical sense she was. The idea was to preserve her for the next ten years, to feed and water her while her implants slowed her brain activity to something just this side of death.

IV tubes had been threaded into both of her arms as well as in her carotid artery beneath the angle of her jaw. A catheter had been inserted into her bladder. She knew her implant was supposed to block all feelings of hunger, despite the fact that she'd had no solid food for a week, but her stomach was rumbling nonetheless. She was uncomfortable, sweaty, ill-tempered, she hadn't had a decent shower since she'd come aboard the *Derna*, and now these . . . these *people* were sticking more tubes and needles into her.

"Relax, Dr. Hanson," one of the cybehibe techs told her.

"This'll just take a moment. Next thing you know, you'll be at Ishtar."

"'Relax.' Easy for you to say," she grumped. She opened her eyes and turned her head as far as the tube in her throat would let her. The hab deck was still crowded with Marines, most of them busily cleaning or working with weapons and other articles of personal equipment. "You have to go through this with every one of those people?"

"Sure do," the tech told her. "That's why it takes so long to work through the list. There's only about thirty of us, and we have twelve or thirteen hundred people to prep this way."

She noticed that her blood was flowing through the tubes in her wrists, and the thought made her a little queasy, despite the suppressant effect of her implant.

"How are you feeling?"

"Okay, I guess," she said. "Uncomfortable. The pain in my arms is going away, a little."

"Good."

"It feels like this damned mattress pad is melting, though. It feels wet, and kind of squishy. Am I sweating that much?"

"No. It's supposed to do that. Think about it. For the next ten years, you're going to be lying here, breathing, eating, drinking, eliminating, filtering your blood, all through these IV tubes. Medical nano and the AI doctor built into these walls are going to be monitoring and handling all of your body functions. The one thing these machines can't do is safely turn you over every couple of hours for ten years. Can you imagine the problems you'd have with bedsores if you just laid on your ass for that long? By the time you're asleep, the pad will have turned into a kind of gel bath. It'll support you gently, just like you were in a pool of water . . . and the gel gives the medical nano access to your back so it can rebuild skin cells and keep your circulation going, keep your blood from pooling, y'know?"

"It feels . . . like I'm sinking." Thoughts of drowning tugged at her mind. She wasn't thinking clearly, and she was having trouble formulating the questions she wanted to ask. "Will . . . I dream?"

"Maybe a little, when you're going under, and when you're coming out. The AI doc will be initiating REM sleep as it takes you down. But most of the time? No."

One of the other techs laughed. "I know I wouldn't care to have to deal with a decade's worth of dreams," she said, "especially knowing I couldn't wake up!"

"I . . . think the Ahannu sergeant is Cydonia at the Institute. Ahannu Buckner is a real bastard. Manipulative. Make me rich . . ."

"I'm sure that's true, Doctor. Would you mind counting backward from a hundred for me?"

"Counting . . . backward? Sure. Saves power. But what about the Hunters of the Dawn? They won't have to wait in line, not with PanTerra. A hunnerd . . . ninety . . . uh, no . . . ninety-seven. Eight . . . nine . . . Ishtar. It's beautiful there, I understand. . . ."

"You'll be able to see that for yourself, Doctor, very, very soon now."

Hab 3, Deck 1, IST Derna
Orbital Construction Facility 1, L-4
1405 hours Zulu

The surface of the world of Ishtar blurred beneath the hurtling Dragonfly, jagged mountains and upthrust volcanic outcroppings among gentler rivers of gleaming ice. This was Ishtar's anti-Marduk side, the hemisphere held in the grip of perpetual winter as the moon circled its primary in tidal lock-step.

But the ice was thinning, the land greening. New Sumer lay just beyond the curve of the red-purple horizon up ahead, another hundred kilometers or so. . . .

"Black Dragons," Warhurst announced over the tactical

net, using the assault force's new call sign. "Stand by . . .
three minutes."

One by one the other dragons responded. Six Dragonfly
reentry vehicles, laden with APC landers, hugged the terrain
as they swung into the final approach, skimming scant meters above the boulders and ice whipping past below.
Abruptly, rocks and ice gave way to open water, and the sex-
tet of deadly black skimmers howled over the sea, raising
rooster tails of spray in their sonic-boom footprints.

Ahead, just visible now, the black, conical mountain designated Objective Krakatoa lifted slowly above the horizon.
Following plans logged with their onboard AIs, the shrieking aerospacecraft began weaving back and forth, spreading
out to make themselves harder targets to hit.

Forty kilometers from the target the sky exploded in dazzling, blue-white radiance. Dragonfly Three, touched by that
nova heat, melted away in an instant. Dragonfly Five, jolted
by the blast's shock wave, lost control and struck the water
in a cartwheeling spray of foam and metallic debris.

Damn, he thought. *Not again!*

It just wasn't working. . . .

And then the mountain was rising to meet them, vast and
black and ominous. Dragons One and Two flared nose-high,
dumping forward velocity, then hovering briefly above flash-
blasted rock and cinder, before releasing their saucer-shaped
payloads—"personnel deployment packages" in mil-speak.
Dragons Four and Six howled low overhead, reaching farther
up the mountain slope before settling with their PDPs.

Each saucer lander, cradled in the gap behind the Dragonfly's bulging nose and intakes and the tail-boom mounted
rear plasma thrusters, carried a section of twenty-five
Marines and their equipment—two to a fifty-man platoon.
The Marines, strapped into wire-basket shock frames, were
jolted hard back and forth within their harnesses as the
saucers plowed into the burned-over side of the mountain.

Then the pilot AIs released the harnesses and cracked

open the side hatchways, and the Marines spilled out into the dim red twilight of Ishtar.

Warhurst followed, though his proper post was the HQ command center in Dragon One's lander. They'd already lost, and there was no sense in continuing. . . .

"End program," he called, and in a flicker of blurred motion the towering mountain, the red and purple sky, the charging Marines, all vanished, and he was again in the simulation couch in his office on Deck One, Hab Three, of the IST *Derna*.

The simulated attack had failed the moment he'd lost a third of his assault team to Krakatoa's searing, antimatter-powered beam.

"You should have continued the assault, Martin," Major Anderson's voice said over his link. "You might have learned something."

"I really don't care to get killed again, Major," he said. "Neither do my people. That sort of thing can't be good for morale."

Actually, he was more concerned with his troops picking up careless habits than about poor morale. Losing your life in a VR simulation like this one was no worse than losing a game sim, but Warhurst wondered if too much reliance on painless simulations led to Marines taking chances on the battlefields of the real world . . . chances that could leave them dead and jeopardize a critical mission.

"So what happened?" Colonel Ramsey asked over the link.

"Same as before, Colonel. We lost two of the Dragonflies going in. We can't take that whole damned mountain with only a hundred Marines."

"Mmm. And we won't have the resources to use human wave tactics. The troops *or* the equipment."

"No, sir," Warhurst replied. Colonel Ramsey wasn't serious about human wave tactics, of course. Marine tactical doctrine emphasized finesse rather than brute force. Ramsey was gently pointing out that this particular tactical problem was not one that could be solved by throwing more troops at it.

"Recommendations?"

"Hard to make any, sir, since we don't really know what to expect. But if these worst-case scenarios prove out, then we're screwed. We need to hit Objective Krakatoa with at least two full companies to be sure of getting through with one."

The only information they had about the An planetary defense weapon had been based on the account FTL-transmitted by a young Marine at the New Sumer compound moments before it was overrun by the An rebel forces. They knew that the An facility, hidden in the mountain they called An-Kur, could shoot down a spacecraft in orbit, and that it could shift the aim of the beam by as much as ten degrees out of the vertical to aim at a specific target.

Could that beam be aimed at a target hugging the surface of Ishtar only a few kilometers away, as well as claw star-ships out of orbit? No one knew. Was the beam generated, as most analyses suggested, by matter-antimatter interaction? Pure conjecture, based on the fact that no one knew of another energy source with the same star-hot output. Was there a recycle time on the beam, meaning a force could slip in after it fired once, while it was still recharging? No one knew. So far as anyone on Earth was aware, the An-Kur beam had fired exactly once. Hell, there was a possibility that the thing was a one-shot weapon, like the old X-ray laser technique that used the detonation of a nuclear weapon to generate the needed X rays, destroying the gun as it fired. The Marines might get to Objective Krakatoa and find nothing left there but a ten-year-old glass-bottomed crater.

But they couldn't count on that, not with so much riding on the question.

Damn it all! How the hell was he supposed to train himself and his company for an assault when next to nothing was known about the target?

Warhurst's stomach rumbled, and he realized again how hungry he was. He didn't notice it when he was in sim, but once he was back in the real world, he wanted to *eat,* and he didn't care what his implants told him he was supposed to feel. This fasting business, he thought, was strictly for the religious fanatics. The thought made him smile, though. He was going to get to see the An in person, which was more than most of Earth's fanatics could hope for, whether they were with the Human Dignity League or the Anist Creators Church.

He just wished he didn't have to starve to do it.

Warhurst covered his face with his hands, thinking. "Okay," he said at last. "If I only have one company, that's all I have. The best approach we've tried was Scenario Five. We only lost one Dragonfly that way. Splitting up over the horizon and angling in from all directions is bound to scatter the enemy's defenses somewhat and may keep our casualties down. The only other possible approach is to land farther out and make the approach on foot."

"Which runs up against the time problem," Anderson put in.

"Agreed."

"I'd throw in a tactical reserve if we had one," Ramsey said, thoughtful. "But we're stretched way too thin as it is. Trying to invade a whole damned planet with twelve hundred Marines . . . it's like trying to empty the ocean with a bucket. We just don't have the assets to spare, in personnel or in logistical transport."

"Don't I know it. I've been thinking about this lots, Colonel. If my people don't take Krakatoa, we're pretty much screwed no matter what . . . unless the whole thing is a paper tiger anyway. And I'm not betting the farm on that possibility."

"Nor am I, Martin. Nor am I. Doesn't make sense to turn a mountain into a gun that's only good for one shot."

"Unless, of course, they have *lots* of mountains around New Sumer, each with its own superpopgun," Anderson said.

"Lovely thought," Ramsey told her. "I'll recommend you for command of the World Pessimists Legion."

"No thanks. I probably wouldn't like that."

"Fortunately," Ramsey said, "there's no indication of more than one planetary defense element. We have to start somewhere, and the Chiefs of Staff are starting this one with the assumption that we have one target—An-Kur—and that the An aren't going to be too eager to point that devastating a weapon at anything below their own horizon. Tell you what. We go with Scenario Five. I'll cut back on the first ground assault at New Sumer by . . . make it two Dragonflies. That's one more platoon. We'll treat Black Dragon as a reinforced company of four platoons. How's that sound?"

"Best we can do, I guess," Warhurst agreed. "Thank you, sir."

"Not a problem. It's my job to make your life and career a living hell. How'm I doing?"

"Quite well, actually. I'm impressed."

"Glad to know we're all doing what we're best at. Okay, Major Anderson and I have to split for a senior staff meeting. Do you need anything more from us?"

"A steak would be nice, Colonel. Rare. With onions."

"You'll have to wait twenty years for that, Captain, but I'm sure it can be arranged when we get back home. Talk to you later."

And the voices in his head were gone.

So . . . not as good as he'd hoped, but better than he'd feared. Hitting Krakatoa with eight Dragonflies instead of six was a little better, anyway. The worst part of the whole situation was the fact that his company included so many relatively inexperienced men and women, the newbies coming out of the past month's crop at Parris Island. The assault on An-Kur was not something he wanted to throw unseasoned people into, not if the idea was to keep down casualties.

But Captain Warhurst was a Marine. He made do with what he was given. Or with what he could steal . . .

Stomach still growling, he linked into Cassius in order to begin working on a rewritten TO&E for the Black Dragon assault.

Hab 3, Deck 1, IST Derna
Orbital Construction Facility 1, L-4
1430 hours Zulu

The virtual meeting space had the look and feel of a large,
Earthside conference room, complete with chairs, American
flag, and a floor-to-ceiling viewall currently set for the GlobalNet Evening news. In the virtual reality unfolding within
his mind, Colonel Ramsey leaned back in one of the glider
chairs at the table, watching the broadcast with the dozen or
so other people in the room.

"Yes, Kate," an earnest-looking reporter said, staring into
the pickup. "Here at New York City's Liberty Plaza, enthusiasm is building for the imminent launch of Operation Spirit
of Humankind, the relief expedition to the world of Ishtar.
Folks have been gathering here for the past twenty-four
hours to show their solidarity with the American forces who
will be departing our Solar system soon, bound for the world
of another star."

At the reporter's back a vast throng of demonstrators
carrying torches sang beneath the reflected glare of floater
lights. Liberty Plaza was a broad, sweeping esplanade built
fifty years earlier to raise the Statue of Liberty above the
slowly encroaching waters of the Upper Bay. The plaza was
filled now with demonstrators, picked up by a far-flung array
of hovering cameras as scene followed scene. Batteries of
powerful, ground-mounted searchlights beamed the reflective floaters a hundred meters up, which scattered a frosty,
blue-white radiance across a veritable sea of singing, chanting, swaying people. In the distance, across the bay, the vast
and translucent city dome of lower Manhattan shone like an
enormous, iridescent pearl in the ghostly glow, as arc lights
sent slender needles of white radiance vertically into the
night sky.

*"Let my people go! Let my people go! Let my people
go! . . ."* The background chanting rose and fell, a muted
thunder of thousands of voices. An enormous projection

screen had been raised at the foot of Lady Liberty, high enough to reach above her waist, displaying a view of the *Derna* floating free at L-4 against a background dusting of stars.

"Satellites counting the crowd here tell us over sixty thousand people have come to Liberty Plaza tonight to witness the historic departure of the first MIEU, scheduled for some forty hours from now," the reporter was saying. "I don't think these camera images can ever possibly convey the sense of excitement and purpose and sheer dedication displayed here in what must be one of the biggest and grandest parties ever thrown in the Greater New York City area. I'm told that deliveries of food to Liberty Plaza exceed 150 *tons* in the past twenty-four hours alone, delivered by air, by hovercraft, by tunnel. At that, most of the people I've talked to aren't eating and aren't sleeping. They've set their implants to take care of their bodily needs so they can concentrate on what one of the demonstration organizers here called, and I quote, 'A group mind experience that will shake the very walls of reality.' And I have to tell you, Kate, that the atmosphere here is like nothing I've—"

"Screen mute," President LaSalle said, and the reporter's voice fell silent. "You see, General, what we're up against. The political repercussions of further delay in this project could be devastating."

General King nodded. "Yes, ma'am."

"This whole thing is wildly out of hand. All of the different religious factions are at each other's throats, either hailing the An as gods or attacking them as demons. And everyone who isn't working to start a new round of religious wars is marching or demonstrating for a crusade to free the slaves on Ishtar. And in addition to all of that, we have the second relief mission being assembled at L-5. They're breathing down our necks right now. So . . . tell me again, in words that I can understand . . . why the new delay?"

General King glanced at Ramsey before answering, then across the table at Admiral Vincent Hartman, who would be commanding the naval assets of the mission. "Madam President . . . the cybernetic hibernation personnel on board the *Derna* are just running too far behind sched. They can only put people into hibernation so fast, you know. And more Marines keep arriving, making for extremely crowded conditions. It's . . . well, it's pretty chaotic up there."

Which was something of an understatement, Ramsey thought, even though King hadn't yet been physically on board the ship. Things *were* chaotic. With crowding, heat, and tempers all rising, there'd been four fights on the lower decks already, and it was only a matter of time before someone got hurt or threw a punch that could not be ignored or downplayed by the officers.

"What can be done to speed things up?" General Gabriowski said. He looked at the President. "If things slip much further, the Europeans and Brazilians will beat us to Ishtar. Then *they'll* dictate to *us* how things are played."

"Unacceptable," LaSalle said. She looked at Ramsey. "Colonel? The bottleneck seems to be in your backyard. What do you propose?"

"Madam President—" He stopped, suddenly uncomfortable. There *was* something that could be done, but he'd been putting off suggesting it. It would be hard on the men, especially the newer ones.

"Go on, Colonel," Gabriowski told him.

"Yes, sir. Madam President, there are still about four hundred Marines on Earth, waiting for passage up to L-4. One reason they're not moving faster is that the D-480s—the personnel transfer shuttles we've been using—can only carry thirty people at a time, and they have a long turnaround time on the ground."

"You can't blame the Navy for that," Vice Admiral Cardegriff put in. Cardegriff was the Navy's representative on the Joint Chiefs, and a senior member of the National Security Council. His word hauled a *lot* of mass.

"No, sir. The Navy's been doing all that's expected, and a hell of a lot more. But we might be able to speed things sig-

nificantly by putting the Marines straight into cybehibe on
the ground and shipping them up as cargo."

"As cargo, Colonel?" President LaSalle said. "That seems
a bit . . . indelicate."

"Marines aren't exactly what you would call 'delicate,'
ma'am. I've been looking at this for a while now, wondering
if we'd need to go this way. With more technicians and
more room on the ground, we can pop out people into hibernation a lot faster than we can at L-4. They've been on
their diets now for several days already and getting the preliminary nano injections, so we can start processing them
through pretty quick. Best of all, they can be loaded straight
into their cells on the *Derna* once they stop the hab rotation.
Zero g'll make things a hell of a lot easier. And they won't
be using consumables—water and air, mostly—if they're
hibernating."

"You don't sound happy about it, Colonel."

"No, Madam President. I'm not. Most of those four hundred Marines are fresh out of recruit training. I was hoping to
start them on simulation combat training once they reached
the *Derna* and were waiting to be dropped into hibe. Besides,
it's kind of a dirty trick to pull on them, shipping them up
like slabs of frozen meat. I imagine a lot of them are looking
forward to the flight up, and now they're going to miss it."

"I'll remind you, Colonel," Gabriowski said, "that this is
the Corps we're talking about, not a travel agency. These
people didn't sign on for a scenic tour."

"No, sir."

"How fast can you do it?"

Ramsey already had the figures stored in his implant.
"Here's the data," he told them. "The short story is that we
can have them all aboard within the next five days. If we
wait for the D-480s, it'll be another nine days before they're
all aboard, and it will be at least two weeks after that before
the last of them are in cybehibe."

"I don't think we have much choice," the President said.
"Do you?"

"No, ma'am."

"Then do it. Do what you have to to get the *Derna* under way within the next week. That's October sixteenth at the latest. *At the latest.* Am I clear?"

"Clear, ma'am."

"Very well. Keep me informed of further developments." And the President of the United Federal Republic vanished from the conference room.

"Dismissed, gentlemen," Admiral Cardegriff said. And the fiction of the conference room faded from Ramsey's awareness.

He was back on board the *Derna*, lying back in his VR couch.

His people weren't going to like this. Not the section leaders who needed to see to it that everyone was up to speed on the training sims. Not the logistics personnel, who were looking forward to the use of a few hundred more backs to help shift cargo into *Derna*'s holds. And not the men and women themselves, who were going to be taken by surprise by this change. Marines were creatures of habit that never liked unexpected change.

How in all of the hells of the Corps was he going to break this to them?

14

INTERLUDE

IST Derna
En route to Llalande 21185 IID

Launch . . .

The trio of starships, IST *Derna* and the two cargo ships
ISC *Regulus* and ISC *Algol*, drifted at L-4 well clear of the
building docks and the *Vesuvius* AM complex. Because AM-
enhanced fusion torch exhaust consisted of *very* high-energy
particles, their torches would not be lit until they were well
clear of heavily trafficked regions of the inner Solar system.
Instead, each was attached to one of the new Cerberus-class
tugs, massive, blocky-looking nuclear-chemical workhorses
with fifty million kilograms of thrust apiece.

Derna's centrifuge rotation had already been stopped and
her three hab modules folded back against her spine as loading work continued in microgravity. The last of *Derna*'s passengers arrived on board already in cybernetic hibernation
and were transferred with the last few hundreds of tons of
equipment and supplies. Meanwhile, cybehibe techs on
board processed the last of the MIEU's waking personnel—
Colonel Ramsey and members of the unit's command constellation—and hooked them into the ship's nanocybernetic
suspension system.

Algol and *Regulus*, unmanned vessels both, were already
cleared for launch.

Across the world a half million kilometers away, humankind seemed to watch with an indrawn psychic breath. Manned expeditions to the stars had been boosting outsystem for fifty years but always on missions strictly limited to science and diplomacy. The Smithsonian archeological expeditions to Chiron at Alpha Centauri and Volos at Barnard's Star, the diplomatic and science legation at Ishtar, and the science missions at Thor and Kali had all been deployed to the stars on strictly peaceful missions. Now, for the first time, humankind was going to the stars armed and armored for war.

Derna's complement of 145 naval personnel remained awake, monitoring the prefire and launch systems, but the launch itself was handled entirely by the onboard AI, unofficially known as "Bruce." The countdown, which had been running now for days, trickled down at last to zero, and the main engines of the three Cerberus tugs flared white-hot.

Fifty thousand tons of thrust seemed barely to nudge the giant starships, but the acceleration, which lasted for all of five minutes, was enough to nudge the trio off-station and start them in a long half-million-kilometer fall toward the Earth.

In Washington, D.C., President LaSalle delivered a speech proclaiming the need to safeguard human life and interests at Ishtar, emphasizing that Operation Spirit of Humankind was not a mission of vengeance or retaliation but one of rescue and recovery.

Elsewhere, riots flared into what amounted to open warfare, as devotees of the An-creator gods battled with the legions of Earth First and traditional religious forces. The Catholic world, already sundered a generation earlier by the election of the Papessa Mary to the seat of St. Peter at the Holy See, was shattered by pitched battles in Asuncion and Ciudad de Mejico, in Madrid and Paris, in Roma, Manila, and even in the suburbs of Boston. The Papessa, in the Vatican, called for a holy crusade to free the human Sag-ura slaves held on Ishtar and to prove once and for all that the

An were neither gods not angelic creative spirits acting as
God's agents. Pope Michael at the Counter-Vatican in Lausanne preached crusade against those who would deliberately bury the scientific evidence that humankind had been
created by agencies from the stars, and urged a dialogue
with the An to reveal at long last the Hidden Truth.

Radical militant Anists, meanwhile, attacked both
branches of the Church, calling for a return of man to his
rightful place at the feet of the wise and powerful Universal
Creators. Anist-led riots in Munich, Belgrade, and Los Angeles killed thousands. The battle in South Los Angeles
alone claimed 918 lives, and the burning of both Catholic
and Counter-Catholic churches triggered a wave of pro-
Aztlan, antigringo demonstrations and rioting.

Four days later *Derna, Algol,* and *Regulus*, still in close
formation and with the Cerberus tugs detached, whipped
past the Earth in a hyperbolic trajectory, accelerated by
gravity. Ten days after that, as the trio hustled outbound past
the ten-million-kilometer mark, the main drives cut in.
Minute quantities of antimatter were fed into the hydrogen
slush entering the aft thruster reaction chambers, triggering
a pulsing chain of fusion explosions at a rate of eight per
second, each one contained, then expelled by powerful magnetic fields. Thrust built steadily until the starships were accelerating at ten meters per second per second, just a nudge
more than one g.

Riding nova flares of incandescence hot with gamma radiation in the 511 keV band of positron annihilation, *Derna,
Algol,* and *Regulus* accelerated out-system. Four and a half
days later, traveling now at four thousand kilometers per
second, they hurtled past the south pole of Jupiter, using that
giant planet's gravity for a second slingshot acceleration and
to swing onto a new course, high up above the Solar ecliptic.
They were aimed now at right ascension eleven hours,
thirty-seven seconds, declination +36 degrees 18.3 minutes . . . in the southern reaches of the constellation Ursa
Major.

Three months after 1 MIEU's departure a second, larger military force departed from the shipyards at L-5. Built around the ISTs *Soares Dutra* and *Jules Verne*, and the cargo vessels *L'Esperance, Sternwind,* and *Teshio Maru*, the International Interstellar Relief Expedition, as it was now called, followed a similar outbound course, picking up a gravitational assist from Earth and then another, stronger boost from Jupiter as they hurtled together into the interstellar night.

Eleven months after launch the three ships of 1 MIEU were traveling at just beneath the speed of light, fast enough that time itself had slowed to a crawl. The Navy crew on board *Derna* had by then joined their Marine passengers in cybehibe, and the operation that followed was carried out entirely by the ships' AIs. Together to the millisecond, the AM drives cut off and the starships fell through an interstellar void strangely distorted by their velocity, with the entire sky appearing to be crowded ahead of their mushroom-cap prows in a doughnut-shaped smear of starlight. Thanks to time dilation, a week of shipboard time was the equivalent of over two months on Earth.

In the outside universe, time continued in its normal fashion. President LaSalle, battered by the politics of secession in the Southwest, lost the election of '40 to John Marshal Cabot, a Boston Neodemocrat who rejected military intervention in Mejico, favored adoption of AI metacontrol of the World Bank, and advocated peaceful negotiations with the Ahannu. The MIEU flotilla by that time, however, was over half a light-year away, well beyond the range of any normal-space communications net. New orders, if any, would have to be relayed to the Marines via the FTL Pyramid of the Eye, if and when they were able to retake it.

In fact, the Cabot administration made no official announcement of policy changes in regard to the Llalande situation. Much could still happen, both at Ishtar and back on Earth. Besides, the poll numbers did not lie. Americans still favored freeing the Ishtaran slaves, and by a whopping majority of seventy-three percent.

Perhaps because he maintained a low political profile so far as the Llalande situation was concerned, Cabot was reelected by a narrow margin in '44. The World Bank Crisis of '45 and the resultant financial crash led to calls for an end to extrasolar adventurism. In fact, the archeological outposts on Chiron, Kali, and Thor were abandoned as funding for them dried up Earthside. Nothing could be done about the expeditions already outbound, however. The MIEU and the Isis Expedition to Sirius were both five light-years out, traveling in nearly opposite directions, both utterly beyond the hope of recall.

Besides, the American public still favored freeing the slaves on Ishtar, by a majority of fifty-eight percent.

On board the *Derna*, the Marines remained unaware of such political niceties, so deeply asleep now that even dreams were banished. The air within their sleep cells was chilled to a constant five degrees Celsius, just warm enough to prevent tissue damage from ice formation.

Meanwhile, the United Federal Republic found itself fighting three nasty little wars, in South China, in New Liberia, and in Nicaragua. In 2146 the situation in Egypt, never wholly settled, exploded into the Great Jihad War, with the EU and the UFR against the Kingdom of Allah. What began as a battle to save world cultural treasures in Egypt swiftly devolved into all-out religious war, with Anists and various antislavery factions in uneasy alliance against the rabidly anti-Anist Islamic militants. The Giza Plateau remained secure in western hands once French, Ukrainian, German, and British commandos took Cairo, but the fighting merely spread to Pakistan, Indonesia, Morocco, and Turkey. Some netnews reporters began calling the conflagration a new world war. Elements of the 1st Marines were committed to fighting in Indonesia and, a year later, in the Philippines. Other Marine units reported to the moon,

Mars, and Jupiter space to protect various xenoarcheological sites, including the Singer in the icy embrace of Europa. The Kingdom of Allah had minimal space capability, but the threat of infiltration and sabotage was thought to be serious.

Perhaps because of the seriousness of the military situation on Earth, interest in the MIEU was waning fast. In October of 2146, a netnews poll reported that only four percent of Americans now favored military intervention at Ishtar. Nearly ten percent felt that the expedition should refuel and return to Earth as soon as it reached the Llalande system, without even awakening the sleeping Marines.

By the middle of 2147 the Great Jihad War had officially been elevated in status to World War V, at least by the various news media. Opinion polls indicated that forty-one percent of Americans now favored military intervention in An affairs and that, significantly, seventy-three percent admitted to strong anti-An political or religious views. Some thirty-one percent felt that negotiation with the An was the better way to go, a figure that had doubled in the past ten years; almost twenty percent were unaware that human slaves were held by the An, and twenty-eight percent more knew but didn't care. In July, President Cabot called an emergency cabinet meeting to discuss the fact that a military mission was entering an alien star system intent on waging a war that no longer enjoyed a broad base of popular support at home. The only agreement reached was that the greatest threat to the mission now was the International Interstellar Relief Expedition six months behind the *Derna*. The troops on board included both KOA and anti-An Traditional Catholic forces from Brazil. They might well pose a greater threat to the Marines than the An, now that they were enemies in the world war raging back home. A full briefing was prepared, both for standard radio transmission and for FTL relay through the Cydonian facility on Mars.

The question was when—and if—the Marines would get the word, and whether the enemy troops in the IIRE, who would also have access to the FTL site at New Sumer's

Pyramid of the Eye, would learn of their change in status first.

Eight light-years away, the *Derna, Algol,* and *Regulus* all had spun end for end, folded their hab modules, and refired their AM drives. Backing down the acceleration curve, now, they were less than half a light-year from their destination. This was, arguably, the most dangerous point of the flight. For three years of shipboard time the crew and passengers of the *Derna* had been protected from high-energy impacts by the vast bulk of the reaction mass storage tank forward. Now, though, with the AM drives pointed at the destination and with the craft still moving at close to *c*, the hab modules were exposed to stray bits of matter incoming at relativistic speeds. The drive flare itself, together with the magnetic fields used to focus the exhaust plume, was *supposed* to clear the way, but the technique was still highly experimental. Inflatable balyuts—a doughnut of balloons filled with water—unfurled aft of the hab modules to provide some extra protection, but mission experts on Earth could only cross figurative fingers and wonder what was happening. *Derna* should be slowing now, but they wouldn't know about it on Earth until either the Pyramid of the Eye was recaptured intact or a radio signal made it back to Earth in another eight and a half years.

The Marines remained asleep, though by now *Derna*'s medical AI had begun warming the sleep cells slowly to body temperature, as nano injections prepped their brains for reawakening. The Navy crew would be revived first. They'd been lucky on this passage; out of 145 naval personnel, only seven had failed to survive the trip.

By March 2148 the *Derna* and her escorts were falling into the Llalande system, still decelerating at one g. Drives were focused to initiate end-course corrections that would bring the trio of vessels into Marduk space. Potential disaster was averted when *Algol*'s ship AI failed to make the necessary course changes; high-speed particles had degraded elements of *Algol*'s navigational software, deleting key commands. *Derna*'s crew transmitted software patches over the laser communications link, however, and brought the cargo vessel back onto the proper course.

Derna, meanwhile, deployed twenty-five Argus probes—robot fliers cocooned inside ceramic-sheathed TAV transport modules. They would arrive at the objective days ahead of the hard-decelerating starships.

Another month passed, and giant Marduk loomed huge beyond the flaring drive plumes of the slowing ships. The end-course corrections had in part been designed to bring the vessels in a long, looping passage across Marduk's day side, burning off the last of their excess velocity in an aerobraking maneuver that slung them into a tight, hard loop back into deep space, then back on an infalling path toward Ishtar's night side. The drives switched off and the hab modules extended and began rotating, generating one g of spin gravity in the outer decks.

And on the 24th of June, 2148 by Earth time, but only a bit more than four years after launch by shipboard time, the first of *Derna*'s Marine passengers began waking up.

Deck 3, Hab 3, IST Derna
12 million kilometers from Ishtar
0950 hours ST (Shipboard Time)

Strange thoughts and images flooded Garroway's brain. *I thought we weren't supposed to dream*, he thought, struggling against a thick, hot, and oppressive sense of drowning. He'd been falling . . . falling . . . falling among myriad stars toward a dazzling red beacon at the bottom of an infinitely deep well. The beacon was growing brighter with each passing moment, but somehow he never seemed to reach it. . . .

The strangling sensation grew sharper, and then he was awake, coughing and gasping, struggling to clear his lungs of a viscous jelly plugging nose and mouth and windpipe. He gave a final convulsive cough and hit his head against the roof of his cell. It took him a few moments to connect with where he was. His last memories were of the processing center at Seven Palms, of being led into a cavernous room with perhaps half of his graduating boot company, of being ordered to remove all clothing, jewelry, and personal adornments and log them in with a clerk, of lying down on a thin mattress on a hard, narrow metal slab that made him think about morgues and autopsies. A voice had been talking to him through his implant, having him count backward from one hundred. And then . . .

His arm burned slightly, and a robotic injector arm withdrew into a side compartment. "Lie still and breathe deeply," a voice told him. "Do not try to leave your cell. A transition medical team will be with you momentarily."

He was aware now of more and more sensations, of a growing light in his sleep cell, of the feeling of weakness pervading every muscle of his body, of the warm and wet stickiness of some kind of gel melting beneath his hips and back, of ravenous hunger in the pit of his belly, of the incredible *stink* filling the coffin-sized compartment. Goddess, what kind of hell was he awakening to?

Struggling against a paralyzing weakness, he managed to roll onto his left elbow and found he could breathe a bit more easily than he could while flat on his back. His shrunken stomach rebelled then and he tried to vomit, but his retching produced only more of the all-pervasive jelly, a kind of translucent slime mingled with white foam.

Abruptly, the end of his sleep cell cracked open with a sharp hiss, and his pallet slid partway out into the hab compartment. After the claustrophobic confines of the cell, the open space of the hab deck was dizzying.

Two Marines in utility fatigues, a man and a woman, peered down at him. "How ya doin', Mac?" the woman asked him. "What's your name?"

"Garroway," he replied automatically. "John. Recruit private, serial number 19283-336—"

"He checks," the man said. "He's tracking."

The woman patted his shoulder. "Hang in there, Marine. Welcome to 2148."

The two moved away then, edging along a walkway hugging the face of the hab module bulkhead to the next open sleep cell in line.

Garroway tried to make sense of the confused thoughts clogging a brain that simply wasn't working yet. What, he wondered, had gone wrong? They'd all been told that there'd been a change of plan, that they were to enter cybehibe while still on the ground. The compartment looked like the interior of a fairly large hab module. Was he still on Earth? Or was he on the transport, and something had gone wrong while putting him under?

No . . . no, one of the Marines had said something . . . had it been *Welcome to 2148*?

Realization washed over him, leaving him feeling cold and dizzy. Somehow, in the time between when he'd been counting backward on that pallet in Seven Palms and now, ten years had slipped away. He sagged back down on his pallet, working to assimilate that one small bit of overwhelming information.

Ten years. What had happened during that time to his mother . . . to Lynnley . . . to Earth herself?

And did that mean . . .

Urgently, he thought-clicked, opening his cerebral implant. The link must be working; he'd heard a voice a few moments ago telling him to stay put.

"Link," he thought. "Query. Navigational data."

"Please wait," the voice said in his mind. "The system is busy."

Well, that made sense. If a whole transport-load of Marines was waking up around him, they must be accessing the onboard AI pretty heavily. Even a shipboard intelligence like the one running the *Derna* would have a bit of trouble processing twelve hundred simultaneous requests for data.

He waited for nearly five minutes by his internal clock before the voice said, "Navigational data now open, Private. This is Cassius speaking."

"Cassius. Did we make it?" he asked aloud. "Are we at Llalande?"

"The *Derna* crossed the arbitrary astronomical delineation of the Llalande 21185 system 2,200 hours ago," the voice told him, "and is currently slightly less than twelve million kilometers from the objective world of Ishtar."

A diagram unfolded within his mind, showing the MIEU's inbound course as a blue line drawing itself across the black backdrop of space. Llalande 21185 was a bright red point of light along the way, and Garroway thought he knew now where the half-forgotten dream imagery of a red beacon had come from. He saw how the *Derna* and her consorts had already looped past giant Marduk and were falling now back toward the miniature solar system that was Marduk and its whirling collection of moons. Snatches of alphanumerics floating next to the ship symbols showed the flotilla's velocity and delta V.

"How come I was able to see that red star in my dreams?" he asked, suddenly curious.

"The human mind seems designed to extract information from its surroundings, no matter what the circumstances," Cassius replied. "A number of Marines in the MIEU have reported dream imagery that appears to have leaked across the data interface with the ship navigational AI. This does not appear to represent a problem or a fault in the nanoimplant hardware. Is there another question?"

"How—How long until we debark?"

"H-hour for the main assault group has yet to be determined. The special assault task force code-named Dragon will be debarking in twenty-two hours, fifteen minutes. Debarkation of the main force will depend at least partly on the success of the special task force. Is there another question?"

"Uh . . . I guess not." He felt the connection in his head go empty.

He knew he'd been assigned to TF Dragon. They'd told him as much during his final briefing on Earth. But he didn't know anything about the mission or what was expected of him, didn't know most of these people, didn't even know who his commanding officer was.

He felt very much alone, very much lost.

"Those of you who can move, shake a leg!" someone bellowed from the deck below. "C'mon, you squirrels! Out of your trees! That's reveille, reveille, reveille! All hands on deck!"

The familiar litany galvanized Garroway into movement. He still felt sluggish, and every muscle in his body ached, but he was able to sit up on his pallet, sling his legs over the side, and find the nearest set of rungs set into the bulkhead, allowing him to shakily climb down to the deck.

Dozens of Marines were already there, talking, standing, sitting, exercising in a tangled press of nude bodies. A line had already formed in front of the shower cell, a passageway in the bulkhead leading through to the shower head and dry compartment and back out again to the main deck. Others were gathering in front of the chow dispensers, accepting with grumbling ill grace the squeeze tubes of lightly flavored paste that would be their food for the next several days, until their digestive systems got used to the sensations of dealing with real food once more.

Garroway wrestled for a moment with the choice . . . clean or food? His body was coated with a thin, slick film of mingled sweat and the residue from the support gel he'd been lying in for the past decade, and he felt as though he were choking on his own stink. But at the same time his stomach was twisting and growling in spite of the punishment it had just taken. Food, he thought after a moment. He needed food more.

"All personnel with last names beginning A through M will fall in for showers," the voice in his head said. "Personnel N through Z will report for chow."

Yeah, figures. The Corps likes to run every detail of your life, he thought with a wry inner shrug. And no matter what you wanted, the Corps would tell you to do something else.

In a way, though, it was pleasant to have someone tell him what to do, even if the someone was only a disembodied voice in his head. He was still feeling a bit muzzy, like he'd just awakened after a night of pretty heavy drinking, and didn't entirely trust his own thought processes.

"Haven't seen you around," a muscular, naked man told him as he stepped into the shower queue. "Newbie?"

"Yeah," he admitted. "Company 1099."

"Don't mean shit here," the man said. "You're 1st Marine Div now. How'dja make out on the pool?"

"Pool?"

"Yeah. The death-watch pool."

"Don't pay any mind to this shithead," a flat-chested woman in line behind Garroway said. "Some of these jack-offs think it's cute to run a pool on how many people don't survive cybehibe. Everybody puts in five a share and picks a number. The closer your number is to the CH attrition, the more money you get."

"What'd you win, Kris? Zip, as per SOP?"

"Ten newdollars profit."

"Eat shit, Staff Sergeant. Twenty-five."

"Screw you."

"Your place or mine?"

"Wait a second," Garroway said, breaking into the exchange. "You're saying people died during the passage?"

"Sure," the man said. "Whadja expect?"

"Thirty-seven Marines didn't make it," the woman said. "Three percent attrition. That's actually not that fucking bad. Sometime's it's as high as five."

"Hey. One cybehibe passage to Europa lost twelve out of sixty," the man said with infuriating nonchalance. "One out of five. That was a real tech-fuck."

Garroway felt as though a cold draft had brushed the back of his neck. He'd not realized that nanotechnic hibernation was that much of a crapshoot.

"Stop it, Schuster," the woman said. "You're scaring the kid." She extended her hand. "Staff Sergeant Ostergaard," she told him. "The jackoff in front of you is Sergeant Schuster, and don't let him get to you, he's a teddy bear. Welcome to the Fighting 44th."

"Sir, thank you, sir. Recruit Private Garroway."

"Don't sir me," Ostergaard told him. "I work for a living."

"You can drop the boot camp crap, kid," Schuster added. "Officers are 'sir.' NCOs are addressed by rank or last name. The quicker you stop sirring everything that moves, the quicker you'll fit in."

"Aye aye, s—uh, Sergeant."

"That's better. You're not 'recruit private' anymore, either. You're a private first class now, unless they Van Winkle you."

"Van Winkle? What's that?"

"Promote you on the basis of your time served subjective," Ostergaard said.

"Objectively," Schuster told him, "you've been in the Corps ten years. Subjectively, you've been in for four, even though you were asleep for most of that time. Can't have a PFC with four-slash-ten years in. Looks real crappy on his service record."

Garroway remembered downloading that information in boot camp . . . hell, it seemed like a month ago. It *had* been a month ago, so far as his waking mind was concerned. This was going to take some getting used to.

"So I might have gotten a promotion already?"

Ostergaard shrugged. "You'll just have to wait and see what the brass hats say. But . . . you know? Out here rank isn't quite as important as they made it out to be back at Camp Lejeune."

"Heresy," Schuster said.

"S'truth. Way out here? The Corps is more like family than military."

The line moved forward enough that the three were able at last to file through the shower area, bombarded by water and by ultrasonic pulses that melted the accreted slime from their bodies. Hot air let them dry without requiring laundry facilities, and by the time they emerged back on the Hab Module deck, a laser sizer and uniform dispenser had been set up and was cranking out disposable OD utilities. The food paste tasted like . . . well, Garroway thought, like food paste, but it staunched the hunger pangs and helped him begin to feel more human.

Which was important. It was slowly starting to dawn on him that he was eight light-years from home, twelve from Lynnley, surrounded by strangers . . . and utterly unsure of his chances of survival over the next twenty-four hours.

Somehow, as thorough and rigorous as boot camp had been, it hadn't prepared him for this—a devastating loneliness mingled with soul-searing fear.

15

Lander Dragon One
Approaching Ishtar
1312 hours ST

". . . and *four* . . . and *three* . . . and *two* . . . and *one* . . . release!"

A surge of acceleration pinned Captain Warhurst against his seat as powerful magnetic fields flung the TAL-S Dragonfly clear of the vast, flat underbelly of *Derna*'s reaction mass tank and into empty space. Seven additional Dragonflies, each with its attached lander, drifted out from the transport's docking bays at the same moment, the formation perfectly symmetrical with *Derna* at the center. *Derna*'s massive AM drive had been shut down, since the gamma emissions from matter-antimatter annihilation would have fried the landers and all on board.

Long minutes passed, and the landers continued to pace the *Derna*, sharing with the huge transport her current velocity toward the planet ahead. Once the landers were well clear of the deadly kill zone of *Derna*'s AM drive venturi, the transport and her two consorts again triggered their drives, continuing to decelerate.

From the point of view of the eight landers, *Derna*, *Algol*, and *Regulus* appeared to be accelerating back the way they'd come at ten meters per second per second. In free fall, the

Dragonflies hurtled toward the looming curve of the planet, now some two million kilometers ahead.

Dragon One's microfusion plasma thrusters kicked in as the craft pirouetted into its proper alignment, accelerating. They would hit Ishtar's atmosphere six hours before the transports decelerated into orbit, a critical timing element of the Krakatoa mission.

Still strapped immobile in his seat, encased in his Mark VII armor and with his LR-2120 clipped to its carry mount on his front torso, Warhurst closed his eyes and reviewed the op program.

"D-day, the sixth of June 1944," the voice of General King echoed in his noumenal reality, a replay of the general's address of some hours before. "The Allied invasion forces were threatened by massive shore battery emplacements at Pointe du Hoc, west of Omaha Beach. Elements of the U.S. Army Rangers assaulted the battery from the sea, scaling forty-meter cliffs with mortar-fired grapnels trailing climbing ladders and ropes."

In his noumenal display Warhurst could see the grainy, black-and-white images of historical documentary films, showing primitively clad soldiers climbing sheer cliffs from tiny, tin-box boats bobbing in the surf at the base of the rocks as King's voice droned on.

"After a fierce firefight at the top of the cliffs, with opposing forces at times only meters apart, the Rangers overran the position, suffering heavy casualties in the process. Their heroism and dedication to achieving their mission were in no way lessened by the fact that the shore batteries thought to have been mounted at Pointe du Hoc had, in fact, been removed. The gun emplacements were empty."

One of the great minor ironies of military history, Garroway thought, but not the sort of thing to inspire the troops before the big fight. Marines liked to think their actions counted for something.

"Objective Krakatoa is very much of a stripe with the

Pointe du Hoc shore batteries," King's voice went on. The image unfolding in Warhurst's noumenon showed the mountain, An-Kur, seen from the air by computer imagery. "Since it has been ten years objective since the planetary defense batteries within that mountain fired, we can hope the facility has been abandoned or fallen into disrepair. The modern Ahannu do not possess the technological prowess of their ancient ancestors."

And that, Warhurst thought, was a royal load of crap. Whatever else you said about the An of ten thousand years ago, they built their machines and tools to *last*. The likelihood of the An-Kur facility being a one-shot weapon was so remote as to be practically invisible. Certainly, the Marine assault team wasn't going to bet the farm on the possibility.

The recitation finally reached the part of the record he was interested in. He could have fast-forwarded through the recorded memories, but he'd wanted to marvel again at King's clumsy exhortation.

All too little was known about the objective, save what had been gleaned from orbit by mapping satellites. Two point heat sources were known, one near the peak, the other on the mountain's east slope, about one-third of the way up from the base. The mountain was clearly a natural landform, but one that had been extensively reworked, probably over millennia. The slopes were preternaturally smooth, and terraced in places, with stacked rocks holding back walls of earth. Absolutely nothing was known of the mountain's interior workings, but infrared scans suggested a tunnel complex of considerable extent and in three dimensions, connecting the two hot spots, which were almost certainly entrances of some sort.

Computer analysis of the IR readings had produced a 3D map of the complex. What could not be analyzed or deduced was what might be waiting for them down there. There were some similarities to underground works discovered during the past century on Earth's moon, especially in the Tsiolkovsky Crater site on the lunar far side. Created by An colonizers ten thousand years ago, the Tsiolkovsky complex was thought to be typical of ancient An military defenses, and as such it might hold clues for an assault on An-Kur. Every man in Black Dragon had a complete set of floor plans for both Tsiolkovsky and An-Kur in their Mark VII armor computers.

But . . . was it defended? That remained to be seen. Pointe du Hoc had been an empty emplacement vigorously defended by German troops; perhaps An-Kur was the reverse, a live weapon not defended at all.

Maybe. And maybe pigs could fly without the benefits of genetic engineering.

The Dragonfly gave a hard jolt as it encountered the first tenuous wisps of Ishtar's atmosphere at a velocity of close to forty thousand kilometers per hour.

Lander Dragon Three
Ishtar, approaching Krakatoa LZ
1620 hours ST

Private First Class John Garroway—his rank had not been Van Winkled after all—closed his eyes, trying to ignore the irritating tickle of sweat between his eyes, unreachable behind his helmet visor. The Dragonfly was trembling, bucking, lurching unsteadily in its descent, the roar of atmosphere building now like a waterfall just beyond the lander's thin hull. The TAL-S was using the lander module slung beneath its wasp-waist belly as a heat shield now, riding the disk-shaped module down on a cushion of flame.

An image was being fed to Garroway's noumenon from a camera mounted forward beneath the craft's bulbous cockpit, but there was boringly little to see. They were coming into Ishtar's atmosphere on the night side, which also, by design, was currently the anti-Marduk side. Marduk itself was invisible, hidden behind the curving loom of Ishtar; the star Llalande 21185 was a shrunken red ember just above the bloody crescent of Ishtar's horizon, little more at this distance than a ruby star. Ishtar's night side was completely black, a featureless darkness swiftly expanding to fill the noumenal feed.

Even so, Garroway couldn't quite bring himself to close the feed window and sever that slender, less-than-helpful link with the universe outside of Dragon Three's shuddering hull. The alternative was the claustrophobic near-darkness of the LM's squad bay, fully armed and armored Marines crammed into seats so narrow they were literally wedged against one another's shoulders and gear packs. Unable even to turn his helmet, Garroway could only stare at the back of the seat in front of him or down at his own lap below the LR-2120 clipped to his torso mount. Watching the darkness blotting out the stars in his noumenon was infinitely preferable to simply waiting out the thunder of reentry, blind as well as helpless.

The men and women around him were not quite the strangers they'd been when he'd emerged from cybehibe. He'd been expecting either the hazing traditionally handed out to newbies in a military unit or the ostracism reserved for men who'd not yet proven themselves in combat. The 44th Marine Regiment, however, was a newly created ad hoc unit thrown together expressly as a part of 1 MIEU. As such, it included both veteran Marines and kids right out of boot camp.

The command constellation, Garroway had learned, had quite a bit of experience, as did his platoon commander, Lieutenant Kerns. Gunnery Sergeant Valdez, who ran 2nd Squad, had fought in Uzbekistan, Venezuela, and Egypt. She was a fifteen-year veteran from Escondido, California, and had the war stories to tell to prove it. The squad's plasma gunner was Sergeant Nathaniel Easton Deere—"Honey" Deere to his squad mates—a kid from El Dorado, Kansas, with a nasty scar on his forehead and quite a few war stories of his own, even though he'd only been in for eight. Sergeants Foster and Dunne, Lance Corporals Womicki and Brandt, and PFC Cawley had had some time in, ranging from two years for Chuck Cawley, a red-haired agroworker from Iowa, to seven years for Sergeant Richard "Well" Dunne, a onetime underdome 'combganger from the wastelands west of the Chicago Desert.

Tom Pressley and Kat Vinita were both brand-new Marines fresh out of boot company 1097, however, and Roger Hollingwood and Gerrold Garvey—"Hollywood" and "Gravy" to their buddies—both were alumni of Company 1099. The five of them were the FNGs of 2nd Squad, Third Platoon; the idea was that five fucking new guys could learn from the seven experienced Marines in the squad, a kind of do-or-die on-the-job training.

But all of them, experienced or not, were quite literally in the same boat. If there were any tendencies toward newbie-baiting in 2nd Squad, they were being well controlled by Gunny Valdez and Honey Deere.

Second Squad had spent most of the past twenty-two hours—all but three hours of forced cybesleep that ship-morning, followed by a twenty-minute sermon by General King—running through training sims downloaded from the command constellation's AI, Cassius.

"You don't need to be fucking heroes," Valdez had told them all as they sat on a noumenal hillside at the edge of an AI-generated Ishtaran forest, a tangled mass of purples, blacks, and reds. The light there was dim, a perpetual red twilight from a ruby-hued, shrunken sun little larger than a bright star. "We want live Marines on this op, not dead heroes. You new guys . . . keep your heads down and stay out of the line of fire. I especially want you to keep well to either side of Honey's thundergun. The fringe-bleed from a PG-90 will fry your ass if you're too close, armor or no armor. You old hands . . . keep an eye on the newbies in your fire teams. Don't let them get lost, don't let them shock-freeze, don't let them play hero. Remember the first time you all were in a firefight, and think about what it's like for them."

That lecture had been a damned sight more useful than the canned talk by General King—a warmed-over hash of platitudes served up around some historical two-vees about Army troops landing in Europe a couple of hundred years before. The pep talk hadn't exactly been encouraging; of the 150 Rangers who'd stormed the Pointe du Hoc cliffs on June 6, 1944, only ninety were left when they were relieved two days later—forty percent casualties to take a battery of guns that had, in fact, already been moved. If that was the stuff of heroism, Garroway wanted no part of it.

Numbers in the lower right corner of his noumenal inner window gave the dwindling range to the LZ and estimated time to landing. Another fifteen minutes to go.

The LM gave another lurch, then dropped sharply, like a string-cut puppet.

Fists clenched in carbon-fiber gauntlets, sweat dribbling incessantly and maddeningly down his unreachable face, Garroway wondered if he was going to be sick inside his armor.

Lander Dragon One
Ishtar, approaching Krakatoa LZ
1625 hours ST

They'd dropped at last below the cloud deck, and Warhurst shifted to his tactical noumenon. A composite image generated by the lander's AI presented the visible spectrum overlaid by infrared and a 3D contour map showing elevations, targets, and way points in lines and symbols of white light. Dragon One was over Ishtar's night side, but the lander's chin cameras rendered the scene with near-noontime illumination; some of the contour lines didn't quite match up with the landforms rushing past below, however. Either the terrain had changed a bit in ten years, or the first expedition's mapping satellites had transmitted less than precise data on Ishtar's topography.

At the moment—and thanks to careful work by the MIEU's planning staff, both human and cybernetic—Ishtar's night side was also the side forever tide-locked, fac-

ing away from the super giant planet Marduk. The red dwarf
star Llalande 21185 provided Ishtar's daylight, but the heat
came from the sullenly glowing super-Jovian gas giant
called Marduk and from the friction of internal tidal stresses.
According to the briefing information downloaded to
Warhurst's implant, surface temperatures on Ishtar ranged
from over forty degrees Celsius on the side facing Marduk,
to minus fifty on the anti-Marduk side, temperatures only
slightly affected by the cycles of night and day induced by
the distant red-dwarf sun.

The landscape below was one of glaciers and ice-locked
mountains. Volcanoes glowed and thundered on the horizon
in every direction, and in some places rivers of lava encountered ice in searing explosions of steam and molten rock. In
a flash, a tortured plain of cracked and fractured ice-rimed
rock gave way to water, huge, dark swells thick with drifting
mountains of ice. Alphanumerics in the corner of Warhurst's
noumenal vision identified the water as the western edge of
the Abgal, the Great Sea that bordered Ishtar's habitable belt
between ice and fire.

None of the other Dragonflies was visible, again according to plan. The eight landers had scattered across half a
hemisphere as they entered Ishtar's atmosphere, with the
idea that the more scattered the targets, the tougher it would
be for the ground defenses to target them. Warhurst was
gladder than ever now that he'd insisted on the additional
landers and troops. So much could go wrong, and they faced
odds that made the Giza Plateau look like a pleasant afternoon in a sandbox.

Lightning flared ahead, illuminating the bellies of thick-
ening clouds. The imbalance of temperatures in the opposite
hemispheres, hot and cold, meant lots of energy in Ishtar's
weather systems, and that meant large and frequent storms
across the habitable belt. Maybe that storm ahead would
scramble the enemy's tracking system.

Maybe . . . maybe . . .

The trouble was, so little was known about the modern

Ahannu, and even less about the ancient An who'd built Ishtar's defenses. Ten thousand years ago they'd forged an interstellar empire and colonized parts of Earth with a technology humankind had yet to match. They'd already thrown a nasty surprise at the first expedition; what other surprises were hidden down there, in clouds and darkness?

The lander gave a savage jolt, rolling hard to the left and dropping sharply. The AI pilot extended the stubby wings a bit, angling them to grab the air, and increased the power to the plasma thrusters in the Dragonfly's belly. Four minutes to the target . . .

Ishtar's planetary defenses were almost certainly automated, running on programs written thousands of years ago. That was both a major problem and a slender hope for the assault team. Automated weapons would have faster than human reflexes and responses; at the same time, they would lack the flexibility of a living mind at the trigger.

That, at least, was the hope. And there was the hope too that after ten thousand years the weapon inside Objective Krakatoa had only one shot in it.

None of the Marines was counting on that, though.

Light flared in the distance far to the north, a momentarily day-bright snap of radiance. Warhurst blinked. Had that been lightning?

The shock wave hit minutes later, slamming the Dragonfly to the right and nearly knocking it out of the sky. The AI boosted power to the rear thrusters, however, and clawed for altitude as the waves below surged past the lander's belly. A quick check of the team's telemetry confirmed the worst: Dragonfly Four had just vanished in a torrent of energy directed from up ahead.

The assault force was under fire.

Combat Information Center
IST Derna, approaching Ishtar orbit
1632 hours ST

"Dragonfly Four is down," Cassius said in maddeningly even tones. "I repeat, Dragonfly Four is down."

Ramsey had seen the point of bright blue light representing Dragonfly Four wink out in his noumenal feed, had read the cascade of data describing energy levels, bearings, azimuth, and angle. Krakatoa had fired a second time and taken one of the Dragonflies out with a burst of raw energy roughly equivalent to a thousand-megaton thermonuclear explosion. The lander and twenty-five Marines must have evaporated like a snowflake caught in the flame of a blowtorch.

So Krakatoa was still very much operational. The question now was . . . how long did it take to warm up for another shot?

"Fuck!"

The explicative startled Ramsey, and he turned to look at General King, floating in harness next to him. *Derna*'s CIC was a relatively small and cluttered compartment located in the ship's spine, aft of the centrifuge coupler, and housed an impressive array of communications consoles and displays. Most of the men and women micro-g floating there at the moment, however—each wearing a harness to keep them from drifting into equipment or other Marines—were linked directly into the ship's noumenal feeds. Ramsey could see in his mind's eye the incoming data from the Black Dragon assault group, could watch the eight—no, now *seven*—blue stars moving across the multispectral map representation of Ishtar's night side, and he could hear Cassius's dry commentary in his mind.

At the same time, however, he could still hear the voices of the people in the compartment around him with his phenomenal—as opposed to noumenal—ears, and with an inner thought-click he could push the visual feeds into the background and see with his real-world eyes. Despite his immersion in the noumenon, General King's verbal anger had fully captured his attention.

"We expected losses, sir," he said quietly. Indeed, the

Dragonflies had gotten a lot closer to the objective than anyone on the planning staff imagined possible before drawing
fire. Dragon Four had been less than forty kilometers from
the LZ. That suggested there was only one defense complex
on Ishtar like Krakatoa, and that its line of fire was limited to
targets above its horizon.

"That strike force had better take that thing down," King
said with a growl, "or we are dead. *Dead.*"

Major Anderson was floating near a console on the other
side of King, obviously aware of the conversation. Ramsey
exchanged a dark glance with her before she shrugged and
looked away.

General King was still something of an enigma, a strange
fact given that they'd met him ten years ago objective. Between time dilation and their long cybehibe nap, it felt as
though they'd welcomed him aboard only a few days ago,
and the only times they'd worked with him were in the
various staff planning sessions, where he tended to be remote, almost disinterested. So far as the mission was concerned, it might as well have been Ramsey and his command
constellation who were actually bossing this mission. King
had a managerial style better suited to a major corporation
than to a Marine Expeditionary Unit. And now . . . hell.
Ramsey was beginning to think that the man was afraid—
no, terrified—and that he was using a remote and delegating
command style to hide his own fear.

That did *not* bode well for the integrity of their mission.

"So much for command by political appointee," Ricia's
voice said over their private link channel.

"Are you as worried as I am?" Ramsey asked her. "He
hasn't been outside of his own orbit since the Dragons
launched."

"More worried, I think. He was telling me earlier that he
shouldn't even be here, that his personal AI could've handled all of this in proxy. Something has him worried, and it's
not just the Ahannu."

"The mission itself, maybe," Ramsey suggested. "There's

a lot of political capital riding on this, including the possibility of war back home if we fail here."

"Well, he'd better get his act together, or we're all in deep shit," Anderson replied. "Uh-oh. Heads up. Dragon Seven is coming over Krakatoa's horizon."

Ramsey wrenched his attention back to his noumenon. The attack plan had called for all of the Dragons to enter Krakatoa's line-of-sight more or less simultaneously in completely different directions, but vagaries of wind, reentry orientation, and navigation could not be predicted with perfect accuracy, and as expected, there'd been some scattering. Dragon Four had approached from the west. Seven was coming into the mountain's line of fire now from the north; Dragon Three would enter it from the southeast in another thirty seconds.

And the seconds continued to flutter past without an outward response from Krakatoa. *Good . . . good!* Maybe there *was* a delay in recharge for that damned thing. If so, they could use it to good advantage by—

Sensors in the Dragonfly landers, the reconnaissance satellites over Ishtar, and on board the *Derna* all picked up the sudden build and surge of an immense magnetic field pinpointed deep beneath the mountain. A surge of radiation—of fusion-hot plasma—and an instant later the blue star marking Dragonfly Seven flared and winked out. Another LM, another twenty-five Marines, gone. Twenty-five percent of the assault force lost already, and the first lander hadn't even touched down yet.

This was going to be rough. . . .

Chamber of Warrior Preparation
Deeps of An-Kur
Third Period of Dawn

He felt the mountain shudder and made the gesture of *gizkim-nam*, the Sign of Destiny, a warning to the universe not to mismanage the affairs of the Dingir. The Enemy was upon them. The only question was *which* Enemy it was.

His name was Tu-Kur-La, and he was *dingir-gubidir-min*, a god-warrior of the second rank, of the house of In-Kur-Dru and a Keeper of the Memories. The particular memory lineage he bore was no less than that of the House of Nin-Ur-Tah herself, and so he remembered the Sag-ura of Kia, remembered the Ahannu colony there and the creation of the Sag-ura, the Blackhead slaves of that world.

Yes, he remembered. . . .

All around him other Ahannu god-warriors were gathering, awakened from the Sleep of Ages to once again defend the sacred vales and mountains of Enduru. Drones and males born for their purpose, they filed into the Chamber of Weapons, taking down the lesser *anenkara* from the racks along the bare stone walls. There were too few of the ancient devices for even one in twelve to carry one; most god-warriors, the drones who could no longer breed, would carry *mitul*, curved *chakhul* and thrusting *shukur*, and blunt-tipped *tukul*, primitive weapons, though effective when deployed in large numbers. And the Sag-ura *gudibir*, of course, had weapons of their own.

He ran a slender, six-fingered hand along the elegantly graven barrel of his *anenkara*. God-weapons. Weapons forged by the gods-who-came-before, forged and stored here in the depths of Enduru against the coming of the Hunters of the Dawn.

Yes. He remembered . . .

The colony cities on the fair, blue world of Kia, like vast, stone flowers unfolded in the sun, remembered especially the great capital of Eridu at the confluence of the two rivers, Buranun and fast-flowing Idigna.

He remembered the skies darkened by the Hunters when they came, remembered the battle over desolate Kingu, Kia's solitary moon, Defender of Kia. At that time, of course, "he" was a she, a biotechnician named Lul-Ka-Tah, storing memories of the conflict for transmission back to Anu.

And he remembered the time of sadness that followed, re-

membered the chunk of rock, like a burning mountain, plunging out of space into the Greater Sea south of Eridu. The Hunters of the Dawn had judged the Gods of An and determined to scour them from existence.

And not just on Kia . . . but on Giris, on Abalsil, on Gal-Mul, even on sacred Nibir-Anu itself . . . on all of the worlds of the Anunnaki, flame, flood, and destruction rained from the skies.

But among the galaxy's suns, numbering in the hundreds of billions, there were so many worlds, worlds enough that a few might be overlooked even by the Destroyers of the Gods. Here, on Enduru, the Ahannu colony had survived, overlooked by the Hunter fleets searching for them among the stars.

Had the surviving An been discovered at last? . . .

Lul-Ka-Tah had been dust for millennia, but her memories survived, regrown in Tu-Kur-La's brain before his birth. In a way, she lived once again, as Tu-Kur-La would live again someday, when the need was great.

Her memories, of course, flocked like birds around the Great Destruction that had come from the stars, the Hunters of the Dawn and their sick thirst for the extinction of all who were not like them. That part of Tu-Kur-La that was Lul-Ka-Tah was certain that the attack threatening Enduru now must be the Libir-Erim, the Ancient Enemy that had smashed the far-flung empire of the gods millennia ago.

But Tu-Kur-La had last been awakened from the Sleep of Ages a mere two cycles ago, when strange Blackheads, ignorant of their place and bearing weapons of power, had descended from the skies of Enduru, demanding equal standing with the gods.

The thought was sheer foolishness, of course. None were the equal of the Dingir, not even the Ancient Enemy who, after all, had failed in his quest for the extinction of the Ahannu. And as for the former *slaves* of the gods, the domesticated creatures of the lost world of Kia, such could never aspire to be gods themselves. Such would be *erinigar-gal*, an utter and monstrous abomination that the universe itself could never permit to exist.

The information coming through now from the Kikig—the control center—suggested that these attackers were the wild descendants of *zah-sag-ura*, no more. They'd been dealt with once before, they would be dealt with again. Permanently.

"To the defenses!" A commander-of-sixties hissed the order, and the Ahannu god-warriors chanted their response and started for the door.

"Not you, Tu-Kur-La," the commander-of-sixties said. "You are a Keeper of Memories, is it true?"

"Truth, Commander."

"Then your place is at Kikig Kur-Urudug. They will need you there, in the Abzu." Kur-Urudug. The Mountain of the Thunderstorm Weapon. "Give your weapon to another."

He handed his *anenkara* to a drone warrior nearby, who dropped his heavy *mitul* with a glad shout at the unexpected gift.

"I serve the sacred memory of Nibir-Anu," Tu-Kur-La said.

"Go, then, Dingir-Gubidir, and serve."

He blinked his eyes twice in the ritual Gesture of Respectful Assent and hurried out.

16

Lander Dragon Three
Ishtar, approaching Krakatoa LZ
1634 hours ST

The Dragon skimmed broken rock and black sand, flashing across the last few kilometers toward the target. The sky was overcast, the clouds boiling in the wake of the mountain's last shot. The strobe of that titanic gun had seared the Dragon's chin camera, leaving the Marines on board momentarily dazzled, but as his noumenal vision cleared, Garroway could see the mountain clearly, a vast, tar-black cone rising from a flame-blasted plain, its top hollowed by a yawning crater.

According to the infrared data coming over the link, the ground had been blast- and flash-heated to almost forty degrees Celsius, while the crater was still glowing red-hot. It was impossible to tell if there were any organic defenders down there; the ground was so hot, their IR signatures would have been swallowed in the background heat. Here and there, scattered points of red and orange glows marked the fall of hot debris from the mountain's summit.

"What a monster!" someone said over Garroway's tac channel.

"Yeah! How're we supposed to fight *that*?"

"Can the chatter," Valdez snapped. "Get ready to jump. Twenty seconds!"

Garroway felt sharp deceleration tug him forward against his seat harness. The Dragonfly was angling toward a broad, open terrace a third of the way up from the mountain's base. Nose high, air brakes spread wide, ventral thrusters shrieking, the lander drifted over the rock shelf in a swirling cloud of grit and sand. Magnetic grapples released the saucer-shaped landing module from beneath the Dragonfly's gently curved, mid-hull strut. Relieved of the lander's weight, the Dragonfly bounded back into the sky, sleek now and wasp-waisted; the landing module dropped to the ground, the leading edge plowing into loose gravel, the impact cushioned by mag floaters and chemical thrusters.

Inside the lander, the shock slammed Garroway against his seat harness, bruising his chest and shoulders even within padded armor. The noise—a grating, rasping shriek—sounded like a world's ending; the saucer bulldozed through loose rock and sand, skewing slightly before it came to rest at a ten-degree list.

Panels all around the saucer's rim exploded up and out, releasing HK-20 combat robots and a cloud of sensor drones. Broader hull panels, shaped like the slices of a pie, unfolded, opening the interior of the module to the outside.

"Grounded!" Valdez shouted over the tac channel. *"Go! Go! Go!"*

Garroway's harness automatically disengaged and he tumbled forward, thrown off balance by the cant of the lander's deck, but he braced himself on an overhead strut, unshipped his laser rifle, and started moving forward. All around him the other armored Marines of 1st and 2nd Squads crowded toward the openings, pounded down the deck gratings of the debarkation ramps, and scrambled clear of the grounded landing module.

Something slammed into the LM's hull just above Garroway's helmet as he stepped into the open. Another something hit the rock nearby with a sharp, metallic crack and a scatter of sparks. It took him an awkward moment to recognize what was happening. *"Shit!"* Hollingwood shouted at the same moment. "They're *shooting* at us!"

Training took over then. *Don't freeze, don't bunch up. Exit the LM and form a perimeter.* Hunched over as if leaning into a stiff wind, Garroway ran through loose gravel, counting out the paces until he was fifty meters from the downed module. Throwing himself down on his belly, he brought his rifle up and thought-clicked the targeting display. Instantly, a bright red target reticle popped into his field of vision, overlaying the multispectral view from his helmet pickups. The reticle, transmitted by his rifle's computer, marked the weapon's precise aim point.

The only trouble was, he couldn't see a target. Ahead, the mountain rose like a solid, jet-black wall, its top still glowing with a fierce red heat. To either side, other 2nd Squad Marines were dropping into place on the perimeter as HK robots strode ahead on scissoring black legs gleaming with an oily, reflected light. Incoming fire continued to snap and crack across the rock plain, but he couldn't see where the shots were coming from. Twenty meters ahead, though, an HK had frozen in mid-stride, its twin-camera "head" smashed into trailing ribbons of torn metal and plastic.

There! Garroway's helmet radar had detected the flash of a solid, high-speed projectile, and the Mark VII's computer backtracked its path, marking the shooter's position at the base of the rock wall with a small red circle. He moved his rifle until the reticle centered on the circle, which twisted itself into a red diamond, indicating a target lock, then pressed the firing button.

The laser's bolt was invisible; with most of its energy in the ultraviolet range of the spectrum, it left only a thin, backscattered sparkle of ionization as it burned through the air. The pulse showed clearly enough in Garroway's optics, but he couldn't tell whether he'd hit the shooter or not. With no fresh targeting data, the target symbol vanished. Damn, had he hit the sniper, or not?

A winking red light on his display switched to green as the rifle's chargers powered up for another shot. Rising, he darted forward another five meters, keeping low, trying to pierce the very rock around him with his electronic senses, searching for a target, any target, any threat at all. He felt nakedly exposed out there beneath the eight-hundred-meter loom of the mountain.

A stuttering flicker of pulsing light snapped from the small dome turret on top of the lander module, a rapid-fire laser mount directed by the LM's AI. Overhead, the Dragonfly swooped and circled against the night, seeking targets, as a second TAL-S drifted in from the north, slowing its descent, releasing its LM in a swirling cloud of dust. Around Garroway, the tortured landscape of rock steamed and smoked in hellish light, an obscene premonition of a dark and flame-shot Hell.

"Squads One and Two, ready," the voice of Lieutenant Kerns said in his head. "Overwatch advance. Squad Two, move up!"

"Right!" Valdez shouted. "Second Squad! You heard the man! We're up! On your feet!"

Garroway scrambled to his feet again and trotted forward. Small arms fire continued to pepper the section, but the defenders appeared to be split now in their attention between his unit and the lander that had just grounded on the terrace plain a hundred meters to the left. The incoming rounds, according to his data feed, were small, solid chunks of metal massing no more than a few tens of grams, but accelerated to velocities of around five hundred meters per second.

Bullets, in other words. Definitely primitive tech, propelled either by chemical explosions or a very low-powered gauss accelerator. One of them slammed into his chest, jolting him hard but causing no damage. If *that* was the best they could do . . .

He stumbled, his boot coming down in a hole, and he fell to his hands and knees, almost dropping his rifle. Private

Pressley stopped beside him, reaching for his arm. "Hey, watch that first step, pal," Pressley said over the tac channel. "It's a real—"

Pressley's armored torso splattered then, a gaping hole opening as his upper body and shoulders ceased to exist save as a thin, red spray of mist.

Garroway screamed; he was holding Pressley's left arm by the hand, an arm no longer attached to a body. Pressley's legs and lower torso, still encased in armor, collapsed steaming onto the rock as his helmet bounced away, his head still inside.

Dropping the dead arm, Garroway folded back onto the ground, still screaming, his universe awash in blood, horror, and death.

Combat Information Center
IST Derna, *approaching Ishtar*
Orbit
1635 hours ST

Ramsey studied the analysis as it unscrolled through his noumenal awareness. "A relativistic cannon," he said, nodding. "I suppose we should have guessed that."

They were within *Derna*'s CIC, floating amid a tangle of feed cables and harness straps. The compartment was growing more crowded by the hour as officers floated in. Admiral Vincent Hartman, the MIEU's naval commander, and several members of his staff had entered and linked in only a few moments before.

"The energies released are within estimated ranges for an AM detonation," Cassius said over the CIC's main noumenal channel. "However, the lack of concomitant radiations clearly indicates no matter-antimatter annihilation is taking place. That, and the presence of an extremely powerful magnetic pulse with each energy release, suggests the acceleration of small amounts of matter to near-c velocities. The resultant high-speed plasma impacts the target with kinetic and thermal effects similar to those of a large-scale thermonuclear detonation."

"That's one way of putting it," Ricia Anderson said.

"So how are they hitting targets just coming over their horizon?" Ramsey asked. "That's a deflection of better than ninety degrees off the vertical."

He was watching one of the video feeds from the surface—a shot from a camera mounted on Dragonfly One's grounded lander module. Marines crouched in the twilight, firing toward the vast black shadow of the mountain called An-Kur . . . and Krakatoa. The mountain had not fired again since the destruction of the second Dragonfly, but time enough had passed for the thing to recharge, if the time delay between the first and second shots was any indication.

"High relativistic masses would be extremely difficult to deflect by more than a few degrees as they emerged from the mountain's throat," Cassius replied. "The plasma bolt would, therefore, be easily directed only at targets within, I estimate, ten to twelve degrees of the vertical, but could not be aimed at targets approaching from the horizon. However, by the time the initial projectile mass approached relativistic velocities, and while it was still within the mountain's central bore, it would have been reduced to an extremely hot, possibly fusing plasma. The magnetic field generating the bolt's velocity could be used to bleed off a small amount of that plasma near the mountain's crater and direct it at any target within line-of-sight."

"So they can throw the equivalent of a thermonuke at targets in orbit," Ramsey said, "or split off a tactical nuke's worth for close-in point defense. Slick."

"But that kind of mass acceleration would require incredible energy," General King protested. "Where are they getting their power? Damn it, the Frogs are supposed to be *primitives!*"

Ramsey wished that King would get off that particular soapbox. The An were what they were, and complaining about their abilities—or their technological inconsistencies—was not going to help.

"Analyses of the subsurface structures beneath the mountain suggest deep thermal sources," Cassius replied. Within their minds, the command center AI unfolded a schematic of the tunnels and shafts inside and beneath An-Kur Mountain, as suggested by *Emissary* gravitometric scans and orbital reconnaissance. A pair of shafts, slender on the computer noumenal display but probably each measuring several tens of meters across, plunged from the extinct volcano's throat deep, deep into Ishtar's crust.

"An energy pump facilitating heat exchange with the planet's deep crust via those twin vertical shafts would be essentially self-contained and self-sufficient," Cassius continued. "Such a system could have been put in place thousands of years ago and remained functional without refueling or other technical intervention from outside, especially if the ancient An possessed sophisticated robotic systems for maintenance and repair."

"Which also means they don't have an antimatter production facility down there," Ramsey pointed out. "That's one piece of good news, at least." A serious concern of the mission planning staff had been that the Ahannu might be able to spit chunks of antimatter at the approaching Earth transports. Not that blobs of plasma accelerated to near-c velocities were all that much better from the target's point of view . . .

"What kind of range does a thing like that have?" Admiral Hartman demanded.

"Unknown, and I am unable to extrapolate from the given data," Cassius said. "We know only that the *Emissary* was destroyed by a single shot while in orbit around Ishtar, at an altitude of approximately 312 kilometers."

"Krakatoa is still over the horizon from us," Ricia put in. "We won't have line-of-sight for another . . . four hours, twelve minutes."

"Then they have that long to take that thing out," King said, his voice grim. "And God help us all if they fail!"

"They won't fail," Ramsey said. "*Failure* is not in the Marine lexicon."

"A brave sentiment, Colonel," King said. "I just wish I could be as certain of it as you. Admiral Hartman? Perhaps you'd best pass the word to have *Regulus* and *Algol* extend their range from us and from one another. We don't want to be caught bunched together up here like shooting range targets."

"It's our men and women on the ground right now that I'm worried about," Ramsey said. "If Krakatoa can divert some of the energy from a shot aimed straight up to cook targets nearby, what's to stop the An from frying the ARLT?"

"Maybe they can't shoot at their own slope," Ricia said. "That would be, I don't know, like shooting themselves in the foot? It might have a minimum range as well as a maximum. Threats any closer would be dealt with some other way."

"Right," Ramsey said. "I'll buy that. So now the question is, what other defenses does Krakatoa have?"

"I imagine our people will be finding out pretty soon now," Ricia said. "And Goddess help them when they do."

ARLT Section Dragon Three
Objective Krakatoa, Ishtar
1642 hours ST

"C'mon, son!" Valdez said gently but firmly. Stooping, she slapped the back of his armored shoulder, urging him up and forward. "You can't help him now!"

Garroway had dropped Pressley's severed arm moments before, but he continued to lie in a shallow depression in the rock a meter away from the Marine's blood-drenched lower torso. Pressley's helmet lay nearby, the man's black-irised eyes and gaping mouth clearly visible behind the blood-smeared visor.

"Garroway!" Valdez rasped. "Snap to, Marine!"

"A-Aye aye," he managed to say.

"Hit your backbone," she told him. *"Do it!"*

Backbone was Corps slang for the nanoneurotransmitters within his implanted technics that adjusted certain key chemical, muscular, and mental responses. They didn't exactly banish fear at a thought-click, but they could help a Marine on the verge of going into shock to pull out of it, to focus on the task at hand, to keep from getting sick or simply having his legs fail beneath him.

Garroway nodded inside his helmet and focused on the mental code that activated the appropriate NNTs. He felt an inner rush, a kind of emotional flutter in his gut, and then he drew a sharp, deep breath. He could still feel the horror of Pressley's death, but it was cocooned somehow, more distant, less immediate. He felt the strength coming back into his legs and belly, felt the shaking stop. "Thanks, Gunny," he told Valdez.

"Keep moving, Marine," she told him. "We have a mountain to take."

She moved off without looking back. He picked up his weapon and followed.

ARLT Command Section, Dragon
One
Objective Krakatoa, Ishtar
1642 hours ST

Captain Warhurst remained harnessed inside Lander One, though he was almost completely unaware of his surroundings. As CO of the ARLT, he was expected to stay safe and give orders, coordinating the attack from the presumed security of the armored LM. The training invested in modern military officers was simply too expensive, too valuable, to allow them to lead from the front; indeed, they'd not done so for two centuries or more.

Warhurst listened to the rattle of small arms fire off the lander module's hull and wondered who they were kidding with that kind of blatant rationalization. The LM was a definite target—a large and quite attractive one, in fact—while individual Marines wearing stealthy armor were able to literally fade into their surroundings and become *very* hard to hit.

And that too, he realized, was his own form of rationalizing things. The fact was, he wanted to be out there with his people right now, not stuck behind in this glorified tin can, watching an AI run the data link switchboard and holding the collective hands of the command staff still on planetary approach.

His noumenal awareness was crowded with images, feeds, and downloads. With a thought-click he could tune in on the helmet sensor array of any of his Marines. At the same time, he was aware of several members of the command staff "riding his link," looking over his virtual shoulder from the *Derna*'s CIC. Majors Anderson, DuBoise, and Ross were all there, as were Lieutenant Colonel Harper, Colonel Ramsey, and both General King and Admiral Hartman. The electronic ghosts of a dozen other command staff officers and technicians were there as well, sifting through the flood of incoming data. Theoretically, they were there to offer advice and watch to see that he didn't miss anything. In practice, it was a micromanagement cluster-fuck waiting to happen. Warhurst concentrated on doing his job and ignoring that particular unpleasant possibility.

An aerial view of the LZ was spread out beneath him in his noumenal awareness. Robotic drones, battlefield management probes, and the sensor feeds from the Marines outside all contributed their data streams to build up a more or less coherent picture of the engagement as it unfolded. Four landing modules—one hundred Marines—were on the ground now and advancing toward an apparent door in the side of the mountain. Two more were angling in from opposite directions, north and south. Enemy resistance was heavy—twelve Marines dead so far, plus fifteen HK-20 robots knocked out—but the troops were advancing. The worst danger at this point of the assault was that the Marines would be pinned down, unable to move; instead, they seemed to have momentum enough to carry them into the mountain, despite sleeting small arms fire.

"We're taking heavy fire from the mountainside," Warhurst said, uploading to the *Derna* CIC. "We need air support!" The Marines on the ground needed firepower, and they needed it now.

"Major DuBoise," Ramsey said. "Scrape that mountainside clean!"

"Aye aye, sir."

Warhurst heard the orders being given over the air support net. All that remained was to wait for them to be carried out.

Kikig Kur-Urudug
Deeps of An-Kur
Third Period of Dawn

It was called the Abzu, a word constructed from *aba*, the sea, and *zu*, to know, and meaning, roughly, "the Sea of Knowing," or possibly "the Sentient Sea." Ancient Sumerian texts had spoken of the Abzu as a land beneath the sea, or as the "Lower World," the place where the god Enki ruled. Perhaps, Tu-Kur-La thought, the Abzu had once been a physical place on far-off Kia, one of the scattered Anu colonies on that world before the coming of the Hunters of the Dawn. The old records read that way.

Or perhaps it had always been *this*, an artificial construct representing the collective unconscious of all of the gods. The records, even the Memories passed down across the ages, often broke at key places, with information forever lost or rendered corrupt. Sometimes it was hard to tell what the old memory texts truly meant.

Rarely, though, was an exact interpretation of the records necessary. The spirit of what was meant, of the information transmitted across the centuries—that was the heart and soul of the thing.

Interpretation of the records was best left to others.

Tu-Kur-La relaxed as the Sea engulfed him. Physically, he was within one of the lower chambers of the Kikig, the command center for the Mountain of the Gods. The Abzu-il, the Gateway to the Lower World, oozed slowly from the cavern walls around him, enveloping him, penetrating him, its artificial nervous system forging billions of connections with his physical brain on countless levels, drawing him swiftly under.

To Tu-Kur-La's senses, the Abzu seemed to be a physical place like any other, a kind of green-lit cavern with dim and far-off walls all but lost in soft fog. Reality coalesced itself from that fog. He saw images . . . other Ahannu . . . and heard voices, as the battle in the world above raged. Information was here for the asking, within a kind of library of the mind. And he could see whatever he willed himself to see. . . .

"Welcome, Tu-Kur-La," a voice said within his mind. "We welcome your soul to the Circle of An-Kin."

"Thank you, Lord," he replied, startled. The voice, the towering figure before him, was none other than Gal-Irim-Let—Kingal An-Kur, the Great Commander of the Mountain of the Gods. An-Kin was a council of the gods, a meeting to determine the future course of the gods' will. Why would the Kingal itself want the advice of a mere second-level god-warrior?

"We desire the advice of all those who faced the Zah-sag-ura two cycles ago," the voice said, answering his question before he could voice it. "Your experience will help us decide how best to bring them down."

"To that end," another voice said, "we bestow upon you the rank of *uru-nam,* that you may take your place with us."

This second speaker was Usum-Gal, a title that was both name and rank—the Great Dragon, the Lord of All. The Sag-ura of Kia referred to it as the High Emperor, a strange and meaningless term.

"I . . . I thank the Great Lord," he stammered. "I will strive to be worthy of the honor." *Uru-nam!* It meant

Guardian of Destiny; this made him a minor *kingal* in his own right.

"You are one of the gods," Usum-Gal replied, "a Guardian of Destiny by nature. It is no honor to do what is your nature, but simple personal responsibility. Now, Uru-nam Tu-Kur-La, tell us how we might destroy the invaders."

Within his inner vision, a scene unfolded, a view of the city the invaders called New Sumer, which the An had always called Shumur-Unu, the "Stubborn Fortress." Strange how the invaders had such trouble with the proper pronunciation of language. Much of the city was burning, as hordes of Anu god-warriors and Sag-uras burst through and over the walls, storming toward the Pyramid of the Eye.

A handful of offworlder warriors gathered at the base of the pyramid steps, holding off the onslaught for long moments as survivors of the attack loaded on board one of the alien flying machines at the pyramid's apex. One by one the defenders fell, as heaps of burned and torn god-warrior bodies piled up in a semicircle about the plaza. At last, like a black sea, the Ahannu god-warriors surged forward, overwhelming the few surviving defenders.

"Our victory two cycles ago," Tu-Kur-La replied, "was one of superior numbers. There were not enough armed Blackheads to withstand our full might."

"These Sag-ura sky-warriors," Gal-Irim-Let said, thoughtful. "What are they called?"

Tu-Kur-La plucked the alien word from the Abzu's knowledge stores. "Marines," he said. "They call themselves Marines."

"These Marines possess a weapons technology that gives them a considerable advantage in combat. Their body armor . . . their weapons-of-power . . ."

"All true, Great Lord," he said. "And there are many more of them this time than last. Victory will not be easy."

"We will suffer terrible losses," Gal-Irim-Let observed. "We have lost twelves of sixties already, simply defending An-Kur."

"But consider," Tu-Kur-La said. "Our god-warriors number sixty sixties of sixties or more. Only a handful of these Blackhead Marines have landed so far. There may be more on the vessels now approaching Enduru, but . . . how many? A sixty of sixties?"

"Half of that," Gal-Irim-Let replied. "According to what the prisoner-slaves told us, a thirty of sixties. No more."

"Exactly. However many god-warriors we lose, we can afford to grow more, as many as are needed. The Marines are a long way from Kia and reinforcements. If our information from the Sag-ura we took two cycles ago is accurate, it will be a cycle and a half before news of their need can reach Kia, another two cycles before more ships could cross the gulf between Kia and Enduru."

"Unless they recapture the Pyramid of the Eye," Gal-Irim-Let said. "They could call for help immediately then, as they did before."

"Perhaps. But their ships sail more slowly than the pictures in the Pyramid. They still require a two-cycle trip.

"And long before then, the last of these Marines will be dead."

ARLT Section Dragon Three
Objective Krakatoa, Ishtar
1644 hours ST

A bullet spanged into Garroway's chest armor, staggering him back a step, but he leaned forward and kept moving. From what he'd heard and downloaded so far about the Ahannu, they were supposed to be armed with spears, damn it, not guns. Someone's intel about this rock was seriously out of date.

At least most of the incoming rounds were small stuff, gauss-gun projectiles accelerated by powerful magnetic fields. The monster high-velocity, high-mass rounds like the one that had taken Tom Pressley apart were pretty rare, thank the Goddess, and most of those were being aimed at the LMs and at the circling air support.

The Dragonfly TAL-S transports, relieved of the burden of their lander modules, were lighter now by fifteen tons each and far more nimble, darting about above the LZ much like their terrestrial namesakes above an insect-infested swamp. Swooping in close to the black mountainside, chin turrets pivoting sharply, they sent fusillades of pulsed laser bursts into each crevice, outcrop, and ledge that might hold enemy gunners. Weapons pods slung under their down-canted wings loosed clouds of high-velocity needles, microrockets, and target seekers. Rock shattered as explosions detonated across the cliff face, sending showers of rock cascading down to the ledge below. The Marine pilots of those Dragons were throwing everything they had on the line to give the ground-pounders below a chance to clear the kill zone.

As he watched, one of the Dragons shuddered from a hit, its left wing and arched tail boom crumpling as black smoke began boiling from the dorsal drive unit. The aircraft banked sharply, then began tumbling, smashing into the side of the mountain. The other Dragons stooped from the glowering sky, electronically noting the location of the gauss launcher that had felled their comrade and searing it with pulsing laser flame.

The fire from the mountainside half a kilometer ahead was slackening now, he thought. Either the air support was doing its job or the defenders were pulling out. "Heads up, Marines," Valdez's voice said over the tactical link. "The Ahannu gunners are pulling back. That could be good . . . or it could mean—"

"Hit the deck, Marines!" Colonel Ramsey's voice shouted in the noumenal, overriding Valdez's words. "We've got a mag reading off the scale. They're going to—"

Garroway fell full-length on the ground. He could feel the rocky surface of the ledge trembling through his torso armor as inconceivable energies deep within the mountain built higher and higher. His audio pickups relayed a shuddering rumble, like far-off thunder.

Then a dazzling blue-white light illuminated the rocks, the murky twilight replaced by blazing high noon. As the light faded he looked up, just in time to see a wall of white mist rushing down the slope from the mountain's peak.

"Shock wave!" Valdez shouted. "Stay down and hang on!"

And then the wave front hit him like an oncoming hurricane. Once when he was a kid, a tropical storm had hit Baja and the Sonoran coast, lashing inland with 160-kilometer winds. This was like that, only worse, much worse, as the howling wind suddenly seemed to turn solid, smashing at the Marines scattered across the storm-seared landscape. The external temperature, he saw on his helmet display readouts, was nearly one hundred degrees Celsius, and the atmospheric pressure had momentarily surged to well over fifteen atmospheres.

Garroway felt himself being lifted, felt himself sliding back across the rock. Reaching out with both gauntleted hands, he grabbed hold of a crack in the rocky grounds and hung on. The wind slammed him down then, rattling him inside his armor.

The pressure wave passed over in another second, leaving Garroway and the other Marines gasping but more or less unscathed. He picked up his laser rifle, checking the settings. "What the hell was *that*?" someone yelled over the tactical link.

"The bastards downed another Dragon," someone else shouted back.

Garroway looked up into the turbulent overcast. The blast had wiped the circling Dragons from the sky. Four were returning now, but one other had vanished.

"Move in, Marines!" Valdez ordered. "Hit that gateway, bearing two-one-five!"

Garroway turned his helmet, watching the bearing indicator numbers sweep around to the indicated direction. There was something there. . . .

He thought-clicked his helmet magnification to ten times and could make out the gateway Valdez was talking about. It looked as though a portion of the rock wall above the ledge LZ had been cut away with a high-energy beam of some sort, leaving a deep crevice. Rock had flowed like water there before cooling and hardening once more, leaving smoothly shaped basaltic flowstone. Within that smooth-walled break in the cliff, a high, narrow, rectangular opening plunged into blackness. His helmet radar confirmed that it was indeed a gateway of some sort, open for at least twenty meters back into the mountain. Elsewhere on the cliff face, to either side of the gate, red light gleamed from slit windows cut into rock—gun ports, he guessed, from which the defenders were sweeping the LZ with deadly fire.

Basic tactical doctrine downloaded into Garroway's implant during boot camp was clear. When you're in the open and in danger of getting your ass shot off, *move!* NNTs sang in his blood, his brain, his thoughts. He thought-clicked his fear down another notch and started running, pounding across the scorched and broken rock surface of the ledge toward the gate.

The other Marines in the ARLT were sweeping forward as well, armored figures to his left and right. His helmet warned of movement ahead. . . .

He was only a few meters away from the gateway in the rock when figures began boiling out of the tunnel and from openings in the ground to either side. It took him a chilling moment to realize that the shapes were not human.

Humanoid, certainly . . . but shorter than men, most of them, with oddly articulated arms and legs and an odd, forward-leaning manner of holding themselves as they leaped into battle. They didn't run so much as *bound*, with powerful leaps driven by strongly muscled legs. What he noticed about them most, though, was their eyes, large and gold, with horizontally and jaggedly slit pupils. They wore an oddly mismatched collection of armor, those that wore anything at all, *primitive* armor almost laughably clumsy and piecemeal compared with the Marines' Mark VIIs. And though a few carried odd-looking guns, most were armed with spears, razor-tipped lances, swords, and even war clubs. It was like stepping from a twenty-third-century battlefield into something out of the Middle Ages . . . worse, like a fantasy in some virtual role-playing sim.

Primitive they might be, but there were a hell of a lot of them, too many to count.

And they were rushing to meet the Marine charge head-on.

17

ARLT Command Section, Dragon
One
Objective Krakatoa, Ishtar
1645 hours ST

Another Dragon gone, snapped out of the air by a burst of
plasma from that damned mountaintop. Four aircraft left out
of the original eight.

Warhurst thought he saw the pattern, though. The mountain fortress could fire at targets in any direction and within
about 140 degrees of straight up. That meant that targets
within a few kilometers of the mountain's base, including
the entire LZ, were safe from direct fire. Dragonfly Two,
however, had circled far enough away from the side of the
mountain to bring it into the defense complex's kill zone.
Secondary fringe effects of the weapon's shots—blast, heat,
overpressure, radiation—were all threats to units inside minimum range, especially aircraft, but not so deadly that they
could not be countered. Armored troops in the open need
only hunker down to be more or less safe; the blast effects
were rough on airborne units, but the Marine flyers were
good at what they did, and the TAS-L Dragonfly was arguably the most rugged aircraft in the sky.

He was already uploading what he'd learned, seen, and
guessed to Major DuBoise, and she was passing it back
down in distilled form to her surviving pilots. They would

have to carefully balance their flight paths, close enough and low enough to avoid becoming targets for the Ahannu gun, yet high enough and far enough out to avoid being smashed by the shock wave from the next shot.

On the ground, the Marines had moved in close to what appeared to be the entrance into the mountain and encountered a wave of Ahannu troops.

This, he decided, was where the Marines would earn their pay.

ARLT Section Dragon Three
Objective Krakatoa, Ishtar
1645 hours ST

John Garroway raised his LR-2120, squeezing off a burst of rapid-fire pulses when his helmet display flashed red on an acquired target. An Ahannu ten meters in front of him shrieked and staggered back into the crowded front ranks of its companions, the elaborately molded plastron of its bronze body armor exploding in glittering motes of white-hot liquid metal. The Ahannu mass continued surging forward, enveloping the dead warrior and trampling it underfoot. Garroway dropped to one knee, steadying his weapon, then fired again . . . and again. Other Marines were firing as well, slashing into the enemy mob, and still they kept coming.

There were just too damned many of them. . . .

"Grenades!" Lieutenant Kerns yelled over the tac link. "Use your M-12s!"

A dangerous option at such close range, but the only one going against such a numerous and densely packed enemy. Garroway thought-clicked his weapon link, engaging the 20mm underbarrel grenade launcher, then setting it to slow full-auto. He braced the rifle's stock against his hip and pressed the firing button, swinging the weapon slowly from left to right.

The M-12 fired with a heavy *thud-thud-thud*, loosing

three rounds per second, each shot slamming the rifle's butt against his armor. Each spin-stabilized round detonated on contact with rock, armor, or flesh with a cheerful lack of discrimination, filling the air with dust, smoke, and a thin scarlet mist of Ahannu blood and body parts.

The Ahannu warriors kept charging, dying by the tens, then by the hundreds, with every few paces. A number of them carried poles holding vertically hung banners, something like the *sashimono* of feudal Japan. They seemed to designate units; banner colors ranged from red and scarlet to orange, brown, and yellow, and each bore a different alien symbol at its center, geometric designs laid out in sharp, black brush strokes. Most, Garroway saw, carried blade weapons of various types. The ones with rifles were the most obvious first targets, and few of them got more than a few meters toward the Marine ranks before being ripped apart by explosive 20mm rounds.

Still, it was a near thing, that desperate firefight in the shadow of the alien mountain. The Marines were putting down a deadly fusillade of high-explosive death, blasting the close-packed ranks of charging Ahannu warriors, but the enemy horde was spilling out of countless hidden doorways and crevices in the mountainside and closing in from all sides. The Marines closest to the mountain gateway had to begin letting their flanks fall back, pulling into a circle, creating a perimeter to keep the charging mob at bay.

And Marines were being hit now by incoming small arms fire. Each time an Ahannu warrior dropped a rifle when it died, one of its companions would scoop up the weapon and keep coming, firing as it leaped across the high-piled stacks of its slain fellows. The smaller Ahannu weapons couldn't penetrate a Mark VII battlesuit, but they had a kind of a gauss railgun, its two-meter length unwieldy for the short Ahannu warriors, and it packed enough power at close range to punch through Marine laminate armor like a high-powered laser. The sound was a hideous cacophony of cracking explosions mingled with the eerie shrieks, wails, and screams of the Ahannu and the deeper, ragged yells of the Marines.

Garroway's entire universe was narrowed down to a tiny slice of ground a few meters across, a space filled with dust and smoke and bodies and the staccato flash and bang of 20mm grenade charges detonating in strings. Lance Corporal Patricia Brandt was on Garroway's left, and Hollingwood was on his right, both Marines leaning into their weapons as they hosed the oncoming charge with grenades. At this range there was no point in locking targets for guided RPG smartrounds; they simply pointed and fired, and the grenades smashed through Ahannu armor, skin, and bone at eight hundred meters per second, often before the grenade ramjet engines could even ignite.

"Heads down, Forty-four!" a voice called over the tactical link. An instant later a shrill sound like tearing paper hissed overhead, and the rock wall tunnel vented a savage, ground-shaking blast filled with flying Ahannu and shredded, scarlet-bloody meat.

"Way to go, Sandy!" someone yelled. "Sandy" was Sergeant Thor Sanderval, the platoon's sniper, taking pot-shots at the gateway with an MD-30 from his lander pod. From the blast effects, Garroway guessed he must be firing mass-driver bomblets instead of the usual steel-jacketed de-pleted uranium rounds. The rock walls of the gateway crevice had amplified the small grenade's detonation into something resembling a shell from an old-style artillery fieldpiece.

A moment later a whirling blast of hot wind and swirling dust enveloped the Marines, and Garroway looked up at the howl of an incoming aircraft. One of the Dragonflies was balancing down on shrieking ventral thrusters, hovering as close to the mountainside as its pilot dared, spraying the Ahannu troops with pulsed laser fire from its chin turret and pod-launched, special-munitions bomblets. Shotgun rounds exploded meters above the Ahannu hordes, slicing through dozens of screaming warrior fanatics.

But those warrior fanatics still had the initiative, were *still* coming despite everything the Marines could throw at them. Garroway's grenade magazine bleeped its dry warning; five more rounds and he would be empty. He switched back to laser fire and burned down a charging Ahannu waving a wickedly curved sword.

Too late, he saw a second Ahannu already bounding high in the air, leaping above the line of crouching Marines, firing his two-meter railgun straight down as he sailed overhead. Garroway fired and missed; the Ahannu landed behind him, spun, raised his rifle . . .

. . . and sagged forward in a crumpling heap as Gunny Valdez pulled a gore-dripping Marine combat knife from the warrior's back.

And suddenly it was very quiet.

The charging Ahannu, what was left of them, had vanished as abruptly as they'd appeared, leaving piled-high heaps of blast-mangled bodies behind. "Goddess!" Garroway said. He slapped Hollingwood's shoulder. "Did you see Gunny with that knife?" Battle lust still sang in his blood; he felt wild and hot and flushed, and incredibly proud of what his squad leader had just done.

Hollingwood didn't respond, and Garroway took another look. That last Ahannu's shot from overhead had punched through the back of Hollingwood's helmet, leaving a fist-sized hole in the dark metal and a visor opaque with blood.

"Oh, *shit!*" He double-checked the armor's med sensors and confirmed that Hollingwood was dead.

His battle lust drained away with that realization, leaving Garroway very weak and very scared in the middle of the dust and smoke-fogged carnage.

Combat Information Center
IST Derna, *approaching Ishtar orbit*
1712 hours ST

Ramsey watched the battle come to its abrupt resolution from the vantage point of a URV-180 battlefield drone, circling a hundred meters above the dust and chaos and death below. The remaining Ahannu warriors seemed to stop almost in mid-stride, as though yanked back by invisible leashes, then scrambled for cover in the surrounding rocks.

"Are you getting those trapdoor locations, Cassius?" he asked.

"Of course, Colonel."

"Good. There're too many of them for me to keep track of. That mountain face must be honeycombed with the things."

"I have noted 217 distinct openings, not counting the main gate," the AI said. "Individual tunnels appear to be less than half a meter in diameter, too narrow to admit a Marine in full armor. It will require special tactics to clear them."

"Roger that." *Special tactics.* The term embraced a number of distinct possibilities, none of them pleasant to think about. Sending small-framed Marines without body armor into those holes was one. Tunnel rat duty was never popular, though Ramsey had no doubt there'd be ample volunteers. Casualties would be high, however, and too large a percentage of his force would be tied down for too long. That was not a cost-effective action.

The use of chemical or biological agents was another possibility. CB warfare hadn't been used on Earth for centuries, originally due to moral injunctions against them and later because combat armor and effective decon countermeasures rendered them useless on the modern battlefield. The Ahannu weren't using sealed armor, however, and were vulnerable. On the other hand, Ahannu biology was still poorly understood, and a gas or bacterial agent would have to be specially tailored to their biochemistry to be effective. There wasn't time for that . . . or proper research facilities on board the *Derna*.

Of course, a few things were known about the Ahannu. They *did* breathe, for instance, and filling those tunnels with smoke might drive them out. *Might*. How long could they hold their breath? Again, not enough data.

Besides, Ahannu moral codes, beliefs, and psychology were even more poorly understood than their biology. Ramsey's orders included a most particular injunction against jeopardizing PanTerra's chances of establishing useful and viable relations with the Ahannu after the mission's primary objectives were met. If gassing them in their holes meant they would begin viewing humans as monsters or war criminals, the PanTerran people might not be able to pick up the pieces.

He made a mental note to have a noumenal conference with both Gavin Norris and Dr. Hanson. If they had *any* further information not included in the regular briefing downloads . . .

In any case, Ramsey wasn't eager to gas the critters. The MIEU One's mission was one of coercion, not extermination. They needed to convince the Ahannu to accept a Terran presence on Ishtar, to release their Sag-ura slaves . . . and, just possibly, to be willing to deal with PanTerra on matters of trade, research, and cultural exchange. Besides, Ramsey had no desire to go down in history as the man who'd annihilated the first sentient species to be encountered among the stars, and a poorly controlled or vectored CB agent could do just that. No, there had to be another way.

Other special tactics included the use of robots—no good, since HK gunwalkers didn't possess the requisite programming. Teleoperating the things was out too, since control signals wouldn't penetrate rock. Besides, there were fewer HKs with the MIEU than there were tunnels, and they needed to be saved for other duties.

Nano agents? As with biological agents, not enough was known about Ahannu physiology. Infecting them all with microscopic machines that put them to sleep or made them

decide to quit fighting was great in theory but still well beyond the technical capabilities of nanotech programming
specialists.

No . . . in this case, "special tactics" probably meant doing things the old-fashioned way, using high explosives to
seal each and every one of the tunnel entrances down there.
Smoke might work . . . and if the Krakatoa tunnel complex
was as extensive as he feared, there might be no alternative
but to use tunnel rats.

In other words, they would use the same tactics that
Marines had used on Saipan and Iwo Jima, in Vietnam and
Colombia, in Cuba and Vladivostok—slow, dirty, and all too
often, costly. It would be simple enough to identify the tunnel entrances on the outside of the mountain. Cassius had already managed that. But the labyrinth inside Krakatoa was
going to be something else entirely.

"How long do you expect the clean-up to take, Colonel?"
General King asked.

Ramsey started. He'd been so deep in the noumenal
awareness, he'd forgotten King's presence there, looking
over his virtual shoulder. "No way to tell, sir," he replied
over the link. "Our people have to go inside that mountain.
They'll have a better picture once they do."

"We can't afford to screw around with fanatic holdouts."

"Affirmative, sir."

"We have a little over five hours—"

"Until we come over Krakatoa's horizon. *Yes,* sir." He
was becoming annoyed with King's hovering, dithering
worry.

King missed the exasperation in Ramsey's mental tone—
or chose to ignore it. "Do you think we'll have to use the
cork?"

"Too early to tell, sir."

"Damn it, Ramsey, you're no help. Who's the ARLT commander. . . . Warhurst, is it?"

"Yes, sir—"

"How do I raise him directly? Ah . . . there's the command channel. . . ."

Ramsey felt King opening up the private link with Captain Warhurst.

"Warhurst? This is General King. You are not to use the cork unless I give explicit orders to that effect."

Ramsey didn't hear Warhurst's reply. Abruptly, he pulled out of the noumenon, returning his full awareness to *Derna*'s CIC. King was floating on the other side of the compartment, secured in his harness. "General King. A private word, sir? *Outside* the noumenon?"

After a moment, King's eyes blinked, then opened. Ramsey unsnapped his harness and pushed off from his console, drifting across the compartment to a point near King.

"This is highly irregular, Colonel," King told him as Ramsey caught a hand grip on the overhead and pulled himself to a halt.

"And everything we say over the noumenal link is recorded by Cassius and the *Derna*'s AI," Ramsey replied. "I wanted this to be private."

King arched a skeptical eyebrow. "Oh?"

"Sir, we have to let our people down there do their job. Anything else is micromanagement bullshit and is going to jeopardize the mission. Let's let it play out and see what happens. Sir."

"I could order you to stand down, you know," King told him. "Insubordination! Those aren't *our* people on Ishtar, Colonel. They're the Marine Corps' people, and since I am the senior Marine officer within eight light-years, they are *my* people. Is that understood?"

"With all due respect, General, that's not how the chain of command works. As regimental commander, *I* have authority over my units, and that includes Captain Warhurst and the ARLT. You have overall command of the MIEU, and it is your job, therefore, to determine overall strategies that you then implement through me. Sir."

"Are you telling me my job, Colonel?"

"I am reminding the general that our people at the LZ know what they're doing and that micromanagement will only confuse, slow, and hamper operations. Sir."

King opened his mouth as if to argue, then seemed to think better of it. "The success of this mission, our very survival, depends on Warhurst and the ARLT, Colonel. At the same time, however, my orders require me to secure certain potential assets on Ishtar, assets of considerable value to . . . to Earth. Using a cork would guarantee the destruction of that planetary defense complex down there. But if we can find some sort of control center inside that thing, or access the computer that controls it. . . ."

"The ARLT officers and senior NCOs have all been well-briefed, sir. And we have ten people down there with special download programming for dealing with any instrumentation they may find. If there's any way to capture the facility intact, they'll manage it. If not. . . ." He shrugged, the motion turning him slightly in zero g. He pulled himself back to avoid bumping the general with his feet. "If not, they use the cork in another four hours. That's the plan, as we all agreed to it."

"God help us if this goes wrong, Colonel. God help us all."

King, Ramsey noticed, was sweating heavily, the droplets of moisture beading up and drifting through the air like tiny, gleaming words when he moved his head. *He's terrified*, Ramsey thought. *What the hell is going on with this guy?*

ARLT Section Dragon Three
Objective Krakatoa, Ishtar
1715 hours ST

Garroway had stopped feeling much of anything. His emotions during the past few minutes had seesawed wildly between terror and elation, and Hollingwood's death had left him feeling utterly spent. He watched in numb emptiness as a spidery-looking walker picked its way over the steaming piles of Ahannu bodies and vanished into the gateway crevice.

"Garroway," Valdez said. "You okay?"

"I . . . think so."

"Brandt bought it. I'm moving Sergeant Foster to the PG team. From now on, you're with my fire team. Understand?"

He nodded, then realized his squad leader couldn't see the nod in his helmet. "Uh, yes, Gunny. Aye aye."

"Good man."

The import of Valdez's words was only now beginning to sink in. Second Squad had been organized as four fire teams of three Marines apiece. His fire team had consisted of Hollingwood and Sergeant Cheryl Foster. Lance Corporal Brandt had been teamed, along with PFC Cawley, with Honey Deere and his plasma gun. Brandt's death put a hole in the plasma gun fire team, which needed three experienced operators—gunner, assistant gunner, and spotter/security. Foster was filling that hole, which left Garroway without a fireteam. Valdez's trio, called the squad command team, included Dunne and Pressley. Now he was replacing Pressley in the SCT.

The reshuffle made sense, he supposed, given the need for three experienced hands on the plasma gun. Still, he felt a nagging worry that Valdez was doing it this way just to keep a close eye on him.

"TBC in place and ready to fire," Valdez called over the tac net. *"Fire in the hole!"* An instant later the crevice in the mountainside lit up with a fierce, blue-white light. The shock wave washing over the Marines crouching outside was as thunderous as the detonation from Krakatoa's peak.

Rock was still clattering down the mountainside when Lieutenant Kerns shouted, *"Go! Go! Go!"*

Garroway scrambled to his feet and advanced toward the crevice. "Mind the walls," Valdez warned. "They're still hot."

Hot enough, indeed, to melt any part of Garroway's armor that happened to touch them, though the special insulation on his boots would let him cross the entrance floor without burning his feet. The rock underfoot was oddly plastic, clinging to him like heavy mud with each step. The Thermal Breaching Charge, teleoperated into the gateway by a small remote walker, had momentarily concentrated the heat of a small star against a portion of the blocking door less than a millimeter across. Much of the gate, as well as several tons of surrounding rock, had been turned into plasma and a great deal of energy, leaving behind a larger, gaping hole with walls and floor still incandescent. Air roared into the tunnel as the Marines filed through, entering the larger chamber beyond.

"We're looking for a control center of some kind," Valdez told her squad. "But stay alert. These passageways'll be full of Frogs."

Garroway thought-clicked his light and heat sensitivity up a few notches. It was dark in the high-vaulted cavern beyond the entrance, with only a dim, reddish glow filtering down from somewhere high overhead. With enhanced vision, he could dimly see the far walls of the place, black and rippled, as though the rock had momentarily flowed like water before hardening into something like glass.

The TBC's effects hadn't reached this far inside the mountain, he knew. These chambers in the heart of Krakatoa must have been melted out of the solid volcanic rock millennia ago by a technology at least as advanced as what humankind currently possessed. He overlaid his surroundings with a virtual image drawn from the maps of the tunnel complex stored in his helmet memory, and dim green ghosts of passages and rooms and chambers floated in the darkness around him, beyond the shadowy rock walls. Hot spots from his IR sensors pinpointed places where some of those tunnels opened into the main chamber. Other Marines were already fanning out in several directions to seal those potentially lethal doorways.

He kept looking ahead, though, wondering if some of

those tunnels up there connected with the core of the mountain. Could the Frogs vent some of the titanic fury of their big weapon into these passageways? Not a pleasant thought . . .

"Second Squad," Valdez called. "With me!"

Garroway trotted along after Valdez and Dunne, trying to look in all directions at once. This was a wonderful place for an ambush, if there was going to be one. . . .

It was then that a portion of the chamber wall dissolved and the Marines were enveloped by hordes of Ahannu warriors.

And this time they had no hope of help from air support.

ARLT Command Section, Dragon
One
Objective Krakatoa, Ishtar
1725 hours ST

"They're coming! Open fire!"

"Third Squad! First Squad! Form perimeter! Second Squad, get your asses the hell back here! You're going to be cut off!"

"Mathorne! Where's Mathorne?"

"Get those PGs firing, damn it!"

"Corpsman! Marine down!"

"Second Squad! Damn it, you're being cut off!"

Captain Warhurst listened to the excited shouts and commands coming from inside the mountain and wondered if he could pull the plug.

The "plug" was a Mark XVII laser-plasma-fired backpack fusion demolition device. There were six of them assigned to the ARLT, and four were currently being worn by four different Marines inside the mountain—Gunnery Sergeants Mathorne and Valdez, Staff Sergeant Ostergaard, and Lieutenant Kerns. The remaining two were stored on the lander modules for Dragon One and Dragon Six. Any or all could be detonated by the Marine carrying one, with the appropriate firing codes provided by one of the LM AIs, by Warhurst himself from Lander One, or by the Command Constellation still on board *Derna*. It was believed that one device, with a yield of 0.7 megaton, detonated inside Objective Krakatoa, would collapse enough of the entire mountain to render the Ahannu planetary defense complex useless.

The plug was decidedly an option of last resort, one to be used only if there was no other way to protect the incoming transports. The things could be given a time delay or triggered immediately. The hope, of course, was that one of the Marines could leave a warhead where it would do enough good and give the ARLT time to evacuate to a safe distance, but no one in on the planning for Operation Spirit of Humankind believed that escape would be possible. The plugs turned the ARLT assault into a suicide mission.

Worse, from Warhurst's point of view, only the Marines actually wearing the deadly packs knew what they carried. The rest of the Marines down there didn't know, and that was just plain wrong, Warhurst thought. A man or woman who was going to die when a *friend* thought-clicked a command trigger ought to know what was going to happen . . . and that instantaneous incineration meant success for the rest of the invasion.

But knowledge of the Mark XVIIs had been locked under need-to-know restrictions. Someone higher up the chain of command had decided that knowing about that part of the operation might degrade unit combat efficiency.

That still didn't make it right.

Four warheads were inside the underground complex now, totaling 2.8 megatons. If he was ordered to fire those warheads in the next few minutes . . . could he? No problem if everyone inside was dead when he punched it, but combat rarely worked out that neatly. There would be survivors in there, not to mention the Marines still outside the mountain who might be caught in the blast. None of them would know. . . .

And as the battle inside the mountain increased in fury, Warhurst knew the moment of decision was almost on him.

Damn the waiting . . . and damn the fact that he was stuck out here, instead of inside that mountain with his people.

18

ARLT Section Dragon Three
Objective Krakatoa, Ishtar
1727 hours ST

Second Squad had been ahead of the others when the Ahannu warriors began boiling out of hidden entrances on all sides of the underground chamber. As a black sea of leaping, thronging figures swirled around them, they were in serious danger of being cut off from the ARLT main body.

Garroway dropped to one knee between Well Dunne and Gunny Valdez, pumping 20mm grenades into the horde of attackers, using single shots to conserve his dwindling ammo. Many of these new Ahannu, he noticed, were different from the ones outside—taller, more muscular, and much darker in color, the green-black of their skin making their large, golden eyes even more prominent in the dim light.

These attackers, in fact, were quite different from those he'd studied in downloads on board the *Derna*. A different species? There wasn't any data on the topic one way or another. Their body armor looked heavier, more ornate . . . and seemed to provide better protection from shrapnel and laser bursts.

But they could still be killed. Explosions chopped and tore through the packed ranks of the attackers. The onslaught wavered as the Ahannu in the lead ranks hesitated, unwilling to press in closer to the deadly ring of fire laid down by the hard-pressed Marines.

Then Garroway's M-12 chimed a tone indicating it was out of rounds.

He reached for his belt pack and pulled out his last forty-round magazine. "I'm almost out of grenades," he told the others. "One mag left!"

"Same here," Vinita added.

"I'm out," Chuck Cawley said. "Nothing left but light!"

The attacking wall surged closer. And beyond the massed ranks, Garroway saw a larger shadow, a hulking, humanoid form rising above the smaller Ahannu like a giant, with massive forearms, stooped shoulders, and gold eyes tiny compared to the broad swath of face, almost hidden deep within bony sockets. It carried a long and clumsy-looking weapon, another gauss gun of some kind, but so long that no smaller Ahannu could have wielded it.

"My God!" Garvey screamed. "What the hell *is* that?"

"Just kill it!" Foster barked. "Pour it on!"

Laser fire snapped and flashed across the monster's heavily armored form, eliciting a scream like doomsday. It raised its weapon; Garroway felt the high-velocity round shriek low overhead, felt the concussion behind him.

"Second Squad!" Honey Deere yelled. "Hit the deck!"

Garroway threw himself forward, landing facedown on the rock floor. An instant later lightning snapped and glared overhead with a stuttering burst of thunder. Outside, he'd not noticed the squad's plasma gun in action in all the swirling noise and confusion. Inside this enclosed chamber, however, the rapid-fire bolts of charged plasma banished darkness in a dazzling explosion of light and sound.

Garroway felt the noise fade out as his helmet compensated, and his visual feed darkened as the input filters snapped in. Deere's plasma gun loosed bolts in such rapid succession that the effect was of a single flickering bolt of lightning.

And whatever that lightning touched vanished, exploding in clouds of vapor and sprays of blood and charred tissue. The giant Ahannu collapsed in a heap; smaller Ahannu were scrambling back, falling over one another in their rush to escape.

Someone cut loose with a wild rebel yell. And then the Marines were alone once more in the chamber, surrounded as before by piles of burned, torn, and flame-mutilated bodies.

Other Marines rushed up then, pushing past 2nd Squad. First Platoon was coming through the tunnel now, surrounding the battered remnants of Third Platoon.

Two more casualties. That single round from the giant's gauss gun had smashed through Chuck Cawley's helmet, obliterating his head, before hitting Cheryl Foster in the torso and tearing her apart. With only seven Marines left out of the original twelve, 2nd Squad was seriously under strength.

"Stand down, Third Platoon," Lieutenant Kerns ordered. "We're pulling back to the entrance."

Odd. Garroway felt a strange combination of relief and disappointment. He was happy to be pulled out of the battle line, yeah . . . but he also wanted to see this thing through.

Mostly, though, he was just too damned tired to even think. He trudged back to the entrance with the others, emerging in what looked like bright daylight until his visual filters accommodated. The cavern battle must have taken place in almost total blackness, and he hadn't even realized it.

Outside, the overcast was beginning to break up, with patches of dark green sky showing through black and deep maroon-lit clouds. His helmet AI informed him that it was dawn at the LZ and would remain so for the next several hours. Ishtar's lazy rotation made for long, long periods of night and day, with a lingering, drawn-out transition between the two.

The rest of the ARLT was completing the job of securing the LZ, setting up a perimeter against possible attacks from off the mountain and laying out guide strips for incoming robot supply landers. A supply dump had already been set up on the north side of the ledge; someone had raised a UFR flag on a makeshift staff there, the red, white, and blue cracking hard in the wind.

"Pick up fresh grenade mags and power packs," Valdez ordered. "And check your battle armor for breaches, feed failures, and power drain."

As they replenished their ammo stores, a squad hustled past in single file, vanishing through the yawning gateway into the mountain.

"What's going on?" Kat Vinita asked.

"Ah, don't sweat it," Womicki replied. "Nobody'll tell us nothin' anyway."

"I just had word come down from the captain," Valdez announced to the squad. "Twenty minutes rest. Then it's back to work!"

"Semper fi, man," Dunne said, laughing. "The Corps is always looking after us."

With a groan, Garroway slumped to the ground and was almost instantly asleep.

Chamber of Warrior Preparation
Deeps of An-Kur
Third Period of Dawn

"Our forces retreat," Tu-Kur-La said. He felt a crushing disappointment, mingled with fear. The scenes they were watching, of a fierce battle within the flame-lit passages of An-Kur itself, were coming from the mind of a Commander-of-Sixties actually participating in the battle. Much of that commander's emotion was transmitted through the organic connection that linked them.

"We lose too many warriors," Gal-Irim-Let said within the warm embrace of the Abzu. "And we are not holding them back. *Still* these Marines come."

"Their weapons . . ." the Great Lord said, sighing. "Against such weapons . . ."

"We still have the mountain itself," Dur-En-Mah pointed

out. It was a senior controller in Gal-Irim-Let's staff, a high-ranking drone, one of the lords of An-Kur. "We have destroyed several of their flying weapons. And soon their ships will be within our reach."

"The Kur-Urudug is largely useless against the Marines that have already landed," Tu-Kur-La pointed out. "And we have only warriors to throw at the Marines that have already entered the gate."

"Those worry me," the Great Lord said. "They may have the means of destroying An-Kur."

"The Abzu has detected Divine Weapons among them," Gal-Irim-Let said. "They are small but would do much damage."

"We must stop them!" Dur-En-Mah exclaimed. "They must not be allowed to—"

"Peace, Dur-En-Mah," the Great Lord said. "If they wished to destroy the mountain, they could have done so by now. I think they wish to learn An-Kur's secrets."

"But we should withdraw to a safe place," Tu-Kur-La suggested. "If we withdraw, they may be deceived into believing they have captured An-Kur."

"Sound strategy," the Great Lord said. "Let it be done."

ARLT Command Section, Dragon
One
Objective Krakatoa, Ishtar
1740 hours ST

"New passageway," the voice said in Warhurst's mind. He could see the scene in his noumenon—a high, narrow corridor with smoothly sculpted walls, intense darkness relieved only slightly by wan red lights. The sensors in Lieutenant Frayne's helmet relayed the scene in rapid, uneven sweeps. "No one—"

The transmission was lost in a burst of static.

"Say again, Seeker," Warhurst said. "You're breaking up."

"How's this, Captain?"

"Much better."

"The mountain's blocking transmission, as we expected," Staff Sergeant Krista Ostergaard's voice added. "The relays work okay, but sometimes we have to face just the right way. The lieutenant was saying this looks like a new passageway but that no one's at home."

"Left at the next intersection," Warhurst told them. "If the layout is anything like at Tsiolkovsky, that'll be the control center."

"Roger that," Frayne said. "We're at the intersection. Geez, are you gettin' all this?"

The passageway was opening up now, with the left-hand corridor debouching into a huge, open chamber. The squad, designated Seeker, spread out, examining everything, weapons at the ready. Various sensors reported elevations in temperature, in magnetic flux, in radiation. The air was wet, heavy with steam. Some sort of organic matter—something halfway between jelly and mold—grew on most of the surfaces.

"Affirmative," Warhurst called back. "What's that wet goo covering everything?"

"Not in the IBB, sir," Frayne replied, referring to the data base of Ishtaran life cataloged and transmitted to Earth by the First Expedition. The Ishtaran BioBook was far from complete. "Looks like someone's not been taking proper care of the place, though."

"This is definitely the control center, though," Ostergaard told him. "I see touch controls here . . . and they match the Tsiolkovsky configurations."

Seventy years ago, during the UN War, U.S. Marines had captured a long-dead Ahannu base discovered in the central peak of Tsiolkovsky, on the far side of Earth's moon. The layout had been similar—except that the lunar weapon had been designed to fire antimatter beams. The two facilities must have been erected at more or less the same time . . . some ten to twelve thousand years ago.

"Roger that," Warhurst said. "Plant the charge, Lieutenant. You know the drill. Set it for detonation on direct command, relay trigger, and tamper-trigger. Your team will stay in place until relieved."

"Aye, sir." The microthermonuke in Ostergaard's back-pack was swiftly mounted beneath one of the smoothly sculpted consoles, and Frayne and Ostergaard began setting the detonation triggers.

"Captain Warhurst," another voice said, coming in through the tactical chat link. "This is General King."

"Yes, sir." What was the general doing calling a captain?

"I just heard you order the nuke set for tamper-trigger. What are your intentions?"

"I was going to set the nuke in place, with a squad to watch it. If we need to blow Krakatoa, the squad can do it themselves, or we can fire it here or from orbit using the re-lay at the halfway point in the caverns. And it'll blow if the enemy tries to mess with it, of course."

"I'm not comfortable with that, Captain. Too much can go wrong. Your men might panic and pull the plug too soon."

"What do you suggest, sir?"

"Put the nuke in place, but no tamper charge. We don't want the enemy taking the initiative from us with this thing. And pull your people out of that control room. I don't want them panicking and setting the charge off prematurely."

"Sir, we need to set guards to protect the charge and the relay. . . ."

"The relay, yes. The relay will feed us sensor data on what's going on around the warhead, and we'll need to pro-tect the relay to keep that feed open and to trigger the charge from here. But *I* want that responsibility. No one else should be able to fire the warhead unless I give specific orders to that effect. Do you understand me?"

"Yes, sir."

"Good. Carry on."

"Aye aye, sir."

Warhurst shook his head. Micromanagement reared its ugly head once again.

Still, he could understand the general's position. Setting

off a nuclear warhead was not exactly on the same level as deciding whether or not to return enemy fire. It was an escalation of force that had to be ordered from the very top of the chain of command.

But he was afraid that the constraints King was putting on the mission were going to jeopardize its execution. The more you tinkered with a plan, the more complex and convoluted it became, the greater the certainty that something was going to go the hell wrong.

"Lieutenant Frayne? How's it going?"

"Just about set, Captain."

"New orders, Lieutenant. Set the charge for relay-detonation only, then get the hell out of there. Set a guard on the relay unit, but do not leave anyone in that chamber."

"With pleasure, sir. This place gives me the crawlies."

Frayne reset the trigger mechanism, using his armor AI. "Relay check," he said.

"I've got a signal," Warhurst replied. The relay was transmitting a steady and unobstructed signal from the backpack nuke to Lander One. "You're clear. Set the gunwalkers and pull out."

"On our way out, Captain."

"And about fucking time," Ostergaard added. The squad began filing back out the way it had come.

Maybe, Warhurst thought, just maybe this crazy operation would work out right after all. General King's micromanagement had made him a bit nervous, but with the backpack nuke in place and the relay guarded, they could still pop the mountain's cork anytime they needed to, and the incoming *Derna* and the supply ships would be safe.

Now he needed to see to the security of the Marine ARLT.

ARLT Section Dragon Three
Objective Krakatoa, Ishtar
2250 hours ST

"Awright!" Valdez exclaimed. "The word's just come through. *Derna* and the transports are in orbit! The next wave of LMs is already coming down."

"Outstanding!" Deere said. "About time those assholes quit lounging about in zero g and got their dead asses down here to give us a hand!"

"Who needs a hand, Sarge?" Womicki asked, laughing. "We got this place secured without 'em!"

"Krakatoa, maybe," Valdez said, cocking an eye on the mountaintop looming above them. "But there's still the little matter of New Sumer and the Legation compound. You feel up to tackling those on your own?"

"Hell, no, Gunny," Womicki said, jerking a thumb skyward. "Like Honey says, let *those* guys upstairs do something for a change!"

What was left of 2nd Squad was seated on the ground in a circle not far from their LM, peeling open their self-heating rations and eating. They'd removed helmets and gauntlets but were still encumbered by the heavy shells of their Mark VIIs.

Some six hours had passed since the battle. After a brief rest, the platoon had been assigned to pickup detail, going over the whole LZ, moving Frog bodies and picking up weapons. A science team off the *Derna*, they'd been told, would examine the bodies. The alien weapons were sorted and deposited in piles for later study. And now there was nothing to do but sit, sleep, eat, and talk, while taking turns with the other platoons on perimeter guard.

The sky was definitely lighter now, and the clouds that had shrouded the LZ earlier were breaking up, but it was still darker than an Earthly twilight to unaided eyes. In the east, a line of scarlet-gold light rimming the clouds masking the horizon marked the rise of Llalande 21185. In the west, swollen Marduk loomed vast and wan and ringed in a green and indigo darkness, its banded face pocked with oval storm patterns, each as big or bigger than the Earth. Overhead, a meteor blazed brightly, scratching a thread of light across a sky already aglow with the soft reds and greens of the Ishtaran auroras.

The literally unearthly beauty of this place, Garroway thought, was hypnotic, supremely compelling. It was possible to lose yourself in that sky. . . .

"So what's on the agenda, Gunny?" Gerrold Garvey asked. "Are we out of the war yet?"

"You wish," Valdez said, and the others laughed.

"I don't think the Frogs beat that easy," Deere added.

"You call that *easy*?" Garroway asked sharply, looking up. "We got kicked in the ass today!"

"We *won*, kid," Sergeant Dunne told him. "Right now, that's what counts."

Garroway stared at his hands. They were trembling, the adrenaline-laced aftershocks of the NNTs he'd ridden.

"You okay, Garroway?" Valdez asked. She sounded concerned.

"I'm okay," he said. "I'm okay." The mental image of Pressley's arm dangling in his hand flashed before him only briefly, but bearing with it all the shock and horror of that nightmare moment. He wondered if he would ever be able to forget. . . .

"We wait for orders," Valdez told them, with a sidelong look at Garroway. "The next assault'll be on New Sumer. We hold this mountain and the BFG for the techies . . . and move to reinforce the main attack if they need us."

"Hurry up and wait," Deere said, grinning. "That's the Corps for you, all the way!"

"BFG?" Garvey asked. "What's that?"

Deere grinned wolfishly. " 'Big fuckin' gun,' kid. A big fuckin' gun."

"We've pulled the fangs on the Frog planetary defenses," Valdez added. "Now we watch the rest of the MIEU mop up!"

Garroway leaned back against a boulder and picked at his meal, watching his squad mates as he did so. Their reactions, he thought, were interesting. The vets among them all seemed to be taking this pretty casually, though he suspected that some of the bravado was a kind of verbal protective shell. Of all of them, Valdez seemed to have the most genuine and matter-of-fact responses—those of a professional doing an unpleasant but necessary job.

The two other newbies left in the squad, though, were taking wildly different tacks. Garvey seemed to be doing his best to imitate the veterans in the outfit, cracking jokes and laughing. Kat Vinita, on the other hand, had said very little since the end of the battle and seemed to be withdrawing into herself. He'd seen Valdez sitting with her, talking quietly a while ago, but she hadn't joined in the banter.

Most of the time she was staring into that incredible, glowing sky.

A bit self-consciously, Garroway got up and walked over to Kat, dropping down next to her. "Can I join you?"

She shrugged, still looking into the sky.

"You okay?"

"What's it to you?"

It was his turn to shrug. "Self-therapy, I guess. I got the whim-whams a bit, back there. I thought talking to someone else might help."

She sagged inside her armor. "Sorry. Didn't mean to bite your head off."

"No problem. Chewy or crunchy?"

"Huh?"

"My head."

"Oh." She looked up into the sky again. After a long time she said, "Why does it glow like that?"

"What, the sky? Auroras. Ishtar has a pretty strong magnetic field." He'd already accessed the *Derna*'s noumenal net, wondering the same thing. "And a good thing too, or we wouldn't be able to uncork our armor. Marduk throws off a hell of a lot of radiation. Ishtar's magnetic field traps a lot of it up there, where it excites free atoms of oxygen and other stuff and gives off that glow. If it wasn't for that—"

"We'd be fried, I know. But I thought planets had to rotate to generate a magnetic field. Ishtar is tide-locked to Marduk. It rotates, but slowly, once in six days. And it has a strong one too, almost five gauss. A lot stronger than Earth's."

"I never thought of that." He reached into the net for an answer but found none.

"I already did a search," she said, sensing his uplink. "Some planetologists think the tidal flexing that keeps Ishtar at livable temperatures also stirs up the core enough to generate the mag field. But nobody knows for sure. There's so *much* we don't know. . . ."

He was surprised. She didn't talk like a Marine . . . certainly not like a private. Of course, neither did he—or Lynnley either, for that matter—but her quiet intelligence seemed out of place. Despite the obvious evidence to the contrary, the Marines still bore the unpleasant stereotype of all muscle, no brains.

"Shit!" Dunne snapped from the other side of the circle. "What do those bastards think they're doing?"

"What's wrong, Well?" Deere asked.

"Apricots! Goddamn *apricots!"*

Garroway exchanged a long, quizzical look with Kat. Apricots?

Dunne pulled the foil cover back from one corner of his ration container. The refrigerated portion contained some pale white-orange slices of soft substance and dubious origin. He flung the tray aside. "Bastards should know better'n that!"

"Settle down, Sarge," Valdez told him. "We're not riding armored vehicles."

"Yeah?" Dunne said. He jerked a thumb over his shoulder at the lander. "What the hell is *that*? Or, Jesus, the *Derna*, for that matter?"

"What's his problem?" Garroway asked.

Deere, seated at Garroway's right, chuckled. "An old, old

Marine Corps tradition," he said. "Nineteenth century, at least. It's bad luck to eat apricots. Your APC is bound to break down if you do."

"They didn't *have* armored personnel carriers in the nineteenth century," Womicki pointed out. "Horses, yes. APCs, no."

"Okay, okay, twentieth century," Deere said.

"Everything's cool, Sarge," Garvey said. "The LMs got us down in one piece, right?"

"Yeah. And how the shit are we gonna get over to New Sumer?" Dunne asked. "Or back up to the *Derna*? Walk?"

At first Garroway had thought it was a joke, but Dunne was genuinely angry and upset. Over a silly superstition involving . . . apricots?

He looked down at the ration pack in his lap. He'd already peeled back the foil from the refrigerated part and eaten half of what was there. Funny. He'd not been very hungry before. He was less so now. He set the pack aside.

"It's just superstition, man," Womicki said. "Don't sweat it."

"Yeah, well," Valdez said, "that's just for track drivers, not spacecraft."

"Still ain't right to take chances," Dunne said. "Not this far from home. . . ."

Relative quiet descended over the circle then, though Garroway noticed that the other Marines either weren't eating or weren't eating *all* of their rations. Marines, he decided, were superstitious critters.

"So, how come you're in the Marines?" he asked Kat quietly.

The other Marine stood up abruptly and rushed off. He'd seen tears in her eyes.

"What . . . ?"

"Let her go, Garroway," Valdez said.

"Is she okay?"

"She joined the Corps because her partner joined the Corps. Goddamned stupid reason to sign up. And a damned stupid stunt, lying about it to Personnel."

"Her . . . partner?"

"Her lover. Tom Pressley."

The name hit Garroway square in the gut. "Oh."

"She's riding some NNTs that should cut the grief, but her emotions are going to be swinging pretty wildly for a while. She needs time, is all." Valdez shook her head. "Damn idiots! If I'd just known!"

"What . . . could you have done?" He tried to imagine what it would have been like if that had been *Lynnley* who'd been blown apart out there; tried, and failed.

"The Corps tries to avoid Sullivans."

A quick check of the net acronym and mil-term listing jogged his memory. He'd heard about Sullivans before, back when he and Lynnley had talked about joining up together, being shipped out together. The Sullivans were five brothers in the U.S. Navy, back in one of the wars of the twentieth century. All had been assigned to the same ship, and all were killed when their ship was sunk in battle. Nowadays the name referred to close relatives or partners serving on the same ship or in the same combat theater.

"If I'd known," Valdez continued, "one or the other of them would've damn well stayed on Earth. I could have at *least* had them assigned to different companies in the MIEU. Now we have two casualties instead of just the one."

"Two casualties?"

"Even with the NNTs, it's going to catch up with Vinita sooner or later. We'll need to evac her out of the combat zone and back up to the *Derna* as soon as we can arrange it." Valdez turned away. "Finish your chow, Marine, and then sack out. I'm putting you on the 0200 perimeter watch, and I want you rested."

"Aye aye, Gunny."

He watched Valdez walk away, a tired, lonely figure. Garroway was beginning to appreciate that she carried the burdens of all of the squad as well as her own.

Goddess. When they shipped Kat back up to orbit, the squad would be down to six. Fifty percent casualties.

And the exchange had left him shaken. Shit, he and Lynn-ley had done the same as Vinita and Pressley—joining the Marines with the idea of staying together.

Where was she right now? Garroway stared again into that impossible sky. Hell, where was *he* right now?

And, more important, why? Finding answers, he was learning, was a lot harder than reaching up into the noume-nal data stores.

Chamber of Seeing
Deeps of An-Kur
Seventh Period of Dawn

A seismic quake sent gentle, rumbling shudders through the An-Kur Deeps, but Tu-Kur-La didn't feel it. He was too lost now in the Zu-Din, the Godmind of the Abzu, to feel anything but exaltation.

More and more Keepers of Memory were entering the Abzu now as they were awakened from the Sleep of Ages and engulfed by the Abzu-il. He could feel their presence, a thronging host of mind and thought and will. As the Zu-Din grew, so too did Tu-Kur-La's power and the scope and depth of his vision. Before, linked with the Abzu, he'd still been himself, albeit with access to seemingly limitless informa-tion. Now, however, as a kind of critical mass was reached by the minds linking in . . .

This was what it truly meant to be a god, omnipresent and omniscient, a thousand minds working together in parallel as one with a speed and clarity impossible for any purely natural sentience. Tu-Kur-La's individuality was fading swiftly now; he was no longer Tu-Kur-La of the House of In-Kur-Dru, but the mind and soul of the Abzu itself, the Godmind summoned from the Deeps to once again defend the world of Enduru.

The Race of the Gods *would* survive.

He watched from a thousand vantage points as the enemy

warriors penetrated the Kikig Kur-Urudug, watched as they placed the package beneath a control panel. Sensors within the Abzu-il, which lay like thick jelly on the floors and dripped from the cavern walls, analyzed the device and identified it as a compact thermonuclear device easily large enough to wreck the upper levels of the An-Kur facility.

He could sense too the electromagnetic signals passing between the device and a series of relays set up in the corridors leading to the outside of the mountain. Traps and sensors within the device would probably detonate it if it were tampered with. The problem would require some thought.

The Godmind was both highly intelligent in its own right and supremely fast. The Abzu-il that lay like a gelatinous blanket through much of An-Kur's underground workings was a biological construct, something created countless cycles ago to connect the various Keepers of Memories. It possessed an artificial intelligence of high order and considerable volition; that AI had been charged with the defense of An-kur, and had responded to the attack a few periods ago on its own initiative. Now, however, that intelligence expanded dramatically as living Ahannu minds linked in.

In the skies over Enduru three large but primitive spacecraft were entering orbit. Through remote sensors scattered about the planet, the Godmind could sense the cloud of smaller ships debarking from the larger. Enduru was being invaded.

Briefly, the Godmind mourned. So much, so very much, had been lost since the coming of the Hunters of the Dawn. These invaders, descendants of the Sag-ura of lost Kia, were primitives, their ships not even capable of faster-than-light travel. Unfortunately, the Ahannu's own assets were badly depleted, their weaponry especially. Enduru's defenders would rely on weapons more primitive than those of the invaders.

No matter. Numbers—and the superior speed and intellect of the Godmind—would be enough to preserve Enduru. And the Godmind saw now what needed to be done to stop the detonation of the nuclear device in the control center.

With a thought, the Godmind summoned again the defenders of An-Kur. . . .

19

Combat Information Center
IST Derna, *approaching Ishtar orbit*
2317 hours ST

Within the link, Ramsey looked down on Ishtar from space, the virtual presences of Dr. Hanson and Gavin Norris hovering by his shoulders. From their noumenal vantage point they seemed to be moving swiftly above the swirl and stippling of a broad swath of clouds, clouds tinged with red and gold from the light of the distant sun. Breaks in the cloud cover revealed glimpses of a tortured landscape, sere desert crisscrossed by vast, yawning fault valleys and rugged mountains; stretches of salty sea filling low-lying rifts like fingers; glaciers clinging to broad, mountain plateaus; savage storms each the size of a subcontinent; and everywhere the black-smudge plumes of active volcanoes.

"Not exactly the sort of neighborhood where you want to raise your kids," Norris said quietly. "You wouldn't think anything could live down there."

"That's almost certainly why the Ahannu colony survived," Hanson explained. "The Hunters of the Dawn must have swept through this part of the galaxy, destroying every trace of sentient life and civilization they could find. We know they wiped out every Ahannu colony on Earth and on Earth's moon.

"But their search wasn't perfect. They missed scattered

bands of human survivors on Earth—overlooked them or ignored them—or else we wouldn't be here to talk about it.
And they missed the Ahannu colony here."

"Why?" Ramsey asked.

He felt her noumenal shrug. "Perhaps they were searching
for evidence of technology . . . radio transmissions, neutrino
leakage from fusion reactors, that sort of thing. That's probably why our ancestors escaped on Earth. Flint-knapping
and campfires don't show up very well from space. Out
here . . . well, like Mr. Norris said, this isn't exactly prime
real estate. Ishtar is five times farther from its star than Earth
is from the sun, and Llalande is a cool red dwarf. Anything
this far out ought to be frozen solid at ten or twenty degrees
Kelvin."

"It's not because Marduk is a brown dwarf, right?" Norris
said. "A failed star."

"Incorrect," the voice of Cassius said. "The gas giant
Marduk is of insufficient mass to be classified as a true
brown dwarf."

"Actually," Hanson added, "the gas giant does give off a
lot more heat than it receives from the star, but not enough
on its own to make Ishtar habitable. Most of Ishtar's heat
comes from tidal sources—volcanism and seismic activity—caused by the constant tug-of-war on it between the gas
giant and the other major satellites of Marduk. It's like Io
and Jupiter in our own Solar system, though not quite so extreme. Instead of the entire crust turning itself inside out, the
tidal flexing gradually liberates heat that is trapped by
Ishtar's atmosphere and oceans."

"Still, you'd think the Hunters of the Dawn would have
noticed the anomaly," Ramsey said. "A planet-sized moon,
warm and with an atmosphere, this far out . . ."

"There are lots of unusual things about Ishtar," Hanson
said. "The tidal friction is *just* enough to create a habitable
band around the Marduk twilight zone . . . not too much, not
too little. The atmosphere is thick enough to trap the heat re-

leased through volcanism and crustal movements. There's enough of an ionosphere and a planetary magnetic field to deflect the worst of the radiation from Marduk. The storms caused by the constant heating of Ishtar's oceans are incredible, but some of the fault valleys in the twilight band offer shelter enough for a small civilization to survive. All things considered, the chances of finding a livable world here must be somewhere between damned slim and nonexistent."

"Is it possible Ishtar is the product of planetary engineering?" Ramsey wondered. "I mean, with that many coincidences . . ."

"We were actually wondering about that for a while," Hanson replied. "After all, Mars shows evidence of having been terraformed half a million years ago. We thought for a while it might be possible that the Ahannu were responsible.

"But the Ahannu don't appear to have ever possessed that level of technology. Star travel, yes . . . but not changing climates and atmospheres on a planetary scale. No, the civilization we call the Builders terraformed Mars 500,000 years before the Ahannu came on the scene. The Builders were wiped out by an even more technically proficient civilization, the race that created 'the Singer' that we found out on Europa."

"The Hunters of the Dawn," Norris said.

"Mmm. Possibly," Hanson said. "It doesn't seem likely that the same folks who wiped out the Builders on Mars and the civilization we found at Alpha Centauri would have survived half a million years, to be on hand in time to wipe out the Ahannu."

"Though both predatory species have been called 'Hunters of the Dawn' in popular literature," Cassius observed, "the time span involved makes it extremely unlikely that the same 'Hunters' destroyed both the Builder civilization and the starfaring Ahannu culture. In any case, the Singer discovered beneath the ice at Europa represents a technology far beyond the probable technology of the destroyers of the Ahannu colonies half a million years later. There are considerable xenoarcheological problems inherent in identifying the two as one."

"Can't you shut that damned thing off?" Norris asked.

Ramsey grinned. "Not likely. Cassius is a part of our Command Constellation. Besides, Cass, you were out there at the Singer, weren't you?"

"Correct. Though there was scant opportunity for exploration. My primary task on Europa was guard duty."

"Yeah, well, there's no sign of the Dawn Hunters nowadays," Norris pointed out, ruffled. "Except for the mess they left behind."

"We hope," Ramsey added. He'd downloaded enough data on the Ahannu and on the Builders to know something of current xenohistorical theory. "From what I've DLed, galactic civilization comes and goes in waves. Things are just starting to tick along smoothly, then along comes a predator race—like the Hunters—who follow the notion that the best survival strategy is to eliminate the competition. *All* of the competition. Then they destroy themselves, and the stage is set for the next turn of the wheel. Is that right, Dr. Hanson?"

"That's the idea. It's called the Predatory Survivors Hypothesis, and it's the best answer we've come up with yet for Fermi's Paradox."

"Fermi's Paradox?" Norris said. "What's that?"

"Look it up on the net," Hanson told him.

" 'Where are they?' was the question supposedly asked by a physicist named Enrico Fermi, back a couple of hundred years ago," Cassius explained. "Basically, it notes that even if faster-than-light travel is impossible, a single technic race could spread out and colonize the entire galaxy in a few hundred thousand years."

"Right," Ramsey said. "Back in Fermi's day there was no sign of alien colonists, none that we recognized at the time, anyway. So the question was . . . where are they? Why aren't they here? If they're not here, what happened to them?"

"It was actually pretty strong evidence that we were alone," Hanson said. "That we were the only technic civilization in the galaxy or one of a very, very few. Since then, of course, we've found out that habitable planets are common . . . and intelligence must be fairly common too. We know of at least three now and possibly four sentient species besides ourselves—the Ahannu, the Builders, and either one or two groups of Hunters . . . all, apparently, in the same corner of a very *large* galaxy."

"The Predatory Survivors Hypothesis suggests that many sentient species arise and develop technology at roughly the same time," Cassius said. "However, in each cycle there is certain to be at least one species that survives by killing off all the competition."

"Yeah," Ramsey said. "Maybe it's something hardwired into certain species by evolution, with the idea that survival-of-the-fittest means survival-of-the-*meanest*. Or maybe it's more random than that. What we seem to see, though, is that every so often a predator species explodes across the galaxy, wiping out every other species in its path. And civilization has to start all over again."

"A pretty grim scenario," Norris said.

"It is," Hanson agreed. "But it's the only theory we've found that explains how intelligence can appear as a matter of evolutionary routine, if given even half a chance, and yet also explains why someone hasn't already snapped up and colonized every habitable world in sight."

"It would also explain why the Ahannu built something like that giant relativistic cannon down there," Ramsey said. "They were *scared*. Scared the Hunters were going to find them. They must've known the Hunters were looking for them, and they couldn't trust that they wouldn't find them."

They were passing over Ishtar's day side now. Marduk hung in the sky almost directly overhead, a vast, golden-rimmed crescent, along with a half dozen of the nearer, larger moons threaded like pearls on the silver thread of the gas giant's rings. The ruby gleam of Llalande 21185 touched the giant's horizon, then swiftly faded out. Stars reappeared as *Derna* and the two transports swept into Marduk's planetary shadow.

Below, night reigned once more. Vast fields of molten lava glowed with sullen, scarlet anger, as volcanoes and lightning illuminated the cloud deck from beneath with eerily shadowed glows and shimmers.

A world of storms, fire, and ice, Ramsey thought. Not a bad analog of Hell.

Closer at hand, TAL-S landers deployed for deceleration. They were due to deorbit in another . . . fifteen minutes. Worker pods unloaded the transports, readying canisters of supplies for guided reentry.

"Colonel Ramsey?" It was General King, entering the noumenon. The discussion between Ramsey and the two civilians was tagged private over the net, but a general's personal security key overrode most encryption lockouts.

"Aye, sir."

"Any change on the situation at Krakatoa?"

"No, sir."

"Mr. Norris? I still don't see why your people are so interested in that damned mountain. It is a menace to this operation so long as it remains intact."

"General, that mountain represents the single piece of useful technology we've seen on Ishtar, not counting the Pyramid of the Eye, of course. That may be the only thing that made this whole jaunt out here worthwhile."

"Don't be an ass, Norris," Hanson said. "*You're* making a pleasant profit. As am I."

"I'm talking about profit for PanTerra . . . and Earth. They've put enormous resources into this expedition. They deserve a payoff."

"I thought we were here to rescue human slaves, Mr. Norris," Ramsey said with a lightly sarcastic edge to his voice. He'd seen little evidence that Norris or his people back on Earth were that interested in freeing slaves. It was technology they were after. Alien technology. And that mountain must hold secrets worth an obscene fortune to PanTerra.

"Give me a break," Norris said. "Social do-gooding is fine, but it doesn't begin to pay for an interstellar mission." He shrugged. "Besides, the Sag-ura have been slaves down there for ten thousand years, right? They can wait a few years longer, if need be."

"I'm sure both Congress and the Marine Corps share your views, sir," Ramsey said. He had to bite down on the words to keep his anger from leaking across the interface into the noumenon. Norris, he'd decided, was a thoroughgoing son of a prick, but the MIEU was stuck with him, whatever his own feelings in the matter might be.

If Norris heard Ramsey's sarcasm, he ignored it. "General, I can't stress enough the importance of that planetary defense base. We *must* have access to its secrets."

"We do," Ramsey told him. "The first phase of the assault has gone smoothly. Surprisingly smoothly, in fact. We've taken the mountain, and an ARLT xenotech team is on-site now, examining the thing. You do realize, though, that any secrets inside that mountain are going to take years of study to winkle them out. Our people have reported they don't understand more than a fraction of what they've found."

"The next phase is to take the Legation area of New Sumer and the Pyramid of the Eye," King said, "which will commence with our next orbit. After that we can begin negotiations with the Frogs."

"If they agree to it," Hanson pointed out.

"Of course, of course," King said. "I suspect this show of force will be sufficient to force them to the bargaining table. But . . . Colonel?"

"Sir?"

"I've posted my standing orders on the net and to every platoon, company, and battalion leader in the task force. If there is even a quiver out of that mountain, we pop the cork. Understand me?"

"Yes, sir."

"I will not risk the entire MIEU to PanTerra's profit motive, however compelling that might be. I'm counting on you, Colonel, to detonate that nuke if it becomes necessary to do so in order to protect the fleet. Clear?"

"Aye aye, sir."

"Good. Carry on." The general's noumenal presence faded from the link.

Around the three noumenal viewpoints, the orbiting fleet emerged again from Marduk's eclipse of the local star. A hundred kilometers below, an ocean steamed and fumed.

"Shortsighted idiot," Norris said, the words barely audible.

"Belay that crap," Ramsey told him. "*He* is in command of this mission."

"That doesn't make him right. You've felt his fear? The man is terrified. He's going to order An-Kur blown if he just *thinks* there's danger. It was a mistake bringing him on."

"Oh? And what did PanTerra have to do with the selection of the MIEU's chain of command?"

"PanTerra organized the international follow-up expedition, Colonel, and to win the cooperation of so many foreign governments, they had to make certain . . . concessions. Among those was to choose as supreme commander for the MIEU, a man all could agree on. General King has had a great deal of experience working in diplomatic circles with various of the other governments, including Brazil and the Kingdom of Allah. He was the best compromise candidate among available senior Marine officers."

"I see." Ramsey hadn't expected a straight answer from the man. "Then if he's that experienced, why—"

"The man has family," Norris said. "Two husbands, a wife, and two kids. He is a deliberate exception to the military's famsit rules."

Which explained a lot. There wouldn't be many senior officers available who were domestically unattached.

"He must have volunteered, surely," Hanson said. Exceptions could always be made in any set of regulations.

"Sure. And to get him, PanTerra is providing very well indeed for the general and for the members of his immediate family—including anagathic treatments that will keep them in step with him over the course of a twenty-year-objective mission. Jesus, you know how expensive *those* are. Just the same, a man isn't as trustworthy out here if he's separated from a family."

"General King is a Marine," Ramsey said. "He'll do what has to be done."

Ramsey cared little for General King and hadn't been impressed with the man so far. He'd never expected to find himself defending King to anyone else.

But Norris was the outsider here. The Marines did not abandon their own.

Chamber of Seeing
Deeps of An-Kur
Eleventh Period of Dawn

The Zu-Din gave the command: *Attack!*

God-warriors spilled from narrow access passageways into the main caverns, shrieking battletruth and grappling with the enemy. The enemy warriors, three of them protected by layers of impossibly tough armor, did not go under with the first onslaught, but the sheer ferocity of the assault knocked them back and swept them along, like wood chips on a flood.

Sag-ura *gudibir*, human slave-warriors, joined the attack this time, rushing forward with shrill yells, brandishing their weapons, and the Godmind noticed an interesting fact. The enemy warriors *hesitated* at the sight of members of their own species, hesitated and held their fire until the advancing mass was almost upon them.

The enemy opened fire at the last possible moment, their

flame-weapons ripping through the packed mass of lightly armored or naked slave-warriors to hideous, shrieking effect. And then the defenders were slammed back against the cavern wall. Through the artificial senses of the Abzu-il, the Godmind watched and listened as the three became two . . . then one. Then the enemy warriors were dead; a human slave danced in the passageway, holding high a bloody head still encased in an armored helmet.

Another held the relay, a small, silver canister resting on tripod legs on the floor of the passageway.

The Godmind communicated its orders, and the warriors returned to the side passages. In moments, as the relay was carried deeper into the mountain, the transmission between the nuclear device and the enemy forces outside was severed.

There'd been a possibility, of course, that loss of signal would trigger the device, but the Godmind felt secure in probabilities. Military devices would be designed to allow for power failures or equipment breakage. With a weapon as powerful as the nuclear device left in An-Kur's control center, the Enemy would want positive control, the ability to trigger the thing deliberately rather than risk an accident with potentially devastating consequences.

It had a great deal of experience with humans and human reactions from which to draw.

The Enemy would be reacting to the Godmind's assault very swiftly now, however. Sensors buried in the surface of the mountain's peak scanned the sky, watching for the spacecraft in orbit. The calculations would have to be extraordinarily precise, with no room for error. . . .

The mountain's sensors picked up the heat and radar signatures of a number of spacecraft coming in from the east . . . but these were too small and too fast to be the primary targets. Another invasion wave, then, landing craft bearing more ground troops. The Godmind overrode the simple and somewhat limited artificial intelligence of the Kur-Urudug. Wait . . . wait . . . there! Rising now above the eastern horizon ... the signatures of three huge, orbiting spacecraft.

The Godmind targeted the lead vessel, as the power within An-Kur's deep core swiftly mounted.

ARLT Command Section, Dragon
One
Objective Krakatoa, Ishtar
2354 hours ST

They'd underestimated the Ahannu, and badly ... that, or the Marine ARLT had just had its legs cut out from under it by one hell of a coincidence. And in Captain Warhurst's experience, coincidence was nothing more than a myth used to explain relationships that no one understood.

He was kicking himself mentally for not having followed his first impulse and deploying a sizable contingent of Marines to guard the nuclear warhead in the alien control center. General King's orders had been specific, though, and he wouldn't have been able to leave troops in the mountain's control center without risking direct insubordination.

But damn it, if he'd even left a ready-strike team in place within easy reach of the nuke, just in case something went wrong ...

And things certainly were wrong now, with the telltale magnetic flux within the mountain building, the relay in Ahannu hands, and all contact with the nuclear weapon lost. Someone with the appropriate trigger codes would have to go inside the mountain again to get within range of the weapon in order to set it off. That meant Lieutenant Kerns, with a fire team in support.

If that was the order to come through from orbit. The trouble was, he'd put through an up-link call to either Colonel Ramsey or General King, but so far neither had responded.

The suddenness of the renewed attack had caught everyone off balance.

If the order didn't come through . . . would he be able to blow that mountain anyway? Against orders? He might have to in order to save the *Derna*.

ARLT Section Dragon Three
Objective Krakatoa, Ishtar
2354 hours ST

The alarm in Garroway's head brought him to full alertness, and he sat upright so sharply his head struck a projecting ledge on the bulkhead beside him.

He'd been trying to get some shut-eye, as Valdez had ordered, lying on a sleeping bag unrolled on the deck inside the Dragon Three LM. A command to his implant had begun to close down the waking portions of his brain, leaving him in a comfortable state of half-awareness when the alert came in.

Rubbing his head, he grabbed his helmet, gloves, and rifle and stumbled from the lander, along with several other Marines who'd been similarly awakened. "What the hell?" Corporal Womicki said. "I can't link through!"

Garroway was trying to download an AI update through his link as well, and also without success. He kept getting the tone indicating a system error. The local node, however, was online, providing the disturbing news that a magnetic field was building inside the mountain's core.

The bastards were getting ready to fire that god-awful gun again.

He saw Valdez, Lieutenant Kerns, and a handful of other Marines running across the LZ toward the gateway to the mountain. "Gunny!" he called out. "Where do we go?"

Valdez turned and looked at him, her face pale and sharp-edged. "Stay here, Private. You're not trained for this."

Trained for what? "I can learn, Gunny. Where do you want me?"

"Stay here! That's an order!" And she was gone, jogging after Lieutenant Kerns.

Combat Information Center
IST Derna, *in Ishtar orbit*
2358 hours ST

The net had jammed.

It hadn't gone down—thank all the gods of technology for that—but data could only flow from node to node through the system so fast, and when the data packets began queuing up, taking their turn in line, bottlenecks were sure to form.

Extremely tight, extremely *dangerous* bottlenecks.

A frequent problem in the early days of the Internet was narrow bandwidth, with too-small channels creating a traffic jam of data. Something of the sort was happening now, as more and more demands were placed on the transmission carriers, data-routing AIs, and relay nodes, both those on board the starships and those already on the planet.

The *Algol* had already launched two of the five communications satellites that would provide for full-time data access, but the net so far was operating only at about forty percent of full efficiency, with most of the storage, switching, and retrieval functions handled by Cassius on board the *Derna*. The streams of broadband data uploading continually to *Derna*'s CIC had already severely taxed the system.

Now, as the alert went out, the system slowed. First to be cut out were the low-ranking data requests—Marines on the ground, mostly, querying the system to see what was going on. As additional ground sensors kicked in to monitor events inside An-Kur, though, the communications blackout spread to upper echelons as well. Cassius was working to pull the system back into balance, but the effort would take a minute or two more yet. . . .

Chamber of Seeing
Deeps of An-Kur
Eleventh Period of Dawn

The Godmind had a firm target lock. *Fire!*

The magnetic flux surged, sparking violet lightnings within the mountain core. A tiny sliver of rock, accelerated to nearly the speed of light, was transformed into a bolt of high-energy plasma flicking up the mountain's throat in a tiny instant of time, deflected at the peak by powerful directional fields and sent searing through tortured atmosphere toward the target.

A hit!

Combat Information Center
IST Derna, *in Ishtar orbit*
2359 hours ST

Ramsey was still trying to open the data-stream channel between *Derna* and the LZ when the bolt flashed clear of Ishtar's atmosphere and struck the *Algol,* in orbit less than fifty kilometers ahead of the *Derna* and the *Regulus.* In the noumenon, he could see the *Algol* as a bright star adrift above the slow-turning expanse of gold and violet clouds that was Ishtar's curved horizon, saw the clouds suddenly burn blue-white . . . and in the same instant the star marking the transport flared to nova brightness.

Another instant passed . . . and then *Derna*'s AI sounded a ship alarm within the noumenon. "Debris on collision course. Debris on—"

Something struck the *Derna,* punching through the reaction mass tank like a bullet through cardboard. The shock sent the huge vessel into a tumbling roll.

Ramsey felt himself slam against a real-world bulkhead just before the noumenon snapped off, draining from his mind and leaving him in a dazed fog of disorientation and pain. It was pitch-black—power failure. He could hear the thrashing and panicked cries of others in the CIC and in the hab deck outside.

"Cassius!" he called. "Cassius! Are you online?"

There was no answer. He tried to rise, but the normal spin-gravity of the hab module was complicated now by the additional vector of *Derna*'s tumble. It made navigation almost impossible in the darkness. A chair broke free of a deck fitting and slammed against a bulkhead a few meters away.

"God damn it!" That was General King. "What the hell happened?"

"We took a piece of the *Algol*, sir," Ramsey replied.

"Lights!" Ricia called in the darkness. "Someone hit the emergency lights!"

Shit. They should have come on automatically. How bad was the *Derna* hit?

And how long before the Ahannu fired their weapon a second time . . . and finished the job?

20

Lander Dragon Three
Krakatoa LZ, Ishtar
0004 hours ST

"Everyone back to your landers," Captain Warhurst called, his voice coming over straight radio now instead of the netlink. "Emergency evac, everyone but Task Force Kerns! Move! Move!"

Garroway froze in place for a moment, uncertain what to do, where to go. His squad and platoon leaders were headed for the gateway leading into the mountain, along with a dozen other Marines from several different squads. Task Force Kerns? Valdez had told him he wasn't trained for this. With a sudden, sharp presentiment, he realized what Task Force Kerns was trying to accomplish.

Private Vinita stood nearby, obviously as lost at the moment as he. "C'mon, Kat. Back to the LM." Overhead, Dragon Three was circling toward the lander, strobes flashing brilliantly on belly and wing tips.

"Where are they going?" she asked.

"At a guess, I'd say to blow up that damned mountain. Our orders are to evac. *Now.*"

"I can't reach the net. . . ."

"Worry about that later. Run!"

Together, he and Vinita jogged toward Lander Three. Womicki, Dunne, and Garvey were the only other members of their squad there. Deere must have gone with Valdez, Garroway and Vinita banged up one of the open ramps, along with several Marines from a different platoon just as the ramps began to slowly close.

The net was definitely down, and he felt an aching loneliness nearly as acute as when they'd yanked his implant in boot camp. Radio messages were coming through on his helmet's communications suite, but they were scattered and erratic, requiring his active concentration to make any sense out of what was being said. The words no longer simply materialized in his head, already filed and processed.

"Move! Move! Get those ramps up!"

"Kerns to ARLT Command! We're inside the first tunnel. We've got bandits in here, Captain. Lots of 'em!"

"Kerns, Warhurst! Don't stop to play. Keep moving to Waypoint One!"

"Roger that. Moving!"

The Dragon nestled down over the landing module with a metallic clang and the thump of grapples slamming home. With a lurch, the module was plucked from the ground, the shock sending close-packed Marines staggering into one another, armor clashing against armor. Garroway tried to uplink to get an image from an outside camera and got the system error signal again. Damn. He'd forgotten.

The next minute was an eternity, crowded into the lander, standing room only, unable to move, unable to see out, unable to know what was happening outside. The comm channels were flooded with radio chatter as other Marines tried to find out what was going down.

"Does anybody have a link connect?"

"What the fuck is going on?"

"Gunny! Gunny Kendrick!"

"Did the bastards nail the *Derna?*"

"They'll target us next."

"Nah. They'll be busy picking the starships out of orbit. Shit!"

"All right, people! Ice it down! Can the chatter!"

"This is Captain Warhurst. Now hear this. Our communications and data nets are down. As near as we can tell, one of the supply transports was hit by a shot from that Frog cannon, but we have also lost direct contact with the *Derna*. Our AI says she's still in orbit but possibly damaged. I'll give you more news as it comes through.

"In the meantime, do not panic. We are Marines. We improvise. We adapt. We overcome, whatever the situation. Right now our greatest enemy is panic.

"You will also remain silent. Do not access the net until I pass the word that it is safe to do so. Keep radio silence except in the strict line of duty. Now stand by. We may be in for a bit of a rough ride here."

And that, Garroway thought, was a sure bet.

Lander Dragon One
In flight, Ishtar
0005 hours ST

Warhurst was struggling to get a partial Net back on-line.

Any net, from the first DARPA Net two centuries before to the GlobalNet that currently enmeshed Earth and various Solar colonies and expeditions in a complex web of computing nodes, linked by data-sharing protocols. Those links could be copper or optical cable, broadband radio, maser, IR laser, or polyphasic quantum entanglement; the important thing was the transmission of data. Until moments before, the fledgling Ishtar Net had consisted of the AI systems on three starships, the relay nodes of two communications satellites, and several hundred smaller processors, from the AIs of the lander modules and TAL-S Dragonflies, to the thumbnail-sized digital assistants in the helmet of each Marine, to the even tinier mesh of nanochelated conductors grown inside each Marine's cerebral cortex.

The MIEU Network, already operating at only a fraction of its full capacity, had been dealt a deadly blow. One of the starship AIs was completely destroyed, while the major complex of processing nodes, *Derna* herself, was offline and also possibly destroyed. The Command Constellation AI, Cassius, which had been overseeing the operation and deployment of the network, had been isolated on board *Derna* and was out of touch. Worse, the relay/router satellites, an incomplete beginning to the necessary full array of redundant communication links, had been linked to *Derna* and were also out of the running. What Warhurst had at his disposal now was a scattered and disorganized array of computers with an aggregate processing power equivalent to perhaps five percent of Cassius and the *Derna*'s network system alone.

What he hoped to do, however, was reestablish the orderly flow of data within a truncated portion of the MIEU Net. He needed to know where each of his Marines was, what his status was, and what he was doing. The Marines all needed to talk with one another and with personnel up the chain of command, as well as interface with their weapons' aiming and ammo programming systems. Ideally, they needed access to everything from basic information on Ishtar and the Frogs to ballistics tables, stores and logistical lists, and interactive maps.

More, Warhurst knew he needed to reestablish a message routing system that would let him talk with any subset of the ARLT he desired, whether that be all of the Marines, only the squad leaders, the officers, the pilot AIs, or any other combination imaginable. To that end, he had the talents of Lander One's AI, a utilitarian Corps-issue, Honeywell-Sony Mark XL that had the personality of a rock and an initiative to match, but a fair set of software tools for jury-rigging a new command/control network.

In the meantime, he had radio communications on twelve available channels. They could work with that . . . at least for now. Given time and half a chance, he might even be able to restore partial linkage through the Marines' neural implants—faster, more secure, and less prone to garbling than straight radio.

The trouble was, they didn't have much time at all. That monstrous gun would keep firing until the starships were destroyed, and then it would turn on the ARLT, unless Task Force Kerns was able to carry out its suicidal mission.

Damn it! Why hadn't he given the order to destroy that damned weapon as soon as they'd had the chance? The hell with the civilians' needs to study everything in sight!

Now everything, *everything*, depended on the next few minutes. . . .

Task Force Kerns
Depths of An-Kur, Ishtar
0007 hours ST

They raced down the stone passageway, searching for the proper turning of the way. Without the net, they no longer had access to the maps and 3D scans either of An-Kur's tunnel complex or of the similar complex at Tsiolkovsky on Earth's moon. What they had instead were their own memories of this alien labyrinth, memories acquired only hours ago under less than optimum conditions.

"This way!" Valdez snapped. "Lieutenant! Down this way!" She recognized the opening in the wall to the right, the basaltic rock to either side scarred by laser pulses and shrapnel from RPG bursts. A pair of Frog warriors emerged from the opening, brandishing spears with curved blades. Honey Deere burned them both down before anyone else could manage a target lock.

There were fourteen Marines in the hastily assembled task force, counting Valdez and Lieutenant Kerns. The rest were a motley collection of NCOs from several platoons pulled from the LZ because they each had a key asset highly prized by Marine field vets: *experience*. The lowest ranking of them all was Corporal Luttrell, and in his six years of service so far he'd managed to see action in Egypt, China, and

Colombia, pick up a Bronze Star and two Purple Hearts, *and* be busted twice for insubordination.

There would be no room in these narrow tunnels for men or women who hadn't been under fire and learned how to cope with it. That was why Valdez had turned Garvey, Garroway, and Vinita away, along with several other newbies who'd volunteered. They'd done well enough in the firefight earlier, all of them . . . but often the *second* time under fire was the telling one, the moment when a Marine steeled himself to go knowingly into Hell's jaws, dead certain of what awaited him there. She'd seen Marines who'd gone through their first firefight without a quiver freeze solid on their second encounter with the demon of combat. She was taking no chances.

Ahannu warriors and human slaves spilled into the tunnel ahead, dimly seen figures throwing weirdly flickering shadows from the Marines' helmet lamps. Deere's plasma gun stuttered, the flashes strobing wildly in the near darkness. Lasers, their beams made visible in the dust and smoke filling the tunnel, crisscrossed in brief, snapping flashes, and an RPG hissed through the air, swerving to turn a corner ahead, then detonating with a savage blast. A naked, tattooed human wielding a massive, double-headed ax charged to within two meters of the Marine column; Valdez triggered her 2120, twitching the muzzle up, the pulse slashing the man from groin to sternum, spilling his intestines to the ground in a bloody gush.

The slaughter in those close quarters was indescribable, a bloody, searing, nightmare of darkness and burned flesh; of hideous shrieks; of bodies piled four deep on the cavern floor, gruesomely burned, blast-torn, and mutilated.

And then the Ahannu forces dissolved away, fleeing as the Marines advanced. The tunnel opened into a broader chamber, and now the Marines came under fire as Ahannu godwarriors carrying a variety of clumsy-looking gauss-fired weapons opened up from perches on the cavern walls and from the cover of a spill of boulders ahead. Sergeant

DaSilva staggered, then collapsed, a neat, round hole punched through her helmet faceplate. Staff Sergeant Stryker screamed as his left arm was torn away by a massive round ripping through his shoulder. And there were more of those damned giant Ahannu up there at the end of the tunnel, firing their bigger-than-life gauss guns.

For the next ten seconds—an eternity in a close and desperate firefight like this one—lasers and plasma bolts snapped and crackled across the cavern. A barrage of grenades crashed among the boulders at the far end of the room.

Valdez feared that the detonations were about to bring the walls of the cave down on top of them all. "Hold the grenade fire!" she called out. "We'll cause a cave-in!"

"I doubt it, Gunny," Staff Sergeant Ostergaard replied, shouting to be heard above the racket. "After a few thousand years of major seismic quakes and the shock of that BFG going off, I doubt there's anything *we* can do worse!"

Valdez digested this, then nodded in her helmet. "Right, Marines! Hit 'em with everything you got!"

Again the Ahannu defenders began to melt away, scurrying off into side tunnels or vanishing up the curve of the main passageway ahead. The Marines advanced, all save Stryker, who was rapidly fading into shock. Sergeant Knowles looked up at Kerns and shook her head. "His suit medic is fried, Lieutenant. I can't stop the bleeding."

"We can't leave him here," Valdez said.

"And we can't spare the assets to send him back," Kerns decided. "Bring him along."

Valdez noticed an amber light blinking weakly on her helmet display. With the net down, they were relying solely on radio communications now. The amber light indicated that they were picking up the signal from the backpack nuke in the control center, somewhere up ahead.

"Hey, Lieutenant—"

"I see it, Valdez."

"Yeah. This is the cavern where we left the relay. The warhead ought to be another two hundred meters up that way."

"We got company, gang," Gunnery Sergeant Horst warned. "Ahead *and* behind!"

Ahannu god-warriors were spilling back into the cavern. The Marines had advanced far enough that that they were in danger of being surrounded, as enemy fighters emerged from tunnel mouths and cave passageways . . . including the opening of the narrow tunnel from which they'd just emerged.

"Perimeter defense!" Kerns ordered. "Fire at will!"

"Bad guys at three o'clock!"

"Pour it on 'em!"

"Task Force Kerns, Task Force Kerns, do you copy? Over . . ."

"Hold it, people!" Valdez yelled. "Quiet! Radio call comin' through!"

"Task Force Kerns, this is Dragon One. Do you copy?" The words were badly distorted, blurred by static.

"We hear you, Dragon One!" Kerns shouted. "You're weak! Repeat, transmission weak!"

"Report— . . . pon   magnetic . . . building . . . hurry—" The static built to a shrill squeal.

"Say again, Dragon One!" Kerns shouted. "Repeat and boost your gain! Your message breaking up!"

"I say again . . . mountain . . . mag . . . field building up. We think . . . Derna . . ."

"Shit," Ostergaard said. "The Frogs are getting ready to fire their BFG again."

The Ahannu rushed the circle of Marines. For several seconds nothing could be heard above the crack and snap of lasers, the shrieks of horribly burned and wounded attackers, the battle yells of the beleaguered Marines.

Valdez's helmet indicators were showing it now, the steady, throbbing pulse of Objective Krakatoa's magnetic field, building steadily toward a deadly climax. She couldn't hear the radio call from Dragon One any longer.

"Lieutenant?" she called. "I don't think we're gonna make it through to the nuke in time!"

"I know," Kerns replied, snapping off a trio of laser pulses as the Ahannu horde surged forward. "Any suggestions?"

Valdez concentrated for a moment on her own fire, coolly taking down one of the giant Ahannu just before it fired its gauss gun. The idea behind Task Force Kerns had originally been to reprogram the nuke with a time delay, enough to let them get out of the mountain before the thing blew. She had to admit to herself that it had never looked like a real good possibility since any attack by the enemy would have thrown a major wrench into the works.

They couldn't trigger the nuke from here. It had been re-set to detonate only with the proper authorization code, a set of alphanumerics transmitted either from Dragon One or from orbit. And without the relay . . .

"I think we have to act as a new relay, Lieutenant," she said, "*if* we can get a clear signal through to the captain."

"Roger that," Lieutenant Kerns said. "I'm afraid I don't see any other way. . . ."

Lander Dragon One
In flight, Ishtar
0011 hours ST

Success! Warhurst felt the familiar tingle of the net going online, the flow of data unfolding itself within his mind. The noumenon opened . . . narrow and poorly defined, but with resolution enough for him to begin directing his efforts toward establishing a stronger radio link with Task Force Kerns. The Lander One AI had done the trick. It might not have the high-powered processing thrust of a CS-1289, Series G-4, Model 8 like Cassius, but it knew how to set up network protocols.

He could see outside now. The Dragon carrying Lander One was racing low across a purple-red forest, skimming the canopy at treetop level. Behind, ten kilometers distant, now, An-Kur rose above the jungle, a vast, black, flat-topped cone.

He was still getting a faint radio signal from within the mountain, transmitted and magnified by a relay left on the ground at the LZ.

"Enhance signal, Channel Five," he ordered over the net. "Boost it!"

Damn, but this pocket version of the MIEU Net was ragged! His internal cerebralink hardware was so much faster than this cobbled-together monstrosity, he felt himself waiting with dragging impatience after each set of commands.

"*. . . Kerns! Dragon One, this . . . Force Kerns. Come in!*"

"This is Warhurst. I copy!" He shot a coded mindclick up the link. *Clean this freaking signal up!*

"This is Kerns. We're surrounded and can't reach the nuke. Suggest using me as a relay for detonation. Over!"

Warhurst stared in sick horror at An-Kur. "Roger that, Lieutenant. I . . . copy . . ."

Task Force Kerns
Depths of An-Kur, Ishtar
0012 hours ST

Again the enemy was falling back, but four more Marines—Knowles, Luttrell, Muhib, and Couture—were dead, brought down by heavy gauss-gun fire. Rounds continued to crack and snap around them, as hidden snipers fired from behind the surrounding rocks.

"This is Kerns. We're surrounded and can't reach the nuke. Suggest using me as a relay for detonation. Over!"

Valdez looked at the lieutenant. She didn't know him that well, but she knew he'd seen action in Colombia. She caught his eye through his visor and nodded.

"Roger that, Lieutenant," Warhurst's voice replied after a pause. "I . . . copy . . ."

They couldn't reach the nuke in time. Warhurst had the trigger code. He couldn't detonate the nuke directly, but he could send the signal through Kerns's comm gear.

"I'm sorry, people," Kerns told the listening Marines. "There's no other way."

"Hell, Lieutenant," Ostergaard said cheerfully. "No way we were gonna get out of here anyway!"

"Yeah," Staff Sergeant Feltes added. "Let's take a few of the bastards with us, straight to Hell!"

The Ahannu were surging into the cavern again. Lieutenant Kerns jerked and fell, half his helmet ripped away. No matter. Any of them could provide the necessary relay.

For an instant the cavern grew extraordinarily bright, as though the rock ahead had dissolved to admit the bright white sunlight of a summer's noon at home. . . .

Lander Dragon One
In flight, Ishtar
0012 hours ST

The mountain seemed to heave higher, its slopes trembling, a gentle fog of dust rising from its flanks. Warhurst watched, in horror mingled with awe, as the mountain shuddered in an uncertain equilibrium between gravity and the titanic forces loosed within its depths.

Then, after a seeming eternity, gravity won and the mountain began to settle back upon and into itself, the crest slumping, the base of the mountain spreading out, a pall of gray-white smoke spewing from the peak.

He could see the shock wave racing out from the crumbling mountain's base.

"All Dragons!" he called over the newly established net. "Up! Go up!" When that shock wave overtook them, it might slam the landers into the ground. They would be safer at higher altitudes. The view in his mind tilted sharply as the Dragon clawed at the sky.

The shock wave, racing at the speed of sound, thundered past, grabbing the lander and shaking it hard, as the strangely shaped and colored Ishtaran trees were uprooted below and tumbled along in a surging sea of devastation. The Dragon trembled and bucked, the bulkheads of the LM ringing with the concussion.

And then . . . a blessed, dazed silence.

Behind them the mountain continued to settle, slumping into a mound about half as high as the original peak. Seams opened in the rock on all sides, emitting boiling, furious clouds of ash and smoke.

Captain Warhurst watched the mountain's funeral pyre with dark broodings.

Chamber of Seeing
Deeps of An-Kur
Eleventh Period of Dawn

Once again he was Tu-Kur-La, *only* Tu-Kur-La. The Abzu-il, the living Gateway to the Sea of Knowing, had recoiled, shrieking, and Tu-Kur-La and his fellow members of the Zu-Din found themselves again in the Chamber of Seeing, deep below An-Kur.

Seismic quakes continued to rattle walls, ceiling, and floor, and a fine mist of dust filled the air. For a few moments the cavern was plunged into an abysmal darkness, but power lines from the Deep Core regrew themselves in moments, and the light, with uncertain flickers, returned. Slowly, slowly, the quakings died away, though ominous rumblings continued to filter down from the upper levels of An-Kur, many *salet* overhead.

A full sixty Ahannu were gathered in the Chamber of Seeing, resting in couches recessed into niches in the circular stone walls, and these, Tu-Kur-La knew, were only a few of the minds comprising an active *Zu-Din*, a Godmind. Some hundreds of others were scattered throughout the region, some as far away as the city of Shumur-Unu.

Across the chamber, dimly seen through sifting dust and wavering light, Gal-Irim-Let rose from its couch. "The Mountain of the Gods is no more," it said.

"Kingal!" Tu-Kur-La cried, rolling from his own couch. He drew a breath, then sneezed sharply in the dust. "Kingal," he said again. "We have lost the Sea of Knowing!"

"The Sea shall return," the Kingal An-Kur replied. "It has been injured but will regrow. But we can do no more here."

"What do you advise, Lord?" a high-ranking warrior named Sha-Ah-Il asked.

"The fight will center now on Shumur-Unu," Usum-Gal told them, interrupting. "We will travel there with all we can find and gather here beneath An-Kur. There, we will find more of the Abzu-il. There we will continue the fight."

"Death to all untamed Blackheads!" someone cried, and the others took up the cheer, a throaty, almost growled susurration filling the Chamber of Seeing more completely than the dust.

"Quickly, god-warriors!" Gal-Irim-Let cried. "To the Deep Ways!"

Shouting and hissing, the Ahannu filed from the chamber.

Combat Information Center
IST Derna, *Ishtar orbit*
0022 hours ST

Lighting was restored, a fitful gleam from emergency battle lanterns at first, but a full-blown artificial daylight as the emergency power plant finally came on line. Moments later the slow tumble of the crippled starship was arrested as automatic thrusters fired. As the ship's spin slowed to nothing, gravity faded away. Ramsey drifted in the wreckage of the CIC with General King, Ricia, and a handful of techs.

"Cassius!" he called, using his cerebralink. He felt, heard, sensed only a dull and faintly horrifying emptiness. Damn. The net was down, the noumenon lost. Still, Cassius would be online within *Derna*'s ship computer . . . *should* be, anyway, assuming the central processor complex hadn't suffered serious physical damage.

"I've got a radio link to Cassius," Ricia told him. She was floating next to one of the CIC consoles, clinging to a desktop with one hand and working the controls with the other.

"Give me audio, Major," he said. "Cassius?"

"I am here, Colonel," the familiar AI voice replied.

"Give me a sitrep."

"Affirmative, Colonel. *Derna* has taken serious damage from an impact with a piece of wreckage from the *Algol*, a mass estimated at 215 kilograms, traveling at 12.4 kilometers per second. The debris passed through our reaction mass tank near the rim at Section Nineteen, causing explosive loss of reaction mass and radical destabilization of our trim. Secondary debris damaged our main power plant, heat radiator fins, high gain antenna and comm laser unit, carousel drive, and an estimated four supply modules. Ship remotes are still assessing damage while beginning repairs on major ship systems."

"But are we going to make it?" King asked.

"Probability of survival is high," Cassius replied, "barring further attacks by the Ahannu planetary defense system. Since there is nothing we can do here to prevent further attacks, our efforts now should be directed at damage control. Of more immediate concern from a tactical perspective, the MIEU data net is offline, as you have ascertained, and we have lost contact with the ARLT."

Cassius fell silent. "What is it?" King demanded.

"Easy, General," Ramsey said. "Cassius has his figurative hands full right now."

"One moment," Cassius added. "One moment . . ."

Ramsey pushed off from the bulkhead and drifted across the CIC cabin, catching himself on the console alongside Ricia.

"I have additional information," Cassius said after a moment. "Ship sensors have detected a low-yield subsurface nuclear detonation at the location of Objective Krakatoa. I surmise that the ARLT has acted on its own initiative and destroyed the enemy planetary defense network."

"Thank God," Ricia said.

King sighed. "Amen to that. I guess that means Norris isn't going to get his toy for PanTerra."

"At this point I don't give a damn about Norris and his toys," Ramsey said. "Cassius, expedite efforts to reestablish a working net. At least get me radio contact."

"Not immediately possible, Colonel. Our exterior antennas were damaged by the collision. Furthermore, the LZ is about to pass below the horizon, and without our constellation of communication satellites in place, we will be unable to maintain line-of-sight contact for radio or laser communications."

"Estimated time to bring the net back online."

"Unable to provide an estimate, Colonel," Cassius said. "But at what humans might call a very rough guess, I would say that we are talking about a matter of several days, at least."

"Okay, Cas. Highest priority to regaining ship-to-ground communications. Let me know what you need in the way of human assistance to facilitate repairs."

"Yes, Colonel."

Ramsey rotated in space to face King. "With the net down, sir, we're going to be flat-out useless up here. I suggest we consider transferring your flag to the ground."

"You mean . . . to New Sumer? Has the assault force taken it yet?"

"I don't know, General, and we won't be able to know until we come around the planet in . . ." He consulted his inner clock. ". . . seventy-one minutes. But I'll say this much . . ."

"Yes?"

"If our main assault doesn't take that city within the next hour, we might as well go downstairs anyway. I don't know about you, but I'd just as soon die on the ground as up here."

"I see what you mean, Colonel," King replied thoughtfully. "Even if we get the *Derna* fully repaired, we're trapped here."

"That's right, sir. With our reaction mass gone and the main drive dead, we're a space station, not a starship. We won't be going home again anytime soon."

"So our only hope is with the Marines on the ground," Ricia said.

"Yup," Ramsey replied. "Things *could* be a whole lot worse."

21

Lander Dragon Three
New Sumer, Ishtar
0032 hours ST

The Dragon descended over the Legation compound, depositing the lander module on the broad plaza in front of the old xenocultural mission. The doors swung up, the ramps came down, and Garroway stumbled into the murky twilight of a city engulfed in battle. It was, he decided, a good thing that the landing was already under way and the situation well in hand; he was feeling dazed after the hurried evac and the destruction of An-Kur, and he would have had considerable trouble snapping to if there'd been anyone here to fight.

In fact, there'd been little fighting in the Legation compound. The first LMs had touched down twenty minutes earlier to find the entire walled-off area deserted. In fact, the purple-red nakaha vines and hairmoss-alga clinging to the facades of many of the buildings, the doorways still gaping open, the holes in walls and windows unrepaired, all contributed to an almost oppressively lonely feeling of utter desolation and abandonment.

A few Ahannu bodies lying in the courtyard behind the main gate gave evidence that the compound had not been completely undefended, but most of the Frogs who'd been here, seemed to have fled.

Outside the compound it was a different matter. The city

of New Sumer—Shumur-Unu, according to remembered downloads—was a vast and teeming sprawl of low buildings, conical huts, flat-topped pyramids, and labyrinthine walls of mud brick extending north and west of the compound on both sides of the slow meander of the Saimi-Id River. Though most of the native inhabitants appeared to have fled, a fairly steady gauss-gun fire from snipers in the tops of pyramids and the taller buildings kept things interesting for the landing force. Primitive rockets hissed through the early dawn sky, exploding randomly within the compound walls with loud reports and clouds of black smoke. Beyond the walls, smoke billowed skyward from five different locations where Marine assault teams or aircraft had already suppressed particularly annoying sniper strongpoints.

"With me!" a waving figure called. "Advance Recon Landing Team, with me!"

Garroway, Vinita, Garvey, and the rest from Lander Three jogged toward the figure, where the other ARLT Marines were gathering as well. Without the net to connect them on a subconscious level, Garroway couldn't tell the man's rank, but when the Marine reached up and removed his battle helmet, he recognized him.

It was Captain Warhurst, the ARLT CO.

"Listen up!" Warhurst called as they fell into ranks before him. His face looked haggard and pale. "The main assault force has the situation well in hand. We're being put into ready-five." That meant they were in reserve, ready to go into action on five minutes notice. "Your orders are . . . stay in armor, keep your weapons ready and powered up, and remain in this general area in front of Building 12. I'll pass the word if we're ordered up.

"I know you're all wondering what the hell is going on since the net went down. I can't tell you a whole lot myself, but here's what I do know: the *Derna* has been damaged but is still in orbit. I don't know how bad that damage is or whether it will affect the ship's ability to transport us home, but I will remind you that we have an international relief force on the way in our tracks, maybe six months behind us. We are *not*—I repeat, *not*—stranded here, so you can belay that scuttlebutt right now.

"I've heard one piece of scuttlebutt to the effect that there's not enough Earth-type food here. Although one of the robot freighters, the *Algol*, was destroyed an hour ago, the other, the *Regulus*, is undamaged. We can assume she's being unloaded now and that fresh supplies, food, and ammo are on their way.

"In addition, let me remind you all that there is a sizable • human population here on Ishtar and has been for at least one hundred centuries. Our ethnoarcheologists have been telling us for some time now that most of the edible grain crops and domestic animals that appeared suddenly in the Middle East ten thousand years ago were gene-engineered by the Ahannu as a part of their colonization effort. Apparently, they use the same nutrients we do. There are Earth-native crops in the surrounding region, and we can eat most of the local food crops as well. We are *not*—repeat, *not*—in danger of starvation.

"And finally, Marines, I have a special announcement. *Comp*'ny, atten-*hut*!"

Garroway came to attention, along with the hundred or so other Marines in ranks.

"Attention to roll," Warhurst intoned, his voice solemn, slow, and deliberate.

"Sergeant Alicia Jane Couture . . .

"Sergeant Kathryn DaSilva . . .

"Sergeant Nathaniel Easton Deere . . .

"Staff Sergeant Kenneth K. Feltes . . .

"Gunnery Sergeant Athena Horst . . .

"Lieutenant Joseph Edward Kerns . . .

"Sergeant Laurel Knowles . . .

"Sergeant Jacob Wayne Lowenthal . . .

"Corporal Jarrett Luttrell . . .

"Sergeant Abram Muhib . . .

"Sergeant Carol O'Malley . . .

"Staff Sergeant Krista Ostergaard . . .

"Staff Sergeant Frank Edward Stryker . . .

"Gunnery Sergeant Maria Ann Valdez . . .

"These fourteen Marines sacrificed their lives in order to safeguard the *Derna* and this mission. At tremendous personal risk, they reentered Objective Krakatoa when the enemy defense complex reactivated, in an attempt to reach and reprogram the nuclear device planted in Objective Krakatoa's control center. When they could not reach the device due to time limitations and massive enemy assaults, they instead served as a communications relay for the triggering signal to detonate the weapon, destroying Objective Krakatoa.

"By calling friendly fire on their position, they saved the IST *Derna* and all of the Marines and other assets still on board from near-certain destruction, at the cost of their own lives. We will observe now a moment of silence in the memory of fallen comrades."

Garroway stood at rigid attention with the others. The silence was not complete, certainly. The cracks and bangs of scattered combat continued to sound beyond the compound walls, a freshening wind sighed among stone buildings, and, nearer at hand, NCOs bawled orders at running Marines. A pair of Marine Wasps, boldly painted black and yellow strike fighters, howled overhead, banking toward the sprawl of New Sumer on the far side of the river.

Somehow, the noise of battle was part of another world, remote in time and space. Here, there was only the still introspection honoring dead heroes and friends.

"It is my intention," Warhurst said, breaking the moment's silence, "to recommend all fourteen members of Task Force Kerns for the Medal of Honor in recognition of their bravery, self-sacrifice, and service above and beyond the call of duty, all in the finest tradition of the United States Marine Corps.

"That is all. *Comp*'ny, dis-*missed!*"

The ranks began to dissolve into individual Marines once more. Garroway turned then, looking west. He could see An-Kur, a slumped, black mound beneath a pillar of angry, gray-black ash dominating the horizon. The cloud nearly obscured the swollen globe of Marduk hanging above what was left of the mountain.

Gunny Valdez, dead? Goddess! He'd talked to her an hour ago . . . had wanted to join her. Shit, he'd known then that whatever she was doing, it was likely a one-way deployment. She'd turned him away, and somehow the rejection was a sour bitterness, burning throat and eyes.

Of their whole squad, only he, Womicki, Dunne, Garvey, and Vinita were left. Five out of twelve. Shit, shit, *shit*. He felt as if he'd just lost his family.

And, he thought, he had. His mother was far away now and ten years older than when he'd last seen her. Goddess alone knew where Lynnley was. The only family he knew now was the Corps, and seven of his eleven closest relatives had just been whisked away in the space of a scant few hours.

By what quirk of the universe, by what *right*, was he still alive and breathing and, worst of all, *thinking,* while they were all dead? It wasn't fair.

He felt as though the waves of loneliness just outside his circle of personal space were threatening to crash through and engulf him.

He became aware of a presence . . . no, of two presences, at his side—Garvey and Vinita, both still in armor save for helmets and gloves, their faces smudged with smoke and grime acquired at some unhelmeted moment in the past hour.

"It doesn't seem fair," Vinita said. Her grief was tangible.

"No one promised us fair," Garroway said.

"Yeah," Garvey said, "but you know? Sometimes the universe just outright sucks big, slimy rocks."

"Maybe so," Garroway said. "And maybe we just have to pretend it all makes some kind of sense."

Trade Factor's Quarters
Legation Compound
New Sumer, Ishtar
1015 hours ALT (Arbitrary Local
Time)

Gavin Norris surveyed the mess that had been the PanTerran office with growing anger, then slammed his fist down on the already cracked case of a computer monitor. The large windows overlooking the compound had been smashed in, and the stringy-fuzzy purplish stuff that passed for vegetation here had invaded the open room. There was water pooled on the floor . . . and cabinets that once had held data storage crystals had been overturned and scattered everywhere. Mold grew on the walls and ceiling, and parts of the wall showed black streaks indicating an old, old fire. A desk safe gaped open and empty.

If Carleton had left any corporate records here, they'd been utterly destroyed by Ahannu mobs and ten years of the wet local weather. Damn it, it wasn't *fair.* . . .

Not that he'd been counting on Carleton's efficiency. His briefings back in New Chicago had begun with the assumption that he would have to basically start over. But if the man had just thought to leave a note scrawled on a wall, perhaps with a clue or two as to the location of a fireproof lockbox with a stash of backup storage crystals . . .

He would have to begin again here, from scratch.

"Did you find what you're looking for?"

He turned at the voice. Dr. Hanson stood in the doorway that had been smashed open a decade ago by rampaging alien mobs.

"No," he replied. "My . . . predecessor didn't keep a very tidy office, it seems."

"Don't blame him. Blame the company he kept. Looks like the Ahannu pretty well trashed the place when they broke in. I'm surprised they didn't burn it to the ground."

"They burned a number of buildings, I gather." He looked

around the office in disgust. "Damn it, what brought all this on? We had a solid rapport with the local nabobs. Things were going so *well!*"

"It's beginning to look like a classic case of Alexander's First Law."

"Alexander's . . . First Law? What's that?"

"An important xenosociological concept," Hanson replied. "Advanced by the guy who came to be known as the Father of Xenoarcheology, back in the twenty-first century. It states that the members of any given culture will understand the customs, attitudes, and worldview of another culture solely within the context of their own."

"I don't get it."

"There were Native Americans who encountered Europeans for the first time who thought the foreigners were traveling inside gigantic black water birds with huge white wings. Sailing ships with sails, you see? And the ancient Sumerians thought the Anunnaki—'Those who came from the heavens to Earth,' as they called them—were gods."

"Well . . . sure. That's pretty obvious, isn't it? Primitive savages are going to think that a computer or a flashlight is magic direct from the gods, right?"

"If their culture allows for the possibility of gods and magic, yes. The point is, *no* culture is free of its own cultural bias. Including ours."

"What are you getting at? I don't follow."

Dr. Hanson sighed. "No. You wouldn't. I think your people are the ones who brought this on." She held up the remnants of a notebook—a low-tech pressure-sensitive paper version. The cover was badly burned, the pages partially charred and water-soaked, but some words could be made out here and there. "I found this in Dr. Moore's lab."

"Dr. Moore?"

"One of the xenobiologists stationed here at the Legation. Looks like she took all of her electronic records with her, but I did find this. It says, 'We've been suckered by Alexander's

First Law. The autos aren't Aztecs and they're not Chinese. Who do they say they are? Who do they say we are?' "

" 'Autos?' "

"Autochthons. The Ahannu. There's been a major debate going on Earth for years now as to whether their culture could best be compared to that of the Aztecs, back in the early sixteenth century, or to the nineteenth-century Chinese at the time of their contact with modern Europeans. Dr. Moore is warning us not to let our culturally biased perspective distort our picture of who and what the Ahannu are."

"That they're not primitives?" Norris gave a dry chuckle. "They proved *that* with that shooting mountain of theirs."

"Their technology isn't the point," she replied. "It's how we think of them . . . and how they think of us. We tended to see them as primitives compared with us, with a complex culture and some high-tech toys left over from the time when they were starfarers. They see us as the slave species they gave civilization to a few thousand years ago, maybe as slaves who got too big for our britches."

"Yeah . . . okay. Who are you saying is right? They *are* primitives."

"No. Neither viewpoint is right, because both viewpoints are locked up inside of the cultural context that created them.

"Look at their side of the equation. We might've been Ahannu slaves once, but we've grown a lot since then. We've changed. But they still see humans as 'Blackheads,' as they call us, because of our hair. As Sag-ura, the creatures they domesticated to work in their mines and farms.

"But it goes the other way too. Our understanding of the Ahannu is going to be crippled from the start because we see them in ways that make sense to us. As primitive savages. As a culture that has somehow lost its moral authority because it lost its technology, as if *those* two ever had anything to do with one another."

"Are you saying they're some kind of super race? They're so advanced they don't need technology?"

"Not at all. I'm saying they're alien, and we shouldn't assume we know the first damned thing about them. The nature of their technology may have changed. Or the way they
think may be so different from us that we can't recognize
their technology when we see it."

Norris laughed. "Honey, you're giving the Frogs *way* too
much credit. We've seen their technology, measured it. Stuff
like those planetary defense systems and the few guns they
have obviously are leftovers from ten thousand years ago.
What they have, what they understand today, is spears,
clubs, and knives. The mission here was brought down by
overwhelming numbers, not some sort of magic, alien tech
that we can't even recognize!"

She shrugged. "Have it your own way. But you're being
anthropocentric. You're measuring everything by the standards of Homo sapiens, as though we were the pinnacle of
creation. We're not, you know. The Ahannu are not *lower*
than us; they're different."

"Great. I'll remember that when I start negotiating with
the High Emperor and the DesFac."

"DesFac?"

"The Destiny Faction. What we're calling the group that
rebelled against the original government here. According to
the data transmitted back before things turned nasty, it was
led by a Frog named Geremelet. They were promoting the
idea that the Frogs were gods."

"I remember the briefing," Hanson said. "But think about
what you just said. We don't know how the Ahannu think of
themselves in groups, so we don't really know that there
was a 'faction' that differed from the government. We don't
understand what they mean by 'government,' so we're probably wrong when we think in terms of rebellions, High Em-
perors, or what they mean by being led. We don't know if
they think in religious terms, the way we do, so we don't
know what they mean by 'god.' Hell, 'Geremelet' isn't a
proper form for Ahannu names, so we don't even know
who we're dealing with here. Do you see? The Ahannu are

alien. We're not going to be able to communicate with them meaningfully until we know exactly what that means. *How* are they alien, different from us? *How* do they think? How do they think differently? You know, human psychologists are still debating what the word *'intelligence'* means. If we can't define it for ourselves, how in blazes are we supposed to define it for something as *other* as the Ahannu?"

"Maybe," Norris said, "it's not going to be that complicated, you know? Europeans didn't understand the aboriginal Americans either, but between firearms, horses, and smallpox, they managed to wipe them out pretty handily. The bleeding hearts might wish it was different, but might *does* make right, you know. It's the winners in any clash of cultures that write the books and program the downloads afterward. Which means it's the winners who decide who gets defined in whose image."

"Does everyone who works for PanTerra have such a wonderfully bleak understanding of intercultural relations?" Hanson asked. "Or is it just you?"

"I'm a realist, Doctor. The people I work for are realists. And we believe in making things happen . . . *our* way, *objective* worldview, not subjective, not blinkered by sentiment or sentimentality."

"I see. I hope you live to enjoy the fruits of your philosophy. Of course, that's not likely now, is it?"

"Of course it is. The Joint International Expedition will be along in another six months, and that'll be our ride home. The Marines will keep us safe until then." He grinned. "Better living through superior firepower."

"Goddess," Hanson said, shaking her head. "You just don't get it, do you?"

"I was going to say the same about you, Doctor. You worry about Ahannu culture and psychology. Make your notes and collect your data. I'm afraid the natives on Ishtar are about to go the way of all primitives once they come in contact with a technically superior culture. It might be that a thousand years from now the only thing people will even know about the Frogs is what you record here now."

She turned and strode from the room then, angry.

Norris chuckled, then returned his attention to the shattered office of his predecessor. Nothing . . . nothing. Stooping, he scooped up a double handful of computer memory chips and let them clatter on a tabletop. Some of the scattered mems might be salvageable, but he didn't have the equipment or the time to find out. Finding the one mem in hundreds dealing with Ahannu slavery was worse than looking for the proverbial needle in a haystack. Besides, what he needed was probably encrypted, and he didn't have the password.

No matter. Things would have been much easier if Carleton had left behind a note for those who might come after him, but in fact its absence changed nothing. The Marines would do their job, crushing the Geremelet faction or whatever the hell it was really called . . . and then he would step in and do *his* job, happily earning his billion-dollar paycheck along the way. Full payment was contingent on a successful outcome in the negotiations with the Ahannu leadership, so he was determined that nothing would interfere with PanTerra's plans, or with his.

Explosions thundered in the distance, and he walked across to the shattered window. Marine Wasps circled, floated, pounced, raising more explosions and additional pillars of greasy-looking smoke into the early morning sky. Beneath the window, Marines lounged in the courtyard, unconcerned by the aerial barrage taking place less than a kilometer away. On the Legation walls, other Marines stood guard, as a patrol passed through the North Gate into the Ahannu district.

At this rate, the city would be secure within another few hours.

He decided that he'd better talk to King about prisoners. He would need one, preferably a high-ranking one, to carry his negotiation demands to Geremelet.

Marine Bivouac
Legation Compound
New Sumer, Ishtar
1625 hours ALT

Thin red sunlight streamed across the city at rooftop level, touching the roofs and upper portions of the higher structures, leaving the streets still in deep shadow. The Llalande sun, little more than a bright ruby spark, showed itself through a narrow slit between the eastern horizon and the cloud deck. The clouds overhead were slate-gray, heavily striated by high-altitude winds into swirling streaks and arabesques.

At ground level, though, the air was calm, hot, and moist. It had rained several times in the past few hours, and the streets were wet. Marine working parties continued to move among the nanocrete domes of the mission compound, bringing the bodies of Ahannu and Sag-ura to a central collection point and collecting scattered weapons and equipment for cataloging and study. Garroway and the other survivors of the squad had drawn light duty—standing guard over the alien bodies to keep the morbidly curious and the souvenir hunters at a distance. At the moment, Garvey had the duty. Dunne, Womicki, Vinita, and Garroway had joined him, though. No one felt like sleeping. The air was too charged, too pregnant with unrealized promise and danger.

"There," Womicki said. "You feel that?"

The others shook their heads. "I think you're imagining it, Womicki," Garroway said.

"Fuck you. Here. Look." Womicki pulled a canteen from a hip pouch in his armor, pulled off the cap, and dribbled a bit of water into it. Carefully, he set it on the ground. "Watch."

The other Marines stared at the cap for a moment. Sure enough, minute ripples were stirring the surface of the water. Garroway held very still, trying to feel it. *There.* A faint, faint quivering vibration through the pavement stones at his feet.

"Earthquakes," Womicki explained. "They're almost continuous but so faint you can hardly feel 'em. Once in a while they get strong enough to notice."

"Not Earthquakes," Vinita said. "Ishtarquakes?"

"Seismic events," Dunne suggested.

"Yeah," Garvey agreed. "I wonder how all these buildings stay standing so long with this kind of shaking going on all the time."

"That's why the locals build pyramids and domes," Dunne pointed out. "And nothing over a couple-three stories tall, except for the big pyramids." He joined his hands together, steepling his fingers in a rough pyramid shape and working it back and forth. "The stones tend to fall together and hold one another up. Unless a *really* big quake hit, the buildings stay stable."

"I remember something from a download," Garroway said, "about there not being any major fault lines on Ishtar, so you don't get the sudden slippage that makes major earthquakes, like in California. You just get a lot of little tremors from the tidal flexing as Ishtar goes around Marduk."

"Y'know," Garvey said, "if we had the damned net online, we'd be able to link in with the data feed from orbit and all the ground stations and see how widespread it was, where the center of it was. . . ."

"Shit," Garroway said. "We're doing okay without the net. We just don't have as many people looking over our shoulders as we used to, is all."

His own words surprised him. For a time there, back on the mountain, he'd felt nightmarishly alone and isolated without the MIEU Net, much as he'd felt when they'd deactivated his Sony-TI 12000. The nanohardware in his head handled a good many minor and routine tasks—math coprocessing and direction sensing, for instance—and all he was really missing was the ability to download large amounts of data with a thought-click or talk to other Marines with an inner voice akin to telepathy.

He was just now realizing, though, that losing his high-powered hardware in boot camp had gotten them all used to making do with whatever was at hand. Womicki's trick with the canteen lid, for instance. That was damned *clever* . . . and didn't require data feeds from orbit or the local node to tell him what he wanted to know.

Maybe people were getting too damned reliant on their techy toys.

But then again . . .

He stole a glance at Kat Vinita. She seemed okay now, if a bit distant, a little floaty, a bit too placid. She was riding high on NNTs, he guessed, holding her emotions at bay, anesthetizing them until professional psychs could help her deal with them. The tech was holding her together now, but what would the cost be later on?

"Halt!" Garvey called out. "Who goes there?"

A woman, a civilian in a dark green jumpsuit emblazoned with the Spirit of Humankind logo, had approached the group. "I'm Dr. Hanson," she said.

"This is a restricted area, ma'am," Garvey told her.

"And I have authorization," she replied, holding up a scrap of white paper.

Garvey accepted the paper clumsily in a gauntleted hand and peered at the writing. "Signed by Colonel Ramsey," he said, handing the paper back. "I guess it's okay."

"Goddess, of *course* it's okay," Hanson replied. She sounded tired and on edge. "What did you think, I'm here to steal the bodies?"

"No, ma'am. Sorry, ma'am."

"Feeling a bit low-tech, there, Gravy?" Womicki asked with a chuckle.

"It's a hell of a lot easier when you can interrogate the net for pass authorizations," Garvey replied, stepping aside. "How are we supposed to know that pass is genuine?"

"Don't sweat it, kid," Dunne said with a shrug. "She don't look like the kind t'want to cut off Frog ears for souvenirs. Let her do her job."

"Frogs don't have ears," Garvey said. "Just those damned big staring eyes."

"The civilians are here to study the Ahannu," Vinita said. "We're just supposed to keep other Marines away from this stuff."

Hanson was picking her way through a triple line of bodies, each lying on its own length of plastic tarp.

"Can I give you a hand with anything, ma'am?" Garroway asked her.

"I'm looking for signs of rank," she told him. "You're sure these bodies haven't been tampered with? Stuff taken?"

He shrugged. "Not since they were brought here. I can't speak for what happened when the collection parties picked them up."

"They should have left the bodies in place," Hanson said, grimacing with distaste. "How are we supposed to learn anything with you people pawing over them and going through their stuff?"

"We're *Marines*, ma'am," Garroway said, his voice stiff. What the hell was this *civilian* implying?

She looked up at him, then stood. "I'm sorry, Marine," she said. "It's been a rough day. No offense."

"None taken, ma'am." He relaxed a little then, but only a little. "Just what is it you're looking for?"

She sighed. "Anything the leaders might use to mark them as leaders," she said. "I don't know . . . a badge, a medallion, special markings on their armor, anything to make the boss Ahannu stand out from the rest."

"I don't know, ma'am," he said. "The ones I've seen have come in all different kinds of armor, different weapons. It's more like fighting a mob than an army." He pointed at a partially charred body twice the size of the others lying nearby . . . one of the big Ahannu the Marines had begun calling *trolls*. "Even their soldiers are different from one another, you know, in size and color and stuff. Maybe those big guys are the leaders?"

She shook her head. "I don't think so. Those appear to be specially bred mutations, a warrior class, if you will.

They're not very smart. How about some sort of baton or staff?"

"Ain't seen nothing like that," Womicki said, joining them. He pointed to a pile of weapons and standards lying on the ground nearby. "Unless you mean those battle flags some of them carry."

"No," Hanson said. "Those appear to be clan insignia of some sort, but the ones who carry them aren't leaders. The thing is, we think the Ahannu passed on a lot of social conventions to our ancestors back in ancient Sumeria besides agriculture and hygiene . . . things like kingship and caste systems and the idea that someone has to be on top. If that's so, we'd expect to see some emblem of rank among them, some way they could recognize one another and know who was in charge."

"Well, some of them do have fancier body armor," Garroway said. He pointed at another Ahannu body. "And some don't have any armor at all."

"Hell, I thought the Frogs weren't supposed to have any sex," Garvey said, amused. He poked at a tentacular, bulb-headed member between the legs of the Ahannu corpse with the muzzle of his rifle. "What's this?"

"Oh, they have sex," Hanson said. "Our first contact with them here at the mission was just with drones, and we thought they were hermaphrodites. But there are males and females too."

"No balls," Womicki observed.

"Internal gonads. Apparently, they're like some species of fish on Earth, and change sex when they need to, either because there aren't enough of the opposite sex available at the moment, or maybe it's part of a regular cyclical life-change." She shook her head. "There's so *damned* much we don't understand about them."

"Maybe the sex differences are what you're looking for," Vinita suggested. "You know, the males are the leaders? Or the females?"

"No. We haven't been able to correlate sex with their so-

cial ordering yet," Hanson said. "Although it is possible
there are other sexes or somatypes we haven't seen yet."

Garroway noticed something and stooped, awkward in his
armor. Reaching out cautiously, he touched the head of the
Ahannu corpse, turning it to the side.

The head was long and narrow, gray-green in color and
very lightly scaled, with a bony ridge across the top of the
skull that extended over the nasal opening all the way to the
lipless mouth. There were no external ears, though a bone-
ringed opening behind the jaw showed where the hearing or-
gans were located. The golden eyes, each the size and shape
of a pear, dominated the upper face, with jagged, horizontal
slits for pupils.

This one had taken a death wound to the right side of its
skull. A ragged gash opened the head from the deeply cleft
chin almost to the skull crest, revealing white bone, yellow-
ish blood and tissue, and a stringy mess of red-purple jelly
slowly oozing from the wound onto the pavement.

"Look at this," Garroway said. "Is that blood? Brains?"

"No," Hanson said, immediately interested. She knelt beside the body, looking closely. "Their blood is yellow-
orange. See that yellow liquid? I don't know *what* that is."
She pulled a vial from a jumpsuit pocket and began collecting some of the purple jelly.

"Careful, ma'am," Dunne said. "We don't know about
their chemistry yet, and you don't have gloves."

"Ahannu body chemistry is pretty much compatible with
ours, Marine," she said. "If this stuff didn't poison him, then
it shouldn't poison me."

"You can't be sure of that, ma'am," Womicki pointed out.
"Some toxins will poison one species and not another. These
creatures aren't even *mammals*."

"I think it's safe enough," Hanson said. Still, she used
care in securing the sample, wiping the vial carefully on a
rag when Dunne offered one to her. "This stuff is organic,
but it's not part of normal Ahannu biochemistry, as far as we

know. Damn, I wish I had access to the net! This is important! I think—"

A sharp crack sounded across the courtyard and something struck the front of Building 10 across the street, striking sparks bright against the shadows.

Garroway lunged forward, knocking Hanson off her knees and flat on the pavement, covering her with his armored body. Another crack sounded, closer this time.

"The east pyramid!" Womicki yelled, raising his laser rifle to his shoulder. "It's coming from the top of the pyramid!"

The other Marines brought their weapons to bear, triggering a barrage at the presumed sniper's nest. The white-stone pyramid—Garroway remembered it was called the Pyramid of the Eye—glowered down into the Legation compound from the eastern edge of the city, offering a magnificent view of the goings-on within.

"Now hear this, now hear this!" came over Garroway's armor radio receiver. "Battle stations, battle stations! We are under attack!"

And then the first crude rockets began arrowing into the compound.

22

Marine Bivouac
Legation Compound
New Sumer, Ishtar
1642 hours ALT

Garroway rolled off Hanson, snatching up his rifle and taking aim at the pyramid to the east. Linking his helmet display to the LR-2120's optics and damping the input down to infrared, he could see movement in the small peaked hut high atop the building's truncated tip. He magnified the image and caught a glimpse of a face, a *human* face, strangely painted in the yellows and greens of the heat-sensitive sight, leaning into a bulky gauss rifle as the sniper took careful aim. It looked like he was drawing a bead directly on Garroway's faceplate.

But Garroway was faster by a fraction of a second, his thought-click triggering the laser and loosing a five-megajoule pulse. The enemy soldier's head exploded in a burst of brilliant yellow and green, and the figure toppled backward into the purple and blue shadows of the building.

Something hissed into the courtyard, trailing a streamer of white smoke, struck the side of a building, and exploded with a sharp bang. Bits of metal pinged off Garroway's armor. *"This way, lady!"* he yelled, grabbing Hanson's arm above her elbow and bodily dragging her across the pavement.

"Let go! Let *go!*" she yelled. "I can move by myself!"

Pivoting, he propelled her forward, sending her flying into the open doorway of Building 10. Another rocket exploded behind him, picking him up and catapulting him sideways into the street.

His armor absorbed the punishment and he lurched to his feet, laser at the ready. Where the hell was that fire coming from?

Over the wall. Rocket contrails were arching high above the northern wall as projectiles came raining down on the Legation compound. He jumped into the open doorway himself as part of the roof crumbled in a savage blast, showering onto the street in an avalanche of debris, water, and smoke.

"Are you all right?" he asked. The woman nodded. Her eyes were wide and there was a bloody scratch on her cheek, but she appeared unhurt. "Good. Stay here, stay down!"

He ran into the street again, where other Marines were gathering, moving in a running surge of armored shapes toward the northern wall.

At first he thought they were going to go out through the high, arched gate on that side and find the rocket launchers, but a Marine with a massive handgun waved them toward a flight of stone steps leading up the inside of the wall. "To the parapets!" he yelled, using his suit speakers to boom the command out across the courtyard. "Repel the assault!"

Garroway pounded up the steps and took his place alongside a half dozen other Marines already there. The Legation compound wall was broad and heavy, four meters tall, five meters wide at the base, and nearly four wide at the top, the faces slightly concave to render them quakeproof, with a meter-high crenellated parapet along both the inner and the outer sides. Crouching behind the low outer barricade, he peered down into the northern quarter of the city.

Marine Wasps were already zeroing in on the launcher positions, smashing them with deadly accurate missile and Gatling laser fire. There was no need for ground troops to go beyond the walls.

But the streets were filled with Ahannu god-warriors and

their Janissary slaves, a vast throng of figures crowding toward the northern wall and gate beneath a small forest of black and red *mon* banners. He didn't need a target lock; he rested his 2120 on the crumbling stone parapet and began triggering the weapon, cycling in quick, sharp, three-pulse bursts, sweeping the front ranks of attackers as they thundered down the streets leading toward the gate.

Those front ranks wavered as the laser fire from the wall before them grew heavier in volume, more concentrated. Ahannu god-warriors crumbled, staggered, or burst into flame beneath that deadly caress of coherent light. A pair of Marine plasma gunners joined the line, and the brilliant blue-white sparks of energy tore gaping, fire-laced holes in the charging masses.

The ranks behind began slowing as they were forced to scramble over the high-piled bodies of their comrades. Many crouched behind those grisly barricades in the streets, firing up at the Marine defenders with gauss weapons or rising briefly to hurl spears or rocks.

A handful of human Ishtarans rushed the wall carrying four-meter poles with notches chopped along their lengths—makeshift scaling ladders. Laser bolts snapped and hissed through the crowd, setting ladders and warriors alike aflame and scattering survivors in shrieking retreat. Two ladders slammed up against the northern slope of the wall and as quickly toppled again as the defenders at the top shoved them back with rifle butts.

Garroway paused, surprised. The shakiness, the nightmare fear he'd felt earlier, was gone, replaced by a steady, almost preternatural calm. At first he wondered if the NNTs he'd popped were helping to steady him, but decided that it was simply training kicking in. Hell, it didn't matter—training or nanoneurotransmitters. He was a Marine rifleman, crouched shoulder-to-shoulder with other Marine riflemen, doing what he'd been trained to do.

Join the Marines! he thought with an edge of hysteria as

he recalled the old Marine-recruiting joke. *Travel to exotic places! Meet fascinating people! Kill them! Kill them all!*

Another rush, more humans with ladders accompanied by a surging gray-green mob of Ahannu god-warriors, many holding makeshift shields above their heads to ward off the deadly bolts from above. The shields, made of wood, hide, and sometimes sheets of thin metal, only extended the life expectancy of the attackers by a few precious seconds; shields exploded into flying splinters or caught fire, but the attackers beneath them kept coming. Many Marines switched to RPG smart rounds, detonating them beneath the shields with bloody effect.

Garroway saw the Marine who'd led them onto the parapets off to his right, recognizing him by the massive pistol— a Colt 15mm Puller firing explosive rounds—in one gauntleted hand. The guy was standing in full view behind the parapet, coolly snapping off rounds at the attackers at the base of the wall. When more Marines clambered up the steps, he turned his back on the fighting long enough to direct them to weak points on the wall, then returned to the fighting with a businesslike demeanor that was positively inspiring.

A warning tone sounded in Garroway's helmet, accompanied by a flashing yellow light. His laser's power supply was being overtaxed. His backpack power unit needed to be recharged.

There wasn't anything to be done about that now, though. He thought-clicked an override command and kept firing, trying to fire more slowly, more deliberately, and making certain that each shot counted.

Another rocket streaked in, slamming into the middle of the wall twenty meters to Garroway's left with a roar, flinging two Marines into the street. Both landed on the pavement in front of the surging tide of Ahannu, one lying motionless, the other trying to stand, obviously hurt.

Without orders, the defensive fire from the wall shifted to

cover the two stranded Marines, burning down warrior after warrior as they ran across the broad promenade that surrounded the outside of the Legation compound. That open stretch, perhaps ten meters wide, became a bloody killing zone as more and more Ahannu tried to reach the two wounded Marines.

Garroway's HDO was flashing red at him now. He had only a few dozen shots left before his power pack went completely dead. He switched to RPG fire from his M-12 arpeg-popper, giving his power pack a chance to recycle. Other Marines were making the same decision, apparently, as guided 20mm RPGs streaked overhead, exploding among the attackers in stark, blood-splattering detonations. Laser and plasma gunfire burned broad swatches of death through the enemy warriors, while Marine snipers armed with high-energy gauss rifles marked down every Ahannu carrying a firearm they could see. A pair of Wasps joined the battle, circling low overhead, blazing away with Gatling lasers, until the enemy ranks broke and tumbled back in wild disorder.

To his left Garroway spotted a couple of ropes uncoiling as they were tossed over the parapet and into the street at the base of the wall. An instant later two Marines appeared, the two of them rappelling down the face of the wall as the laser fire from overhead increased in intensity to a savage crescendo. They reached the stranded, injured Marines in seconds. One scooped up the unconscious Marine in his arms while the other helped the wounded one along in a one-arm carry. The enemy, seeing their prize on the point of escaping, surged forward again, venting war cries that grated eerily on the nerves like the shrill wail of steam whistles. Again the barrage of laser and plasma-gun fire from the ramparts cut them down, sending the survivors tumbling backward in headlong retreat.

More Marines were dropping down the ropes over the wall now, surrounding the rescue effort, helping the wounded personnel back toward the northern gate. The gates

swung open, spilling more Marines into the kill zone to
cover the retreat of their comrades.

All of this played itself out on the periphery of Garroway's awareness. His entire universe had narrowed down
to his HDO's target picture. With the mass charge broken
now and his backpack power coming back online, he'd re-
verted to a sniper's role, using the magnified image on his
helmet display to pick out individual Ishtarans armed with
weapons more effective than spears and cutting them down.
If enough of the enemy's gauss gunners died, maybe the rest
would get the idea that it was extremely unhealthy to carry
those things anywhere within range of a U.S. Marine.

More minutes passed before he realized that there were
no targets left he could see, and that the fire from the wall
was beginning to dwindle away.

The Marine he'd seen earlier, the one with the 15mm
Puller, held up a gloved hand. "Cease fire, Marines! Hold
your fire!"

An eerie stillness descended over the north wall then,
broken only by the crackle of flames in the kill zone, the
rush of a freshening wind, and the whimperings and isolated
cries of wounded Ishtarans. The Marine with the pistol
reached up, unfastened the catches on his helmet, and pulled
it off.

Garroway recognized him, now—the close-cropped,
sandy hair, the sweat-streaked features. It was Colonel
Ramsey.

He'd suspected that it might be Captain Warhurst. The
idea of a regimental CO taking part in a firefight was startling, well outside the perimeter of approved doctrine in
modern combat. Colonels were supposed to lead from the
safety of a command center. Hell, he hadn't even realized
the Old Man was on the ground yet. TAV-S Dragonflies
were still shuttling between New Sumer and orbit, bringing
down the rest of the MIEU; he'd expected the command
constellation to stay on board the *Derna* until the last possible moment.

The discovery filled Garroway with an inexplicable but undeniable surge of pride, esprit, and camaraderie, and with the feeling that he would follow Colonel Ramsey anywhere.

Damn, they were going to *beat* the Frogs, starship or no starship!

"Good work, Marines," Ramsey called out, his voice booming out across the compound. "Everyone on the north wall, sound off by threes!"

"One!"

"Two!"

"Three!"

"One! . . ."

Each Marine in turn called off a number. Garroway was a "three."

"Okay!" Ramsey bellowed. "Ones, stay on the wall! We'll get recharges up to you that need them. Twos, you're ready reserve! The rest of you, fall in down below in the courtyard. We're going to get this walking cluster-fuck *organized!*"

Garroway grinned behind his helmet visor. Pretty slick . . . and straight out of boot camp. With a working net, an AI would have sorted the Marines out, perhaps keeping those with the most fully charged power packs on the walls while directing the rest to other duties. Without the net, they would have to rely on older, more traditional techniques—like the handwritten paper pass the civilian woman had carried earlier.

Heart pounding, he fell into line and filed down the stone steps into the courtyard, following the colonel.

Beneath the Pyramid of the Eye
Shumur-Unu
First Period of Early Light

Tu-Kur-La slipped again into the comfortable embrace of the living, sentient sea. The *Abzu-il* flowed softly over his skin, penetrating his ears and nostrils, seeping in through the spaces between and beneath his scales, and as key connections were made within his brain, new vistas of sight and sound and sensation unfolded within his mind.

He sensed the presence of at least two sixties of other Keepers of Memory and of the souls and awareness of the *kingal*, Gal-Irim-Let, of Usum-Gal, and of other elders of the *An-Kin*, the Council of the Gods. As more and more minds entered the far-flung organic web of the *Abzu*, awareness expanded, the sense of self dwindled, and Tu-Kur-La again approached the single-minded unity of consciousness of the *Zu-Din*, the Godmind.

He became other minds. In particular, he felt a Keeper of Memories, a drone named Zah-Ahan-Nu, crouching in the shadows of the Chamber of the Eye, peering out through the opening and down into the walled-in rectangle of the off-worlder compound. The bodies of several Ahannu and Sagura lay sprawled about on the stone floor, testimony to the deadly accuracy of the Blackhead warriors below.

Slowly, Zah-Ahan-Nu raised its head, surveying the alien compound. It appeared to be filled to overflowing with Blackheads—wild slaves escaped from Ahannu care. These would be the remote descendants of the Blackheads left behind on Kia after the coming of the Hunters of the Dawn.

Its horizontal, slit pupils widened until nearly the entirety of the golden eyes showed glassy black. Zah-Ahan-Nu had become the eye of the *Zu-Din*.

Regimental HQ
Building 5, Legation Compound
New Sumer, Ishtar
1920 hours ALT

"Attention on deck!" Captain Warhurst called, standing. The several dozen Marines in the room came to attention as Colonel Ramsey, Major Anderson, and General King strode in.

"As you were, as you were," King said, waving a hand. "This is your HQ, Colonel?"

"Yes, sir. It's not much, but it's home."

Until a few hours before, the former supply room had been an empty, junk-filled shell. Working parties had cleared out the debris and brought in chairs of various descriptions salvaged from other parts of the compound, which were set up around a makeshift boards-on-nanocrete-block map table. Someone had painted sheets of plyboard white and drawn rough topo maps on them using colored markers. Chips of painted wood with unit designations printed on them were scattered about the board, blue for Marine forces, red for known or suspected concentrations of the enemy.

Most of the men and women in the room were still in their armor, with their gloves, helmets, and weapons stacked in military order along the wall next to the smashed-open door. The only civilian present was Gavin Norris, and he was wearing a green *Derna* jumpsuit with the Spirit of Humankind patch on the front.

Captain Warhurst stepped to one side, making room for the newcomers. He could sense the tension in the air; Ramsey was making nice to the general, but the politics of the situation were obviously costing him in stress.

"*This* is your answer to the noumenon?" King asked, looking down at the table. "How the hell can you see what's going on?"

"It's not as bad as you might think, sir," Ramsey replied with a thin smile. "It's true, without remotes giving us data from all over the battlefield, without linked-in team leaders, this is the best we can manage. But Marines were playing war games on computers, on paper, and with sticks in the sand long before we had noumenal sims."

"Show me."

"We've reorganized the MIEU in order to spread out the effect of casualties from the initial assault. Five companies in two lightweight battalions—768 Marines altogether— plus our air wing, another twenty-three. The rest—about two hundred, including both physical and psych wounded—have been assigned to an ad hoc reserve company."

He began pointing out the different features on the map: the walls of the Legation compound, the city proper, the river, and, squarely to the east, a black square representing the Pyramid of the Eye.

"Right now we have the walls secured and patrols inside the compound. This," he said, tapping the representation of the pyramid to the east, "is our big problem."

"The so-called Pyramid of the Eye," King said. "That thing has a Priority One for this mission, you understand."

"Yes, sir."

"Damn it, it should have been among the first objectives taken."

"That possibility was discussed, General. It was decided, you'll recall, that it was more urgent that we take Objective Krakatoa before the main landing, and it seemed unwise to divide our forces among too many targets."

"I am *not* senile, Colonel. I remember the briefings, even if they *were* ten years ago." The weak attempt at humor fell flat.

"Yes, sir. In any case, we had no way of knowing how strongly held the pyramid was when we made the landings inside the Legation compound."

"Some of your men reported taking fire from it."

"Yes, sir. We think the Ahannu may have tunnels or secret passageways inside the structure. Our spotters have seen some movement up there during the past few hours and have taken a few shots. We believe they're using it to watch us, rather than as a strongpoint. At least so far.

"That could change, however, at any time. And, as you've pointed out, General, the pyramid is a high-priority target."

"It's more than high priority, Colonel," Gavin Norris said from the back of the room. "It's our only hope for communicating with Earth. We need to reestablish FTL communications with the folks back home."

"That would be desirable, of course, Mr. Norris, but that's not a good reason for risking additional casualties. The International Relief Force is six months behind us. There's nothing Earth can do to speed them up . . . or even to warn them if something goes wrong here."

"The FTL link is vital to our work here, Colonel."

Who the hell had the bright idea of inviting a freaking civilian on this joyride? Warhurst thought, angry. He'd had his fill of micromanagement and ROEs—the ubiquitous Rules of Engagement—in Egypt. He'd expected eight light-years to be more than enough breathing room, at least when it came to interpreting orders. Evidently, he'd been wrong.

He was tired. His body ached inside the unrelenting embrace of his armor. The Mark VII's microtubule filtration system was supposed to suck up the sweat he'd been dumping into the suit, but he still was sticky, hot, and miserably filthy, and he felt damned close to being ready to negotiate a deal involving his soul and a hot shower. During the attack earlier on the north wall, he'd been in the Lander One CP, trying to coordinate communications . . . and perhaps drag the makeshift net online, without success.

And, damn it, he was jealous of Ramsey. The colonel had seen some of the fighting, and he'd been stuck in the damned LM.

He wasn't Wayning this thing, he didn't think. It was the principle involved. Half of his assault force had been killed taking that mountain. He was a company commander, not a REMFing general. And he thought he saw a way that would let him set things straight.

Listening to King's petty bitching and Norris's corporate kibitzing, Warhurst wished he could scratch beneath his armor or, better, peel it all off and take a long hot soak.

"Another thing, Colonel," Norris was saying. "Your men reported firing on the pyramid. If a stray round hits the Eye, that could wreck the facility's usefulness. I'd like you to pass the word to your troops not to fire into the Chamber of the Eye."

"Again, Mr. Norris," Ramsey said quietly, "we'll do our best . . . but no promises. So far as I'm concerned, your precious FTL communicator is not worth the life of a single

Marine. But it is my intention to take that pyramid in order to deny its use to the enemy."

"I can't say I'm impressed with your spirit of cooperation, Colonel. General? You know what I'm talking about."

"Yes, Mr. Norris. I do. And I remind *you*, sir, that Colonel Ramsey is in operational control of this MIEU, while I have responsibility for the overall mission. At this point, until we can induce the Ahannu leaders to begin negotiations with us, or unless we regain a significant orbital capability or an operational Net, I'm just along for the ride. I can offer criticism, I can offer advice, but *he* is in charge of the routine operations on this beachhead. Is that clear, sir?"

Warhurst opened his eyes at that. *This* was new. Maybe old King wasn't such a flaming son of a bitch after all.

"Thank you, General," Ramsey said. "Captain Warhurst? You have an operational plan sketched out, I gather?"

"Yes, sir. I think we have the means for a vertical envelopment."

He began laying out the plan he'd worked out during the past few hours. It was risky in some ways but held a fair promise of success.

City fighting—close-quarter combat in built-up urban areas—was the dirtiest, nastiest kind of fighting there was, with every building a potential bunker, every wall a stronghold, every window a possible sniper's nest. Multistory buildings were the worst, with attackers having to fight their way up each stairwell against a well-covered enemy who had gravity on his side. Modern combat doctrine stressed attacking strongly defended buildings from the top down, when possible—vertical envelopment, it was called—using VTOL/hover landers like the Dragonflies.

"We employ two Dragons," Warhurst explained, moving four wooden chips, stacked two and two. He placed one on the pyramid, the other nearby. "One for the assault, one in reserve. I have some of my people working now on rigging a bunch of twelve-pack sling harnesses with quick-release catches. Secure a couple to the tail boom of each TAV, and

we can have twenty-four Marines on top of that pyramid—
forty-eight if we need them—in a couple of minutes. We
place our snipers inside the compound—here . . . here . . .
here . . . maybe on the rooftops of some of the Legation
buildings—and have them cap anything that moves on the
pyramid during the Dragon's approach."

He continued moving other squares of blue-painted wood.
"Meanwhile, we push a team of gunwalkers around to the
east side of the pyramid . . . here, to give us a tacsit on that
side. It'll help compensate for not having remote probes, and
they'll be in a position to intercept enemy reinforcements
moving to the objective.

"At the same time, we'll have two full companies on the
ground, ready to roll at the east end of the compound. As
soon as the lead Dragon makes its move, they rush the base
of the pyramid and start moving up. They'll throw up a defensive perimeter around the pyramid itself and catch any
Frogs coming down the pyramid trying to escape the airmobile assault."

"I wish to stress that the taking of prisoners is vital at this
stage of the mission," General King said. "We need to capture and identify their leaders if we wish to open negotiations with them."

"Does anybody know what their leaders look like yet,
sir?" Warhurst asked with a smile.

"We're . . . working on that," Ramsey replied. "If we can
take some live prisoners this time and if our Sumerian experts can talk with them, we have a chance. Ideally, we've
hurt them bad enough already that we can negotiate a truce,
hang on to what we have here, until the relief expedition arrives." He looked squarely at Norris. "That assumes, of
course, that the Ahannu can be reasoned with."

"I'll be blunt, gentlemen, ladies," King said. "This is the
critical stage of Operation Spirit of Humankind . . . critical
to our survival, not just the success of the mission. Most
naval personnel have remained on board the *Derna,* with
Admiral Vincent Hartman directing salvage and recovery

operations. However, it is unlikely at this juncture that they will be able to repair the ship's main power plant. With luck, they may regain sensor and communications capability— which means access to the net once again. We cannot afford to wait for that eventuality, however.

"With the destruction of the *Algol*, our supply situation is precarious at best. I believe Major Anderson has some figures for us?"

"Yes, sir. From what I've been able to ascertain so far, water supplies in the city are adequate. We have access to the Saimi-Id River at the west end of the compound, and nanoprocessors are being set up to filter out pollutants . . . and to watch for any unpleasant surprises the natives may slip into the water upstream.

"Expendable ammunition is tight on the ground right now, especially smart-grenades and DNM-85, but the situation will ease as more supply LMs come down from the *Regulus*. Total expendable ammunition is not a problem at this time.

"Food, however, is. We have enough packaged food for perhaps six weeks, mostly T-rations and hotpacks. I'm told that with strict rationing, our nanoprocessors may be capable of extending that limit to two, maybe three months, but they have a limited daily output . . . not enough to handle over a thousand people for six months."

"There you have it," King said. "If we are to survive until the relief expedition arrives, we *must* gain access to native food sources and ascertain which ones are safe for human consumption. That means we either capture and hold the region surrounding the city in order to forage for our own supplies, or we negotiate with the locals for native food shipments."

"Assuming we can trust them not to poison us," Master Sergeant Vanya Barnes said, a growl in her voice. "You ask me, the only way to secure this fucking mudball is to wipe 'em out to the last freakin' Frog."

"That will do, Master Sergeant," Ramsey said sharply.

"The Corps is not in the business of genocide." He looked at Norris. "However, we will employ whatever level of force is necessary in order to safeguard the mission and our personnel."

"*That's* obvious," Norris said with a bitter laugh. "You've already used nukes."

Ramsey ignored the comment. "Captain Warhurst. It appears to me you've already made personnel selections for your operation."

"Yes, sir. First and 3rd Companies for the ground assault. The airmobile element will be volunteer, of course."

"Who do you have in command of the air assault?"

"Me. Sir."

Ramsey raised an eyebrow at that. "Not exactly according to doctrine."

"With respect, sir, there's damned little about this operation that's going down according to doctrine. I can't ride herd on my people through the net, can't maintain a coherent picture of the battlefield from my LMCP. So I'm going along. Sir."

Ramsey nodded. "Very well, Captain. I understand. And . . . good luck to you."

"Thank you, sir."

"Timing. Have you worked out a timetable yet?"

"Since it's going to be daylight for the next three days, sir, the light's not an issue. I would like to give all of our people time for some shut-eye, though."

"Agreed. Shall we say, H-hour in . . . twenty hours from now?"

"Yes, sir."

"Very well. I'll leave the final planning with your staff—code names, communications protocols, and so on. Just one more thing, though. Do you have a designation for the objective? The command constellation has been calling that thing 'the pyramid.' Shall we name it Objective Giza, after the Great Pyramids?"

"I've been at Giza, sir." He shook his head. "Those pyramids are nothing like this one. Actually, I have another suggestion."

"And that is?"

"We've been calling it Objective Suribachi, sir."

Ramsey smiled, then chuckled. "I like it. Objective Suribachi it is."

Suribachi was the volcanic mountain on the south end of a black speck of an island in the Pacific Ocean where six thousand Marines had given their lives two centuries before, a place called Iwo Jima.

Mount Suribachi had been the site of the famous flag-raising during the battle, a Corps icon. Watching from a ship offshore, James Forrestal, the Secretary of the Navy at the time, had declared to General Holland Smith, "The raising of that flag on Suribachi means there will be a Marine Corps for the next five hundred years."

Well and good. All *this* Suribachi would determine was the survival of the MIEU for the next six months.

23

Marine Bivouac
Legation Compound
New Sumer, Ishtar
0053 hours ALT

He was *Lance Corporal* Garroway now. Funny. He'd not even gotten used to being a PFC, and now he'd been advanced to pay grade E-3.

The announcement had come down from HQ with a blizzard of other announcements and promotions. Sergeant Tim Logan and Hospitalman First Class "Doc" McColloch—one of the Navy corpsmen assigned to the Marines as medics—had been put in for Medals of Honor for their daring rescue of two wounded Marines at the north wall earlier that day. And the newbie PFCs had all gotten their promotions . . . not, as it turned out, by being Van Winkled, but as meritorious field promotions. Van Winkling would have required confirmation from Earth; Colonel Ramsey had chosen to make those promotions immediate.

It didn't matter, really. The experience of combat, of surviving his first firefights, had changed Garroway far, far more deeply than any bureaucratic waving of the wand possibly could.

Out of his armor at last and clad in Marine utilities, Lance Corporal Garroway stood beneath the Ishtaran sky. It was, for him, the end of a very long day, even though technically the sun was still rising. This was his down time; in a few minutes he would try to go get some sleep. First, however . . .

Facing east, in the direction of the red-spark sun close beside the towering pyramid at the edge of the compound, he held the athame, ritual blade high, point toward the sky, and intoned the old formula. "Brothers and sisters of the east, spirits of air, spirits of mind and intellect . . . hail, and welcome." Sketching the outline of a pentagram in the air with the blade, he then turned in place to the right, drawing an imagined quarter circle of blue fire. "Brothers and sisters of the south, spirits of fire, spirits of directions, of paths, of passions . . . hail, and welcome . . ."

It had been a long time since Garroway had performed ritual and cast a circle. He had been raised Wiccan by his mother, though he'd lost interest in all religion and drifted away until about four years ago, when the workings of the craft had become yet another way to defy his staunchly Catholic father. "You won't practice that pagan crap in my house!" the elder Esteban had stormed . . . and so he'd taken warm satisfaction in holding ritual outdoors in secret, at a private stretch of the Guaymas beach.

Often, his mother had joined him.

"Brothers and sisters of the west, spirits of water, spirits of emotions, of relationships, of family . . . hail, and welcome . . ."

The beings he invoked, spirits representing the traditional elements of air, fire, water, and earth, he understood as metaphors that let him grasp the unknowable; if they had any objective reality at all, they were not bound by the limits of time and space. Still, the hard, rationalist, left-brained part of him questioned if the ritual made any sense at all.

If there were such things as elemental spirits, or gods, or guardians of the soul . . . could they hear him out here, so far from home?

He felt a bit self-conscious, aware that there were Marines lounging nearby who could see him.

The hell with them. Freedom of religion was an absolute

and basic right in the Corps, even back in boot camp. Lots of
the other men and women in the MIEU were Wiccan, World
of the Goddess, or pagan of various other stripes, and he
knew he could have found others to join him in this ritual.

But he wanted to do this one solo, just him and the universe. Normally, he would have performed it inwardly, a
simulation within the noumenal world, but with the net
down he was left to do it in the phenomenal world instead.
His father hadn't allowed him to use the Sony-TI 12000 for
Wiccan rites either, so he'd learned how to do it the traditional way, with athame blade and imagination. He'd found
as private a corner as he could, off on the south edge of the
open compound area they were now calling "the grinder," an
out-of-the-way spot for the ritual that would make this patch
of ground sacred space.

"Brothers and sisters of the north, spirits of earth, spirits
of practical things, of daily life . . . hail, and welcome . . ."

He completed the imagined circle of blue fire, a perimeter
around him now sealed by four pentagrams. Stooping, he
touched the ground with the point of his blade.

"Great Mother . . . Goddess . . . Maiden, Mother, and
Crone, I invite you to this circle. Be here now."

In many Wiccan traditions the Goddess represented Gaia,
the spirit of Earth herself. Could she find her way across the
light-years? Or did Ishtar have its own goddess spirit? The
thought stirred sudden inspiration, and he added, "Goddess
of ancient Sumeria and Babylon, Goddess who is called
Inanna, Astarte, and Ishtar . . . Goddess of Love and Goddess of Battles, hail and welcome."

Standing, he raised his blade high. The gas giant Marduk
hung vast and banded in the west. "God of Light, God of the
Sun, known as Utu, Shamash, and Marduk, be here now.
Hail and welcome." He wasn't entirely sure that Marduk
could properly be linked mythologically with the earlier
Mesopotamian gods of the sun, but it didn't matter. It was
the idea behind the words that mattered.

He closed his eyes and imagined Ishtar and Marduk,

queen and consort, standing within his circle within a blaze of radiant light. A small but rational part of his mind noted that those deities likely had their origins with the An colonists in ancient Sumer ten thousand years ago. Most of the oldest Sumerian gods, it seemed—Utu and Enki, Ea and An and Nanna—had been real beings, or at least personalized composites drawn from actual encounters between early proto-Sumerian nomads and the Anunnaki, "Those Who Came from Heaven to Earth."

Not that this mattered either. Humankind had long ago refashioned all of the gods in its own image. He doubted that the modern Ahannu would recognize what he called upon now.

More disturbing, the rational part of him thought, was the idea of a twenty-second-century high-tech Marine invoking spirits in a ritual two centuries old, one drawn, it was claimed, from beliefs and practices thousands of years older—older even than the starfaring gods of ancient Sumeria.

He pushed the intruding thought aside, focusing instead on the inner pacing of the solitary ritual, on the metaphors that allowed him to tap deep, deep into his own unconscious, to draw on the guidance, the symbols, the energy residing there. Religion, the religious impulse, whatever its outward trappings and whatever its origin, was undeniably as much a part of humankind as language, politics, or even breathing.

"By the earth that is her body, by the air that is her breath, by the fire of her bright spirit, by the living waters of her womb, this circle is cast."

He opened his eyes, turning them toward a momentarily clear, crystalline blue-green twilight sky alive with pale auroras and the banded beauty of ringed Marduk. A meteor flared briefly at the zenith. "I stand now between the worlds."

He smiled at that. In a sense, he *was* between the worlds. But more . . . he might be light-years from Earth, but the connection he sought with the divine was something he carried within himself, the god and goddess both parts of his own being. The deities he called to this place were not so distant after all. They were a part of his own noumenal world, as opposed to the phenomenal world of sight, sound, and matter.

Facing east once more, he concentrated on raising inner energy for the working he had in mind. He heard laughter and opened his eyes. Yeah . . . he was being watched. A group of Marines offloading supplies from a cargo LM nearby were taking a break, and several were watching his ritual. Let them. This was *his* time, his sacred space, and their laughter meant nothing.

The spiritual feeding of the men and women of 1 MIEU was an undertaking nearly as complex and as daunting as feeding them physically. There were a number of chaplains with the MIEU, all of them tasked with multiple spiritual duties. Captain Walters, for instance, served as priest for both the Catholics and the counter-Catholics, as well as the Episcopalians—a reconciliation of viewpoints that, Garroway thought, must require a fascinating set of mental gymnastics. Lieutenant Steve Prescott was chaplain for the less fundamentalist Protestants, the Church of Light, the Spiritualists, the Taoists, the Neo-Arians, and several other faiths, while a staff sergeant from C Company named Blandings took care of the fundy sects, Four-Squares, Baptists, and Pentecostals. There were two rabbis for the Jews, two imams for the Muslims, a priest for the Hindus, and a young lieutenant named Cynthia Maillard who watched out for the spiritual needs of the pagans, the Native American shamanic traditions, the Mithraists, and five different ancient astronaut sects. He'd heard somewhere that there were all of sixty-five different faiths represented among the MIEU's personnel complement, not counting the atheists, agnostics, and personal faiths. Arguably, the only major religion *not* represented were any of the radical Anist sects. While the Corps was enjoined by law not to discriminate on the basis of religious belief, people who believed that the An were literal gods or that humankind was intended to be a slave race were not the best recruits for a Marine deployment to an Ahannu world.

If he needed counseling during the deployment to Llalande, Garroway's assigned chaplain was Lieutenant Maillard. He doubted that he would need to talk with her, however. Wiccans, for the most part, handled their own priestly duties without the need of clergy.

He did wonder why this ritual, this time set apart, was so important to him now but decided he didn't need to look further than the bewildering avalanche of sights, sounds, emotions, and impressions of the past twenty-some hours. Pressley's shocking death . . . the news that the *Derna* had been crippled in orbit . . . the destruction of An-Kur . . . the battle at the north wall . . . He felt as though he'd lived years in a day's span of time.

Now *there* was an interesting twist on the whole question of objective versus subjective time.

An old, old saying held that religion was for those who feared Hell, while *spirituality* was for those who'd been there.

He felt the faint, nails-on-blackboard tingle on his spine that he thought of as energy rising from the earth, filling him, recharging him. He needed this as much as he needed sleep; it was a reminder of who he was, of *what* he was, and why. An old military saying held that there were no atheists in foxholes.

If his religion had not been important to him before, save as a weapon to wield against an abusive and drunken father, it was vitally important to him now.

He was scared. Alone and scared.

The word had come down from the LM command post earlier that day, along with the news of the promotions and medals. They were looking for forty-eight volunteers for an airborne assault on the pyramid in the east. He'd given it some thought, then decided to put in his name.

He still wasn't entirely sure why he'd done it. Hell, "never volunteer" was the unwritten cardinal rule for all enlisted personnel, a rule probably going back to the time of Sargon the Great. But he was still feeling a bit . . . *detached* was the only way he could phrase it. Numb. The loss of so many men and women he'd come to know over the past subjective days had left him feeling as though he needed to reach out and reattach himself, to put down new roots, forge new bonds.

Volunteering for what they were calling Operation Suribachi seemed the best way to do that.

Of course, they might turn him down for lack of experience, the way Gunny Valdez had. Somehow, though, he felt now as though he carried an entire world of experience squarely on his back.

The Wiccan ritual was a good way to ground himself with earth and with *now* as well.

"God and Goddess, Marduk and Ishtar . . . speed the passing of friends and comrades from this world to the next. Make bright their ways. Strengthen those they've left behind . . ."

A long time later—all of thirty minutes, perhaps, though it seemed like hours—Garroway closed his circle and returned to the phenomenal world of space and time.

He still felt numb, but he did feel stronger. A little, anyway.

He sheathed his athame—a standard Corps-issue Mk. 4 combat knife once again—and returned to the patch of open ground in front of Building 12, where he'd stowed his sleep roll and gear.

Now, he thought, he might be able to sleep.

MIEU Command Center
Legation Compound
New Sumer, Ishtar
1545 hours ALT

"The walkers are through the east gate," Major Anderson reported. "No contact."

"Very well, Major," Colonel Ramsey said as he continued watching the big monitor screen mounted on one bulkhead of the command LM. The view was of a dusty New Sumer street, a view that lurched unsteadily from side to side as the camera platform stalked ahead on two scissoring plasteel and carbon fiber legs. The legend at the bottom of the screen reported that the image was being transmitted from Gunwalker Seven. A red crosshair reticle floated about the scene, marking the aim point of the walker's Gatling laser.

To Ramsey's left a line of seven Marine technicians sat at a long, makeshift console with bread-boarded processor blocks and salvaged monitors. Each watched his or her own screen closely, making moment-to-moment adjustments on the joystick controls in front of them.

"So far, so good," General King said, edging up beside Ramsey and peering up at the big screen. "How much farther?"

"Half a kilometer, General, thereabouts."

"Coming up on East Cagnon and Rosenthal Street, Colonel," one of the techs said. "Making the turn north onto Rosenthal." The image on the screen swung sharply as the teleoperated walker veered left; Ramsey caught a glimpse of another walker making the turn—an ungainly looking device that reminded him of a neckless ostrich cast as modern sculpture. The Gatling laser, slung beneath the body and between the legs in blatantly phallic display, pivoted left and right, seeking targets. "Still no contact."

Ramsey checked a small, hand-drawn map taped to the console in lieu of a noumenal map feed. The streets around the Pyramid of the Eye had been given names for ease of navigation—Souseley, Block, Cagnon, Hayes, Strank, Bradley. Those six were the names of the men—a PFC, three corporals, a sergeant, and a Navy corpsman—who'd raised the famous flag on Suribachi on 23 February 1945. Rosenthal was Joe Rosenthal, the Associated Press photographer who'd snapped the icon photo. Other streets—Schrier, Thomas, Michelis, Charlo, Lindberg, Hansen—were named for the Marines who'd raised the *first* flag on Suribachi, before Rosenthal had arrived on the scene.

Marines remembered their own, with a body of histories, parables, and mythologies as passionate as that of any religion.

Ramsey felt a small shiver of presentiment at that thought. Men of Third Platoon, E Company, of the 28th Marines, had raised both flags on Suribachi. Of forty men in the company, only four had avoided being wounded or killed in the fighting. Three of the six photographed by Rosenthal that morning—PFC Souseley, Corporal Block, and Sergeant Strank—were later killed on Iwo. Of the six who'd raised the first flag, three had been killed and two wounded; only Lieutenant Schrier emerged from the fighting unscathed.

A small bit of Corps trivia, that . . . and a testament to the ferocity of the fighting on Iwo Jima, one of the bloodiest amphibious assaults of World War II. But a bit of superstitious worry gnawed at Ramsey as well. The Pyramid of the Eye was a natural defensive position.

Might that damned pyramid turn out to be a second Suribachi, in bloody kind as well as in name?

Something clanged from the side of Walker Seven, sending the image lurching heavily to the side. "Contact!" the technician announced. "We have hostiles inbound, moving in from north, east, and south."

The monitor image jarred again, nearly falling over, then pivoted sharply, the crosshairs locking onto a running, human figure. The Gatling fired with a shrill whine, and the running figure exploded in a gory red spray.

"Walkers One, Three, Five, and Six, move to block east and south," Ramsey ordered. "Two, Four, and Seven . . . keep moving north, double-time. Punch through them!"

One of the technicians gave a loud exclamation, something between a curse and a groan, and threw up her hands as her screen went dead. "Walker Two is down!"

"Thank you, Sergeant," Ramsey told her. "Stand by your station, please."

"Aye aye, sir."

"Walker Six is out of the running, Colonel," another technician said. "They're nailing us with high-velocity gauss rifles."

"Understood."

"This is too expensive," General King said. "We don't have the gunwalkers to spare for this sort of thing."

Ramsey looked at King. "Better this than sending Marines out there, sir. I do not want to send in the airmobile detachment without seeing the east side of Suribachi."

"Agreed," King said, though with some reluctance. "But they're a damned expensive substitute for floater remotes."

Ramsey smiled. King was painfully aware of the logistical limitations 1 MIEU faced. With a small supply of teleoperated gunwalkers on hand, there were none left when those were gone.

After flirting with robotic weaponry for almost three hundred years, the American military still maintained a remarkably tentative relationship with military robots. Arguing that only a human could make kill-or-spare decisions in combat, true robot soldiers, running sentient AI programs, had never been wholeheartedly embraced, even though robot mines, robot bombs, antimissile guns, even robotic fighter aircraft all had been employed in combat since the end of the twentieth century. The fact of the matter was that robotic senses were far superior to those of human warriors in the smoke and confusion of a firefight, their reaction times were far shorter, and they were unaffected by shortcomings such as fear, pain, anger, or traumatic shock. Fearful that general purpose military robots could be hijacked by a technically proficient enemy and turned on their creators, the Pentagon had rejected sentient robotic soldiers time after time. The closest thing to a true robot so far adopted were robot sentries, which guarded set fields of fire and couldn't move, and hunter-killer gunwalkers, which had only a limited decision-making capacity. Walkers had extremely quick reactions and a deadly aim, but they were best employed as teleoperated weapons . . . with a human driver behind the lines, piloting the machine through a link via the net.

With the net down, of course, they'd lost full function on the walkers, but by posting Marines on the far northern and southern portions of the compound's east wall, they were able to maintain line-of-sight communications with the walkers. The reception was good enough that they were running seven walkers at about eighty percent of their usual performance capacity.

Correction. *Five* walkers.

"I've got the objective in sight, sir," one of the techs called. "Walker Four."

"Punch it up," Ramsey told Anderson. "Let's see it on the big screen."

The scene shifted to the vantage point of another walker, farther up Rosenthal Street. The walker had halted in the middle of the street and was rotated slightly to the left, looking up at the gleaming white slope of the Pyramid of the Eye.

The pyramid was enormous. It measured 106 meters along each side at the base and was nearly sixty meters tall, which made it almost as broad and as tall as the smallest of the Great Pyramids at Giza. The slope of the walls felt more like that of a typical Mayan pyramid, much steeper and more precipitous than the slopes of the pyramids at Giza. The five-tier construction was reminiscent of the step-pyramids or ziggurats of ancient Mesopotamia. Broad, half-meter-high stone steps ran up the center of each of the four sides.

From the vantage point of the HK gunwalker, the Pyramid of the Eye seemed to tower overhead, giving the vertiginous impression that it was about to come crashing down on the street.

The walker's point of view dropped back to street level, focusing on a handful of human Sag-ura rushing toward it armed with clubs, spears, and gauss guns. The Gatling laser opened up, shredding the charge in bloody disarray.

But more and more rounds were striking home, knocking the walker to left or right. Walker Four took another dozen steps forward, then the screen filled with static and went black.

"Four is down," Anderson said. "Bringing up Walker Seven."

"Walker One is down. Enemy forces advancing from the east."

"Damn them," King muttered as the camera view of the last remaining northbound walker winked on. "Why gauss rifles when the sons of bitches are still carrying spears? Why not black powder?"

"Gauss guns are remarkably simple in concept, General," Major Anderson pointed out. "And pretty hard to break. A hollow tube with a mechanism for sending a powerful electro-magnetic pulse down the barrel at high speed . . . as long as they have a way to recharge the power pack, they could store those things for thousands of years. Gunpowder would go stale before too long, especially in a humid climate like this one."

"Makes sense, I guess," Ramsey added. "What about plasma guns and lasers, though? Those don't require chemicals that would go unstable after a few centuries."

Anderson shrugged. "They may have some, and we just haven't seen them yet . . . lasers, anyway. Plasma guns require a pretty sophisticated mechanism for fusing water or some other projectile mass, though, and they need to operate at such high temperatures and muzzle velocities that a primitive culture simply couldn't support them. That's just a guess, though. Gauss guns . . . all you need for a projectile is something with iron in it or wrapped around it. A nail would work. And you don't need really high muzzle velocities. A few kilometers per second would be just fine for a nail or a small iron slug."

"Coming up on the east side of Suribachi, sir," the Walker Seven technician reported. "But I'm taking some damage."

On the big monitor, the watching officers had a clear view now of the pyramid from street level, with no intervening buildings. The steps leading up the steeply sloping east face were clear, and there was no sign of any enemy warriors at the top.

"That's what we needed to see," Ramsey said. "No nasty surprises waiting for us on the side we can't see from here." He looked at King. "General? Permission to commence the assault on Suribachi."

King looked at the monitor a moment, then sighed. "Permission granted, Colonel. Give 'em hell."

"Aye aye, sir!" Ramsey picked up a microphone. "Dragon Flight, this is Dragon Nest. The word is go! Go! I say again, go!"

"Roger that, Nest," a voice came back over the speaker system. "Dragon Flight One, en route."

"Here we go, then," Ramsey said. "Watch that first step!"

Dragon One
New Sumer, Ishtar
1557 hours ALT

Garroway was snapped into the air, the ground dropping away beneath his dangling feet. He closed his eyes until he could get used to the sharp, stomach-dropping feeling of acceleration, then opened them again. They were airborne.

Encased in full armor, his LR-2120 strapped across his torso, Garroway was suspended from the tail boom of the Dragonfly by a harness securing his thighs, back, and shoulders, with a quick release at his waist. Twenty-three other Marines dangled with him, two by two, facing outward as the Dragonfly canted nose down and streaked low across the eastern reaches of the compound, banking sharply toward the Pyramid of the Eye. Looking down, he saw the streets and buildings and the eastern wall of the Legation blurring past less than a hundred meters below.

He was hanging literally shoulder-to-shoulder with Corporal Womicki and a sergeant from First Platoon named Couch. He could hear a retching sound over the squad tactical net and knew someone was being sick inside his helmet, with its sound-activated mike. He tried not to think about that.

"Hey, the Marine Corps is great," he heard Dunne say as the retching subsided. "First-class accommodations all the way!"

"Cut the chatter, people," Master Sergeant Barnes said. "Jennings! Cut your damned mike so we all don't have to listen to you and your breakfast!"

The Dragonfly went nose high and started to climb sharply. Garroway wished he could tap into the net for a camera feed to his helmet display . . . then thought better of it. There were some things he might be happier not seeing.

"Okay, people," Captain Warhurst's voice said over the tactical channel. "I can see the objective . . . range, another two hundred meters. No sign of bad guys on the top."

Garroway heard a loud clang from somewhere forward and above him and realized they were being shot at. There were bad guys down there, and they knew the Marines were coming.

"I think the gunwalkers drew off some of the pyramid defenders," Warhurst went on, his running commentary oddly comforting. Garroway closed his eyes and focused on the captain's words. "I see two . . . three humans on the south steps, halfway up. There are some Annies inside the Chamber of the Eye on the west side. I can see them peering out at us."

Garroway felt momentarily weightless as the Dragonfly began descending. Looking down past his feet, he saw the gleaming white stone of the pyramid's south slope fifty meters below, coming up fast. . . .

The Pyramid of the Eye had a broad, open, truncated peak fifteen meters across, with a small temple or sky observatory, a dome-topped building rising from the center. Despite the obstruction, there was plenty of room for the TAV-S to set down, but the operational plan called for a quick drop-and-go so the Dragonfly was free to become a ground-support asset as soon as the Marine assault force hit the pyramid roof.

"Twenty seconds, Marines," Warhurst called. "Remember. Keep your knees loose. Don't lock 'em. Fifteen seconds . . . we're at thirty meters . . . get ready. Five seconds . . . four . . . three . . . two . . . *release*!"

Garroway stabbed at the quick-release buckle on his waist and felt the suspension harness open around him. He dropped, a dead weight, falling perhaps three meters to the stone surface of the upper platform of the pyramid. His armor took the shock of the landing, cushioning him as he fell into a loose-kneed tumble-and-roll.

He came out of the roll with his laser rifle at the ready, bracing himself on his elbows as he scanned the pyramid roof. The twenty-four Marines had dropped in a ragged double row on the south side of the upper tier. The Dragonfly hovered just overhead, its thrusters shrieking as the pilot gunned it into a swift climb away from the drop zone.

"On your feet, Marines!" Warhurst yelled. "Perimeter defense!"

Hot wind swirled clouds of dust about them as the Dragonfly gained altitude. Garroway leaned forward into the blast and started moving. He heard shouts and the snap of laser fire but could see no targets ahead of him.

To his right, five meters away, was the small domed structure at the center of the pyramid's peak, a kind of cupola with four arched, wide-open entryways facing the four quarters of the compass.

And then he saw the large, hulking figures spilling out of

the building. "Trolls!" he yelled, bringing his 2120 to his shoulder. "Trolls at three-six-zero!"

There were a lot of the creatures, and they all appeared armed with massive gauss weapons at least two meters long.

"Fire at will!" Warhurst yelled . . . and the Battle of the Pyramid began in earnest.

24

Lance Corporal Garroway
Pyramid of the Eye
New Sumer, Ishtar
1612 hours ALT

"Let's go, Marines! Take 'em down!"

Garroway triggered his 2120, sending a burst of rapidly pulsed laser fire through the tangle of Ahannu trolls spilling from the domed building. Overhead, the Dragonfly circled, banking hard, bringing its chin Gatling to bear on the threat. The trolls were still falling into a ragged line, aiming their weapons together in a fair re-creation of a musket firing line from the eighteenth or nineteenth century on Earth, when the deadly scythes of coherent light sliced through them in bloody execution.

Firing as he moved, Garroway jogged across the stone platform, while the enemy line—what was left of it—dissolved and rolled back. Parts of the domed building flared into an incandescent spray of molten stone as Sergeant Tomlin, the assault team's plasma gunner, turned his weapon on the archway. Scattering beneath the onslaught, Ahannu troll-warriors shrieked and burned in the deadly cross fire between air and ground, and the central building collapsed in smoking ruin.

And not the building alone. A portion of the stone pavement beneath the building canted suddenly, spilling debris into a gaping hole that rapidly grew larger. More and more stone blocks fell into the widening gap beneath a boiling cloud of dust and smoke. Garroway skidded to a stop at the edge of the dropoff. The collapse of a portion of the pyramid's roof had revealed a sunken, open chamber five meters across, partially filled now with fallen blocks of stone and with a squirming, crawling mass of Ahannu struggling up out of the pyramid's depths and into the light.

Dropping to one knee, he brought his laser rifle up and began triggering it . . . before switching to RPGs with the idea that repeated explosions would cause more damage to that writhing mass and concuss the survivors.

The other Marines in the charging line had the same idea, concentrating their grenade fire, and in seconds the crater in the pyramid's roof was a thundering, bloody pit of chaotic flame and detonations, blast following savage blast with murderous effect. The circling Dragonfly added to the slaughter hovering above the pit and spraying the opening with Gatling fire.

"Cease fire!" Warhurst commanded. "Marines, cease fire! We want prisoners!"

Most of the movement within the pit had stopped now, but a few dazed survivors were pulling themselves out from under shredded Ahannu bodies and fallen stone blocks. Garroway grabbed one by the wrist, pulled him roughly to the pavement, and pinned him there facedown while Corporal Hazely tied his hands.

The second Dragonfly was inbound now, with twenty-four Marines dangling two by two beneath the slender, slightly arched boom between its forward fuselage and the power plant at the tail. It settled toward the smoking pyramid roof, nose angling up, belly thrusters shrieking, coming to a hover two meters off the pavement.

The Marines dropped from their harnesses in a ragged spill and spread out, joining the first section. The Dragonfly continued its descent and gentled onto wide-splayed landing jacks on the roof.

"Section Two," Warhurst ordered the newly arrived Marines. "On the perimeter, south and east sides! Section One . . . 1st Squad, take the north side. Second Squad, keep digging out those Annies."

More and more Ahannu warriors were dragging themselves up the fallen blocks of pavement stone to the pyramid roof, where 2nd Squad Marines grabbed them, pushed them down, and used plastic stripper-ties to secure their hands behind their backs. None appeared to be in any shape to put up a fight, but as quickly as each was secured, a couple of Marines would drag the captive across the roof to the grounded Dragonfly and secure the prisoner to an open harness. In moments they'd collared five of the regular Ahannu, two trolls, and three human slave-warriors.

Garroway was 1st Squad, so he joined the others and trotted across to the northern edge of the pyramid roof. From that vantage point, he had a spectacular view of the city of New Sumer and the Legation compound to the west. Marines were spilling out through the east gate in the wall, sixty meters below, and rushing toward the pyramid's base. Ahannu warriors were everywhere down there. The sudden attack on the Pyramid of the Eye appeared to have had the effect of kicking over an anthill, sending the defenders scurrying. The movement seemed random at first, but as moment followed moment, it was clear that the enemy was gathering for a concerted rush of the pyramid.

Garroway joined the eleven other Marines in his squad, marking down individual running Ahannu. If enough of them died, shouldn't the others scatter?

Perhaps that was what was written in the manual, but the Ahannu, evidently, hadn't read it. From the top of the pyramid it appeared that a black tide was surging up the north and west faces of the structure.

"Pour it on 'em!" Sergeant Barnes bellowed, and the volume of fire from the pyramid's top swept through the climbing horde with hot-burning fury. Dozens of the Ahannu and Sag-ura in the leading ranks toppled backward, but there were hundreds, thousands, more to surge forward, scrambling over the bodies, snatching up banners and weapons, keening a piercing battle cry that was part hiss, part shrieking wail.

For Garroway, the universe again seemed to dwindle to a tiny slice of its former scope and depth and richness. He heard the infernal noise—the screams, shrieks, battle yells, the incessant snap and hiss of lasers and plasma bolts. His awareness narrowed down almost solely to the enhanced and magnified image projected within his helmet visor, to the faces—human and nonhuman—scrambling up the steps of the pyramid in a headlong charge.

He fired . . . fired . . . fired again, sweeping his weapon back and forth as he loosed triple bursts into the oncoming horde, confident that *any* bolt loosed at the attackers would find a target, if not in the front rank, than in the one behind . . . or the one behind that. Ahannu god-warriors stumbled and collapsed as they advanced, the bodies crumpling onto the steps and immediately engulfed by the surging rush of Ahannu and Sag-ura still living, still howling and hissing their battle rage.

The pyramid steps, he noticed with detached interest, were each a half meter high . . . higher than most of the diminutive Ahannu could manage comfortably. Those precipitous steps were wearing even on the trolls and humans in the attack . . . though they were quickly outdistancing the Ahannu god-warriors in their mad race up the sides of the pyramid. More and more of the front-rank attackers glimpsed through the magnified HDO scope projection were screaming, grimacing, tattooed human faces, mingled with Ahannu troll faces, blunt, thick, and heavy, or the visages of a few of the hardier or more determined of the Frog god-warriors. For a time, Garroway tried to spot the ones with god-weapons—gauss rifles or other modern weaponry, some of it obviously of recent human manufacture—and kill the ones carrying them. Before long, though, all he could do was point and fire, point and fire . . . until the red light on his hel-

met display winked red, warning of power drain and overheating. He switched to smart RPGs to let the weapon cool.

With a shrieking roar of high-pitched thunder, one of the
Dragonflies howled low overhead, arrowing toward the
Legation compound. Garroway glanced up and noted that it
was the TAV-S bearing Ahannu and Sag-ura prisoners from
the initial fight atop the Pyramid of the Eye. The other
Dragonfly orbited slowly over the alien city north of the
pyramid, turning its Gatling laser on the hordes at the pyramid's base, burning down the attackers in broad, scything
sweeps of destruction.

As he watched, oily black smoke began spilling from the
forward fuselage of the second Dragonfly. Ahannu gauss
gunners must have been concentrating their fire on it from
across half of the city. The TAV-S started to turn back toward
the compound, then appeared to stagger in mid-flight, its
bank turning into an ungainly roll. It crashed half a kilometer north of the pyramid, throwing up a tremendous pillar of
smoke and cascading debris.

There was no time to think about that, however, beyond a
numb acceptance of the fact. Ahannu and Sag-ura were
more than halfway up the north side of the pyramid now. As
quickly as the Marine defenders could burn them down,
more appeared to take their place. *Where* were they all coming from?

Radio chatter crackled over his helmet earphones. "Hey,
it's another great day on the firing range! Let's have some
more targets!"

"Can that, Lassiter."

"Yeah, these targets are shooting back!"

"This is Nakamura, on the west side! We need more people over here, ASAP!"

"Nakamura, Warhurst. Roger that. Hold your line."

"We're not stopping them! We're not stopping them!"

"Lower your fire, people. Aim for the front ranks!"

A cascade of rockets sprayed into the sky on twisting
white contrails, arcing over, descending. Several exploded

inside the compound to the west. Others detonated on the sides of the pyramid, hurling chunks of broken stone into the crowds below. One exploded squarely atop the pyramid, and Garroway heard a Marine scream with pain.

"Hell, I think we went and made the bastards mad at us," Sergeant Dunne said at Garroway's left.

"What makes you think that, Sarge?" Garroway asked. His helmet warning display shifted from red to amber, and he thought-clicked back to his laser to save his fast-dwindling supply of RPGs.

"I dunno. Something about the hate mail they're sending us."

The screaming over the radio net abruptly stopped. Either someone had killed the wounded man's open mike or the wound had been fatal.

"Whose bright idea was this, anyway?" Lance Corporal Jennings asked. He was kneeling at Garroway's right, calmly pumping laser pulses into the oncoming warriors.

"Beats me," Garroway replied. "If you find him, let me know so I can thank him personally!"

The idea had been to land on the roof of the Pyramid of the Eye and fight down, a vertical envelopment, in classic Marine tactical doctrine, while Marines from the Legation compound emerged from the east gate and fought their way up, trapping the Ahannu defenders between the two groups. Somehow, though, things were going badly awry. There were way too many of the Ahannu god-warriors, hordes threatening to overwhelm the human defenders in a black, rolling tide.

A volley of gauss-gun fire from the north ripped through the line of Marines. Three fell. Lance Corporal Jennings tottered a moment, fist-sized holes in his faceplate and the back curve of his helmet spilling smoke and a splatter of blood. He started to fall over the edge, but Garroway snagged him by his power pack harness and yanked him back. Fighting down the urge to retch, he pulled the RPG magazine pouch from the right side of Jennings's armor. He also checked the backpack power indicator on Jennings's 2120. Hell, Jennings wasn't much better off than Garroway in the power department.

Garroway continued to fire his own weapon, alternating now between laser pulses and M-12 RPG rounds. He tried to slow the pace of his fire; the temptation was to blaze away as quickly as possible, but that, he reasoned, was a great way to end up dry and empty by the time those hordes reached the top of the structure.

And they *would* reach it. He had no doubts whatsoever about that. If anything, there were more Ahannu god-warriors, trolls, and Sag-ura slaves below than there'd been at the beginning of this engagement. Garroway accepted that with a Marine's stoic inner shrug. Either the Ahannu would break themselves on this rock, or the Marines themselves would be broken.

If there were other alternatives, he couldn't see them at the moment.

MIEU Command Center
Legation Compound
New Sumer, Ishtar
1635 hours ALT

Ramsey listened to the incoming radio messages from the top of the pyramid. The battle was not going well . . . not going well at all. Task Force Warhurst was on top of the building, but a major enemy counterattack was developing. The Marine company deployed through the east gate to relieve the Suribachi assault force had met heavy enemy forces and been stopped cold.

This he thought, was the make-or-break moment.

King looked at him, arms folded, his face bleak. "Well, Colonel? What's your call?"

"Only two ways to play it, General. We reinforce Suribachi or we pull them out. Recommendations?"

King shook his head. "This one is yours, Colonel. Purely tactical. If you're asking for *advice*, I'd say we've obviously kicked them where it hurts, so keep on kicking."

Ramsey nodded. "That was my feeling, sir. We—"

"Colonel!" Major Anderson called from one of the communications consoles nearby. "Heavy enemy forces approaching the north wall. It looks like they're making an attempt to overrun the compound!"

"Acknowledged." He cocked his head, listening to the radio chatter for a moment.

"Godawmighty, lookit 'em come!"

"Pour it on 'em, people! Burn 'em down!"

"I've got Frogs coming in on the northwest corner! There's too many! We need help!"

"Let 'em come! Let the bastards come!"

"Pick your targets, Marines. Make every shot count!"

"Fox Seven! Fox Seven! We're being flanked!"

"Tomlin! Get the pig up there on the northeast corner! Move it! Move it!"

"Dragon Nest, Dragon Nest, this is Echo Two! We have Frogs, lots of Frogs, rushing the north gate! We've got humans with climbing poles down there! They're rushing us! They're . . ."

The situation was growing increasingly desperate. If he didn't reinforce Task Force Warhurst atop the Pyramid of the Eye, he could lose all forty-eight men up there. But if he took men out of the compound to reinforce Warhurst, he would weaken the defenses here and open the MIEU to the possibility of being completely overrun.

He realized that King, Anderson, and most of the others in the cramped combat center were watching him.

"Major Anderson."

"Yes, sir."

"Pass the word to Captain Sanders," Ramsey said, naming the Bravo Company commander. "He's to reinforce the attack at the east gate."

"Aye aye, sir!"

He locked gazes with King. "Might as well be hung for a sheep as a lamb," he said. "We win this thing here and now."

"I concur," King said. "And God help us all."

Lance Corporal Garroway
Pyramid of the Eye
New Sumer, Ishtar
1645 hours ALT

Odd. Garroway felt as though he were two people . . . one very present, completely engulfed in the sound and fury of the battle, the other detached . . . not numb, exactly, but not entirely present, not connected to what was happening. His body went through the movements of aim-and-fire automatically, with mechanical precision and almost completely unconscious control. He responded to orders, hearing the radioed shouts of comrades and officers, and yet he heard them all as if from a tremendous distance. At first he wondered if he were still feeling the effects of the NNTs, but those should have been broken down and reabsorbed by his body long ago. It was . . . interesting to be engaged in the firefight, yet without the nearly paralyzing fear that had gripped him the day before.

The panorama view from the top of the pyramid, the detached portion of his mind thought, was an eldritch scene from some old-fashioned Christian hell, brooding, a red-lit nightmare sprawling beneath ominous black clouds, rising pillars of smoke, and the swooping drift and stoop of Marine Dragonflies.

The loss of one TAV-S, Garroway was delighted to see, had not deterred the others. Four of the aircraft were in the air, laying down heavy close-support fire despite gauss-gun volleys and rocket fire from the city streets below. Their efforts seemed to be stemming the flood of enemy reinforcements from wherever they were coming from and zeroing in with laser-targeted accuracy on the launch sites of those primitive rockets.

"Fall back! They're coming over the edge! Fall back!"

Garroway had dropped his own overheated LR-2120 and picked up Jennings's weapon, the cables still attached to the backpack of the dead Marine. Now, though, the order had come to fall back from the rim of the pyramid roof. He didn't want to leave Jennings's body . . . but he couldn't handle that and both weapons as well.

The Ahannu warriors were nearly at the top of the pyramid, scrambling ever higher despite devastating losses to their ranks. He could see their huge, golden eyes shining in the red light as they climbed. To his left Garroway sensed a wild, swirling struggle as the Frogs reached the top and began spilling onto the paved rooftop of the pyramid, grappling hand-to-hand with the defenders.

He triggered another couple of bursts into the Ahannu god-warrior horde, then tried to wrestle with Jennings's body. Shit, this *wasn't* going to work.

"I've got him." Sergeant Dunne stooped, grabbing the body by the handhold on the back of Jennings's power pack, and started dragging him across the pavement. Garroway picked up his own laser, checked temperature and power supply, then backed up alongside Dunne, covering the other Marine as he retrieved the body.

Marines did *not* leave their own behind, whenever that was humanly possible.

The Ahannu reached the north edge of the pyramid roof and started scrambling over the rim, hundreds of them, most waving scythe-tipped lances, elaborate war clubs, or curved-bladed iron swords. Many carried black and red banners, while a few had gauss guns.

One Ahannu god-warrior in green and black leather armor brandished a particularly grisly trophy—a mutilated human head spiked on the end of a long spear, the mouth and empty eye sockets gaping. It must, Garroway thought, be the head of one of the Marines lost yesterday inside An-Kur, when the Frogs overran the relay inside one of the tunnels and killed the people guarding it.

Or . . . was that the preserved head of one of the Marines who'd died defending the Legation compound ten years ago? Either way, it was one reason why Marines did not abandon even their dead. Furious, he triggered his 2120, sending a burst of coherent light through the Ahannu's armor and setting it ablaze. The Frog shrieked and fell backward off the edge, dropping its trophy into the crowd of its comrades.

And there was another trophy, of sorts . . . an Ahannu wearing a Marine-issue power pack and awkwardly lugging a Sunbeam LR-2120 in splayed, six-fingered hands. Half a dozen Marine lasers cut that warrior down before it had a chance to fire.

The Ahannu, obviously, were technical enough to be able to use captured Marine weapons, though it seemed a bit reckless of them to risk losing them again in front-line combat. Maybe they were getting desperate, throwing everything they had into a do or die effort.

Well, the Corps could play that tune as well. Slowly, begrudging every step, the Marines fell back across the top of the pyramid, continuing to rake the oncoming enemy with volley upon volley of laser, plasma gun, and smart-grenade fire. As their perimeter contracted, they began crowding one another, armored shoulders bumping shoulders as they created a solid and unbroken wall of polylaminate Mark VII armor. They backed to the place where a portion of the roof had caved in and swiftly began dropping down onto the canted stone blocks, using the crater and broken slabs as cover as they continued to burn down the charging Ahannu god-warriors.

There was no place else to go.

Kneeling in the crater, his laser dangerously overheated, Garroway kept firing. He'd switched to single shot when his breech core temperature redlined and his coolant reserve be-

gan steaming, but he knew he didn't have many shots left
before the weapon malfunctioned.

He had two magazines of smart grenades left. He snapped
one into the magazine receiver and chambered a round.

The Ahannu god-warriors rushed forward, keening their
shrill battle cries. . . .

Captain Warhurst
Pyramid of the Eye
New Sumer, Ishtar
1650 hours ALT

"Dragon Nest, Dragon Nest, this is Suribachi," Warhurst
called over the command channel. "Come in, Dragon Nest!"

"Suribachi, Dragon Nest. Go ahead." It was the colonel's
voice.

Warhurst stood on the steeply canted slab of cut stone,
balanced on the edge of the crater atop the Pyramid of the
Eye. The Ahannu and their human slave-warriors were scant
meters away, rushing the Marine perimeter from north, west,
and south.

"Dragon Nest, they have us pushed into a pocket. We're
taking heavy casualties. Request air strikes, repeat, air
strikes in close support of this position."

"We copy that, Suribachi. Our air reports it's hard to see
what's happening up there. They don't want to cause
friendly fire casualties. Over."

"Fuck that!" Warhurst yelled into his mike. He was firing
his laser rifle in quick, steady pulses, burning down the
charging Frogs one after another, and *still* they kept coming.
*"The Annies are all over the fucking pyramid! Dust the
whole area! Now!"*

There was a brief hesitation. "Roger that, Suribachi.
Dragons deployed in close support. Keep your heads down!"

He didn't answer. The wall of Ahannu hit the western arc

of the Marine perimeter first, then the north, god-warriors leaping high above the line and coming down behind and among the struggling Marines.

Suddenly, the fight was a swirling hand-to-hand melee at knife-fighting range, as the Marines at the edge of the pit battled for survival.

Lance Corporal Garroway
Pyramid of the Eye
New Sumer, Ishtar
1657 hours ALT

An Ahannu god-warrior hit Garroway full-on, knocking him backward. He dropped his laser but was able to hold the writhing Frog off long enough to drag his combat knife from its sheath on his chest and plunge it up to the hilt into the being's throat. He turned the blade and slashed to the side, and the Ahannu's head flopped back, gape-mouthed, in a spray of pale blood. Garroway rolled to the side, scooping up his laser in his left hand, clutching the bloody knife in his right. He was shoulder-to-shoulder with Garvey as a dozen Ahannu closed on them from all sides. More god-warriors were emerging from inside the crater, clambering up out of the shadows of a small tunnel. Damn it, they were everywhere, and the Marine line had dissolved into tiny and isolated teams of squad mates fighting hand-to-hand.

More Marines were falling as impossible numbers overwhelmed technology, swords and lances piercing armor joints. Sergeant Couch vanished beneath a thrashing pile of Ahannu warriors. Tomlin's plasma gun fell silent as the Marine gunner was torn to pieces. Half the assault force at least was down now, and the rest would be dead in seconds.

Garroway raised his laser and triggered it as an enemy warrior rushed him; the weapon gave a crackling hiss and failed as status lights on his helmet display warned of power failure, overheating, a ruptured coolant coil, and a burned-out feed coupling. Pivoting sharply, he brought the 2120's butt up and around sharply, connecting with the side of the Frog's head. He felt rather than heard the satisfying *crunch* as the skull caved in.

He swung again, taking down an Ahannu waving a wickedly curved sword. And again . . . and again . . .

"John! . . ."

Four Frogs swarmed onto Garvey, knocking him down. Razor-tipped lances and swords plunged, seeking the flexible joints between hard-shelled carbon-polylaminate sections, at shoulders, neck, hips, and waist. Garvey shrieked. . . .

Garroway swung his rifle level, like a baseball bat, connecting with one of the Ahannu and knocking it away from his friend. Something struck him hard in the left arm, spinning him back and away. "Gravy!" he shouted. "Hang on!"

Garroway tried to swing his rifle again and found his left arm heavy, numb . . . he couldn't move it. Awkwardly one-handed, he tried swinging the battered weapon and saw it shatter against the breastplate of a looming Ahannu troll. He dropped the weapon, reached for his knife . . . and realized he'd dropped it somewhere in the last few seconds. Screwing his face into his best boot-camp war mask, he screamed a Marine battle cry as he charged the towering creature. *"Ooh-rah!"*

He collided with the thing and drove it back, toppling it over. It vented a throaty, hissing grunt and twisted, knocking him aside like a discarded rag doll. It stood then, over two meters tall even when stooped forward, its golden eyes deeply recessed in heavy bony orbits that gave it a hulking, Neanderthal look as it raised a two-meter club edged with razor-sharp shards of volcanic glass.

"Duck and cover, Marines!" Captain Warhurst's voice yelled over the tactical channel. "Everybody down and freeze!"

Garroway was already down and unable to move. The troll shrieked, its club raised high. . . .

And then the sky flashed, brighter than Earth's sun. The

troll stood transfixed for an instant as flesh and armor dissolved in searing white flame.

Somehow, Garroway managed to roll to the left as the burning carcass crumpled and fell forward, landing on the spot he'd occupied an instant before. All around him other Ahannu were burning . . . burning . . . falling, running, shrieking and burning, as fiery death exploded from the sky.

Take something flammable—fertilizer will do—in finely powdered form. Disperse it in air and ignite it. The result is a fuel-air explosive, or FAE, a weapon first developed two centuries before, occasionally referred to as a "poor man's nuke," or as a "daisy cutter" for its ability to quickly clear large areas of forest.

The upgraded version of the FAE were Dispersed Nanomunitions, in the form of DNM-85 thermal microbomblets. Each bomblet, accreted from supplies of thermite, aluminum, magnesium, and trace elements, was smaller than a grain of sand, and individually, each carried less explosive force than an igniting match.

Disperse millions of DNM bomblets from delivery canisters set to explode two meters above the ground, and the air itself burns, briefly, at a temperature of well over a thousand degrees.

A pair of Marine Dragonflies howled low across the top of the pyramid, racing west to east scant meters above the corpse-littered pavement, scattering DNM-85s into the Ahannu swirling hordes. For an instant the top of the pyramid blazed in unholy flame. Dozens of Ahannu caught fire or exploded in that deadly incendiary storm.

"Stay down, Marines!" Warhurst yelled over the tactical channel. "Friendly fire incoming!"

A second pair of Dragonflies shrieked in from north to south, scattering more bomblets in a deadly, burning footprint, setting fire to stacked heaps of bodies, causing broken pavement stone to crack and explode. Garroway pressed himself to the pavement as hot gravel rattled off his armor, as his suit's internal temperature briefly soared in the inferno. Designed to withstand high temperatures, even Mark VII armor could not shed that kind of heat for more than seconds without melting.

Most of the firestorm burned itself out a meter or more above the pavement, though, and as the fireball rose, temperatures on the surface of the pyramid fell. Garroway heard the laboring of his suit's refrigeration and drew a hot breath of relief as his HDO's temp gauge dropped from the unbearable to the merely uncomfortable.

Looking up, he saw Garvey lying on his back a meter away; he crawled that meter and threw himself over the unmoving Marine as the first pair of Dragonflies swung around for another pass.

"Corpsman!" he yelled. "Corpsman!" But there were no medical corpsmen in Task Force Warhurst, and Gerrold Garvey was already dead.

Garroway lay there, stretched across his friend's body, waiting for the world to end. . . .

25

Lance Corporal Garroway
Pyramid of the Eye
New Sumer, Ishtar
1705 hours ALT

But it didn't end.

The thunder, scorching heat, and whirlwind of death, however, faded. Garroway looked up, astonished, in a numb and distant way, at being still alive. Somehow, the airstrike had burned over the upper reaches of the pyramid, and yet he and a scattered handful of other Marines were still moving, standing slowly and looking about, all with the same dazed and lost demeanor.

The Ahannu were dead . . . their bodies stacked and scattered and strewn in grotesque and interlocked tangles across the upper surface of the pyramid, most of them charred into unrecognizable abstracts of ash and cinder, many still burning.

No . . . not all were dead. As Garroway turned, he saw several Ahannu at the bottom of the crater, wiggling into the darkness of a small, open tunnel. They must have been coming up inside the Marine perimeter at the same time they were breaking the line. He looked around for a rifle but saw only the twisted fragments of his own lying on a black-scorched chunk of paving stone. An Ahannu lance, three meters long and tipped by a curving blade, lay nearby. He picked that up in lieu of any more modern weapon.

But it didn't look as though he would need it. The Ahannu in the crater had vanished down their hole, and the only ones atop the pyramid now were dead. He walked unsteadily across to the western edge of the pyramid roof and looked down. Hundreds, perhaps thousands, of Ahannu and Sag-ura bodies were strewn up and down the broad steps, but that fiery rain of airborne death had left none alive. In the streets below, Ahannu were fleeing as the Marine relief force out of the compound rushed the base of the Pyramid of the Eye.

The enemy attack had been broken, *decisively* broken.

Another Dragonfly was angling in out of the west, but this time coming in nose high on a landing approach instead of in attack attitude, with twenty-four more armored Marines slung from the harness on its spinal strut. Reinforcements . . . a little late, perhaps, but unexpected and very welcome. He looked about, wondering. Forty-eight Marines had landed atop the pyramid a little over an hour ago. He saw only eight others standing now in the swirling gray smoke, all looking as isolated and as lost as he felt.

He saw an LR-2120 on the pavement and walked over to pick it up. His left arm, he realized, wasn't working . . . a dead weight. Exploring the surface of the armor with his right hand, he found a hole punched through the thickly layered body glove fabric at the shoulder, but he couldn't feel a thing.

Training told him he should seek medical assistance, perhaps lie down to avoid the effects of shock . . . but in his current state of mind, that level of coherent thought simply wasn't possible. Instead he stood at the edge of the pyramid roof, leaning on his captured spear and watching as the incoming Dragonfly drifted lower on whining belly thrusters. The double line of Marines harnessed to its spinal boom dropped free in a ragged spill. The armored forms hit the ground, rose to their feet, and began spreading out across the pyramid.

"Marine! Hey, Marine!"

A gloved hand slapped his right shoulder, startling him. "Wake up, son."

He turned quickly, dropping into a defensive crouch before he saw that it was Captain Warhurst, his helmet tucked under one arm.

"Sir!" Garroway came to attention.

"At ease, at ease," Warhurst said. "I just wanted to requisition your pig sticker."

"My . . . what?" Then he realized Warhurst was talking about the three-meter spear he carried. Several other Marines had gathered nearby . . . Corporal Womicki, Sergeant Schuster, Sergeant Dunne, Lance Corporal Vinita. Kat Vinita was carrying an American flag, still folded in a tight blue triangle with the white stars showing.

"Flag-raising time," Warhurst said. "Gotta let 'em know down below we're all right."

Schuster and Dunne attached the flag to the butt end of the spear. Together, then, the six of them planted the spear tip in a crack between paving stones close to the western edge of the pyramid's top, wedging it in tight. They stepped back and came to attention as the flag unfurled in the freshening Ishtaran breeze, thirteen stripes and fifty-eight stars representing the United Federal Republic. Captain Warhurst saluted for the six of them.

Those stars, arranged in three concentric circles on the blue field, suddenly and irrationally and almost painfully reminded Garroway of home. The referendum to determine statehood for Sinaloa and the other three Mexican territories had been scheduled for six years ago. He wondered if this flag with its fifty-eight stars was out of date now.

It still represented home, no matter how many stars it bore.

He felt something catch in his throat and swallowed to clear it. Flag-raisings. There was a particularly emotional connection with this one, as he remembered photos of two other similar flag-raisings, one at Cydonia on Mars during the UN War a century ago, and the one on the original Suribachi a century before that.

His ancestor, Sands of Mars Garroway . . . what would he think if he were here now, watching this simple ceremony?

Garroway's helmet external mikes were picking up a strange sound. He tried to identify it—a low-pitched rushing or roaring—and failed. Damn, if he just had a link to the net. . . .

"Detail, dis-*missed*!" Warhurst said.

Garroway unfastened his helmet and pulled it off one-handed, trying to make out the source of the sound with his own ears. It was coming from . . .

Ah. That was it. Looking down on the Legation compound from his vantage point atop the Pyramid of the Eye, he could see a huge crowd of Marines in the courtyard near the north gate. The sound . . . he was hearing cheering, the sound of hundreds of Marines cheering the flag atop this alien Suribachi.

"I need volunteers," Warhurst said. "We're going down to the Chamber of the Eye. Who's with me?"

The other four all had their hands up, and Garroway raised his own. His arm was beginning to hurt now, a dull, pounding throb in his shoulder, but nothing serious. He felt fine . . . maybe a bit light-headed.

"Where's your weapon, Marine?" Warhurst asked him.

"It kind of got bent on a Frog's skull, sir," he replied.

"Is your arm okay? There's blood on your armor."

"I think I got winged by a gauss round, sir. Doesn't hurt, but I'm having a little trouble moving it."

"Okay. Here." Warhurst unholstered his sidearm, a heavy, 15mm Colt Puller, and gave it to Garroway. He unslung his other weapon, a Sunbeam LC-2132 laser carbine, a light-weight weapon that was low-powered compared to a 2120 but didn't need the three-cable connection with a shoulder-carried power pack. "Okay, Leathernecks. Move out!"

Together, they began descending the pyramid's western steps. Behind and above them the flag continued to flutter in the breeze.

Chamber of the Eye
Pyramid of the Eye
Shumur-Unu
Third Period of Brightening Day

Tu-Kur-La emerged through the inner passageway from the Deeps, stepping into the Chamber of the Eye. He felt a bit light-headed, mildly dizzy, almost, with the shock of the past few periods. The Memories had not prepared him for this . . . not at all.

The Ahannu were gods. *Gods.* Beings who once had strode among the far-flung stars, wielding lightnings that could render whole worlds barren and lifeless. How was it that these Blackhead warriors—these *Marines*, as they called themselves—could defeat the combined will and consciousness of the Zu-Din?

He found the charred and broken corpse of Zah-Ahan-Nu near the outside entrance to the Chamber. The Blackhead fliers had seared this entire side of the pyramid with their light weapons, burning down hundreds of god-warriors swarming up the steps. Zah-Ahan-Nu, the Keeper of Memories serving as an eye of the Zu-Din, had gotten too close to the sky outside and been caught in the firestorm.

Tu-Kur-La began reestablishing his own connections with the Abzu-il, slender threads of organic molecules trickling down his back and seeking companion threads growing in the cracks between the stones of the chamber. As the Abzu-il made its myriad interlocking connections, Tu-Kur-La again felt his own personality fading, felt again the growing awareness of the Godmind, of thousands of other Keepers of Memories joining with him, mind to mind to watching mind.

Cautiously, he peered from the open doorway. Blackhead Marines thronged within the walled enclosure below, shouting madly. The Ahannu attack on their fortress had failed, as

had the counterattack against the pyramid. The enemy warriors, evidently, were celebrating their victory.

Victory. Against the *gods*.

The thought was almost literally unthinkable, a concept
not easily put into words. Not since the time of the Hunters
of the Dawn had such a concept even been considered.

Uneasily, the eye of the Godmind watched the Enemy
thronging below.

Lance Corporal Garroway
Pyramid of the Eye
New Sumer, Ishtar
1736 hours ALT

They made their way down the steps as quietly as they
could manage, no conversation, with each step past crumpled,
charred Frog bodies carefully considered before the step was
actually taken. Two Marine Dragonflies circled at a distance,
ready to provide close support should that be necessary.

Half a dozen more Task Force Warhurst Marines had
joined the six of them descending the west face of the pyramid. Twelve of them had survived the Ahannu attack, it
turned out . . . exactly twenty-five percent of the original
forty-eight. Garroway remembered General King's ill-
advised pep talk before the landings . . . was it only yesterday? Marine losses on Suribachi had been high, higher in
terms of percentages, certainly, than those Army Rangers
had suffered at Pointe du Hoc.

He caught himself wondering if King had somehow
jinxed the assault with his speech.

Superstitious nonsense, Garroway thought with wry
amusement. *Might as well blame the fucking apricots.*

The entrance to the Chamber of the Eye extended from
the center of the pyramid's western steps, a squared-off
white stone structure with ornate, apparently abstract designs engraved in the sides. The carvings looked like they

might represent something—beings, perhaps? But they followed an artistic tradition alien indeed from both human and Ahannu thinking. It was difficult to make sense of the swooping, curving, interlocking knots and patterns.

It was possible, even probable, that Ahannu warriors were inside. The chamber provided too valuable an observation post overlooking the Legation compound for the enemy to have left it unoccupied . . . especially since there apparently were hidden tunnels and passageways within the pyramid's massive structure. God-warriors had emerged from the pyramid's interior during the battle . . . and done so in surprisingly close support of the attackers outside. That suggested sophisticated lines of communications, a high degree of efficient command control, and the Ahannu equivalent of scouts and officers overseeing the unfolding battle. With the top of the pyramid under Marine control and the sides scoured clean of the enemy, the Chamber of the Eye was the only vantage point the Ahannu had left on the pyramid.

Following Warhurst's silent hand gestures, Garroway, Dunne, Schuster, and Vinita had moved around to the left, coming up on the entrance from its southern side. The rest approached from the other side, squeezing up close against the comforting stones for cover. This, Garroway thought, would be a great situation for smart grenades . . . except that you had to show the RPG a target for it to lock onto and follow. And standing orders for Task Force Warhurst were not to use explosives inside the Chamber of the Eye.

Again following Warhurst's signed commands, he crouched beside the entrance, pistol in hand, ready to move. On the other side of the door, Warhurst apparently had decided to ignore his own orders. He took an RPG from one of the other Marines, twisted its tail-fin assembly to manually arm it, and gently tossed it around the corner. There was a loud *bang* as the 20mm grenade detonated inside. Garroway rolled around the corner and into the cool darkness of the entranceway . . .

. . . and found himself face-to-face with the enemy.

The Ahannu was sprawled on the floor of the chamber,

just rising, as though it had been knocked down by the grenade blast. Its eyes—huge, pear-shaped, and golden in the poor light—blinked rapidly as the creature held up one splayed, six-fingered hand. Other features—lipless mouth, twin-slit nostrils, finely scaled skin, bony head crest, the lack of any external ears at all—all added up to something that looked far more reptilian than human, despite the humanoid number and arrangement of limbs and other body parts.

Strangest, perhaps, was the mass of purplish, translucent jelly riding on the creature's shoulders and the back of its slightly elongated neck. A thin slime of the stuff coated the being's skin and seemed to be leaking from nostrils and the openings at the base of its jaw that must be its ears. Threads of the gel stretched from the Ahannu's shoulders to the floor and the back wall of the room, like a spider's web made of glistening mucus.

Garroway brought the Colt Puller up, aiming it at the creature's flat face, his finger tightening on the trigger.

"*Nu!*" the creature shrilled. "*Sagra nu!*"

Without the net, there was no hope of a translation. What the hell was *sagra nu*?

But as near as Garroway could tell, the being was unarmed. It wore torso armor that looked like green-stained leather, and some bangles on its arms that might have been gold. Unless that purple crap on its head and shoulders was dangerous . . .

"*Sagra nu,*" the Ahannu said, still holding up its open hand. "*Ga-me-e' din!*"

Primitive the being might be, but it was afraid of the pistol. "You'd better not even twitch, Frog," Garroway said. He knew damned well the Ahannu couldn't understand, but he tried to throw enough authority and menace into his voice to get the message across anyway.

"I . . . no . . . twitch . . . frog . . ." the Ahannu said, its voice raspy and hard to make out, but intelligible all the same.

"Jesus!" Sergeant Dunne said at Garroway's side. "The

thing speaks English!"

"We . . . thing . . . speak . . ." it said. "A few of . . . we . . . thing . . . speak. . . ."

"Who are you?" Captain Warhurst demanded, keeping his laser carbine aimed at the Ahannu's chest. "What do we call you?"

"We are . . . Zu-Din," the being replied. "We are . . . the Mind of God."

"No weapons," Garroway said. "He must either be a scout . . ."

"Or what?" Warhurst asked.

"Or an officer, sir. I don't think he's a regular warrior."

"We'll let Intelligence sort that out," Warhurst said. "Schuster! Evans! Dumbrowski! March our friend here up to the top. Ride with him back to the compound and tell the colonel it speaks English. Sort of."

"Aye aye, sir!" The three Marines led the Ishtaran out.

Warhurst, meanwhile, was studying the only piece of equipment in the small, black-walled stone chamber, a football-shaped object two meters wide suspended from the ceiling by a cable that appeared too slender to bear its weight. A dark red cloth had been draped over the top, covering it. Carefully, he used the muzzle of his laser to tug the cloth off.

Underneath, an oval screen glowed softly deep within black crystal. A human in civilian clothing was visible on the screen, apparently reading an e-pad in her hands.

"Excuse me," Warhurst said. The woman didn't react. Warhurst reached out and touched the bottom of the device with his gauntlet; there was supposed to be a touch-sensitive volume control there. "Excuse me," Warhurst said again.

This time the woman jumped. She turned her head and stared at the Marines with eyes widened in shock. *"Mon Dieu!"* she exclaimed. She launched into a torrent of something sounding like French.

"Whoa, whoa, there," Warhurst said, holding up his hands. Reaching up, he removed his helmet. "We do not have net access here, so I can't understand you. Uh . . . *non comprendez*. Do you read me?"

The woman blinked. "I understand," she said in heavily accented English. "I am Giselle Dumont of the Cydonian Quebecois Research Team. And you are . . . ?"

"Captain Martin Warhurst, First Marine Interstellar Expeditionary Unit, 1st Division, 44th Regiment, UFR Marine Corps," he replied. "Can you patch me through to the UFR Military Communications Network, Code one-five-alpha-three-echo, Priority One, please?"

"I am sorry, sir, but the WorldNet interplanetary relays are offline at this time. We have had a period of bad solar weather. . . ."

Garroway stood to one side of the chamber, beyond the FTL communicator's pickup field. It figured. Communications between Llalande 21185 and the vast underground facility on Mars were obviously crystal clear. The ordinary speed-of-light channels between Earth and Mars, however, seemed to be out of commission.

Or . . . was that really the whole story? The woman was Quebecois, and the nation of Quebec was allied with the EU, had been ever since the UN War. What if there'd been some political or military changes back home in the past ten years? What if the Cydonian complex was under EU control now? Hell, how were they supposed to know *anything* was as it seemed?

As Warhurst continued speaking with the woman, Garroway noticed something on the floor . . . a folded piece of fabric that apparently had been pulled from the top of the FTL comm device when Warhurst had dragged the red cloth cover off. Stooping, he picked it up.

It was a small, folding monitor display, fifteen centimeters by twenty-one, with a tiny camera woven into the smart-threads of the upper border. Printed on the bottom were the words SURVIVALCAM: UFRS *EMISSARY*.

"*Emissary*," he said aloud.

Warhurst turned from the screen and looked at him.

"What was that, Marine?"

He looked up. "Sorry, sir. *'Emissary.'* I found this on the deck."

Warhurst took the cloth and studied it.

"Emissary," Kat Vinita said. "That was the Terran Legation ship, wasn't it? The one that was destroyed?"

"That's the one. I wonder who—" He stopped. "My God!"

Warhurst stepped beyond the FTL unit's pickup field, holding the display screen taut in his hands. Garroway was close enough to see a face, a human face looking up out of the cloth, a face as surprised as the captain's and perhaps even more delighted.

"You came!" the face said, the voice thin and reedy over the folding screen's smarthread speakers but clear enough to be understood. "My God, you came! We *knew* you would!"

"I'm Captain Martin Warhurst, UFR Marines. Who are you?"

"Uh . . . sorry, sir! Master Sergeant Gene Aiken, UFR Marine Corps! Currently assigned to the Terran Legation, Ishtar!"

"Goddess! *Where* are you?"

Aiken grinned. "The Ahtun Mountains, sir. Roughly fifty klicks east of New Sumer. We've been holed up here ever since the Frogs chased us out."

"Ten years . . . ?"

"I reckon so, sir. But we knew you wouldn't forget us. We've just been waiting for the Marines to land and put the situation well in hand!"

"Stay on this line, Master Sergeant," Warhurst said. He handed the cloth to Garroway, then stepped back in front of the FTL screen. "Um, Madame Dumont?"

"Yes, monsieur. I could not catch what you were just saying. Is there interference at your end?"

"My apologies, Madame Dumont. Something urgent has come up. We'll be in touch shortly."

"But, monsieur—"

"Let's go, people."

Wondering just what the hell was going on, Garroway followed Warhurst and the others out of the Chamber of the Eye.

Regimental HQ
Building 5, Legation Compound
New Sumer, Ishtar
1924 hours ALT

"This Dumont person didn't tell you anything more?" Ramsey demanded.

"No, sir," Warhurst replied. "She seemed helpful enough and surprised to see me. But she would not make the connection for us with Washington."

Ramsey rubbed his chin. "She *could* be telling the truth, of course. Solar weather does play hob with the comm relays sometimes. But I don't like this."

"Neither do I, sir." He pointed at the unfolded screen on the table beside them, with Aiken's bearded face looking up at them. "That's why I decided to keep this quiet, at least until you decide otherwise."

"Well done, Colonel." Ramsey looked at General King. "General? I suggest we defer further communications with Earth until we can transport the Legation survivors back here."

"I agree, Colonel. A communications malfunction right now is just a little too convenient."

"So, Master Sergeant," Ramsey said, looking down into Aiken's face. "How would you like to come back to the compound?"

"We'll have to bum a lift, sir," Aiken replied. "We got all our people out here on board three old Starhauler TAVs. We had to make a bunch of trips, though, to get everyone out, and ten years sitting in the jungle afterward didn't do their power plants any good. They're just rusty junk now."

"Not a problem. We can deploy a Dragonfly with a landing module and bring at least some of you back. How many survivors are there?"

Aiken pursed his lips. "Well, sir . . . our current roster has eighteen Marines and 158 civilians. Twenty-seven of those last are children."

"Children?" Ramsey exclaimed. "*What* children? . . . Oh."

"Yes, sir. It *has* been ten years." He grinned. "And the natives are friendly."

"Natives?"

"Yes, sir. We're living at a village of . . . well, they call themselves *dumu-gir*. It means a native child in the Ishtaran common tongue . . . but it means 'freeborn.' "

"You mean these are humans? *Free* humans? Escaped from the Ahannu?"

"Some are runaways, yes, sir. Most of them have always been free. They're descendants of humans who got away from the Frogs, oh, over the past few thousand years, I guess. Maybe going all the way back to when humans were first brought here as slaves. A few must have escaped even back then and set up communities out in the jungle. The Ahannu . . . they don't come out in the wild all that much. They tend to be content to stay where they are, inside their cities and tunnel complexes."

"The Ahannu try to recapture them, surely."

"Oh, once in a while. Sometimes the Frogs band together and try to catch them or stomp them out, but the *dumu-gir* have learned a few things, living out here in the jungle all these years. Sir, they're *good*. The Marines could learn a few things from them."

"How many natives are there?"

"Oh, about a hundred at last count. In this village, anyway."

"A hundred? A hundred free Ishtaran humans?"

"There are other villages, of course. No one knows how many. They don't go in much for governments and such here. Nothing more than a tribal council, anyway. They took us in when we got out of Dodge . . . uh, I mean, when we re- treated from New Sumer. We've been teaching them a few tricks, helping them develop weapons and tactics against the Frogs."

"You speak the local language, then?"

"A bit, sir. Our expert is Dr. Moore. She was our xenosoc expert, and she's gone on to learn a lot about the Ishtarans, both the humans and the Ahannu. And a lot of the *dumu-gir* speak pretty good English now. They've been learning it for ten years."

"Master Sergeant, you may have just saved this expedi- tion's collective ass. Whose bright idea was it, anyway, to leave a survivalcam screen in the Chamber of the Eye?"

Aiken grinned. "Mine, actually, sir. I figured the Marines would be coming, and one of the first things they'd do was get the Chamber of the Eye back, so they could talk to Earth. One of our locals, Kupatin, volunteered to sneak in and put it in place, since he could look the part of a Sag-ura, with all those tattoos and stuff, and I couldn't. That was maybe . . . oh, a year ago, maybe. When we began to think that you guys would be showing up any day now. And actually, sir, to tell the truth, I was under the impression that it was you who were saving our ass."

"Either way. That was damned good thinking on your part. We're sending a Dragonfly for you. Please report to me . . . with your Marines and any senior Legation people who want to come. We'd particularly like to see Dr. Moore, if she's available."

"She sure is, sir." He grinned. "Happens I married the lady, a few years back."

"Ah! Well. Congratulations."

"Thank you, sir. But our people have been intermarrying with the locals too. There haven't been any problems at all in that regard. The biggest difference between Earth hu- mans and Ishtaran humans is in the psychological conditioning. And the *dumu-gir* have managed to break most of that conditioning."

Gavin Norris had been watching and listening in silence to the entire exchange. Suddenly, he stepped up close to the table. "Master Sergeant Aiken," he said. "Is Randolph Carleton among the survivors, by chance?"

"Who are you?"

"The PanTerra Dynamics trade representative on this planet."

"I see. Yeah, Carleton's here."

"Tell him to come along as well."

Aiken looked at Ramsey, who nodded. "Tell him, Master Sergeant. We'll see you in a few more hours."

"It's gonna be good, Colonel. Damned good! Five years we were here since *Emissary* arrived, and then ten more out in the sticks. I tell you, sir, we've gotten more than a little tired of the same old faces!"

"We'll see you soon, Master Sergeant. New Sumer out!" He turned to Warhurst. "Quite a stroke of luck," Ramsey said. "If one of your men hadn't spotted that comm cloth . . ."

"Yes, sir. Although Master Sergeant Aiken indicated that they have been expecting us. They've probably had locals watching New Sumer for our arrival and would have been able to contact us sooner or later."

"Right. But we're in contact now. And we need people who speak the language." Ramsey looked across the room. Their most recent captive, the unarmed Ahannu taken in the Chamber of the Eye a short while ago, was tied to a chair, his face and expression unreadable.

"You said you did hear that Frog speak English?" General King asked. "I haven't heard anything from him except gibberish."

"Yessir. Clearly. He hasn't spoken since we got him back down here?"

"Not since I ordered some of our people to clean him up."

"Sir?"

"That purple jelly. It must've been rolling in the stuff, or something. I thought at first that it might be blood and had a corpsman start washing—"

Warhurst's eyes widened. "General . . . I don't know what that purple stuff is, but we've found it on several Ahannu corpses. Not on all of them, but on a few."

"You think it's something for communication?" Ramsey asked.

"Yes, sir. I do. Look, for primitives, these guys have been doing pretty damned good at coordinating their attacks. Up there on top of the pyramid, they started coming up out of a hole behind us at the same instant they were coming up over the sides of the building. Some of their other attacks have shown a high degree of synchronization too. *Somehow* they manage to talk to each other. That guy was up in the Chamber of the Eye, which gave him a perfect OP from which to watch us. He wasn't armed. He wasn't a sniper . . . which means he was watching us and passing on information to his HQ."

"But how would that help him speak English?" King demanded.

"Well, we know some Ahannu spoke English ten years ago. They learned it from the Terran Legation, right?"

"Right."

"So . . . what if the Frogs have something like our net? A means of transmitting data among themselves very quickly? An Ahannu who knew English could have been listening in when we captured this one and been telling him what to say." Warhurst shrugged. "Or maybe the purple gunk is just the local equivalent of a computer translator. Whatever it is, we've got to be damned careful not to make assumptions about things we don't understand based on our human experience."

"Good advice, Captain," Ramsey said. "What do you suggest so far as talking with our friend here goes?"

"Well, sir, like you said, we have some people coming now who speak the lingo. But if you want to talk to the

Ahannu leadership, our best bet might be to take our friend here right back up to the Chamber of the Eye."

"Hmm." Ramsey considered this. "I'm not sure I want to trust him up there. Like you said, we can't afford to make assumptions about things we don't understand. That includes what passes for their technology. We'll wait and see what a translator makes of it."

"Yes, sir."

Ramsey stared long and hard into the unblinking golden eyes of the prisoner.

What was it thinking? *How* did it think? Like humans . . . or in some way utterly and fundamentally different—*alien*, in other words?

What did it know?

And would it ever be possible to communicate with something that alien?

26

*Pyramid of the Eye
New Sumer, Ishtar
1930 hours ALT*

"You know, they used to call this kind of party a steel beach," Dunne said.

"Steel beach?" Garroway asked. "How do you mean?"

"Navy and Marine personnel on big, oceangoing ships," Dunne replied. "Like aircraft carriers, y'know? They'd have some time off, they'd go out and sun themselves on the deck, maybe smuggle in some liquid contraband." He raised a can of beer in explanation. "They called it a steel beach 'cause all there was to lie on was steel."

"We're not on a ship, Sarge," Vinita pointed out.

"Sure, Kat. But remember your basic Marine terminology. It's a 'hatch,' not a 'door,' a 'ladder,' not stairs. Even ashore." He waved the beer can to take in the Legation compound, the alien green sky, the distant purple jungle, the untidy sprawl of New Sumer. "We're ashore. We treat the place like a ship, anyway. Hence . . . 'steel beach.' "

"With not a single bit of steel in sight," Womicki said, looking around at the flat expanse of the pyramid's top. "Makes as much sense as anything in the Corps."

"Fuckin'-A!" Dunne exclaimed. He drained the last of the beer, then smashed the can against his forehead, crumpling it flat. A small pile of flat, crumpled disks on the ground in front of them paid mute testimony to beverages already consumed.

Garroway still wasn't sure how they'd managed it. Dunne claimed that he and Honey Deere had smuggled a couple of cases of brew onto a supply pallet destined for the *Regulus* before their departure from Earth. Those cases had been hidden inside supply containers marked "dietary supplements" and seemed to have survived the four-years-subjective voyage in reasonable taste. Beer smuggling was by now a grand tradition in the spacefaring Corps. Old-timers liked to regale newbies with the exploits of a Marine unit at Cydonia seventy years ago. Some of old Sands of Mars Garroway's Marines, it seemed, had managed to smuggle a few cases of beer to Mars. Garroway's famous ancestor had appropriated it and turned it into makeshift chemical weaponry against the occupying UN forces.

Modern Marines delighted in finding new and original means of smuggling beer to remote duty stations, an activity still listed as very much a crash-and-burn in both Navy and Marine Corps regulations. If they were caught, the standard excuse was, "We were just following Corps tradition, *sir!*"

Sometimes it even worked.

Garroway took a sip from his can, grimacing. He didn't really like the taste of the stuff but didn't want to admit it to the others. Besides, it was a kind of honor, a right of passage, even, to be included in this simple Corps ritual.

And it *was* a ritual, one every bit as meaningful and as sacred as anything Garroway had performed as a Wiccan. With each can opened and held toward that glorious sky, the name of another fallen comrade was toasted. Dunne had toasted Valdez and Deere, and Kat Vinita had remembered Chuck Cawley and Tom Pressley. Womicki toasted Brandt and Foster, while Garroway saluted his two comrades from boot camp, Hollingwood and Garvey.

The four of them were seated on the pavement atop the Pyramid of the Eye, in armor because they were on call, but with gloves and helmets off. They'd been reorganized once again into a new unit—First Platoon, Alfa Company—all from veterans of the fight for Objective Suribachi three weeks before.

Members of the company had taken to calling themselves the "Pyramidiots," and the name had stuck.

Garroway turned his head, studying the darkening panorama around them as the eclipse slowly deepened. He thought-clicked his visual center, opening his nano-enhanced irises wider to suck in more light. Other members of the company stood guard around the top of the pyramid or lounged in front of the nanocrete dome erected beside the crater as a firebase HQ. The American flag fluttered from a much taller mast now, above the HQ building. Native work-ers, *dumu-gir* from the free village of Ha-a-dru-dir, contin-ued to clear the crater of loose stone and rubble under Marine engineer supervision. In the distance, a pair of Wasps circled high above New Sumer on ever-vigilant patrol.

Somehow, he managed to gulp down the last of his beer and hand the empty across to Dunne.

"Ooh-rah!" Dunne said, and crumpled the can flat.

"Your turn for a toast, Gare," Womicki told him, handing him another can from the opened supplement container.

"What?" He almost didn't recognize his Corps handle. "Gare Garroway" wasn't all that inspired, but for him it was a final break from his old civilian identity as "John," a name he hadn't used, it seemed, in centuries.

"Your turn. Who's next?"

Shit, who was left? They'd toasted all of the fallen in the old assault force squad. And there were so many more . . . Marine men and women he'd never gotten to know but who'd fought and died for this small and distant patch of alien soil. "I think you're just trying to get me drunk," he told them.

"Of course," Dunne replied, grinning. "That's part of the ceremony."

"Well . . ." He thought for a moment, then popped the tab

and raised the can. "To fallen comrades, past and future," he said. "*And* to the cease-fire. Long may it hold!"

"Amen!" Womicki called.

"Most righteous," Dunne added, raising a new can of his own. "*Ooh-rah!*"

They chugged the toast. Dunne accepted Garroway's empty can and smashed it against his forehead.

"How do you *do* that?" Vinita asked.

Dunne grinned. "Got an implant here," he said, running a hand across his forehead. "Solid nanochelated carbotitanium replacing a chunk of my skull. From a little present I picked up in Colombia, y'know?" He knocked his forehead with a fist. "Hard head."

"Figures," Womicki said. "He *is* a Marine, after all."

The sky was rapidly darkening as the Llalande sun settled behind Marduk in its once-in-six-days eclipse, scattering brilliant sunset colors halfway around the gas giant's full-circle horizon. Theoretically, this was the third eclipse since their landing twenty-one days ago, but thick clouds and rain had blocked both of the others.

Yeah, like they said. If you didn't like the weather on Ishtar, just wait a minute.

The cease-fire still seemed too good to be true. Three shipboard days after the fighting on Suribachi, however, Sumerian-speaking Marines from the old Legation expedition had met with a delegation of Ahannu leaders, a meeting arranged by the Frog they'd captured in the Chamber of the Eye. They said his name was Tu-Kur-La.

According to Tu-Kur-La, the Ahannu had been terribly hurt by their failed assault on the pyramid, a battle that had cost the Marines fifty-one dead and thirty-eight wounded, including the casualties in the compound fighting as well as those at the top. Exact Ahannu casualties were unknown but were believed to exceed twelve hundred Ahannu god-warriors, seven hundred Sag-ura, and nearly two hundred of their specially bred *kur-gal-gub*, the "mountain-great-warriors" the Marines called "trolls."

Twenty-one hundred dead Ishtarans at least; the full number might never be known, since so many bodies had been utterly destroyed in the fighting. After the first arranged truce meeting ten days ago, a vast panoply of Ahannu warriors had appeared north of the Legation compound, holding high a forest of *urin* battle standards and keening in their strange, rasping voices. The Marines learned later that the Ahannu song had bestowed an honor of their own upon the men and women of 1 MIEU, as well as a new name.

They called the Marines *nir-gál-mè-a*, which according to Aiken and the other old Ishtar hands, meant "respected in battle." The Fighting 44th had immediately adapted the name to its own use—the Nergal May-I, or Nergs for short.

Garroway smiled at that. The Corps carried a number of nicknames handed to it over the centuries. Leathernecks, for the stiff collars worn by Marines in the nineteenth century, supposedly to protect the throat from sword cuts but actually a means of making recruits stand up straight. Jarheads, a pejorative for the "high-and-tight" haircuts of the twentieth century. Devil Dogs, from Teufil Hundin, a name bestowed on them by their German enemies after the Battle of the Marne, originally as an insult, since *hundin* meant "bitch," but ever after one of the proudest of the Corps' noms de guerre.

And now they were Nergs.

The Marines had made their mark, it seemed, out here among the stars. The folks back home would never understand, but that didn't seem to matter anymore.

The folks back home. Garroway swallowed and bit back the stinging in his throat and eyes. Two days after the fight on Suribachi, communications had at last been established with Earth through the FTL screen in the Chamber of the Eye. There'd been all kinds of scuttlebutt flying through the MIEU about mysterious delays or problems in opening the channel, but the link had been established at last, with an instantaneous two-way connection with Mars, and an added twenty minutes for the Mars-to-Earth link one-way. Regular calls for the Marines hadn't been authorized yet, but a few familygrams and special messages had been routed through from Quantico.

And one of them had been a 'gram for Lance Corporal John Garroway, from his aunt in San Diego. His mother was dead.

He was still having trouble wrapping his mind around that one. According to the brief message, limited to a barren and emotionless twenty-five words or fewer, she'd been found dead a year after the *Derna* had boosted out of Earth orbit. The death was listed as accidental, of course . . . a fall down the steps in front of the Esteban home.

Garroway didn't believe *that* for a moment. He knew she'd gone back to Esteban before he was shipped up to the *Derna*. He'd dreaded this very possibility, that she would go back to that abusive bastard one time too many. . . .

There wasn't a lot he could do now, except grieve. His mother had died nine years ago, while he'd still been asleep in cybehibe on board the *Derna*, outbound from Earth. As for his father, well, apparently there wasn't much news. According to CNN briefs relayed over the net from home, the abortive Aztlan Antistatehood Insurrection of 2042 had driven the ringleaders into hiding.

Carlos Esteban among them, apparently.

Garroway found himself fervently hoping his father was dead.

No . . . No, on second thought it would be better by far if the bastard were alive. That way, he might be able to present his biological father with a bill of reckoning someday. He looked down at his hands, flexing them. His left arm—broken by a gauss round in the battle—was still sore, but it was working now, thanks to the calcium nanochelates and fastheal the corpsmen had given him. He was going to survive this deployment, and he was going to get back home.

And someday, he would meet his father again.

Someday . . .

He looked up into the darkening sky. The brightest stars were beginning to show as the eclipse deepened the twilight. He uplinked to the net to check which stars were visible and where.

At least the net *was* working now. The Navy personnel left on board the *Derna*, plus the command constellation's AI, had brought the full net back online only three days ago. Garroway and the others were still getting used to having that much information a thought-click away once more. In some ways, things had been simpler when they'd had to rely on their own memories and on such primitive-tech anachronisms as radio, human and robotic scouts, and sign language.

Data flowed through his thoughts. Yes . . . that bright one there, low in the north. The brightest star in what at home would be the constellation Scutum, just north of Sagittarius.

The sun of home.

Yeah. Someday.

Gavin Norris
Chamber of the Eye
Pyramid of the Eye
New Sumer, Ishtar
1935 hours ALT

Gavin Norris was puffing hard by the time he clambered up the last step and leaned against the entrance to the Chamber of the Eye. A Marine sentry was there, but he thought-queried Norris's e-pass, snapped to attention and said, "You are recognized, sir."

Good. He'd not expected trouble, but you never knew with these damned jarheads.

Portable lights illuminated what had been the black interior of the Chamber of the Eye. The Eye itself was aglow, showing the interior of the so-called Cave of Wonders at Cydonia, eight light-long light-years away. As promised, the *Quebecois* Giselle Dumont was on duty at the other end.

"Hello, Madame Dumont."

"Ah, Mr. Norris," she said, turning to face the screen. "I was told to expect you about now. Is everything in order?"

"It is. I think we're finally ready to begin." He stepped aside as the others filed into the chamber behind him—Carleton, Dr. Hanson, and Tu-Kur-La the Frog. *"Friar Tuck,"* Norris had been calling the thing, making a joke of the alien name. The Ahannu didn't appear to care.

"I'm still not convinced this is a good idea," Carleton said. "I don't trust the Frogs. Not after ten years in that damned jungle."

"That's not your concern, Carleton," Norris said. "Tell Tuck to do his thing."

Carleton grimaced, then gargled something at the Frog. It gargled back, then sat itself on the chamber floor, holding both six-fingered hands out above one of the cracks between the polished stone blocks.

"What's happening?" Dumont said. "I can't see."

"Sorry," he told her. "We have with us the Frog we used to make contact with the Frog leadership. He's going to connect himself up to a kind of organic computer network the Frogs have grown all throughout this part of the planet. They call it the . . . what was it, Dr. Hanson?"

" 'Abzu-il,' " Hanson replied. "The 'Gateway to the Sentient Sea.' "

"Yeah. Abzu. He's going to put us in touch with the Frog High Emperor, and we're going to pitch the deal straight to him."

Dumont cocked her head. "An organic computer? Pan-Terra would be *very* interested in that."

"Sure, sure . . . but the real payoff's going to be in the human natives. Right, Carleton?"

The other PanTerran executive nodded, though he kept watching Tu-Kur-La with a suspicious glare. "It's like we thought, Madame Dumont," he said. "The humans they brought back here from Earth ten thousand years ago have been bred for all those centuries as slaves. Docile. Completely obedient. The wild ones, the ones who couldn't be easily trained, kept running off into the jungle, and it's a damned good thing they did or I wouldn't be here now. But the ones who stayed with the Frogs, they've been conditioned to do anything their masters tell them. *Anything*."

"He's right," Norris added. "It's no wonder the Ahannu didn't let us see much of the Sag-ura slaves when we first came here. They'll do whatever their 'gods' tell them to do, and like it. Their warriors are absolutely without fear. The women . . . well . . ." He chuckled. "The Frogs don't go in for that sort of thing, of course, but the women do whatever they're told. They're totally centered on pleasing their master. It's almost like they don't have a will of their own. They're brought up that way from birth. I guess that's why things haven't changed here at all in a hundred centuries. It's the status quo from Hell, only it's going to be pure heaven for PanTerra."

"Yes, but will the High Emperor go along with what you tell him?"

"He has to," Norris said. "He agrees to sell us Sag-ura slaves for technology, and we promise not to unleash our Marines on him. My God, you should have seen the slaughter! Over two thousand Frogs killed in that last battle, against fifty Marines! And that's not counting all the Frogs that were killed in the first assault. Yes, I think the Frog Emperor will be *very* willing to listen to reason."

"And PanTerra ships a few thousand agreeable domestic servants back to Earth for a most tidy return on their investment."

"But that . . . that's *slavery*!"

Norris turned to face Hanson, who was staring at him in horror. "Let's not use such loaded terminology, my dear," he told her. "They are slaves now, under the Frogs. We're here to *help* them."

And he smiled.

Dr. Traci Hanson
Chamber of the Eye
Pyramid of the Eye
New Sumer, Ishtar
1944 hours ALT

Hanson could not believe what she was hearing. The bastards! The unmitigated, grade-A scum-gargling *bastards!*

"The people of the Terran Commonwealth want the slaves freed and repatriated to Earth," Norris was telling her. "That is exactly what we are doing. But think about the poor Sagura. They know nothing but slavery . . . ten thousand years of it, in fact. They've been raised thinking of themselves as slaves. The best thing we can do is acclimate them gradually to a new way of life. Letting them work as domestic servants, trained and hired out to certain wealthy clients by PanTerra, seems a most agreeable and decent way of breaking them in, don't you think? I mean, Jesus, they don't even understand the concept of money here. They know nothing except doing what they're told. How do you expect them to live on Earth? How are they even going to *survive* unless we provide this working shelter—this work assistance program, if you will—for them?"

"You bastards," Hanson said quietly. "You fucking bastards! You're going to buy them from the Ahannu, hire them out on Earth, and pocket the profit. That's slavery, no matter what weasel words you attach to it!"

"Nonsense. PanTerra paid for this expedition and helped put together the international coalition behind it. We are going to assume the costs of shipping all those freed slaves back to Earth and for training and feeding them until they can decide what they want for themselves. And PanTerra is paying me—and you, for that matter, Dr. Hanson—*very* handsomely indeed to put this deal together. They deserve a return on their investment."

"You also know that those poor Sag-ura are never going to

get free. How are they supposed to be reintegrated into human society when you have them working for new masters eight light-years from their homes? Are these rich clients you talk about going to just let them go? Or are you going to start shipping slaves from Ishtar on a regular schedule?"

"Dr. Hanson, please," Carleton said. "There's no need for emotional outbursts. A free market, a free economy, finds its own morality."

"Morality!" Hanson screamed. "Goddess!" She held up her right arm, pinching the skin. *"What fucking color is this?"*

"Brown," Carleton said, puzzled. "Dark brown. You look Latino, or maybe—"

"My ancestors were *slaves*, you son of a bitch. I was born in North Michigan, but some of my ancestors came from Gambia, Ivory Coast, Brazil, and Haiti! Some of them were *slaves*, Mr. Carleton, and you expect me not to be emotional?"

"That will be quite enough, Dr. Hanson," Norris said. He'd produced a small, 8mm handgun and was pointing it at Hanson. "I'm disappointed in you. I thought you were a loyal PanTerran employee."

"There are some things even a billion newdollars won't buy."

"Really?" He shook his head in amusement. "Who'd have thought it? Guard!"

The Marine sentry stepped inside. "Yes, sir?"

"Please put Dr. Hanson under protective arrest. I have reason to believe she is in the pay of radical anti-Ahannu church elements."

"It's a lie, Marine!" Hanson cried. "These bastards are trying to—"

"I don't much care what they're trying to do, miss," the Marine said, pointing his laser carbine at her. With his free hand, he reached up and pulled off his helmet.

It was General King.

"*You!*"

"Of course."

"Traitor!"

He scowled. "That's a negative, Doctor," he said, his voice sharp. "A traitor betrays his national allegiance. I have done nothing of the sort. The Federal Republic, in its infinite wisdom, decided to send me out here because I was acceptable to all Commonwealth political factions. To do that, I had to leave my wife and my children on Earth . . . people who have not seen me now for ten years and who will not see me for another ten." He shrugged. "This is my last command, obviously. I have only retirement to look forward to. PanTerra is providing me with my retirement package, that's all. A nice set of investment portfolios at home. The promise of a well-paying job when I get back. And anti-aging treatments for my wife and kids. The deal was too good to pass up."

She sagged. "But . . . they're going to—"

"As I said, I don't really care what these gentlemen do. They are not harming the Corps, and they are not threatening the government. If you'll step back against that wall, please?"

She did so, thoughts whirling. The net. Her only chance was to uplink to the net.

Hanson blasted out an electronic cry for help. "*Colonel Ramsey!*"

Gavin Norris
Chamber of the Eye
Pyramid of the Eye
New Sumer, Ishtar
1948 hours ALT

"Fuck! She's using the net to call for help!" King yelled. He raised his carbine. "Stop it, bitch!"

Norris spun, raising the 8mm and pulling the trigger. The weapon's sharp report rang from the polished black stone of the chamber, and Hanson was slammed a step backward into the wall.

"Damn it," King shouted. "You didn't need to shoot her!"

"Fuck her," Norris said. "You get back out and stand guard. Make sure she didn't put out an alert." He turned to the screen. "Madame Dumont? Sorry for the delay. We had a . . . situation."

"So I gathered. What the hell is going on? Have you made contact with the Ahannu leadership yet?"

Norris looked at Tu-Kur-La. The Frog was seated, cross-legged, in the back of the chamber, his hands still out-stretched, his huge, golden eyes nictated shut. Something was growing rapidly up from the crack in the stone flooring before him, something like the uncoiling head of a fern but a deep and translucent purple and moving with a most un-plantlike agility. Parts of the purplish mass were flowing up the Frog's arms, pooling on his shoulder, gathering at the back of his neck.

"Not yet," Norris replied, "but any minute now. . . ."

Cassius
IST Derna, *in Ishtar orbit*
1948 hours ST

Artificial intelligences were not necessarily *superior* to organic intelligence, but they were different . . . and immensely faster. On board the *Derna*, Cassius had been engaged in monitoring and upgrading the newly restored Ishtar Data Net when he heard Dr. Hanson's uplinked cry for help. In point of fact, he recognized that something was wrong as her first shrill word came through—*"Colonel . . ."*

Stress levels in her mental voice spoke volumes, alerting Cassius to the fact that this was a serious emergency. He required .03 second to isolate that one voice out of the babbling sea of hundreds he was monitoring at the moment and to narrow her position to the general area of the Pyramid of the Eye. There was a slight speed-of-light time delay, but he downlinked with her neuralink hardware, pinpointing her location and seeing the situation through her eyes. A total of 2.4 seconds passed before Cassius sounded the . . .

Lance Corporal Garroway
Pyramid of the Eye
New Sumer, Ishtar
1949 hours ALT

. . . *alert.*

Garroway's eyes came wide open as the thought exploded in his brain. The company was going on full alert. Was it a Frog attack?

"Okay, you Pyramidiots! Fall in on the double! We're rolling!"

It was Captain Warhurst, wearing his armor sans helmet and rushing across the top of the pyramid from the firebase HQ. Garroway and the others scrambled to their feet, snatching up weapons, gloves, and helmets.

"What the hell?" Dunne exclaimed.

"You four!" Warhurst snapped. "Grab your weapons and follow me! You three over there! With me!"

Garroway uplinked a query and was met with a terse *"Net silence!"* Something big was going down, but damned if he could figure out what. Warhurst was gathering in more and more Marines, dragging them along in his wake as he raced toward the western edge of the pyramid roof, then started down the steps.

Garroway snapped his helmet latch to the locked position and brought up the helmet display. Fifteen Marines showed on the little map view in the corner, racing down the pyramid's western stairs. His 2120 was at full power, his Mark VII systems all green.

"Here's the straight download," Warhurst's voice said in his mind as he ran. "Hostage situation in the Chamber of the

Eye. The PanTerran people are trying a fast one. The orders are to take them down. Alive if possible, but take them down! We don't have time for finesse. Just move in and knock them down. Is that understood?"

"Yes, sir," the Marines chorused back.

They approached the entrance to the Chamber of the Eye from above. A lone Marine in full armor raised a laser carbine. "Halt!" he called, using his external speakers. "Don't come any closer!"

"Stand down, Marine!" Warhurst ordered, raising his own 2120. "Safe your weapon and stand down!"

"I . . . can't do that, Captain."

"General King?"

"Trust me, Captain. I know Dr. Hanson got a partial message out. She became . . . unstable. You don't understand the situation here."

"The hell I don't, sir!" Warhurst said. *"Stand down!"*

"Who's going to make me, Captain? You?"

"No, sir. Someone named Cassius."

It was not something the Marine Corps spoke of publicly or discussed with recruits. NCOs and officers were aware of the technology, of course, but rarely thought about it. Why should they? Mark VII suits required sophisticated arrays of microprocessors to sense and follow the wearer's movements. Though built of ultralight alloys, carbon fiber, and plastic laminates, a Mark VII suit was heavy and required considerable power to enable the wearer simply to move, even to *stand* without becoming exhausted. It was a simple thing for Cassius to take every microprocessor in King's Mark VII offline, turning it into an inert mass of very heavy metal and plastic.

And General King collapsed on the steps like a sack of meal, just like a simulated casualty back in boot camp.

Gavin Norris
Chamber of the Eye
Pyramid of the Eye

New Sumer, Ishtar
1951 hours ALT

Norris crouched next to the Frog, sweat beading on his forehead. "Yes, you understood me," he said. "We'll give you technology for your Sag-ura slaves, as many as you want to send us."

"What . . . would we want with . . . Blackhead technology?" the Frog said, its English broken and hesitant, but understandable. "We are the Godmind. We *are* your gods."

A clatter of falling armor made Norris look up. "Shit. What's going on out there?"

"I'll check," Carleton replied, hurrying toward the door.

There was no time for this ponderous back and forth. Norris had watched Friar Tuck make his connection, allowing the purple goo to flow over his neck and head. It was unappetizing, sure, but no worse than a lot of things he had done. Suddenly, impetuously, he shoved his left hand into a mass of the translucent jelly and pulled a glob of it to the side of his face.

The Abzu-il was not intelligent, of itself. It was, in fact, a gene-tailored organism created by the Ahannu many thousands of years before, a living creature without a mind of its own, which could connect the minds of the gods.

The Sentient Sea itself, however, a kind of internal dreamscape of melded minds and stored memories, had its own intelligence, its own awareness.

And it was utterly unlike anything Gavin Norris had ever seen or felt before.

He felt . . . tendrils of writhing ice penetrating his ears, his nose, the pores of his skin. There was a piercing stab of agony across the left side of his head as the thing worked its way through bone with lightning speed and settled into the contours of Norris's brain.

Norris's *human* brain. Humans and Ahannu were much alike in many ways, but they were not the same species or even remotely related. Aspects of their biologies, which they shared, by chance or design, included such basics as a shared left-handedness in amino acids and a shared right-handedness in sugars. They could eat many of the same foods . . . a fact that the ancient Ahannu had taken advantage of when they'd enslaved early humans to raise crops for them in the fertile river valleys of distant Kia long ago.

But the thought processes were mutually alien, so much so that very little of the Abzu was at all intelligible to Norris.

He saw—*felt,* rather—fragments of Memories . . . a whirling chaos of thoughts and alien language and symbologies so distant from his ken he could perceive it only as a kind of storm of color; of nightmare shape; of violent and throbbing scent and taste; of shrieking atonal chords of sound; of a prickling rain of fire across his skin; intense sexual lust; of sadness, fear, joy, despair, greed . . .

He heard the colors, shrill blues and reds and purples.

He smelled the music, alien and deafening, a cacophony of odor.

He heard the touch of living flame as his skin charred.

He screamed. . . .

Lance Corporal Garroway
Pyramid of the Eye
New Sumer, Ishtar
1951 hours ALT

Warhurst and another Marine tackled the civilian outside, dragging him down, as Garroway spun around the corner of the entranceway and jumped into the cool darkness of the Chamber of the Eye. He wasn't sure at first what he was seeing . . . one of the civilians lying on her back by the wall, blood on the front of her coverall; a Frog seated cross-legged at the back, his head encased in purple goo; another civilian kneeling next to the Frog, head back, eyes wildly staring, shrieking at the top of his lungs as purple gunk rippled over his face.

That civilian held a small handgun. Garroway nearly

threw himself across the chamber, swiping at the gun with one gauntleted paw and sending the weapon clattering in pieces across the floor.

The civilian—Norris—kept screaming, oblivious to the Marines now crowding into the chamber. "What do we do, sir?" Garroway asked Warhurst. "It's killing him!"

"No." The single word came from the seated Ahannu. It raised a hand, and the purple mess began draining from Norris's ears and face. Flowing from his skin. "No. We are . . . sorry. We did not mean . . . this one harm."

"What did you do to him?" Warhurst demanded.

"What did . . . he do to himself?" the alien replied. "We fear . . . he was not . . . ready for . . . enlightenment within the Sentient Sea."

"Enlightenment?" Garroway said. "Is *that* what they call it?"

Norris was still screaming, his mind blasted, utterly gone.

Eight days later Garroway lay at the edge of the jungle with Kat Vinita, relaxing after their last bout of lovemaking. He and Kat had become close these past weeks, very close, though he doubted the arrangement would become permanent. How could it, when they had no idea where they would be deployed next, or if they would be deployed together?

Besides, there was still Lynnley, somewhere out there among those stars.

Hell. Was what he felt for Lynnley nostalgia for a distant friend? Or something more? It was impossible to tell. He'd changed so much.

"There's Sol," Kat said, pointing. "The Relief Expedition must be along that line of sight too."

"That's what they say," Garroway replied. "Another five months and they'll be here."

She laughed and snuggled closer in his arms. "I wonder if when they get here they'll approve of our . . . solution?"

He smiled and lightly stroked her breast. "I doubt it. From what Hanson and Carleton told the brass, PanTerra was set to keep the Ishtaran humans in what amounted to slavery." A Navy corpsman had arrived in time to slap some fastheal nano on Dr. Hanson's wound. She'd lived, and she was telling everything she knew about PanTerra's scheme. Carleton had joined her in the revelation, probably to cover his ass.

And King as well, though he still didn't see anything wrong with his stand. Why should he? he asked. PanTerra had been operating with the best intentions of the Ishtaran humans at heart. King had accepted house arrest with ill grace and temper. He would be vindicated, he claimed, at the court-martial.

Unfortunately for him, a board of senior officers would not be available until they returned to Earth. In the meantime, Ramsey had assumed full operational command of 1 MIEU. The Marines themselves joked about the "mutiny." Some had taken to wearing makeshift eyepatches or peppering their speech with piratical *arrrrs*.

They gave the AI Cassius credit for carrying out the coup.

"I think they'll have to accept it as a *fait accompli*," Garroway told her after a moment. "I think the colonel is a damned genius, myself."

"Let's hope the brass back home agrees," Kat replied.

Colonel Ramsey's solution *was* elegant. The Marine Corps was not supposed to set government policy, but the government was 8.3 light-years away right now, and the nearest other representatives of that government would not be there for another five months. With the sudden Ahannu declaration of peace, something had to be done *now*.

Ramsey had put together a working plan. As senior officer for 1 MIEU, he'd formally recognized the free Ishtaran humans as a separate state, an independent state on Ishtar, supported by the U.S. Marines. They would be the ones who talked to Earth's representatives about any repatriation or emancipation of humans in the Llalande system, and they would approve any travel of Ishtaran humans back to Earth.

Further, the Ishtaran state—*Dumu-gir Kalam*, as it was to

be called—would have access to the Sag-ura under Ahannu control. Earth would supply the diplomats to begin peaceful negotiations between the two groups, with an eye to helping the Sag-ura gain some measure of self-determination. The Ahannu had agreed—reluctantly, but they'd agreed. The Marine *nir-gál-mè-a* carried a fair mass in the way of moral authority. Dr. Hanson had compared it to the Marines being thought of as co-equal gods with the Ahannu.

Gods of battle.

That was quite a promotion, Garroway thought.

Frankly, he doubted that the Sag-ura would ever choose self-determination. According to the xenosoc experts, they didn't think of themselves as slaves but as people who merely served their gods, who had served them since time had begun. What, he wondered, would happen when the government's desire to free the human slaves on Ishtar collided with the laws against interfering with people's religion? The social firestorm that raised would likely burn for another century or two, at least.

But the Sag-ura would have time to become adjusted to some new ideas, like the fact that they could choose a path for themselves. Maybe in a few more centuries . . .

"You know," Garroway said, "once this story gets out, none of the other nations on Earth will have anything to do with PanTerra. They'll be finished."

"Maybe," she said. "Though with that much money, I doubt it."

"Aren't you the little cynic?"

"Fuck you."

"Again?"

She let her hand run down the hard-muscled curve of his belly. "Maybe. Depends on whether or not you're up to it."

He laughed, pulled her closer, and kissed her. Glowing, fragile gossamers danced in the night sky above them.

And later still, while Kat slept, Garroway queried the net for the location of Sirius and was disappointed to learn that

that bright star, Alpha Canis Majoris, was halfway across the heavens, invisible now from Ishtar at this longitude.

He wondered if Lynnley was there now.

He wondered if she was thinking of him. Or if she, like he, had found another lover.

He wondered if the sky where she was could be as spectacular as this.

Well, it scarcely mattered. She was a Marine and went where she was sent.

Just like him.

Epilogue

Star Explorer Wings of Isis
Sirius System
1550 hours ST

Lance Corporal Lynnley Collins floated in the wonder of the noumenal projection, apparently free in empty space, actually receiving the feed from the forward cameras of the *Wings of Isis.*

The sky around her was . . . incredible. Sirius was a young star system, still dusty and littered with debris, and the dust created a background glow of silvers, blues, and whites. Sirius A was embedded in that glow, a dazzling, actinic disk too brilliant to look at comfortably even within the artificially subdued medium of the noumenon.

Closer at hand, Sirius B was a white-hot spark, a white dwarf little larger than Earth. There were no planets . . . only rubble, the debris of what might one day be, or once had been, a solar system. Sirius A was far too hot a star to allow for a comfortably Earthlike world; Sirius B had been nearly as bright before it vomited part of its mass and collapsed into its present shrunken state.

Radiation—deadly if *Wings of Isis* had not been well shielded—seared local space, visible in the noumenon as a faint purple glow.

The system abounded in mysteries. One mystery in particular had drawn *Wings of Isis* here, across 8.6 light-years of space. The star Sirius, brightest in the skies of Earth's northern hemisphere, had long figured in human mythology. The Egyptians had identified it with the goddess Isis and noted that its rising coincided with the flooding of the Nile. Their gods claimed a special connection with Sirius . . . and with the constellation Orion, which they called Osiris.

One tribe of primitives in sub-Saharan Africa, the Dogon, worshiped gods from Sirius. When Europeans had first contacted them in 1931, they'd known astonishing details about the Sirius system—including the fifty-year orbital period of Sirius B and the fact that it was the tiniest of stars but with tremendous "weight," a fair description of a white dwarf.

The fact of Sirius B had been unknown to modern astronomy until the mid-1800s, when its existence was deduced by perturbations in Sirius A's path. Sirius B was not even seen optically until 1862, with the use of technologies utterly beyond the Dogon's understanding.

Perhaps the Dogon had gotten their unusual understanding of astronomy from European missionaries whose visit had been otherwise forgotten.

Or perhaps not. There were no Church records of any missionaries visiting the Dogon until 1931.

Berosus, the Babylonian historian, had recorded myths and legends of the peoples who'd preceded the Babylonians in the Tigris-Euphrates Valley. Among them had been the story of Oannes, a being described as a "semidemon" who'd emerged from the waters of the Persian Gulf to teach the locals agriculture, mathematics, medicine, and the alphabet, and who claimed to be from the star Sirius.

All the stuff of myth and nonsense, of course. So archeologists had assumed, until discoveries on Earth, Mars, and Earth's moon in the twenty-first century had proven that early humans had entertained visitors from the stars.

The Isis Expedition had been dispatched to Sirius to learn more about whoever had taught the pre-Sumerians, the

Egyptians, the ancestors of the Dogon. Perhaps they were starfaring Ahannu.

But the description left by Berosus sounded like they might be something else.

And the evidence of that something else hung in space before the *Wings of Isis*, still ten kilometers distant but large enough to fill a quarter of the sky.

Lynnley stared at the object, her sense of wonder stirred. If this was an example of the technology of the ancient visitors to Earth, no *wonder* they'd been welcomed and worshiped as gods.

From her vantage point it appeared to be an immense wheel, thick-rimmed, twenty kilometers across. The outer surface was broken and black, like a cinder; apparently the thing had been built of asteroidal material gathered from Sirian space . . . and yet gravitometric readings suggested that the thing was unimaginably dense.

It was impossible to tell what the huge structure was for, but telltale lights gleamed on the rim, constellations of power usage and life.

Somebody lived there.

"So what do you think it is, Paul?" she asked.

Sergeant Paul Watson gave a noumenal shrug. "I think it's a giant habitat of some kind," he said. "You know, like the O'Neil colonies they used to talk about building someday. You make a big wheel or cylinder, rotate it to provide artificial gravity . . ."

"But that thing's not rotating."

"Maybe it was destroyed in the same war that wiped out the Builders," he suggested. "It's dead."

"Then what are those lights?" she insisted. "*Someone's* alive over there."

"Geez, how the hell should I know?" he growled. "Be patient! We'll find out soon enough."

She laughed. Paul was her current shipboard lover. He was a bit slow on the uptake sometimes, but a decent guy.

He carried just enough arrogance on his shoulders that it was fun to deflate him with an impossible question every so often.

She did wonder, sometimes, about John. Where was he now? In the Llalande system?

What was he doing?

What was he thinking?"

"My God!" Paul said.

"What?"

"Look! There in the center. You'll need to magnify. . . ."

Something was drifting out of the center of that massively rimmed wheel . . . a ship, but such a ship as human eyes had never before seen, at least not in historical times. Comparing it to the known diameter of the wheel suggested that it was huge, a couple of kilometers long at least, needle-slim, and made of something that looked like purest beaten gold.

"What . . . is it?" she said.

"A ship!" Paul said. "Obviously, a ship!"

"Why obviously?" Lynnley said. "We don't know who these people are. Or what they are. We can't take anything for granted!"

"Bullshit," Paul replied with a mental snort. "It's a *ship*. That wheel must be some sort of enormous habitat or space station. I think we're about to meet Berosus's friends!"

"I hope they're friendly," she said. "The *Wings of Isis* wouldn't make a decent lifeboat for that thing!"

"Of *course* they're friendly!" Paul replied cheerfully. "All the legends about gods from Sirius emphasized that they were friendly, taught humans how to plant crops, that kind of thing. They're just coming out to greet us!"

The shipboard alert clamored in their minds. *Wings of Isis* was going to battle stations. "I hope to the Goddess you're right, Paul," she said. "But whoever they are, they must be damned old, and someone once said that the old are often insanely jealous of the young. And . . . there are the Hunters of the Dawn, remember?"

She felt his noumenal touch. "Nah. It's Oannes's descendants, and they're coming out to see how their offspring have done. Everything'll be fine. You'll see."

"Damn," she said. "I sure hope you're right."

She wished that John Garroway were here.

We hope you've enjoyed this Eos book. As part of our mission to give readers the best science fiction and fantasy being written today, the following pages contain a glimpse into the fascinating worlds of a select group of Eos authors.

Join us for exciting adventures and fascinating discoveries, as Juliet McKenna spins a tale of magic, intrigue, and danger, and as new author Mitchell Graham begins a fantasy adventure of epic proportions. Be drawn into the past as award-winning author Michael Swanwick takes on *Jurassic Park*—and looks at what really would happen!—and venture into the future as Ian Douglas begins an action-packed trilogy of first contact, *Interstellar Marines*-style. And don't miss Sheri Tepper's spellbinding tale of discovery, imagination, and peril in a post-apocalyptic earth, or Sean Russell's wonderful new high fantasy saga of the battle to rule the One Kingdom.

THE FIFTH RING

Mitchell Graham

"My lord, this was found while we were digging by the fountain," the man said holding out the box.

Annoyed at the interruption, Duren slowly looked up from the book he was reading.

"You said to bring you anything we found at once, my lord," the man prompted.

Duren looked at the box and then at the man.

"Have you looked in the box?"

"Yes, my lord," the man said simply. "There are four metal rings of a strange color. They bear some kind of writing on the inside of them that I have never seen before."

Duren's hands started to shake, and he was forced to grip the table to keep it from showing.

"Who else saw you recover this?"

"No one, Sire. I swear it. Those were your instructions."

"You are sure?" Duren said quietly.

"No one," he repeated.

Duren got up from the desk, rising to his full height. Despite his age, he was still a tall, imposing figure, and it rather pleased him to have people look up when speaking to him.

"I do not tolerate deception in anyone who serves me," he said, bringing his face close to the workman's.

"Sire, I do not deceive you. I am speaking the truth. I swear it."

For a full minute Duren searched the man's face, seeking some sign of disloyalty. Finding none, he relaxed, smiled, and put his arm around the man's shoulders.

"You have done well—very well. What is your name?"

"Roland, my lord."

"Yes . . . Roland, of course. Yours will be an honored name above all others." Duren's fingertips lightly touched the other man's face. "Yes . . . yes . . . an honest face . . . a loyal face. I know where loyalty is to be found, Roland. You know that, don't you?"

"Your people love you, my lord."

"I know," Duren replied absently, looking at the box.

He cupped the worker's face in both of his hands, and stared intently into his eyes. Roland was at a complete loss as to what he was supposed to do, so he just stood there. Over the years he had learned that where lords and ladies were concerned, the best thing was to say as little as possible.

"Yes, I can see it in you. You are an honest man—trusting and honest. Come with me, Roland."

Duren put his arm around the man's shoulders and led him over to the crystal.

"Have you any idea what this is," he asked.

Roland shook his head.

"No . . . no . . . of course you don't." Duren chuckled under his breath. "This was the source of the Ancient's powers. They were like gods, Roland. They could do anything, using only their minds," he whispered in the man's ear.

Roland's eyes grew wider and he stared at the crystal in wonder.

"Do you have any idea what this box contains?" Duren asked.

"Rings, my lord?"

"They are the links to this very crystal," Duren explained patiently, as if he were talking to a child. "Attend." Without hesitation, Duren opened the box and slipped a ring onto his finger. He closed his eyes for a moment, and then fixed his attention on a chair standing nearby.

"Rise," he commanded.

The chair remained where it was.

"Rise," Duren repeated again, with greater force than before.

Roland looked at the chair expectantly, and then he looked at the floor, wishing with all his heart that he were someplace else at that particular moment.

In annoyance, Duren tried again using the second and the third rings, with the same results. He was positive that he was correct. These rings *were* the links. They had to be! When he took the fourth ring from the box and placed it on his finger, his face had already begun to darken. This imbecile had brought him trash, he thought. Perhaps he *wanted* him to look foolish. Anger began to seethe deep inside Duren's chest. He could see that the man was pretending to look at his feet, all the while laughing silently at him. Slowly, Karas Duren's hand crept toward the jeweled dagger in his belt.

What happened next didn't occur immediately, but then an odd tingling sensation began emanating from the ring and coursed through his arm.

Duren's eyes widened in surprise.

The sudden explosion of the chair shocked them both. One minute it was there, and the next it was a pile of splinters. Roland's mouth fell open and he backed away, flattening himself against the wall. It took virtually all of Duren's considerable willpower to regain his own composure. After a moment, when his breathing returned to normal, he ran his hands deliberately through his long hair, and made an elaborate show of adjusting his black velvet cloak as if nothing out of the ordinary had occurred. Roland stood there, gaping, as Duren casually flicked a few tiny pieces of wood from his sleeve. Though the king was exultant, he deliberately kept his face serene. There was still the problem of Roland.

BONES OF THE EARTH

Michael Swanwick

If the whole tangled affair could be said to have a beginning at all, it began on that cold, blustery afternoon in late October when the man with the Igloo cooler walked into Richard Leyster's office. His handshake was firm, and he set the cooler casually down on a tabletop between a lime-green inflatable tyrannosaur and a tray of unsorted hadrosaur teeth without asking permission first. His smile was utterly without warmth. He said his name was Griffin and that he had come to offer Leyster a new position.

"Let me begin by spelling out the terms of the contract, just to save me the trouble later on. You'll be allowed to stay in your present position, and arrangements will be made to borrow your services for the project six aggregate months out of the year. You'll continue to be paid by the government, so I'm afraid there won't be any increase in your salary. Sorry."

He's enjoying this, thought Leyster. Science bores him to death, but having opposition to overcome brings him back to life. Ordinarily, Leyster didn't find people very interesting. But Griffin was different. He studied the impassive planes of the man's face, looking for a point of entry, a beginning to understanding, the least flicker of a hint as to what made him work. Leyster knew himself to be a methodical researcher; give him one end of a tangled thread and he wouldn't let go until he'd unraveled the entire snarl. All he needed was enough time and that one loose end.

And then Griffin did an extraordinary thing. It was the smallest of gestures, one Leyster wouldn't have noticed under ordinary circumstances. Now he found it riveting. Without looking, Griffin brushed back his sleeve to reveal a thick stainless steel watch. He clamped his hand over it, hiding the dial completely. Then he glanced down at the back of his hand.

He didn't release the watch until he had looked away.

Leyster had found his opening. Prodding gently, he said, "So far, you haven't made much of a case."

"It gets worse," Griffin said. So he had a sense of humor! Astonishing. "There are restrictions. You won't be allowed to publish. Oh, findings based on your own fieldwork, of course"—he waved a dismissive hand at the HDTV screen— "that sort of stuff you may publish whenever. Provided it is first cleared by an internal committee to ensure you're not taking advantage of information gained while working for us. Further, you won't even be allowed to talk about your work with us. It will be classified. We'll need your permission to have the FBI run a security check on you. Strictly routine. I assure you, it will turn up nothing embarrassing."

"A security check? For paleontology? What the hell are you talking about?"

"I should also mention that there is a serious possibility of violent death."

"Violent death. This is going to start making sense any minute now, right?"

"A man comes into your office"—Griffin leaned forward conspiratorially—"and suggests that he has a very special job to offer you. By its very nature he can't tell you much about it until you've committed yourself heart and soul. But he suggests—hints, rather—that it's your chance to be a part of the greatest scientific adventure since Darwin's voyage on H.M.S. *Beagle*. What would you think?"

"Well, he'd certainly have my interest."

"If it were true," Griffin said with heavy irony.

"Yes," Leyster agreed. "If it were true."

Again, Griffin clamped his hand over his watch. Glancing down at it, he said, "You'll take the position anyway."

"And the reasoning upon which you base this extraordinary conclusion is—?"

Griffin put the cooler on Leyster's desk. "This is a gift. There's only one string attached—you will not show it to anyone or tell anybody about it. Beyond that—" He twisted his mouth disparagingly. "Do whatever it takes to convince you it's genuine. Cut it open. Take it apart. There are plenty more where that came from. But no photographs, please. Or you'll never get another one to play with again."

Then he was gone.

Alone, Leyster thought: I won't open it. The best possible course of action would be ditch this thing in the nearest Dumpster. Whatever Griffin was peddling, it could only mean trouble. FBI probes, internal committees, censorship, death. He didn't need that kind of grief. Just this once, he was going to curb his curiosity and leave well enough alone.

He opened the cooler.

For a long, still moment, he stared at what was contained within, packed in ice. Then, dazedly, he reached inside and removed it. The flesh was cool under his hands. The skin moved slightly; he could feel the bones and muscles underneath.

It was the head of a *Stegosaurus*.

Author of the popular *Heritage* series, military sf
author Ian Douglas begins a
new trilogy of exploration, discovery,
and military action.

STAR CORPS
Book One of the Legacy Trilogy

Ian Douglas

12 MAY 2138

Firebase Frog
New Sumer
Ishtar, Llalande 21185 IID
72:26 local time

Master Sergeant Gene Aiken leaned against the sandbag barricade and stared out across the Saimi-Id River. Smoke rose
from a half dozen buildings, staining the pale green of the
early evening sky. Marduk, vast and swollen, aglow with
deep-swirling bands and storms in orange-amber light, hung
immense and sullen, as ever just above the western horizon.

The gas giant's slender crescent bowed up and away from the horizon where the red sun had just set; its night side glowed with dull-red heat, as flickering pinpoints, like twinkling stars, marked the pulse and strobe of continent-sized lightning storms deep within that seething atmosphere.

The microimplants in Aiken's eyes turned brooding red dusk to full light, while his battle helmet's tactical feed displayed ranges, angles, and compass bearing superimposed on his view, as well as flagging thermal and movement targets in shifting boxes and cursor brackets.

The sergeant studied Marduk's blood-glow for a moment, then looked away. At his back, with a shrill whine of servomotors, the sentry tower's turret swiveled and depressed, matching the movements of his head.

He could hear the chanting and the drumming, off to the east, as the crowds gathered at the Pyramid of the Eye. It was, he thought, going to be a very long night indeed.

"How's it going, Master Sergeant?"

Aiken didn't turn, not when he was linked in with the sentry. His battle feed had warned him of Captain Pearson's approach.

"All quiet on the perimeter, Captain," he replied. "Sounds like the Frogs're pretty riled up down in the 'ville, though."

"Word just came through from the embassy compound," Pearson said. "The rebels have seized control in a hundred villages. The 'High Emperor of the Gods' is calling for calm and understanding from his people." The way he said it, the title was a sneer.

"Do you think they'll attack us?"

"It could happen. The ambassador still hasn't answered Geremelet's ultimatum."

A gossamer flitted in the ruby light, twisting and shifting, a delicate ribbon of iridescence. Aiken lifted the muzzle of his 2120 and caught the frail creature, watching it quiver against the hard black plastic of the weapon's barrel in bursts of rainbow color. Other gossamers danced and jittered in the gathering darkness, delicate sparkles of bioluminescence.

"They're not talking about . . . surrendering, are they?"

"Not that I've heard, Master Sergeant. Don't worry. It won't come to that."

"Yeah. The Marines never surrender."

"That's what they say. Keep a sharp watch. There've been reports of frogger slaves trying to gain entrance at some of the other bases. They might be human, but we can't trust them."

"Aye, aye, sir." The Ahannu slaves, descendants of humans taken from Earth millennia ago, gave Aiken the creeps. No way was he letting them through *his* part of the perimeter.

"Good man. Give a yell if you need help."

"You don't need to worry about *that*, sir."

Aiken turned and looked into the southern sky, where the first stars were beginning to appear. Eight light years from home had not much altered the familiar constellations, though the dome of the sky was strangely canted against the cardinal directions. There was a bright star, however, in the otherwise dim and unremarkable constellation Scutum, not far from the white beacon of Fomalhaut.

Sol. Earth's sun. As always, the sight of that star sent a small shiver down Aiken's spine. So far away, in both space and time. . . .

Eight point three light years. Help from home could not possibly arrive in time.

THE VISITOR

Sheri S. Tepper

caigo faience

Picture this:

A mountain splintering the sky like a broken bone, its western precipice plummeting onto jumbled scree. Below the sheer wall, sparse grasses, growing thicker as the slope gentles through dark groves to a spread of plush pasture. Centered there, much embellished, a building white as sugar, its bizarre central tower crowned by a cupola. Like a priapic wedding cake, it poses amid a garniture of gardens, groves, mazes, all halved—west from east—by the slither of a glassy wall, while from north to south the tamed terrain is cracked by little rivers bounding from the snowy heights toward the canyons farther down.

Picture this:

Inside the towered building, galleries crammed with diagrams and devices; atria packed with idols, images, icons; libraries stacked with reference works; studios strewn with chalk-dust, marble-dust, sawdust, aromatic with incense—cedar and pine and sweet oil of lavender, yes, but more mephitic scents as well; cellar vaults hung with cobweb, strewn with parchment fragments, moldering cases stacked high in shadowed corners. All this has been culled from prior centuries, from wizards now dead, sorcerers now destroyed, mysterious places no longer recognized by name or location, people and places that once were but are no longer, or at least can no longer be found.

Even the man who built the place is no longer. He was Caigo Faience of Turnaway (ca 701-775 ATHCAW—After The Happening Came And Went), once selected by the Regime as Protector of the Spared Ones, Warden of Wizardry, but now well over a century gone. Upon his death the books were audited. When the results were known, the office of Protector was abolished and the function of Warden was transferred to the College of Sorcery under the supervision of the Department of Inexplicable Arts. DIA has taken control of the place: the building, the walls, the mazes, the warden's house (now called the Conservator's House), the whole of Faience's Folly together with all its very expensive conceits. It is now a center for preservation and restoration, a repository for the arcana of history. When The Art is recovered, Faience will become a mecca for aspiring mages under the watchful eye of the Bureau of Happiness and Enlightenment, yet another brilliant in the pavé crown of the Regime.

Picture this.

A Comador woman, her hazelnut hair drawn sleekly back into a thick, single plait, her oval face expressionless, dressed usually in a shapeless shift worn more as a lair than a garment, a shell into which she may at any moment withdraw like a turtle. She is recently come to womanhood, beautiful as only Comadors can be beautiful, but she is too diffident to let her beauty show. Possibly she could be sagacious, some Comadors are, but her green eyes betray an intellect largely unexplored. Still, she is graceful as she slips through the maze to its center, like a fish through eddies. She is agile as she climbs the tallest trees in the park in search of birds' nests. She is quiet, her green eyes ingenuous but speculative as she lurks among shadows, watching, or stands behind doors, listening, the only watcher and listener among a gaggle of egos busy with sayings and doings.

Picture her on a narrow bed in the smallest bedroom of the

Conservator's House, struggling moistly out of tangle-haired, grit-eyed sleep, lost in what she calls *the mistaken moment* when her heart flutters darkly like an attic-trapped bird and she cannot remember what or where she is. This confusion comes always at the edge between sleep and waking, between being here now, at Caigo Faience, and being . . . other, another, who survives the dawn only in echoes of voices:

"Has she come? Has she brought all her children? Then let her daughter stand upon the battle drum and let war begin . . ."

"Can you smell that? The stink wafts among the very stars; the spoor of the race that moves in the direction of darkness! Look at this trail I have followed! This is the way it was, see why I have come . . ."

"Ah, see there in the shadows! This is a creature mankind has made. See how he watches you!"

"A chance yet. Still a chance you may bring them into the light . . ."

And herself whispering, *"How? . . . why? . . . what is it? What can I do? . . ."*

Waking, she clings to that other existence as a furry infant to an arboreal mother, dizzied but determined. She is unwilling to let go the mystery until she has unraveled it, and she tries to go back, back into dream, but it is to no purpose. With sunlight the voices vanish, along with the images and intentions she is so desperate to recover. Though they are at the brink of her consciousness, they might as well be hidden in the depths of the earth, for she is now only daylight Dismé, blinking, stretching, scratching at the insistent itch on her forehead as she wakens to the tardy sun that is just now heaving itself over the sky-blocking peak of Mt. P'Jardas to the east.

"I am Dismé," she says aloud, in a slightly quavering voice. Dismé, she thinks, who sees things that are not there. Dismé who does not believe in the Dicta. Dismé who believes this life is, perhaps, the dream and that other life the reality.

Dismé, she tries not to think, whose not-sister, Rashel Deshôll, is Conservator of the Faience Museum, tenant of the Conservator's House, and something else, far more dreadful, as well.

THE ISLE OF BATTLE
Book Two of the Swans' War

Sean Russell

Torches guttered and flared, haloed in the mist that boiled above the river. No body had surfaced, though that was of little comfort to Prince Michael of Innes. He walked knee deep in the slow-moving river, feeling the mud give softly beneath his boots, half afraid that he would stumble over Elise Wills motionless on the bottom.

"What a foolish act!" he whispered to himself. Foolish and desperate, but had he not considered the same thing himself? Escape from Hafydd—escape at all costs.

He found the whole evening strange and unreal. Even his feelings seemed veiled, as though this same cold mist was all that moved within his heart. Elise was gone . . . yet he didn't believe it. Her own father had said she couldn't swim. She'd gone into the river rather than let their marriage serve Hafydd and his ambitions. *Rather than marry* me, the Prince reminded himself.

Voices sounded along the shore, muffled in the murk, but there was no elation in those calls, no sudden joyful discovery to blow the clinging mist from his heart.

The Prince set one foot down in the ooze, then the other. A

ghost of anger made itself felt, though distant and unformed.
He cursed Hafydd under his breath, the words swirling out in
a fine mist.

A blunt-ended punt loomed out of the fog, its masked and
costumed inhabitants drawing quick breaths of surprise as
the prince appeared in the haze: a man, strangely costumed
walking on water. A ghost.

After all the madness at the Renné Ball, a ghost should
have been expected.

One of Hafydd's revenant honor guard hurried by along
the bank, a torch held high, forcing back the night and illuminating the wraiths of mist that swirled around them. Prince
Michael prayed that they would find Elise alive—and prayed
that they would not. Such a courageous act should not end
with being dragged from the river, drenched in failure. She
deserved better than that. It was selfishness alone that made
him hope she would be found, still among the living.

The party that had come with the Wills family were desperately searching, running this way and that, even the men
at arms choking back tears. They had known Elise all her
short, sweet life, he reminded himself. They wouldn't feel
this numbness that penetrated his heart.

Torches wavered above him suddenly, and he realized he'd
come back to the bridge. A small knot of dark-robed men
gathered on the bank, their whispers barely distinguishable
from the river's voice. They glanced up as the Prince appeared, but then ignored him, as they did habitually. Hafydd
was there, at the center, tall and proud. He moved down to the
river's edge and crouched—the motion giving the lie to his
years. He glanced at Michael, then away. A gray man,
Michael thought, dressed in black, grim and hard as stone.

For a moment he didn't move, his men arrayed about him
silent and intimidated. But then he stood, drawing out his
sword. Prince Michael felt himself step back, though he
hadn't willed his limbs to do so. Hafydd slid down the small
bank into the water. He plunged the blade into the smooth
back of the river and held it still, his eyes closed. None of his
minions dared speak.

"She's gone," Hafydd said, but then his arm jerked as if

the river had shuddered. His eyes opened. "*Sianon*," he whispered. He seemed about to collapse, crumpling over the blade he still held in the river. Two of his guards stepped forward to support him but the knight shook them off and drew himself up.

Hafydd turned and strode up the bank, disappearing into the fog, his minions following after like so many shadows.

THE BATTLE FOR
THE FUTURE BEGINS—IN
IAN DOUGLAS's
EXPLOSIVE
HERITAGE TRILOGY

SEMPER MARS
0-380-78828-4/$7.50 US/$9.99 Can

LUNA MARINE
0-380-78829-2/$6.99 US/$9.99 Can

EUROPA STRIKE
0-380-78830-6/$7.50 US/$9.99 Can

AND DON'T MISS
THE LEGACY TRILOGY

STAR CORPS
978-0-380-81824-2/$7.99 US/$10.99 Can
In the future, Earth's warriors have conquered the heavens.
But on a distant world, humanity is in chains . . .

BATTLESPACE
978-0-380-81825-9/$7.50 US/$9.99 Can
Whatever waits on the other side of a wormhole must be
confronted with stealth, with force, and without fear.

STAR MARINES
978-0380-81826-6/$7.99 US/$10.99 Can
Planet Earth is lost . . .
but the marines have just begun to fight.